Critical acclaim for Robin Lee Hatcher's sweeping Historical Romances:

"PIRATE'S LADY has it all—a beautiful, headstrong heroine, a handsome, dashing hero, white slavery, wild desire and heartstopping adventure."—ROMANTIC TIMES

"Robin Lee Hatcher writes a fast-paced story with much intrigue, romance and adventure. She draws her characters so well, the reader hates to say goodbye to them."—AFFAIRE DE COEUR

GEMFIRE is "utterly delightful! A rousing Western Historical Romance and a real page turner. Robin Lee Hatcher at her best!"—ROMANTIC TIMES

And now, praise for THE WAGER:

"You'll fall in love with this tender romance!"—ROMANTIC TIMES

NIGHT OF PASSION

She felt the cool air against her hot flesh as the robe was pushed from her shoulder. There was a flash of shyness, a desire to cover herself once again, but it was quickly forgotten as his lips began a slow journey down her neck, across her shoulder, down her arm to the inside of her elbow, then back again.

The words were whispered near her ear. Unexpected and so soft she might only have imagined them. "Marry me, Bethany."

Marry him? Had he really asked that? Had he actually spoken or was it only part of the spell he was weaving around her?

Yes, Hawk, her mind and heart replied. *Yes!*

But she was still unable to speak. His mouth was moving again, leaving a path of tingling flesh wherever his lips touched. Her head fell back, her hair falling toward the floor. She didn't know what he was doing to her. She only knew she never wanted him to stop. . . .

Other Leisure books by Robin Lee Hatcher:

STORMY SURRENDER
HEART'S LANDING
THORN OF LOVE
HEART STORM
PASSION'S GAMBLE
PIRATE'S LADY
GEMFIRE

The Wager

ROBIN LEE HATCHER

LEISURE BOOKS  NEW YORK CITY

To Jerry Neu,
for proving heroes don't live only in novels,
and for showing me love and romance
aren't just fiction.

Now and always,
R.

A LEISURE BOOK

May 1989

Published by

Dorchester Publishing Co., Inc.
276 Fifth Avenue
New York, NY 10001

CHAPTER ONE

Despite the early afternoon hour, riotous laughter and the brassy tinkle of piano keys filtered through the swinging doors of the Plains Saloon and spilled into the lone street of Sweetwater, Montana. At the far end of town, Bethany Silverton carefully swept her lime-green and white striped gown out of the way and closed the picket gate of her new home. Petite gloved fingers opened a matching striped silk parasol.

"It is shameful the way that noise never stops," Ingrid Johnson said in her rolling Swedish accent. "I do not know why the good reverend wanted to build his church in Sweetwater. He was asked to stay in Denver, and there were so many other pretty towns along the way. . . . "

Bethany hid her sudden smile with her parasol. She couldn't admit to her friend how much she already liked this raw frontier town which her father had chosen as the site for his new church. If she told Ingrid, Ingrid would tell her father, and Reverend Silverton was the last person Bethany wanted to know. After all, she had complained fiercely and loudly when he announced they were to leave Philadelphia to go west. She had made it clear from the very beginning that she would never forgive him for removing her from Miss Hendersen's School for Young Ladies and from all her fine society friends. Now, two years later, she could admit to herself how much she preferred the freedom, even the danger, of this country to the staid and very proper existence she had led back East. But she still refused to admit it to her father. Bethany Silverton was more than just a little stubborn.

Controlling her amusement, Bethany shifted the parasol to her other shoulder and turned sea-mist green eyes on her friend. "There are saloons in every town, Ingrid. Even Denver. You just have to get used to them or ignore them." That said, she began walking toward the center of town, and Ingrid had to hurry to fall into step beside her.

Sweetwater was nearly two years old, a town flowering suddenly to life to serve the needs of the ranchers who were snatching up the vast grasslands of Montana. Already proclaiming itself prosperous, its single street was lined with false-fronted wooden buildings, including two mercantile stores, four saloons, a small restaurant, a livery, an apothecary and doctor's office, and even a sheriff's office and jail. When the Silverton family had arrived less than one week before, the reverend had immediately purchased a small, two-story home on the edge of town from a widow woman who was returning to Missouri. This, he had said, was where they would stay.

The first business the two young women reached was the apothecary. Bethany opened the door, causing a small bell to ring overhead as she and Ingrid entered.

A green-visored man looked up from his paper-strewn desk. His weathered face cracked into a friendly grin. "How do, ladies. Can I help you?"

Bethany stepped forward. "I'm Bethany Silverton, sir. My father is Reverend Silverton."

"I heard we'd got us a preacher. Glad to meet you, Miss Silverton. My name's Wilton. John Wilton. My brother's the doc here in Sweetwater."

"It's a pleasure to meet you, Mr. Wilton. Miss Johnson and I don't want to take up too much of your time. We came to tell you that my father will be holding services this Sunday morning in a field tent behind our house. Service will start at ten."

"Me and my missus will be there. My Sarah's been praying for a pastor to come through these parts ever since we settled here. She'd want me to tell you she's been eager to meet you and your mother, but she's been feeling a might poorly lately. We've got us a new baby coming real soon now."

Bethany offered one of her dazzlingly sweet smiles. "How wonderful, Mr. Wilton. Please tell your wife I'm looking forward to meeting her. Good day."

"Good day, miss."

At the livery stable, Bethany tacked up a notice of church services, then the two young women crossed the street to Mrs. Jenkin's restaurant. Once again, Bethany introduced herself while Ingrid waited silently in the background. She repeated the same introduction and invitation to the proprietors of the mercantiles and the bakery, then tacked more notices outside two of the saloons.

They had just left the sheriff's office when they found their way suddenly blocked by a grinning man with a week's worth of whiskers on his chin.

"Well, would you look at what we got here. Ain't you a couple pretty little fillies."

Bethany leveled a cool stare upon the grizzled, trail-dusty cowpoke. "A gentleman, sir, would step aside and allow us to pass." Although a good deal shorter than the man, Bethany's voice carried a note of superiority which seemed to add inches to her diminutive height. Her eyes never wavered, almost daring him to refuse to obey her silent command.

His smile disappeared. His face reddened. His eyes darted quickly about to see if anyone had noticed what was transpiring. Then, mumbling an apology, his gaze fell to the boardwalk as he stepped down into the street. "'Scuse me, ma'am."

Bethany nodded curtly but deigned not to speak to him again. "Come along, Ingrid."

Ingrid's pale blue eyes widened as she stared at her friend before looking back over her shoulder. "Are you never afraid of *anything*, Bethany?"

Bethany sniffed her disdain and tossed her head, causing burnished auburn curls to sway against her back. "I have nothing to be afraid of from the likes of him. I learned how to deal with men who have no manners when I was at Miss Hendersen's."

Bethany stopped at the far corner of the Plains Saloon and tacked the church notice to the board siding. The music and laughter coming from inside were louder than ever. Twice she glanced toward the door of the saloon, feeling a terrible, almost irresistible temptation to peek inside and learn what was causing so much merriment. But, of course, she couldn't do anything so foolish and unbecoming. After all, she was the reverend's daughter. She had a position to maintain.

And, if she admitted the truth, what truly kept her from following her impulse was Ingrid's presence more than propriety. While she still occasionally acted the part of the society lady, the role somehow didn't quite fit her anymore. She wasn't sure why. It just didn't.

She glanced once more toward the saloon doors, curiosity growing, but she had to resist. Ingrid might tolerate a lot of things from Bethany, but she would go straight to the reverend if his daughter were to do anything so brash as entering a saloon.

Perhaps some other time, when Bethany was alone. . . .

She turned from her task, ready to head for home, then stopped as she felt her dress catch. She cringed as she heard the tearing of fabric. This was one of her favorite dresses. If it were to be ruined, she would be heartsick.

"Allow me."

She heard the deep voice even as she turned to see the stranger bending over to free her skirt from the troublesome nail. When he straightened, she found her head tilting backward, ever backward.

Well over six feet tall, the man was rawboned and lean, his weight distributed in hard muscles across his broad shoulders and chest. She had never felt so slight, so utterly tiny as she did this moment, standing before this stranger. There was a toughness in his boldly spaced features, a toughness that intrigued yet alarmed her. His skin was dark, his jaw smooth and square. Shaggy blue-black hair brushed the collar of his shirt and fell across his forehead. His expression was fathomless, but his midnight-blue eyes seemed to look right inside her, reading her mind, judging her thoughts.

Bethany uttered a belated gasp and stepped backward, pulling her skirt away from him.

One corner of his full mouth lifted, suggesting a smile without ever becoming one. He turned his back toward her.

"Bethany?" Ingrid's hand clasped over her arm.

She took another step backward, her eyes still on the dark stranger.

"Look at this, Hawk," a second man said,

pointing to the church notice. "They're startin' up a church here in Sweetwater. We really are gonna get civilized. You gonna go?"

The man named Hawk glanced over his shoulder, his enigmatic eyes meeting Bethany's once again.

Unconsciously, she held her breath, awaiting his reply.

"No," he said simply, then walked past her and into the saloon, followed quickly by his friend.

"Come on, Bethany." Ingrid tugged at her arm.

"Did you see him?" she asked breathlessly.

"Of course, I saw him. I was standing right here."

"Have you ever seen anyone so . . . so . . ." She didn't know what she wanted to say about him. So handsome? So mysterious? So dangerous?

"You'll never see *him* in church, Bethany Silverton," Ingrid said in an ominous tone. "Now let's go home."

At last she did as she was bid and turned to walk toward the white house at the edge of Sweetwater. "Why do you think we'll never see him in church?" she asked, her thoughts still back at the Plains Saloon.

"You just never will, that is all. Not even if you should invite him yourself. He is just not the type to be found in church, I think."

"There was something rather—" Bethany stopped abruptly. A sudden twinkle lit her green eyes as a mischievous smile curled the corners of her mouth. "I'll wager I could get him to church if I wanted to."

Ingrid's blond brows drew together in a frown. "Bethany, what are you thinking?"

"I'll wager five dollars I can get him to come to church within thirty days, Ingrid Johnson."

"The reverend would not approve of your betting," Ingrid admonished her.

Bethany held out her hand. "Are you saying I can't do it? Then shake my hand and accept my wager."

As Ingrid's fingers closed around Bethany's, she sighed. "I have a feeling we will regret this moment."

Hawk Chandler drank his beer in silence, then motioned for Rand to follow him and left the saloon. His dark blue eyes glanced at the clear sky of late afternoon. It would be nearly dark before they were back to the Circle Blue Ranch. He swung into the saddle of his copper-colored stallion and pressed his heels against the sleek steed's sides. The horse jumped forward, then settled into a smooth canter. Rand Howard drew his pinto gelding alongside, and the two men rode in silence toward the ranch.

Hawk's dark eyes scanned the grasslands that stretched a hundred miles in nearly every direction. The land undulated with benchlands and cutbacks, draws and coulees. It was a land rich in native buffalo grass, a grass like no other. It withstood the heat and drought of Montana summers. It survived the freezing, snow-covered Montana winters. It was unharmed by the trampling of hooves. It grew and flourished and filled the bellies of Circle Blue cattle.

It was good land. From the moment Hawk laid eyes on this range back in '78, he had known this was where he was going to call home. It had all the buffalo grass and blue joint he could ask for. It had lots of natural brush shelter in the form of plum thickets and chokecherry trees. And most important of all, it had water. Hawk had laid claim to his 160-acre homestead tract, beginning at the springs at the foot of the mountain range that bordered on the west. Rand had filed on the adjoining stretch of land and turned it over to Hawk, giving the Circle Blue Ranch plenty of room to grow.

Hawk had brought up his starter herd in the spring of 1879. For three years, he'd watched his herd grow. He'd introduced some shorthorns from Oregon to the range, and he'd practiced mowing hay for feed in the winter, ignoring the scorn of other ranchers who let their cattle fend for themselves. He'd built a small but sturdy house to withstand the frigid Montana winters. Hawk was proud of the Circle Blue. He was proud to call this range his home. He'd thought there wasn't much more a man could want to make him happy.

That's what he'd thought right up to the moment he'd looked into those silvery green eyes and heard her startled gasp as she drew away.

Rand would have been surprised by the turn of his friend's thoughts, but he couldn't have been more surprised than Hawk himself. He had learned his lesson years ago about young ladies like that one. Besides, he didn't need a woman. Not any woman. He'd told himself that plenty of times. He'd believed it up until . . .

Hawk shook his head as if to loosen the delicate image lodged in his mind, but she wouldn't leave him. He kept seeing the fiery auburn curls cascading from beneath her saucy green hat. He kept seeing the heart-shaped mouth, the lower lip full and enticing, the upper lip thinner and gently bowed. Once again he saw the delicately arched brows and the dark sable lashes surrounding eyes a color he'd never seen before. He saw the bright flush of her cheeks and the slightly upturned nose. He saw the generous swell of breasts and the narrow waist.

His jaw clenched. Instinct told him he wasn't going to forget this young woman as quickly as he dismissed others. Warily, he wondered how soon he would see her again.

"We thank You, Lord, for bringing us safely to our new home. We ask now that You bless Your work in Sweetwater. Amen."

Nathaniel lifted his head even as a chorus of three soft "amens" echoed his from around the supper table. His hazel eyes settled first upon his bride of twenty years. To him, the former Virginia Braddock was as lovely as the day he'd taken her to wife. Her dark sable hair was now highlighted with strands of silver, but he never thought of the gray as a sign of age; it was more like a crown or, perhaps, a halo. For twenty years, she had worked beside him in his calling to Christ's church, never questioning him, not even when he told her he wanted to come west to build a new church on the frontier. She had turned her back on the wealth and ease of their former life without a backward glance.

The same had not been true with his daughter.

Nathaniel's gaze shifted to Bethany. In this moment, she seemed as submissive, as gentle in spirit as his beloved Virginia. Ah, but looks could be deceiving. She was filled with a fire for life, that one. If he could, he would protect her, shelter her from what he feared was before her, from the trials that would come—most of them of her own making. Of course, if he must confess, he had spoiled her outrageously as a child —and still spoiled her to this very day. He had never been able to resist her impish grins. She had always had charm and she had always known how to use it to her advantage.

She looked up at him, her misty green eyes filled with a light that warned him her mind was at work. Bethany was up to something; he was sure of it. She grinned, and his heart melted. Then she looked away once more, turning her attention back to the meal.

The reverend returned her smile even as he mentally shook his head. She'd forgiven him long ago for taking her away from Philadelphia and the only life she'd ever known, but she still hadn't allowed herself to tell him so. She was far too stubborn to admit such a thing, even to the father she adored. Nathaniel had never known anyone more stubborn than this daughter of his. He could only hope and pray that her stubbornness would not bring too much sorrow into her life before she learned the price of it.

His gaze moved on, this time stopping on Ingrid. Where Bethany's coloring was bright and vibrant, with her burnished auburn hair and glittering green eyes, Ingrid was pale. Her blond hair was more silver than gold, her blue eyes so light as to be almost gray. Where Bethany's short body was perfectly curved by young womanhood, Ingrid was tall and straight with little to distinguish her waist from her bust or hips. Likewise, their personalities were as night to day. Bethany seemed ever in search of mischief; Ingrid was ever in search of peace.

Again he smiled to himself, remembering the Silverton family's first meeting with Sven Johnson and his daughter back in Minnesota. They had all become fast friends, yet none so quickly as these two girls who were such opposites. When Ingrid's father died suddenly on their way west, it had been only natural for the Silvertons to make her a part of their family.

"Papa?"

Nathaniel turned his head toward Bethany. "Yes?"

"Ingrid and I met as many of the townspeople as we could today, and we posted notices about church services. But what about the ranchers? What if they don't come to town for weeks on end? Shouldn't we try to seek them out and let them know Sweetwater now has a church and its own minister of the gospel?"

"Well, I . . ."

"I'd love to go with you, Papa. I could meet the women and encourage them to come."

"Perhaps your mother . . ."

"Oh, of course. If Mother wants to come, it would be all the more fun. And Ingrid too."

The nagging suspicion lingered—she was up to something. Yet, even as he acknowledged it, he acquiesced. How could he not when she turned pleading eyes upon him and offered one of her dazzling smiles.

"I think it's a fine idea, daughter. If the weather's good tomorrow, we'll take the buggy and go calling." He turned toward his wife. "Virginia, will you join us?"

"If it's all the same to you, Nathaniel, I'll decline. There's so much still to do here before I'll feel settled. You and Bethany go and have a good day together."

"How about you, Ingrid?" he asked as he glanced in her direction.

There were small circles of pink on Ingrid's cheeks. She was watching Bethany with a strange look in her eyes even as she shook her head, saying, "No, Reverend Silverton. Thank you, but I will stay and help Mrs. Silverton."

"I guess it's just you and me, Bethany. We'll leave right after breakfast." That settled, Nathaniel turned his attention to his cooling supper.

"I can't wait," Bethany said softly.

Hawk yanked the pump handle up and down until cool water gushed from the pump's mouth, then he leaned over and stuck his head beneath the icy flow. He straightened, shaking droplets of water from his blue-black hair and drawing in a deep breath.

It was hot for May. Too darned hot for his liking. He glared up at the golden sun.

Water trickled from his wet hair down his neck and throat, mingling with the sweat that beaded across his bare shoulders, back and chest. He grabbed the tin cup hanging on a nail near the pump and filled it with water. He drained the refreshing liquid quickly, then cast a reluctant gaze toward the barn. He still had one more horse to shoe before he could call it quits.

He returned the cup to its nail, then turned on the heel of his boot and started across the dusty yard, long strides eating up the distance. He stopped suddenly and turned, sensing a movement before seeing it. A horse and buggy approached at a smart clip, the identity of the buggy's inhabitants hidden in the shadow cast by the fringed black top.

Standing with his hands resting on his hips—a stance that looked more casual than it was—he waited as the buggy drew near. He heard the driver's "Whoa!" as the horse slowed to a walk, then stopped not far from where he stood. He squinted into the shadows, still trying to make out the faces of his visitors.

"Good afternoon," a friendly male voice said as a man stepped down from the buggy. He was dressed in a fine black suit, a suit too hot for the day. "I'm Reverend Nathaniel Silverton of Sweetwater."

"Afternoon."

The reverend held out a hand toward the buggy. "This is my daughter, Bethany."

He watched her alight, a delicate flash of

ankle and the tiniest shoes he'd ever seen peeking from beneath her flounced and ruffled gown of sunshine yellow as she stepped from the buggy. When his gaze returned to her face, he found her staring at his bare chest with intent green eyes, a hint of color in her cheeks.

"I was just shoeing a horse," he said, his voice sounding a bit gruff.

"We didn't mean to disturb you, Mr. . . . ?" The reverend stopped and waited.

Hawk wiped his hand on his jeans, then held it out as he took a step forward. "Chandler. Hawk Chandler. This is my ranch, the Circle Blue." He shook the reverend's hand.

"As I said," Nathaniel Silverton continued, "we don't want to disturb you. We just wanted to introduce ourselves and to extend our invitation to attend church services in Sweetwater this Sunday."

Hawk's gaze moved once more to the mere slip of a girl at her father's side. Bethany. The name fit her. Ladylike. Elegant. Lovely. Her rosy lips parted ever so slightly as he watched her. He felt his stomach tighten in response.

"Thanks for the invitation, Reverend, but I don't think I'll be there." He stepped back one length and nodded. "Good day to you." Then, without waiting, he turned and headed for the barn.

Bethany didn't think she'd ever seen anyone like him before. He was so tall, more than a foot taller than her five feet two inches. His skin was smooth and bronze-colored, and it glistened with sweat, enhancing the corded muscles of his chest and arms. The sight had left her feeling a little breathless and uneasy. She'd never seen a man's bare chest before, and she hadn't been able to take her eyes from that magnificent, almost frightening body from the moment she'd stepped from the carriage.

Now he was walking away from her, and she hadn't said even one word to him.

"Come along, Bethany," her father was saying now, his hand on her elbow. "We've a long way yet to go today."

Hawk Chandler. She recalled the sculpted angles of his face, the heavy black brows, the deep-set, almost hooded eyes. Blue eyes, yet so dark they were nearly black. Yes, he was like a hawk. She had felt his fierce strength as she stood before him. She could imagine his swiftness, his cunning.

"Hawk Chandler," she said softly as the buggy turned in the yard. "The name doesn't sound . . . Do you think he's an Indian?"

"I'd guess there's some Indian blood in him, though I could be wrong. But God doesn't look at the color of a man's skin, Bethany. He looks at the heart, and so should we. We'll be in prayer for him. We'll pray he'll join us in services one day soon."

Bethany glanced over her shoulder at the receding ranch house and barn. "I'll do everything I can to see that he comes," she whispered inaudibly.

CHAPTER TWO

· — ·

Vince Richards leaned against the high-backed leather chair, a vague smile playing across his lips. But he wasn't concentrating on the reverend's words.

His thoughts were locked on the auburn-haired beauty seated beside her father. From the moment she entered the room, his body had been alert with desire. Never had he seen a face so perfect. Never had he seen a body more ripe with womanly curves, yet so obviously young and virginal. He'd always liked young, innocent girls. They were so uncertain, so frightened.

"Well, we've taken up enough of your time, Mr. Richards. It was a pleasure meeting you. I hope we'll see you in church on Sunday."

Vince rose. "I'll most certainly be there, Reverend Silverton." He stepped forward and shook the reverend's hand. "I look forward to seeing you and your lovely daughter again."

Nathaniel took Bethany's arm. "Until Sunday then. Good day, Mr. Richards."

"Please, call me Vince. No point in so much formality between new friends. Right, Reverend?"

"Of course. And you must call me Nathaniel."

Vince saw Nathaniel and Bethany to their buggy and waved to them as they drove away. A self-satisfied smile slipped into the corners of his mouth. There was a girl he would take great pleasure in possessing. And who better for his wife than a reverend's daughter? One day he meant to be governor of Montana. Not just the territory either. He would see that it became a state and, when it did, he meant to be governor. Bethany Silverton would be the perfect wife to have at his side. Beautiful, cultured, refined . . . and virginal. Yes, he would have her for his own. He must have her.

He turned back toward his house. Vince Richards was proud of the massive, two-story brick structure. It had taken him two years to build and furnish it, but it was the finest home in all of Montana Territory. He was sure of that. A home fit for a cattle king and the future governor of Montana.

Again he thought of Bethany Silverton. This time in his bedroom. This time in his large four-poster bed, her fiery auburn hair loose and spilling over her creamy shoulders. His grey eyes lit with feral delight. He rubbed sweaty palms together as he stepped up onto the porch. It seemed a long time until Sunday.

He drew in a ragged breath, bringing his lustful thoughts back to the present. He sat in a chair on the porch and took a cigar from his shirt pocket. As he smoked, his gaze roamed over the rolling countryside that made up the Bar V Ranch. Five thousand Bar V cattle roamed the range. Soon there would be ten, then twenty thousand. Perhaps even more. All he needed was time and more grazing land—and more water.

Water! He bit down on the cigar, teeth clenched, eyes narrowing thoughtfully as they slid toward the mountain range to the west. Hawk Chandler's ranch was at the foot of those mountains—Hawk's ranch and a spring that never ceased to flow, providing life-giving water for cattle for miles around. Control of that spring and river gave the Circle Blue control of the range for fifteen to twenty miles on either side of it.

Damnation, but he needed that water. If he planned to own the largest cattle operation in Montana, he had to have control of Spring River, from the mountains all the way to the Musselshell. He had to find a way to drive that dirty, thievin' redskin from his ranch.

Angry now, Vince tossed his cigar into the dusty yard and jumped up from his chair to storm into the house. It always made him angry to think of a redskin owning what should be his. He didn't care how watered down the Indian blood was in Hawk Chandler. It wasn't right for a breed to own land that should, by right of superiority of race, belong to a white man. Hawk Chandler ought to be on a reservation somewhere instead of running his own cattle ranch and being free to associate with decent white folks.

Someday, he thought. Someday, as surely as

he meant to possess Bethany Silverton and make her his wife, he meant to kill Hawk Chandler and take possession of the Circle Blue and its spring.

"Had some visitors today." Hawk sat down at the table with his bowl of stew.

Rand looked at him with questioning eyes, tension in his voice. "Who?"

Hawk shook his head. "No. It wasn't Richards or any of his men." He lifted the spoon filled with steaming beef and potatoes toward his mouth. "It was the new reverend and his daughter. Came to invite us to church."

"They did, huh? Well, I guess if they're going to go to all that trouble to bring a personal invitation, we oughta go."

Hawk remained silent.

"I don't suppose the reverend's daughter was a blonde, was she?" Rand asked, recalling the tall, thin girl he'd seen outside the Plains Saloon the day before.

"No."

Rand swallowed his disappointment. "Well, I think I'll go anyway. Sure you won't join me?"

Hawk shook his head.

Rand understood his friend's reluctance to mingle with the town's growing population. He'd come to know Hawk pretty well in the five years they'd been together. In bits and pieces, for Hawk wasn't much of a talker, he'd learned of Hawk's childhood in Chicago, of the cruel taunting of children about his father's squaw. His mother, Crying Wind, the granddaughter of a Sioux chief and the daughter of an Indian princess and her white trapper husband, had never tried to teach him the ways of her Sioux heritage. Hawk had always lived among the white men, and the world of his mother's people was as foreign to him as to any other boy in Chicago. But that made no difference to the children who had singled him out to be persecuted for the darkness of his skin and his name, Blue Hawk.

Rand also knew of the girl named Alice, the girl Hawk had fallen in love with when he was sixteen. Lovely, ladylike Alice. Hawk had believed she loved him, despite their different backgrounds—Hawk the son of a working-class newspaper reporter, and Alice the daughter of the newspaper's wealthy owner. For nearly a year, they had seen each other secretly, proclaiming their devotion, planning to be married just as soon as they were old enough. Hawk had assumed Alice knew about his mixed blood, but he was wrong. When she met his mother and learned he was one-quarter Indian, she had rejected him with cutting finality.

Rand knew his friend had never forgotten that rejection. Hawk kept most people, especially women, at arm's length. Rand wondered if the wound would ever heal.

"Some other time, then," Rand said as he reached for a thick slice of bread and dipped it into his stew.

Sleepless, Bethany lay on her bed, staring at the ceiling while the encroaching dawn lightened her room. She twirled a strand of hair around her index finger as she thoughtfully worried her lower lip.

Now that she'd found Hawk Chandler and learned his name, how was she going to get him to agree to come to church? Just because he'd told her father he wouldn't be there didn't mean she was going to give up. She was more determined than ever to win her bet with Ingrid. But it was more than the five dollars she stood to lose. There was something about Hawk Chandler that made her want to know him and know him well. She'd only seen him twice. She'd probably heard him speak fewer than a dozen words, and she had never spoken to him. Yet he filled her thoughts.

Even now she could see him in her mind's eye. He was the most ruggedly handsome man she'd ever seen. So dark, so tall. And his voice, so deep and strong. She wondered why no woman had—

Land o' Goshen! She sat up in bed. *What if he's married?*

She felt the heat rise in her cheeks. She didn't want him to be married. Oh, she could still try to get him to church. She could still win the wager. But somehow she knew it just wouldn't be the same. Her heart raced in her chest. She had to find out if there was a Mrs. Chandler. She had to find out today.

Bethany pushed away the blankets and swung her feet over the side of the bed. She would go for a ride. She would just "happen" by the Circle Blue. It wasn't so terribly far from town. She could be there in an hour or two by horseback.

Of course, she would have to take Ingrid with her, but it would probably be better if she didn't tell her their destination. She glanced out the window at the clear sky. It promised to be another warm day. She would use that as an excuse for an early ride.

Quickly she poured some water from the pitcher into the bowl and performed her morning ablutions. Then she ran a hasty brush through her unruly thick curls before capturing them into a proper bun at the nape. While she was dressing in her riding habit, she heard a door open and close, then the creaking of the stairs, and she knew her father was up for his morning prayer time. She would have to wait until he emerged from his study again before she could leave.

She checked the mirror one more time, approving her appearance in the dark umber riding habit, then left her room, hurrying on quiet feet down the hall to Ingrid's bedroom. She knocked softly, entering without waiting for the grumbled reply which greeted her knock.

"Get up, sleepyhead," Bethany whispered as she neared the bed.

Sprawled on her stomach, her blond hair draped over her face, Ingrid opened one eye to peer up at her early-morning torturer. "What time is it?"

"Time to get up if we want to go for a ride this morning."

"Ride? What ride?"

"Our ride. Don't you remember?" Bethany swept off Ingrid's coverlets. "We wanted to go for a ride today."

Suspicion clouded Ingrid's face as she pushed her hair away from her eyes and sat up. "I do not recall anything about a ride."

"Oh, you're so forgetful, Ingrid." Bethany flounced over to the chair near the window and sat down in it. "Look outside. It's going to be a beautiful warm day, and I'm not leaving this room until you're up and dressed and ready to go riding with me. I had such a lovely time with Father yesterday. The country is beautiful. Even more so than I'd thought before. Especially over by the Cir—" She caught herself. "By the mountains. I want you to see it all. Maybe we'll even see some buffalo today. Wouldn't that be exciting?"

While Bethany chattered, Ingrid got out of bed, washed, then went to her wardrobe. As she dressed, she said, "You do not fool me, Bethany. You are up to something."

"Up to something?" Bethany's voice peaked in feigned surprise and hurt. "Ingrid, must you always be so suspicious?" Then Bethany began to laugh, her eyes twinkling, revealing her suppressed excitement.

Ingrid tried to frown but couldn't. Soon she was laughing right along with her friend, even though she knew there was trouble brewing.

The horse quivered, its black eyes wild with fright, its four legs braced. Rand gripped the rope, holding the animal steady while Hawk stepped carefully into the saddle.

"Okay. Let him go."

For a moment after Rand had stepped backward, the rangy black stallion didn't move, but

Hawk wasn't fooled. He tightened his hold. A second or two later, the horse erupted into the air with wild fury, its body twisting in a vicious attempt to unseat the unwelcome rider. All four hooves struck the hard earth with teeth-jarring impact. Horse and rider grunted in unison.

Hawk heard Rand's yell of encouragement as the wild horse took flight again. The stallion echoed the sound with a shrill neigh as it dropped its head between its legs, back arched. With grim determination, Hawk awaited the abrupt landing. His body reacted instinctively, flowing with the animal's movements rather than against them. His free arm acted as a balance as the stallion bucked and twisted and spun around the corral. Dust filled his nostrils and stung his eyes. Sweat poured from beneath his hatband and down his back.

A stubborn grin curved the corners of his mouth. He would win in the end, but he loved the battle. From the moment he'd sat his first bronc when he was eighteen and as green as they came, he'd loved the excitement of bronc busting.

Suddenly, the horse stopped fighting, standing in absolute silence in the middle of the corral. Hawk was surprised by the abrupt cessation of motion, and his guard lowered. In that same instant, the crafty stallion threw its back legs toward the sky, its nose almost touching the ground.

Hawk parted company with the saddle and somersaulted in the air toward the corral fence. With terrific force, he hit the dirt, shoulder first. The air was knocked from him as he tumbled over onto his back. He lay still, eyes closed, trying to drag a breath back into his lungs.

Rand's laughter reached his ears. "I thought you'd actually gotten some wings, Hawk. You were flyin' all right."

Hawk sat up, his stormy blue eyes turning on the recalcitrant beast. Without comment, he pushed his tall frame up from the dirt and brushed off his jeans as he walked across the corral. The horse's breathing was labored; white rings circled its eyes as it watched Hawk's approach. Hawk could feel the tension in the air.

"Easy," he crooned softly, picking up the rope and reaching for the saddle horn. "Easy, boy."

His leg was scarcely over the animal's back before the twosome was once again airborne.

Bethany could hear the screaming horse and the excited whooping long before she could see where it was coming from. As she and Ingrid rode around the side of the barn, her eyes were met by a wild scene.

The man she had seen with Hawk outside the Plains Saloon was sitting on the corral fence, shouting encouragement and waving his hat. In the corral, Hawk was riding a horse that looked for all the world as if it meant to kill both the rider and itself. The excitement was palpable. Except in brief glimpses, she couldn't really see Hawk's face, yet she knew he was enjoying the insane ride.

She nudged her little mare forward, drawn by the drama of man against beast. Reaching the corral, she dismounted, then stepped up onto the bottom rail of the fence. Her gaze never wavered from Hawk. She had forgotten Ingrid. She was unaware of the other man on the fence nearby. She was captured by the battle of wills transpiring before her eyes.

She wasn't certain how much time passed before the bucking slowed, then stopped. Finally, the animal stood quietly, dragging in noisy gasps of air. Hawk waited a moment, then nudged the belabored sides with the heels of his boots. The horse moved forward at a walk, then a trot. Hawk guided it with the rope and halter, circling the corral.

He didn't look at her as he rode past her place on the fence, yet she knew he had seen her. She felt a tiny thrill race along her spine.

"He's good, ain't he?"

She looked over at the man who had spoken. "Yes. I've never seen a horse ridden like that before."

Rand hopped down from the fence and stepped toward her, pulling his hat back on his head as he did so. "I'm Rand Howard." His brow lifted in question.

"Bethany Silverton. And this is my friend, Ingrid Johnson."

"Pleased to meet you, Miss Silverton." He paused, his gaze lingering a moment on Ingrid. "Miss Johnson."

Ingrid acknowledged his close scrutiny with a nod and a blush.

In unison, they all three turned their attention back to the corral.

Hawk had drawn the lathered stallion to a halt. Slowly, deliberately, he stepped down from the saddle. He spoke softly to the horse, his voice but not his words carrying toward the observers at the fence. His hand stroked the sweaty black neck. Then he placed his foot in the stirrup once again and remounted, talking all the while. The stallion's ears twitched forward, then back, listening to the soothing sound as he stepped out at Hawk's urging. Several more times, Hawk guided the horse in a wide circle around the corral. When he dismounted the second time, he gave the black stallion a pleased pat on the neck, then loosened the cinch and removed the saddle and pad.

It was a pleasant thing, watching him work. Bethany noticed how gently he treated the animal, yet she was keenly aware of the strong muscles hidden beneath his sweat-dampened shirt.

In that moment, he turned toward the corral fence, and his blue eyes captured her green ones. It was a penetrating gaze, seeming to read her thoughts. She felt color rising in her cheeks, but she couldn't look away. He walked toward her, his gait smooth, his stride long. She had the feeling she shrank in size with each step that brought him closer.

She swallowed hard, forcing herself to break free of his mesmerizing gaze. "Good day, Mr. Chandler." She smiled brightly and tilted her head to one side in a flirting gesture she knew was becoming. "My friend and I were out taking a ride and heard a commotion, so we came to see what it was. I'm so glad we did. I've never seen anything so exciting."

Hawk's glance flicked to Ingrid, then returned to Bethany. "You're a long way from Sweetwater."

"I know, but the day was so warm and it's such a lovely ride."

"It's not safe for two women to be out alone this far from town."

She widened her eyes in innocent surprise. "But I was out here with Father just yesterday. I saw nothing to be afraid of."

"You don't always see danger in this country, Miss Silverton." His deep voice sent another wave of shivers down her back.

"I . . . I guess I didn't think of that. Perhaps . . . would you mind riding back with us to Sweetwater?" She was surprised to find how very much she wanted him to do just that. Not because she would be that much closer to getting him to agree to go to church with her. No, she just wanted to be with him a little while longer. She wanted to get to know him.

She also realized he would be a difficult man to get to know. She sensed so much she didn't understand lurking behind those fathomless blue eyes. For some reason, she wanted terribly to understand him. And she realized something else as they stood there. Here was a man she would never control by the flutter of her eyelashes. She would never wrap him around her finger or charm her way into his heart.

Confused by her own thoughts, Bethany dropped her gaze to her hands where they rested on the corral railing.

"How about if we offer them lunch and then I'll see them back to town," Rand offered.

Bethany's eyes darted up once again. Hawk was still staring at her, his face unreadable.

"We wouldn't want to put you or your wife out, Mr. Chandler."

"There is no Mrs. Chandler," Hawk said at last, his voice low. There was no time for her to be happy with that bit of information before he added, "And we'll all go into town. I mean to have a word with the reverend and tell him to keep you at home where you belong before you wind up in trouble."

A quick flash of anger replaced the confusion of moments before. Her silvery-green gaze darkened to the color of a stormy sea. She stepped back from the corral fence, her chin jutting forward in defiance.

"My father has no need of your advice, Mr. Chandler. I assure you I'm not as helpless as I appear."

For the first time, she heard him laugh and saw a full smile spill across his face. It had a startling effect on her equilibrium. And the surprising force of her own reaction to his smile unsettled her even further.

Hawk stepped onto the bottom rail, then vaulted over the fence. "I'm sure you're anything but helpless, Miss Silverton." The laughter and smile vanished as quickly as they'd come. "But I still mean to talk to your father. Next time you might not find the men you meet as friendly as Rand and me."

"Less friendly than you, Mr. Chandler?" She tossed her head as she turned toward her mare.

"I should certainly hate to meet anyone less friendly than you."

Hawk rode along beside Bethany, controlling his amusement with difficulty as he looked at the lift of her stubborn chin. Her eyes still sparkled with lingering anger. He supposed he shouldn't have taken it upon himself to tell her father how to manage her, but now that he'd suggested it, he had to carry through.

Besides, he was right. A woman alone out here, especially without a gun or a rifle, could get into all sorts of trouble, if not from disreputable men, then from snakes or wolves or buffalo or any number of things.

And for some reason which he preferred not to examine at that moment, Hawk especially didn't want anything bad to happen to Bethany Silverton.

Bethany jerked back suddenly on her mount's reins. "What on earth is that?" she asked, pointing toward an enormous mound of sun-baked bones.

Hawk followed her finger. "Remains of a buffalo herd."

"What killed them?"

"Greed."

Rand elaborated on Hawk's simple statement as he and Ingrid pulled up beside them. "Hides pay about three-fifty each in Miles City. Maybe more by now. The great buffalo herds of the southern plains were wiped out in the seventies. Montana's about the last place for the buffalo, and you won't be able to find any here in another year or two."

Hawk touched his heels to his copper stallion's sides. "Cattlemen think they can't raise their herds where there's buffalo."

"And you don't agree?" Bethany asked, catching up with him again.

Hawk shrugged.

Once again, Rand filled the silence. "Buffalo come through, they just sweep away horses and cows right along with them. Chances are you'll never see your stock again. Besides, they eat the grass the cattle need. Now that the railroad's reached Montana, there's going to be more and more men coming north to build their ranches, men with big dreams for the grasslands here. Those dreams don't include buffalo herds. Anyways, as long as there's people willing to buy buffalo hides, there'll be hunters willing to kill them."

"We saw some buffalo on our way to Sweetwater," Bethany said thoughtfully. She turned her gaze upon Hawk. The anger was gone. She looked strangely saddened, like a child who has lost a kitten or a puppy.

Hawk felt a tug at his heart.

"I thought they were magnificent," she added. "They were frightening and yet so noble."

He'd never seen a mouth so made to be kissed.

"Have you ever killed a buffalo, Mr. Chandler?" There was a tremulous quality in her voice.

"No, Miss Silverton, I haven't."

She smiled, and it was as if the sun had just come from behind a cloud. "I'm glad."

In that moment, so was he. Very glad, indeed.

CHAPTER THREE

·——·

I wish I'd never made that miserable wager,"
Bethany complained as she passed a dripping
dish to Ingrid. "If I hadn't, I'd never have to see
that Hawk Chandler again. And the way Papa
carried on! You would have thought I'd stolen
something or killed someone or something really terrible like that."

Softly, Ingrid said, "We can forget the wager if
you would like."

"We will not!" Bethany dropped a dirty skillet
into the wash water, splashing soapy suds onto
her apron. Her eyes narrowed as she began to
scrub, imagining it was Mr. Chandler beneath
the wire brush. "I'll win that wager and I'll make
him pay for the trouble he's caused me."

Even now, five days later, she could still hear
her father's rantings and ravings. "I'll not have a
daughter of mine behaving like some ill-
mannered street urchin. Riding out alone so far
from town. Calling on unmarried men. I won't
have it."

"But Papa—" she'd tried to protest in her behalf.

"You'll not sweet-talk me out of this, Bethany Rachel. You are forbidden to ride that horse of yours for two weeks. And I'll be having plenty of things for you to help me with around here besides."

"But Papa—"

Her protests had been to no avail.

So here she stood, washing dishes like a common servant on a delightfully sunny morning, her mare locked up in the stables, and it was all Hawk's fault. If he hadn't told her father how dangerous it was for her to be out riding . . . If he hadn't told the reverend about their visit to his ranch . . . If he hadn't insisted on coming back to town with her . . . It was all his fault, and by hook or by crook, she meant to get even for the trouble he'd caused her.

Ingrid's hand touched her shoulder. "Bethany, you should not be thinking such things."

"What things?" She scrubbed the skillet even harder.

"You know what things. You should forgive Mr. Chandler. He was only trying to protect us."

"Don't you stand up for him, Ingrid Johnson. Don't you *dare* stand up for him. I'm just about as mad at you as I am at him."

Ingrid's hand fell away. Her already pale complexion whitened even more, and her light blue eyes dropped to the dish she was drying.

Bethany knew she should apologize. Ingrid's feelings were easily hurt. But right now she didn't want to apologize. She was angry with Ingrid. After all, Ingrid hadn't even tried to get Rand Howard to church, but guess who the first person was to arrive at the tent last Sunday morning? Rand. And he had come alone. Hawk hadn't even had the decency to join his friend in church. For two hours, Bethany had had to watch Rand making eyes at Ingrid, and Ingrid blushing so brightly she looked as if she might melt away from embarrassment.

Suddenly, Bethany stepped back from the counter and tore off her apron. "I'm going for a walk. I can't stand it in here one more moment."

She hurried out the back door, not even stopping to put on a bonnet or grab a parasol. What did she care if the sun darkened her complexion. Who was there out here to notice anyway?

Holding her skirts out of the way, she walked swiftly across the open field behind the house, making for the cottonwoods and willows that lined the river running parallel to Sweetwater's single street. On the banks of Spring River, she sat down in the shade of the leafy trees, drawing her knees up to her chin. She hugged her legs against her chest as she stared into the deep-running, clear water.

It wasn't fair. It just wasn't fair. She was fond of Ingrid. Honestly, she was very fond of her. Ingrid was like a sister. Bethany loved her. She was happy there was a young man who found Ingrid attractive. And Rand Howard seemed like a very nice sort. They would do well together.

But, oh! How it stuck in her craw that Rand

should have fallen so obviously for pale, tall, thin Ingrid when Hawk Chandler hadn't even given Bethany a second glance. She knew she was pretty. Hadn't everyone always told her so? Hadn't she always had a flock of male admirers, even when she was just a child? It just wasn't at all fair. Not at all.

"I'll win that wager yet, Hawk Chandler," she whispered. "You'll see."

Rand whistled as he and Hawk rode toward Sweetwater. He couldn't wait to see Ingrid again. In all his twenty-five years, he hadn't felt this way about a girl. It seemed as if he'd suddenly realized he'd been looking for her and hadn't even known it until he saw her. But now he knew, and he wasn't about to let her get away. He meant to sweet-talk that girl into marrying him. He didn't own more than his clothes, his saddle, a couple of horses, and a piece of land Hawk had given him up against the mountains in exchange for his homestead claim. Rand meant to build a little place there, warm and tight against the cold Montana winters. He and Ingrid would be happy there.

He hadn't thought about his family back in Iowa for a long, long time, but suddenly he did. The youngest of fourteen children, seven boys and seven girls, he hadn't taken much notion to being a farmer like his pa. So, at the age of thirteen, he'd struck out on his own, heading West to learn to be a cowpoke. The last twelve years hadn't been bad. He'd learned a lot. He'd made a few friends. He'd never thought he missed the noise and crowd of his large family. Yet, all of a sudden, he found himself wishing for a large family of his own.

He grinned to himself. Perhaps he'd better build a little bit bigger place.

"What's got you so happy?" Hawk asked.

"I'm havin' supper at the Silvertons. You oughta join us, Hawk. The reverend invited you too."

Hawk grunted. "I don't think Miss Silverton would feel the same way."

"So what are you going to do? Spend the evening at the Plains or maybe drop in on Miss Olivia?"

Hawk shrugged noncommittally.

"Miss Silverton's a whole lot prettier than Miss Olivia," Rand added with a chuckle.

Then his thoughts turned back to Ingrid, and he began whistling once again.

Hawk dismounted in front of the Plains Saloon and watched his friend continue down Main Street toward the reverend's house. He refused to admit to himself how much he would have liked to go along, how much he'd like to see Bethany again. Ever since he'd left the Silverton home last week, he'd been haunted by the memory of her icy green gaze following him out the door. He kept seeing her face, flushed with anger.

He turned away from the saloon door. He didn't feel much like a drink. And he didn't feel like spending an evening with Miss Olivia or any of her girls either—as delightfully entertaining as they sometimes could be. What he needed was to clear his head, shake loose of Bethany Silverton's bewitching memory.

Impulsively, Hawk cut between the buildings and headed for Spring River.

The cottonwoods and willow trees were in glorious spring foliage, a stark contrast to the undulating brownish-green grasslands that stretched for miles in all directions. A welcome breeze rustled the leaves overhead as Hawk walked along the river's edge.

He stopped when he saw her, sitting in the shade, hugging her legs against her chest, her chin resting on her knees. Unwillingly he realized she was even more beautiful than he'd been remembering. She had pulled the pins from her hair. The auburn tresses, ablaze with fiery highlights, fell in thick waves down her back, touching the ground behind her. Her eyes were closed, and she worried her lip, deep in thought.

Hawk heard her sigh. Quickly, he stepped closer to a tree, melting into the shadows.

Bethany opened her eyes. She released her legs and stretched her arms high over her head. A grin replaced the worried look of moments before. She pulled up the soft brown skirt, revealing tiny feet and a delightful glimpse of leg. With nimble fingers, she loosened her shoes and removed them, then jumped up from the ground and stepped to the river's edge. She tested the water with one toe, drawing suddenly back with a gasp. But she didn't give up just because of the cold. Her lips pressed together in determination as she lifted her skirt even higher and stepped down into the water.

It was a joy to watch her. Hawk had forgotten how nice it could be just to look at a woman. In the years since he'd left Chicago, he'd avoided women for the most part, except for those occasional visits with ladies of Miss Olivia's ilk, and that just wasn't the same. You couldn't compare those painted, oft-times hardened faces with Bethany's fresh-faced beauty. You couldn't compare their blowsy appearance to Bethany's simple elegance. No, it was a real pleasure just to look at this girl.

It would be better, of course, if he didn't allow himself the enjoyment. There was no room in his life for the likes of Bethany Silverton, and there was nothing to make him think she wanted any part of his life anyway. If he was smart, he would turn around and walk as quickly as he could back to the Plains Saloon. Better yet, he ought to mount up on Flame and race his copper stallion back to the safety of the Circle Blue.

Instead, he stepped out from the shadows and toward the river.

"Afternoon, Miss Silverton."

Bethany gasped and turned quickly. Her foot slipped on the mossy rocks. Eyes wide and arms flailing, she fell backward into the river.

Quickly, Hawk stepped into the water to retrieve her.

She felt his hands closing over hers. He drew her to her feet, then scooped her into his arms, sodden skirt and all. Of their own volition, her arms circled his neck as he carried her out of the river. Never in her life had she felt such an incredible sense of safety as she did at this moment, held closely against his broad chest.

She looked up into his face. His eyes were studying her in a most disconcerting manner. He wasn't smiling, yet neither was he not smiling. She felt her heart flutter.

"I'm getting your shirt wet," she said softly, unnecessarily.

"I know."

"Hadn't you best put me down?"

He seemed to consider it a moment before doing so.

"Thank you."

Hawk's full smile suddenly appeared. "You make quite a splash for such a little girl."

His words begged for an angry retort, yet she discovered she felt no anger. She seemed helpless against the magnetic pull of his wonderful smile. Surprisingly, she laughed aloud and nodded. "Yes, I guess I do."

"I'd better see you home. You should get out of those wet things."

"You'll want to dry off, too, Mr. Chandler."

"I'll be all right."

"You may as well stay for supper. Mr. Howard will be there, you know." Her heart was fluttering again. "You were invited, too. Won't you please stay?"

Hadn't she been furious with him only moments before? She'd been plotting to get even. Shouldn't she let him know how angry she was with him? Yet she knew in her heart she wasn't angry with him any longer. She didn't want to win a bet or get even. She just wanted him to stay. She wanted him to like her. She wanted

him to approve of her. She wanted to make him
smile that glorious smile of his again and again.

"Won't you please stay?" she asked one more
time.

"I guess I can't say no after causing your
dunking in the river."

She shook her head. "No, Mr. Chandler, you
most certainly cannot. Having supper with us
will be the only way to make up for startling me
so."

"Then I'll stay."

They walked side by side in silence back to
Bethany's home. Once inside, she excused herself and left Hawk with the others in the parlor
while she fairly flew up the stairs to her bedroom. She let her water-soaked skirt fall in a
puddle of fabric on the floor and stepped out of
it even as she unbuttoned her blouse. She had
just discarded her undergarments and was pulling on clean drawers when Ingrid's soft tap
sounded on her door.

"May I come in, Bethany?"

"Yes."

Bethany didn't even turn around as the door
opened. She hastily drew on a fresh chemise and
a ruffled muslin petticoat. "What dress should I
wear, Ingrid? Oh, please help me decide."

Ingrid joined her at the wardrobe.

"Do you think he would like the rose satine?
Mother says it brings out the red in my hair. Oh, I
wish I had something new to wear, but it's so
difficult to get fashionable clothes out here."

"You always look lovely in anything you wear,
Bethany."

She glanced up at Ingrid then and felt a blush

coloring her cheeks. "I'm acting foolishly, aren't I?"

"Are you?" Ingrid shook her head, smiling gently. "I think he is very handsome. I would want to look my prettiest too."

"Oh, you *do* look pretty, Ingrid," Bethany insisted, grabbing her tall friend by the shoulders and turning her toward the mirror. She peeked around to meet Ingrid's gaze in the glass. "Mr. Howard can't take his eyes off you. I saw that the moment I entered the parlor, even as wet as I was." This was a lie, of course. She hadn't been aware of anything or anyone except Hawk. But Ingrid need never know that, and it wouldn't hurt to give her some confidence about her appearance.

Ingrid's voice was whispery soft, breathless with hope. "Do you really think so?"

Bethany nodded.

"Bethany?"

"Yes?"

"I am not sorry we came to Sweetwater any longer. Even if the saloons *are* noisy."

Bethany smiled at Ingrid's reflection even as she squeezed her friend's arms. Then she turned away again to pull from the wardrobe the satine gown with its flounced skirt and draped bustle. Ingrid helped her slip it over her head, fussing with the skirt while Bethany buttoned the bodice down to its pointed waist. Then Ingrid brought a towel and dried Bethany's hair as best she could before coiling it into a chignon at the nape and capturing the rich auburn tresses in a rose-colored net to match the gown.

As Bethany cast a critical eye at her reflection in the mirror, Ingrid asked, "You do like him, don't you, Bethany?"

"I . . . I don't know, Ingrid." Her light green gaze met Ingrid's pale blue. "He's so . . . so different from any man I've ever known. He makes me so unsure of myself." She smiled wryly. "And so angry too."

Ingrid nodded, a look of satisfaction on her face. "And you are not just doing this to win the wager?"

Bethany laughed as she rose from her dressing table, her uncertainty vanishing. "Oh, I intend to win the wager, Ingrid Johnson. I most definitely intend to win the wager."

Hawk's watchful eyes turned toward the parlor doorway as soon as he heard footsteps on the stairs and the muffled whispering of feminine voices. He stood as she entered the room at Ingrid's side, but he wasn't even aware of the tall blonde's existence.

A soft blush highlighted Bethany's creamy complexion. Her silver-green eyes seemed darker than usual as they met his, then glanced away. The dress bodice had a modest neckline, yet it couldn't conceal the ripeness of the woman's figure beneath. A sharp longing surged through Hawk. A desire he hadn't felt in a long, long time. A desire not just to take a woman to bed but to cherish her, to hold her, to be a part of her. Not since Alice . . .

He felt the cold wash over him. He wasn't a foolish schoolboy any longer. He'd better learn to be satisfied with the Miss Olivias of this world. A young lady like Bethany Silverton was not for Blue Hawk Chandler.

A gray-haired woman in a black dress and crisp white apron appeared in the parlor doorway. "Mrs. Silverton, supper's ready."

"Thank you, Griselda." Bethany's mother turned toward her guests. "Gentlemen, shall we go in to supper?"

The reverend stepped forward to take his wife's arm even as she spoke, and the couple led the way to the dining room. Rand and Ingrid followed next, leaving Hawk and Bethany alone in the parlor. Almost reluctantly, he held out his arm to her. When she slipped her fingers into the crook of his elbow, he felt her quivering, and another sting of longing shot through him.

He looked down at her, so petite, so utterly delicate and feminine. He could smell a light fragrance of toilet water, something like wildflowers on a spring morning. At that same moment, she leaned her head back and looked upward. Her eyes widened in silent question.

Deliberately, he hardened himself against the tug of her gaze. "Come on," he said roughly and started forward.

Supper was a long, miserable process for Hawk. His pants and shirt were still damp, reminding him of the moment he'd held Bethany in his arms. He wished he'd never taken that walk. He wished he'd never seen her sitting by the river. And he wished he'd never pulled her out. If he hadn't, he wouldn't be here now, fighting this silent battle in his head, resisting the urge to look at her, rejecting the desire to hold her and . . .

"My husband tells me you're a rancher, Mr. Chandler." Virginia Silverton passed him the platter of meat as she spoke. "Is it a family ranch?"

"No, ma'am. My parents are both dead."

"How tragic. I'm so sorry."

Hawk shrugged, trying not to think of the raging fire that had claimed their lives. "It was a long time ago, Mrs. Silverton. Back in Chicago where I grew up."

"In Chicago?" Bethany's voice questioned. "I thought you must have always lived out west."

Hawk glanced in her direction and shook his head.

"Hawk and I met up on a cattle drive from Texas," Rand said with a teasing twinkle in his eyes. "He was still a bit of a greenhorn. Hadn't been out West long enough. Me, I'd been on my own since I was thirteen and I knew all the ropes. So I took a hand in showin' him what it took to be a proper cowboy. He was so grateful, he kept me on when he started his own place. Been together ever since. Truth is, he couldn't've done it without me."

"Why do I have the feeling, Mr. Howard, that your story is slightly exaggerated?" Nathaniel asked with a chuckle.

Rand joined the laughter. "Guess I should know better than to try to pull the wool over a minister's eyes." He winked at Hawk.

But even as Hawk acknowledged Rand's words with a half-smile of his own, he could still feel Bethany watching him. He could sense her wondering about his background. What would she do if she knew about his mother? It hadn't mattered to the cowboys he'd lived and worked with since leaving Chicago so many years ago. But women were different. Would Bethany be as repelled as Alice had been when she learned the truth? Perhaps now was as good a time as any to find out.

He turned his midnight blue eyes on Bethany. Unknowingly, his jaw stiffened and his mouth was set in a firm line, but she didn't look away from the hardness of his gaze.

"My father was a newspaperman. He traveled all over the country when he was young. He met my mother in the Dakotas. My grandmother was a full-blooded Sioux. My grandfather was a fur trapper. My mother, Crying Wind, was raised near her mother's village." He waited for some reaction, not just from Bethany but from everyone around the table. No one said anything. No one moved. "When my father took a job with the newspaper in Chicago, they went there to live. That's where I was born. I don't think my mother was ever happy in the city, but she loved my father so she went where he went."

"Have you ever met any of your mother's family?" Bethany asked, her voice soft.

The question brought back a sudden, long-forgotten memory of his mother. At seven years old, he'd been in a fight with some of the boys at school—the ones who always called him a dirty injun and his mother many things worse—and he had come home with a black eye and bloody nose. Crying Wind had wordlessly cleaned his wounds, then tucked him into bed. She had leaned over him, kissing his forehead and whispering to him, *Never be ashamed that you are of the Sioux, my son. Our people are a proud people. But you are also a white man. Be proud of that as well. There are bad people like those boys in both worlds. It is up to you to be different. Do not learn to hate. Become the best of both peoples.* Her smile had been so tender, her black eyes misty. *If you are a man like your father, you will be the best.*

Hawk shook his head, both in answer to Bethany's question and to shake away the memory that brought a tightness to his chest. "I never tried to find them. I didn't belong in their world." His voice hardened once again, this time in challenge. "But I make no apologies for my Indian blood."

She met his gaze unflinchingly. "Why should you, Mr. Chandler?"

He felt a warmth spreading through him, a soothing sensation, a healing brought about by the simple honesty of her words.

She accepted him as few had done before.

CHAPTER FOUR

. ———— .

Bethany tossed another gown across the bed and eyed it with disgust. "It's not right. Not a one of them is right."

Clad only in chemise and drawers, she turned back to her wardrobe. Surely there must be a dress in her wardrobe that would be perfect for tonight.

"But Bethany," Ingrid said from behind her, "you have so many pretty gowns." She picked up the blue gingham dress from the floor. "What is wrong with this one?"

"Half the women in town will be wearing one just like it tonight, Ingrid. I don't want that." To herself she added, *Hawk will never notice me if I just look like the others.*

"You are doing this for Mr. Chandler then?"

"Of course not," Bethany replied indignantly, irritated that Ingrid had so easily read her intentions.

Ingrid turned toward the bedroom door, a smile in her voice as she said, "Of course not. He may not even come, you know." Then she left the room.

Bethany flounced down on the bed, pushing the pile of clothes onto the floor. "He'll come," she said aloud. "He's *got* to come."

As soon as she'd learned about the barn dance, Bethany had sat down and written a note to Mr. Chandler and Mr. Howard, telling them how much she had enjoyed their company at supper and how she hoped they would see each other again at the barn dance. Her father would have been appalled had he known. He never would have approved of such bold behavior. But how else was she going to win her wager with Ingrid if she didn't have more opportunities to see the elusive Hawk Chandler?

Cupping her chin in her palms, elbows resting on her legs, Bethany recalled once more the way she'd felt when Hawk pulled her from the river. She wanted to feel that way again. She would if he were to dance with her. She knew she would.

A glance toward the window told her the hour was growing late. She would have to decide on something to wear now or she would never be ready in time. She scrambled off the bed and returned to her wardrobe. She simply must own something suitable to catch his eye.

It was against his better judgment, but somehow Hawk had let Rand talk him into going into town for the dance. He knew he should have stayed at the ranch. Rand just didn't understand that Hawk didn't fit in at times like these.

But Hawk understood. He'd lived with it too many years. He was a good man with his hired help, and most of them considered him a friend. But cowpokes were cowpokes. A different breed.

Town folks liked him well enough. After all, his money was as good as the next man's. But a barn dance was different altogether. They would be socializing, talking to the ladies. And most folks just didn't think a man with Indian blood in him was fit company for a white woman.

Yet, when he'd glanced once again at Bethany's note and imagined seeing her there, he just couldn't help himself. He'd wanted to come. He'd wanted to see her, even if all he could do was stand by the punch bowl and observe her as she danced with the men of Sweetwater.

Phil Potter's new barn at the edge of town still smelled like fresh lumber. The hard-packed dirt floor had been swept free of straw. A long table, covered with a white tablecloth, was set against the far wall. It was stacked high with cookies and pies and a large crystal punch bowl. Laura Potter was standing alone behind the table, filling cups with punch, when the Silverton family entered the barn.

"I'm going to give Mrs. Potter a hand," Virginia told her husband and hurried across the barn.

As they moved farther into the building, Bethany glanced quickly around the large, airy structure, searching the faces for one in particular. She was scarcely aware of the admiring looks she was receiving from nearly every male in the room. She nodded automatically when her gaze chanced to meet with someone else's, but she didn't really see the person.

When her search had come full circle, she felt a terrible disappointment and dropped her gaze

to the floor. He wasn't there. He hadn't come.
She had been so certain . . .

"Good evening, Miss Silverton."

She saw the shiny black shoes first, then raised
her eyes to meet Vince Richards' steely gray
ones. "Good evening, Mr—Mr. Richards, isn't
it?"

"I'm flattered you remember, Miss Silverton."
He turned toward her father. "Good evening,
reverend. It's good to see you. I wanted to tell
you how much I enjoyed your service on Sunday. Inspiring. Very inspiring, indeed."

"I'm glad you thought so, Mr. Richards."

"Vince, please."

As the two men exchanged pleasantries, Bethany's attention wandered once more, this time
taking a moment to study the people filling the
barn.

The first person she recognized was John
Wilton, the pharmacist. Short and wiry, with
thinning hair and a weathered complexion, he
was hard to imagine as the husband of Sarah
Wilton, whom she'd met after church on Sunday. Sarah was at least twenty years her husband's junior, pretty and plump with pregnancy
and obviously deliriously in love with John. But,
of course, Sarah wasn't with her husband tonight. Her time for delivery was fast approaching, and, as she'd confided earlier to Bethany,
she was much more comfortable at home in her
rocker than anywhere else.

Standing next to John Wilton was Sweetwater's doctor. She only knew him as Doc
Wilton and wondered if anyone knew his first

name. Doc was taller than his older brother and still had a full head of brown hair, graying now at the temples. Like his brother, he wore spectacles and was constantly pushing them up the bridge of his long, narrow nose.

Moving on, her gaze settled on Martha Eberlie. Fifteen and blossoming, Martha showed all the signs of insecurity every young girl felt when her thoughts turned to men and marriage. It was easy to see Martha's thoughts had turned in that direction. Her brown eyes were fastened on a tall young man in a too-large suit standing near the punch table.

Bethany felt a sting of jealousy as she watched the fellow return Martha's gaze. Then he set his cup on the table, straightened his shoulders, and walked across the barn toward the now blushing girl. Bethany wished the same thing was happening to her, only with Hawk.

A fiddle began to play, and Bethany followed the sound to the loft where several musicians had positioned themselves, fiddles and mouth organs in hand. As they warmed up, more people began entering the barn, and soon the building was echoing with happy voices and shared laughter.

Ingrid tugged at Bethany's elbow. "They are here," she whispered, leaning close to her friend's ear.

Bethany's head turned quickly, her pulse already beginning to race. There were five of them—Hawk and Rand and three others. But Bethany only had eyes for Hawk. He was wearing a white shirt that contrasted starkly with his dark skin. She noted again his broad shoulders and muscular arms.

Rand said something to him, and his mouth curled in a half-smile as he nodded. His blue-black eyes quickly scanned the room. When they met hers, they stopped. Her stomach tightened and her mouth went dry.

"Look," Ingrid said softly. "Rand is coming over."

Rand had, indeed, stepped away from the other cowboys and was crossing the barn. He whisked his hat from his head, ran a quick hand over his slicked-back hair, then came to a halt in front of Ingrid. "Evenin', Miss Johnson."

"Good evening, Mr. Howard."

"Evenin', Miss Silverton," he said to Bethany without even looking her way.

"Good evening."

He glanced toward the table. "Care to join me for a glass of punch, Miss Johnson?"

"I would like that very much."

Rand was grinning from ear to ear as he offered his arm and escorted Ingrid away.

Bethany drew a deep breath, hoping that when she turned her head she would see Hawk coming to ask the same sort of question. But she was in for a disappointment. He and his friends had moved away from the door and were leaning against the side of the barn, visiting among themselves. He wasn't even looking her way any more. At that same moment, the musicians struck up a lively tune. It wasn't long before the center of the barn was filled with twirling couples. Bethany waited hopefully, casting surreptitious glances toward the four men, but Hawk seemed oblivious to the music and the dancers.

"Miss Silverton? May I have the pleasure?"

She didn't want to dance with Vince Richards. Still, if Hawk saw her dancing with other men, saw her laughing and having fun, maybe then . . .

"Thank you, Mr. Richards. I'd be delighted."

Beneath hooded eyes, he watched her. Hawk didn't think he'd ever seen a lovelier woman than Bethany. Her glossy auburn curls were gathered in a fiery cluster at the back of her head, revealing a stretch of white throat. Her shimmery mint-green gown exposed straight shoulders and just a hint of cleavage. When she'd glanced his way, he'd caught the misty quality of her eyes and thought how a man might drown in their sea-green depths. And he wasn't a man given to such thoughts.

He tensed when Vince walked over to her. He waited, unconsciously hoping she would refuse his offer to dance; his jaw tightened as he watched Vince putting his hand on the small of Bethany's back. If there was any man in this town she shouldn't be dancing with, it was Vince Richards.

It's none of your concern, he told himself, but still he couldn't look away. He watched as Vince guided her around the large floor. He noted the possessive expression on the man's face, and it started a burning anger in the pit of Hawk's stomach.

"Evening, Hawk." Fred Eberlie stepped up

beside him. "Haven't seen you in the mercantile lately. Glad you could make our little party."

Hawk pulled his gaze away from Bethany. "The ranch keeps me pretty busy these days."

"So I hear. Things are going well for you then? Good. Good." Fred's attention turned toward the dancers. "Have you met the reverend and his family? I'd be glad to introduce you."

Hawk's gaze followed the merchant's, settling once more on Bethany. "Reverend Silverton and his daughter called on me a week or so ago." The music had stopped, and Vince was escorting Bethany back toward her father. "In fact, they had Rand and me to supper this week."

"That so? They're nice folks. We're glad to have them in Sweetwater. Course, they're a little green about how we do things out west, but they'll catch on soon enough."

Hawk understood Fred Eberlie's meaning. The Silvertons didn't know you didn't socialize with a breed, not at your own supper table, not with two unmarried white daughters at the table.

"Guess you must know we're going to be building us a church now."

"No, I hadn't heard."

Fred grinned as he took a step away. "Well, we'd like to have your help if you can spare the time. I'll let you know when we start to raise her."

"You do that, Fred."

She had danced twice with Vince Richards, three times with her father, and one dance each with several young men whose names she had already forgotten. And still Hawk Chandler stood in that dim corner of the barn. It appeared as if she would have to make the first move if she were to have the chance to talk with him tonight.

Squaring her shoulders, Bethany slipped away from the refreshment table where she had been helping her mother and Laura Potter serve punch and cake. She didn't falter in her approach. The time was now and she was determined.

As she neared, she saw his head turn. His eyes met hers. She saw the slight lift of one eyebrow, then watched him push himself off the wall he'd been leaning against. He was so tall, it nearly made her head swim to look up at him. She stopped a few feet away. The other men had ceased their talking too. Blood was pounding in her temples, and her mouth had gone dry for the second time this evening.

"Hello, Mr. Chandler."

"Miss Silverton."

His voice sent shivers up her spine.

"I'm glad you came tonight."

He simply nodded. He wasn't making this any easier for her. Well, she wasn't about to back out now.

"I was hoping you would ask me to dance, Mr. Chandler."

Out of the corner of her eye, she saw two of the men jabbing each other in the ribs with their elbows.

Hawk's expression was difficult to read. "I'm not sure that would be . . ."

"Please, Mr. Chandler."

The strains of a waltz began from the loft.

"Go on, Hawk. Don't disappoint the lady."

Hawk cast a harsh glance toward the cowpoke. "You're no help, Rusty."

Her courage was increasing. He wanted to dance with her. She just knew it. Maybe he wasn't a good dancer. That must be it. Well, she didn't care. "I simply won't take no for an answer, Mr. Chandler."

He hesitated a moment more, his dark eyes boring into hers, warning her of something she didn't understand. Then she was suddenly in his arms and floating effortlessly across the dance floor.

Bethany Silverton had been introduced to Philadelphia society two seasons ago. She had danced beneath glittering crystal chandeliers to the music of full-piece orchestras. She had glided in the arms of elegant young men from the finest families in the East. Clad in yards and yards of satin and lace, she had whirled past walls lined with gilded mirrors. But never could she remember an evening so brilliant, a moment so breathless as the one she knew now.

And he was a marvelous dancer besides.

Her head back so she could look up at him, she tried to think of something witty and flirtatious to say to him, but her mind was blank. She wanted merely to look at him and enjoy the moment. There would be time later to win her wager.

*   *   *

"That's not too smart of him," Fred Eberlie said as he watched Hawk dancing with the reverend's daughter.

Vince Richards relaxed his clenched fists. "Perhaps I should speak to her father."

"Wouldn't do for that pretty gal to have folks talkin' loose about her. Seems like she should know about consortin' with Indians, though, don't it?"

"The problem, Fred, is that he doesn't think of himself as a redskin. And the folks here in town haven't helped matters any. You treat him as you would any white man. Like he's as good as the rest of us."

Fred Eberlie looked insulted. "Listen here, Richards. That fellow owns a lot of land and cattle 'round these parts. He's a good sort, too. I happen to like him. Not his fault his father took a squaw for wife. It just ain't right for him to be thinkin' he can be courtin' a white woman, that's all."

"It's only one dance, Fred." Vince's eyes narrowed. "And you can be sure, I mean to protect Miss Silverton from any further unwelcome attentions by Mr. Chandler."

Hawk could sense their eyes upon him, could almost feel the disapproval in the air. He knew he should stop dancing and escort Bethany back to her father, but he just couldn't turn her loose from his arms just yet. She seemed to fit so perfectly.

The cessation of the music made his decision

for him. He stepped back from her and reluctantly let go of her hand. "Thank you for the dance, Miss Silverton."

Her cheeks were flushed with color. Her silvery green eyes seemed almost to glitter. "It was my pleasure, Mr. Chandler."

For a moment, his gaze lingered on the fullness of her bottom lip. The urge to kiss her was growing almost irresistible. Swallowing the unwelcome thoughts, he placed a hand beneath her elbow and steered her across the barn toward her father. Then, without another word, he turned to leave her.

"Wait!"

Her breathless cry stopped him in his tracks. He turned his head.

"I . . . I hope we'll see you in church Sunday."

With a noncommittal nod, he turned and left the barn.

CHAPTER Five

· ——— ·

Bethany awoke long before the sun was up the next Sunday morning. The moment her eyes opened, she was thinking of him. Her heart pattered erratically, and she touched her chest, wondering at the crazy sensation.

From sunup to sundown, she'd thought of nothing but Hawk since the moment he walked away from her in the Potters' barn. And one question kept running through her mind. Would he come to church on Sunday as she'd asked?

Bethany slipped from her bed and padded on bare feet to the window. She swept aside the lace curtains her mother had brought with them from Philadelphia and gazed out the window.

Her father's white tent reflected the last traces of moonlight. A gentle, early-morning breeze ruffled the canvas flaps and stirred the buffalo grass. Overhead, a canopy of fading stars filled the lead-gray sky.

Bethany leaned her elbows on the windowsill and cupped her chin in her palms as her gaze moved past the tent and toward Spring River.

She didn't even have to close her eyes to imagine herself back there again, to remember the deep timbre of his voice and the way it made her heart leap. And when he looked at her, she always had such a queer feeling. It started in the pit of her stomach, everything quivering, and then it moved up her spine and seemed to wrap tight fingers around her heart.

No one had ever made her feel this way before. At least she didn't remember it, and surely she would remember anything so terribly wonderful. She thought back to Philadelphia, to the parties and the boys she had known. She had always been surrounded by boys and young men, for as far back as she could remember. She had always loved to flirt and laugh and enjoy herself in male company. It was great fun to be the center of attention. But there had never been anyone who came close to making her feel the way Hawk Chandler did.

She remembered being kissed by Martin Phillips when she was thirteen. The flirtation had been great fun, watching him growing more and more frustrated, but she hadn't thought much of the kiss, all wet and hurried. No, Martin had never made her feel this way.

Then there had been Stephen Patrick. She was fifteen when he'd asked her father for permission to call upon Bethany. Their families, the Patricks and the Silvertons, had been friends for many years, and Virginia had told Bethany often how wonderful it would be if she would take an interest in Stephen. He had certainly been handsome enough, but for some reason, she had always been glad when their visits ended. She had never even allowed him close enough to try to kiss her. No, Stephen had never made her feel this way either.

Of course, she couldn't ignore her brief flirtation with Harold Masters in Denver. Harold had been the spokesman for the folks who wanted her father to stay in Denver and start his church there. Harold was fairly tall, with sandy blond hair and cool gray eyes. His family had made considerable money in the gold and silver mines of Colorado, and he was building a fine mansion in Denver. Harold had actually proposed marriage to Bethany, which had quickly ended any amusement or enjoyment she had gained from the relationship. No, Harold had definitely never made her feel this way.

Hawk Chandler. Even his name made her skin prickle with gooseflesh. Could it be that she had really only seen him five times in the last eleven days? How could anyone fill her thoughts so completely in so short a time?

Bethany gasped. Could she be falling in love? Is this what it felt like?

She turned from the window and sat on the floor, tucking her feet beneath her as her hands clutched her stomach, calming the sudden flutter of butterflies within.

She couldn't be in love with him. She didn't even know him. Her mother had always told her that love needed to grow slowly if it were to last. Virginia and Nathaniel had known each other many years before he approached her as a suitor. Surely that was the way one fell in love. It couldn't happen so quickly. It couldn't possibly happen with a virtual stranger.

She closed her eyes and saw him, standing beside his corral at the Circle Blue. His dark face was dusty, his shirt sweaty, his black hair tousled. He was so tall and strong. His face was so stern, his blue-black eyes so unreadable. And then, unexpectedly, he smiled at her. Even in her imagination, the look made her go all weak inside.

Could this, indeed, be what it felt like to fall in love?

"I'm going to church. You comin', Hawk?"

Hawk peeled another strip from the wood he was whittling. "No. Another time maybe."

Rand put on his hat and stepped away from the house. "Miss Silverton will be disappointed."

Hawk grunted a reply without looking up. He was relieved to hear Rand walking away.

He wished Rand hadn't mentioned Bethany Silverton. He had almost managed to put thoughts of her out of his head. Almost, but not quite. Ever since last Tuesday, he'd been thinking of the way she'd looked at him and said, "Why should you, Mr. Chandler?" He kept thinking of the way it had made him feel. Ever since the dance, he had thought of how perfectly she fit within the circle of his arms.

But that was no reason to go losing his head. He had a ranch to run. Spring roundup was over, but the season of hard work was just beginning. He didn't have time to get mixed up with a woman. Not any woman. Not even Bethany. Especially not Bethany.

It hadn't taken him long to figure out the Reverend Silverton was not your usual itinerant preacher. Their home was beautifully furnished. They had their own maid, brought with them from Philadelphia. The women all wore finely tailored gowns of the latest fashion. Even if he wanted to entertain thoughts of courting a girl like Bethany, what had he to offer her? His spread was only a small beginning. He had some prime land and plenty of water and some good livestock. But it was only a beginning. It would never do for a girl like Bethany, a girl used to the finer things, a girl perhaps too much like Alice. . . .

Hawk suddenly threw his pearl-handled knife at the cabin. Its sharp point slid with ease into the wooden door. The handle sprang back and forth for several seconds after impact.

Women.

Hawk stared at the knife a moment as if it were the troublesome woman he referred to. Then he got to his feet, a dark scowl still furrowing his brow. He jerked the knife from the door and slipped it into the sheath he always wore on his belt. Turning abruptly, he headed for the barn, spurs jingling with each step.

The last thing I need, he reminded himself, *is to get mixed up with some woman.*

Taking her eyes briefly from the hymnal, Ingrid cast a furtive glance toward the man at her side. Just as she'd suspected, Rand was watching her. He stopped singing and grinned. She quickly dropped her gaze back to the music as the heat of embarrassment rose from the neckline of her gown all the way to the cowlick in the middle of her bangs.

Never in her seventeen years had Ingrid Johnson had a suitor. And never would she have dreamed a man would single her out when he could have chosen Bethany. It nearly made her dizzy with happiness.

The hymn ended, and the congregation sat down on the wooden benches as Reverend Silverton took his place at the makeshift pulpit. Ingrid tried to concentrate on the reverend's words. She always loved his sermons. He spoke of a loving, caring God. He spoke of a wonderful, miracle-working Savior.

But today she couldn't keep her thoughts from straying to the man seated on her right. She knew already that he was going to ask her to marry him. She also knew she was going to accept. It would be difficult to leave the Silvertons. They had been so kind to her. They had made her a member of the family. But her life was destined to be lived by Rand Howard's side. She knew that now.

Bethany had never spent a more miserable morning. Not only hadn't Hawk come to church again, despite her personal invitation, but for the second week in a row, she was forced to sit beside Ingrid and Rand and witness their lovesick glances.

She wavered between anger and despair. Why

hadn't he come? She'd made it clear how much she wanted him to do so. Why hadn't he done it just for her? Didn't he like her? Oh, why did she even care? He wasn't so very special. She could find a dozen men more interesting, more handsome, more entertaining. If it weren't for her wager, she swore she wouldn't care if she never saw him again.

Well, she *didn't* care. She had been mistaken about her feelings for him. She didn't care any more for Mr. Chandler than for any other man she'd ever known. In fact, she probably cared less. It was just because of her wager that she minded his not coming. That was all. She just hated to lose the wager. And she *wasn't* going to lose it.

As soon as her father spoke the last amen, Bethany was headed for the back of the tent, determined to escape to a place where she could be alone and begin plotting a course of action regarding Hawk Chandler. Her intentions were thwarted by Vince Richards.

"Good morning, Miss Silverton." He tipped his hat. "Wonderful sermon your father gave."

"Yes," she mumbled hurriedly, sidestepping to go around him.

Vince's hand caught her arm. "Miss Silverton, I was hoping you might do me the honor of having lunch with me. I had my cook prepare a basket lunch, just in case you were agreeable. I thought we could dine along the river."

"Well, I . . ." Bethany glanced behind her, looking for an excuse to refuse his offer. But all she saw was Ingrid and Rand, their heads close together as they spoke softly to each other. It sparked a note of jealousy in her, causing her to reply contrary to her own wishes. "I'd be happy to join you, Mr. Richards." Realizing what she'd done, she tried to undo her own words. "But I will have to get my father's permission first."

"Allow me, Miss Silverton. I'm sure he won't mind. We'll be within view of the house, and if you or he would prefer, we can bring your friend along as well. There is plenty of food."

A short while later, much to her chagrin, Bethany found herself walking beside Vince down to the river. His first choice of a picnic site was the same spot where Hawk had pulled her from the river just a few days before. She had to work to recall the anger Hawk's name was supposed to stir in her, and she found it impossible to sit down to picnic with Vince in the shadow of his memory.

"I think there's a much better spot down that way," she suggested quickly and began walking in the opposite direction.

Vince followed after her, carrying the blanket and picnic basket. The trees were more sparse in the spot she selected. The clear view of her house and the church tent gave her a feeling of security.

"Here would be nice," she said, offering her escort a fleeting smile.

She watched as Vince spread the blanket over the level ground, wishing all the while that she hadn't accepted his invitation. She had no desire to encourage his apparent interest in her. For one thing, he was much too old for her to entertain any thoughts of a flirtation with him. Vince Richards had to be close to her mother's age if he was a day—not that her mother was that terribly old at thirty-six, of course. There was no arguing he was a handsome enough man. His dark brown hair had only a touch of gray at the temples, giving him a rather distinguished look, as did the thin mustache over his mouth. His figure was trim and without flab, and he was always superbly dressed. He was obviously a man of considerable means. Yet there was something about him she just didn't like.

Besides, he wasn't Hawk. Everything about him paled in comparison to Hawk. Dark, irritating, wonderful, enigmatic Hawk.

Unconsciously, she sighed.

"Is there something wrong, Miss Silverton?"

"What?" She looked at him as if seeing him for the first time. "Oh, no. I—I was just daydreaming. I'm sorry."

"No need to apologize. Come and sit down, and we'll see what Ming Li has prepared for us."

Hawk spotted Rusty Andrews' sorrel in the distance. The horse was grazing quietly at the edge of a draw, reins dragging the ground, rider nowhere in sight. Hawk nudged Flame into a gallop and rode toward the sorrel. His eyes scanned the countryside, alert for trouble. The riderless horse started and shied backward as Hawk drew near, but it didn't run away. Hawk's hand moved instinctively toward his rifle and drew it from the scabbard. He rested the rifle in front of him.

"Rusty?"

"Down here."

He followed the sound of the cowboy's voice, finding him crouched over a dead cow in the dry creek bed. "What happened?" he asked as he dismounted.

Rusty Andrews turned to look up at Hawk, his weathered face crinkling as he squinted into the sun. "Neck's broke."

"What from?"

"Must've fell over the edge there."

Digging his heels into the loose soil, Hawk descended into the draw. His eyes studied the brindled cow. It hurt to lose even one, especially a cow that looked as good as this one did, already fat this early in the season.

"There's some tracks up there you oughta look at, Hawk." Rusty straightened, pushing his hat back on his forehead. "I'd say she slipped when someone was trying to drive her down into the draw here."

"Rustlers?"

"'fraid so."

Hawk removed his hat and drew his shirt sleeve across his forehead, wiping away the beads of sweat. He didn't have to voice his suspicions about who would be behind rustling on the Circle Blue. It could be Indians; it happened occasionally. But chances were more likely it was someone others might call neighbor.

"I tried to follow 'em," Rusty continued, "but

the tracks disappear down the creekbed a ways. Too many rocks."

"How many riders?"

"Couple of them, it looks like."

"Any other cows?" Even as he asked, Hawk followed Rusty down the draw to study the signs for himself.

"I'd say only two or three. Probably this mornin'. The brindle hasn't been dead all that long."

Two or three cows weren't all that serious. But chances were it wasn't going to stop with just two or three. Not if the brains behind the rustling wore the name Richards.

Hawk turned abruptly back toward the dead cow. "Let's get what meat we can from her. No point in it being a total loss." He trusted Rusty. If the rustlers could have been followed, the old cowhand would have done it. "Tell the boys to keep a sharp eye out for any signs of visitors."

"I'll tell 'em."

Hawk knew the chances were slim they would find anything. Besides himself and Rand, the Circle Blue employed only Rusty and two other cowboys. They weren't enough. With the acquisition last spring of two more homestead claims along the Spring River—from Rusty and his son, Gabe—the Circle Blue now controlled nearly forty thousand acres of rangeland. Five men just weren't enough to tend three thousand head of cattle over forty thousand acres. Not if Richards was ready to wage an all-out assault on Hawk's cattle.

Rusty seemed to be reading his mind. "With

that new herd of shorthorns you got comin' in from Oregon next month, you're gonna be needin' some more men on this place."

Hawk nodded.

"Matt says there was some boys in the Plains last night on their way to Miles City, lookin' to hook up with some outfit on the Big Dry. Might see if you can still catch 'em."

Hawk glanced up at the midday sun. "Think I'll do that."

"You go on. I'll finish up here."

Again Hawk nodded, turning silently to scramble up the side of the draw and remount his grazing stallion.

CHAPTER SIX

·—·

Bethany smoothed her skirt over her knees, then folded her hands in her lap, consciously relaxing the muscles in her face to hide her impatience. Would her father never stop asking Vince questions about his ranch and Montana Territory? She longed to get up from her chair in the parlor and excuse herself from their company, but she knew such rudeness would never be tolerated by her father.

She could have kicked herself for ever accepting Vince's invitation to eat with him! It had been the most intolerable hour of her life. And then, just when she thought he was leaving at last, her father had invited him inside and struck up this conversation.

She glanced longingly toward the doorway. What she wouldn't do for a solitary ride on Buttercup this afternoon. To feel the sunshine on her face and the wind in her hair. To canter her buckskin mare across the rolling plains or walk her along the river's edge. To be anywhere else but here, in fact.

Oh, why didn't he just go home?

"Well, Reverend, it's been a pleasant afternoon, but I must be getting back to the Bar V." Gray eyes turned upon Bethany. "I hope we can do this again soon, Miss Silverton."

Bethany forced a smile as she quickly rose to her feet. "Perhaps we shall, Mr. Richards." She moved toward the doorway, her eagerness to be rid of him scarcely contained.

Her father and mother bid Vince a good afternoon and turned in unison toward the rear of the house, leaving Bethany alone with her guest. He opened the front door, then stepped back to allow her to precede him onto the porch. As he stopped before her, he took one of her hands in his and lifted it very slowly to his mouth. He brushed dry lips across the back of her hand, then held it in midair while his gray eyes stared into hers.

"You're a remarkable young woman, Miss Silverton. Just the kind of woman this country needs. You'll make a place for yourself here."

Uncomfortable, she pulled her hand from his grasp, but before she could reply, he spoke again.

"The Bar V was built with a woman like you in mind."

Bethany paled at his words. There was something oddly threatening about his compliment. She tried to disguise her distress as she answered, "And I'm sure one day you'll find the woman you had in mind, Mr. Richards."

Vince's voice dropped to a near whisper. "You *are* that woman." He reached for her hand once again.

Bethany drew quickly away. With all the right-eous indignation she had learned at Miss Hendersen's School for Young Ladies, she turned a cool gaze upon her would-be suitor. "I assure you, Mr. Richards, I am *not* she. I am quite happy to live here with my parents and help my father with his work. You will have to look elsewhere."

"Don't be so quick to reject me," Vince replied with a sharp laugh. "You're young. You don't know what's best for you. But I do, and you'll see that I'm right. I have a great future in this territory, Miss Silverton. You would do well to join me." That said, he placed his hat on his head and turned away, descending the three steps. He didn't look back even when he reached the gate.

Bethany stayed on the porch, watching as he climbed into his carriage and drove away. As his horse jogged out of town, a small cloud of dust stirring behind the carriage wheels, she let out a long sigh. She rubbed the back of her hand against her skirt, as if to remove any trace of his kiss. If she had anything to say about it, he wouldn't have the opportunity to kiss her hand again.

She turned to look toward town. The instant she recognized the copper stallion tethered out-side the Plains Saloon her heart began a staccato beating in her chest. *He* was in Sweetwater. He hadn't come to church, but he was in town now. She felt an aching desperation well up inside, a need to see him. Yet she couldn't seek him out in the saloon, and there was no reason for her to be out walking in town on a Sunday afternoon with everything except the saloons closed for the day.

Bethany moved to the porch railing and leaned against it, her gaze still locked on Flame. She didn't even try to stir up her earlier anger with Hawk. She didn't even try to convince herself that all she wanted was to win her wager with Ingrid. It would have been pointless to try. She wanted to see him. Everything inside her willed Hawk to come walking out of the saloon at that moment, willed him to look toward her house, willed him to want to see her as much as she wanted to see him. But it didn't happen. The laughter and the music wafted through the swinging doors, but no one entered or departed.

If she was, indeed, falling in love with Hawk Chandler, it wasn't the happy feeling she'd always been told it was. Bethany couldn't think of any time in her life when she'd been less happy than she'd been since meeting Hawk Chandler.

Hawk shook hands with the two cowpokes. "Matt here'll show you how to get to the ranch and where to bunk. Glad to have you with us, Caleb. You, too, Westy."

Hawk had worked one drive with Caleb Moore back in '76. Caleb was a good hand and would fit in well with the other men at the Circle Blue. While Hawk didn't know the other man, Westy had a stark, lean look about him that spoke of experience on the range. Hawk trusted Caleb's judgment, too. If Westy weren't a good cowboy, Caleb wouldn't be riding with him.

"You comin', Hawk?" Matt asked as he pushed away from the bar.

"Not right away. Thought I'd wait and ride back with Rand if he's still in town."

"Oh, he's still here, all right." Matt flashed a crooked grin. "Been at the parson's house since services. His horse is still tied out back by the tent. You ask me, he's sweet on that Swedish gal in a bad way." Matt motioned for Caleb and Westy to follow him and left the saloon.

Hawk stood alone at the bar, his thoughts already gone ahead to the white house on the edge of town. When he rode into Sweetwater about an hour before, he'd recognized Vince's carriage hitched outside the reverend's house. Remembering that, Hawk's jaw tightened.

Hawk had a lot of reasons to dislike and distrust Vince Richards. The man had been making trouble for the Circle Blue ever since he arrived. Hawk knew Vince's goal was to drive him from his land. Vince wanted the water rights to the spring and all the land it controlled. He was an ambitious, ruthless man. He would own all of Montana Territory if it were possible for one man to do so.

But Hawk wasn't the sort to run from a fight. He wasn't out to be the biggest rancher in Montana, nor did he mean to be the wealthiest. But he wasn't about to give up the land he'd laid claim to, either. The Circle Blue was his home. He meant to live out his life there. He meant to make it a success. Maybe, one day, there would even be a son to inherit what Hawk had built.

He stopped himself. It was better not to think such things. Especially not when such thoughts brought with them the image of an auburn beauty with flashing silver-green eyes. No, it was better not to think such things.

He spun on his heel and strode quickly through the doorway of the saloon. Narrowed eyes turned east. The carriage was gone. As soon as he knew Vince was no longer with Bethany, the tension eased from his shoulders, tension he hadn't even been aware he'd felt.

He stepped into the stirrup and eased himself into the saddle.

Wouldn't hurt to let Rand know I'm in town so we can ride back together.

And if he should chance to see Miss Silverton at the same time . . . well, so be it.

"I've got to be gettin' back to the ranch soon." Rand cast a furtive glance at Ingrid, walking by his side.

"I thought you must."

"It's been an awful nice day."

"Yes, Mr. Howard. It has."

Rand stopped. His hand reached out to lightly brush her elbow. "You think you could bring yourself to call me Rand?"

She blushed and dropped her gaze to the ground.

"Course, if it's not proper . . ."

She smiled, even though she still wasn't looking at him. "I would like very much to call you Rand, Mr. Howard."

He almost chuckled at the way she used both his names.

Her eyes lifted to meet his. "And you will call me Ingrid?"

"It'd be my pleasure . . . Ingrid."

He loved the soft rolling sound of her voice. He wished she would continue to speak. Like most cowboys, Rand hadn't learned the fine art of conversation. Words weren't easy for him to come by, especially sweet-talkin' words. At the dinner table after church, it had been the reverend and his wife who had kept the conversation alive. Rand had been satisfied just to look at Ingrid. And even once he asked her to take a walk with him by the river, he'd spent most of the time thinking of what he wanted to say to her without knowing quite how to say it. Now it was time for him to head back to the Circle Blue, and he still hadn't said anything important, he still hadn't said any of the things he'd planned to say when he left the ranch that morning.

Rand motioned with his head toward the grassy spot near the river. "Care to set a spell 'fore I take you back to the house?"

Ingrid nodded, the hint of pink returning to her cheeks.

He waited until they were settled, both of them turning their eyes upon the swift-flowing water. Then he cleared his throat and made an effort to speak his piece. "I been driftin' ever since I left Iowa back when I was a kid. I always liked movin' around, seein' new things. Never thought of settlin' in one place 'til I met Hawk

and he was comin' up this way to start his own
ranch."

"You are very close to Mr. Chandler."

"He's about the best friend a man could ask
for. I'd trust him with my life . . . and have a
time or two." He glanced at her quickly, then
looked away again. "Anyways, I got me a piece of
land near the mountains. Nothin' to ranch with.
Just a spot to build me a house of my own. Plenty
of trees and a fine view of the range."

"It must be lovely, Mr. Howard."

"Rand," he reminded her. "Anyways, I hadn't
thought much of buildin' a house there. Seemed
just as easy to go on bunkin' with the other boys
at the Circle Blue." He cleared his throat again.
"But, here lately, I been givin' it a lotta thought.
Seems like a good idea to get busy with it while
the weather's good. Wouldn't be too fancy. I'd
probably build it of logs. But I want it to be big.
Lots of rooms. A place I'd be proud to call home
and . . . and a place a woman might not mind
too much callin' home either." His last words
came out in a rush.

There was a lengthy silence that followed.
Rand couldn't bring himself to look at Ingrid.
He knew he'd made a mistake. He'd spoken too
soon. What was she going to want with some log
cabin anyway? She was used to living in a fine
house and having servants waiting on her. And
why would she ever want to settle down with a
man with nothing more to offer than a tiny patch
of ground in the middle of this vast territory?

When she spoke, it was as if she'd been
reading his mind. "My father and mother came

to America from Sweden. We had a farm in Minnesota. When my mother died, my father did not want to stay there any longer, so after a few months he sold the farm. It was hard work, farming, but it was a good life. We were a close family." She drew a long, deep breath, then sighed. "The Silvertons have made me a part of their family, and I love them, but sometimes I feel too idle. I wish I were building something for myself as you are going to do."

Their heads turned toward each other in unison. There was a glimmer of light in Ingrid's blue eyes, a glimmer telling Rand she understood the things he still hadn't been able to say, telling him she wanted the same things too. It was all he could do in that moment to keep from letting out a whoop for joy and grabbing her and kissing her smack on the mouth. But, of course, he couldn't do that. Not yet. He had to have something more to offer her before he could ask her to marry him.

Rand got to his feet and held out his hand. "I better get you back before the reverend comes lookin' for us."

Ingrid laid her hand in his and allowed him to draw her up. She offered a tentative smile, then placed her hand in the crook of his arm as they started walking.

Rand couldn't help grinning. "Yep. I think I'll start work on that place this week. That's what I think I'll do."

Bethany opened the door in response to the knock. The man's tall frame filled the doorway, blocking out the rays of late afternoon sun. "Hawk," she whispered inaudibly, her blood pounding in her ears at the first sight of him.

"Afternoon, Miss Silverton. Is Rand here? His horse is tied out back."

"He . . . he and Ingrid took a walk by the river. They should be back soon."

He frowned and turned his head to glance back toward town. "Well . . . I guess I could wait for him at the Plains."

"No!" she said quickly. Too quickly.

He turned around again, his frown deepening, his dark gaze studying her intently.

Bethany hated the pleading sound of her voice, but she didn't want him to leave. "I mean, I'm sure they'll be back any minute. Won't you wait for him here? You could sit on the porch if you'd like." Before he could answer, she slipped by him, pulling the door closed behind her. "There's more shade around on the side."

She started toward the side porch, waiting breathlessly to hear his footsteps following her. When she heard them, she released a tiny sigh as she felt a rush of relief. He was staying, and they were alone for the moment. Her self-confidence came flooding back. Now was her chance. Hawk Chandler was different from the other men of her acquaintance, but he couldn't be *that* different. There had to be some way to make him like her. He couldn't be totally indifferent to her flirtations.

She settled gracefully into a cane-backed chair. She took a moment to smooth the skirt of her floral-embroidered dress, all the time aware of Hawk as he leaned against the porch railing, stretching his long legs out before him. Everything in her seemed to respond to the very maleness of him. She'd never felt this way before, and she wanted him to feel it too. He just *had* to like her. She had to make him like her or . . .

Her pulse quickened as she lifted her green gaze toward him. "I looked for you in church today." Her voice was pleasantly sweet, the invitation in her smile open and honest while at the same time carefully calculated.

"I had work to do at the ranch." He glanced toward the river.

"It keeps you very busy, doesn't it?"

"Yes." Hawk nodded without turning his head in her direction.

How could she flirt with him if he wouldn't even look at her? Besides, any moment he might see Rand and Ingrid walking back from the river, and her chance would be gone. Her determination grew. She was not about to let him leave without showing he cared for her, just a little.

Bethany rose and moved swiftly across the porch to stand before him. Her action drew his gaze again. She sensed more than saw the question in his dark blue eyes.

Boldly, she reached out and touched his hand where it rested on the post. "It would mean so much to me if you would come to church next Sunday."

"Miss Silverton, I'm not—"

Impetuously, her hands flew up to clasp his

neck and she pulled his head down toward her. Her lips pressed purposefully against his, sending a shock wave down the length of her body. On the heels of the delightfully terrifying sensation came surprise and then horror at her brashness. She drew quickly away, her eyes wide with mortification as she looked into his bemused face.

"Oh!" she gasped, one hand flying to cover her mouth as she whirled to race into the house.

Hawk stared after her. A frown pulled down his dark eyebrows, and his eyes narrowed as he mulled over Bethany's actions. Then, ever so slowly, the dark look eased, replaced by a wry half-smile. An abbreviated chuckle rumbled deep in his chest. It hadn't been much of a kiss as kisses went but he'd liked it all the same.

He pushed away from the railing and headed for his tethered stallion. He didn't have time to wait for Rand. There was lots of work to do before next Sunday, especially if he was going to take the morning off to go to church.

CHAPTER SEVEN

On Saturday night, Hawk dragged out the washtub and set it in the middle of the kitchen. Then he put several kettles of water to heat on the stove. In the meantime, he filled two buckets with water from the pump to rinse with.

Finally, washtub filled with warm water, he shed his clothes and stepped in. There was no room for a man of his size to stretch out in the round tub. Hawk's knees were forced to remain bent, leaving the better part of his legs in the open air. He lathered his blue-black hair not once but twice. He scrubbed every inch of his dark, muscled body with the harsh soap. Finished at last, he stood and poured the icy water from the buckets over his head, rinsing away the last traces of soap as he gritted his teeth against the cold.

It had been a long time since Hawk had taken such great care with his bath. He was usually satisfied with a soaping in the creek. But that wasn't good enough this time. Not this time. He grinned and began to whistle as he imagined Bethany Silverton in her Sunday finest.

"You're right pretty, Mr. Chandler. Right pretty."

Hawk opened his eyes, water still running in rivulets from his hair. Rand lounged in the doorway, a grin splitting his face.

With a laugh of his own, Hawk tossed the empty bucket at Rand. "If you plan to sit with Miss Johnson tomorrow in church, you'd better do some bathin' yourself. You smell like you've been tangling with a grizzly, and you don't look much better than you smell." He stepped out of the tub, dripping water across the floor as he reached for a towel and began to dry off.

Rand didn't argue with him. He shucked his own clothes and stepped into the half-filled tub, the tepid water a murky white color from the soap. "Any special reason for a bath on Saturday night, Hawk?"

Hawk wrapped the towel around his lean hips. "Same reason as always. To get clean."

"No. I mean on *Saturday* night."

"No time to take one before church tomorrow."

"Thought that might be the reason."

Hawk grunted, the sound a verbal shrug.

"Got a minute 'fore you turn in, Hawk?"

"Sure." Hawk poured himself a cup of thick black coffee and sat in a chair at the kitchen table.

Rand stuck one foot on the edge of the tub and soaped it as he talked. "I spent some time up on that piece of land this week. Laid out some plans for the house I'm gonna build." He glanced at Hawk, then switched feet and washed the other one. "Thought I'd try and get a start on it this summer. Have somethin' to live in before the first snow maybe."

Hawk waited silently, but he knew what was coming.

"I'm gonna ask Ingrid to marry me. Figured we'd do it as soon as I've built us a decent place to call our own."

"I thought you might." Hawk offered one of his half-smiles. "I'm glad for you, Rand. She's a nice girl." He glanced around the kitchen. "You know, I could move into the bunkhouse with the men and let you and Ingrid have this place."

"Thanks, Hawk, but I'd rather wait 'til we have our own place on the mountain. 'Sides, it'd be more private. You understand."

"Sure." Hawk stood, picked up the buckets and went out to fill them with rinse water from the pump.

Funny how having the words spoken aloud made him feel. He was glad for Rand. He'd noticed how happy his friend had been ever since he first met Ingrid. He'd known it was only a matter of time before the two of them tied the knot. However, he hadn't expected to feel envious—which was exactly how he felt.

He turned from the pump and gazed back at his house. It wasn't much to look at. Just a log cabin with four small rooms. It was enough for two bachelors who did little more than eat and sleep there. He'd always had plans to build a bigger place, but there hadn't been any hurry.

But now he looked at the log cabin and thought how it would appear to a woman's eyes.

Just a shack. Certainly not a place a man would want to bring a bride. No wonder Rand had turned down his offer. It wasn't just because they'd want to be alone. Rand wanted to build something special for Ingrid. Just like Hawk would want to do if he . . .

He turned abruptly and started pumping the handle, sending out a sharp stream of water as he tried to blot out the sudden image in his mind. But she wouldn't go away. He felt his stomach muscles tighten as he remembered their last meeting and the way Bethany had unexpectedly kissed him. Time and again this past week, he had imagined that she hadn't escaped from him so quickly, that he'd been able to hold her tightly in his arms and return the kiss. And that wasn't all he'd been imagining when it came to the delightful Miss Silverton.

He swore softly beneath his breath. A preacher's daughter, no less. Instinct told him he was headed for trouble.

Hawk picked up the pails of water and carried them back into the house.

Bethany stood on the porch, her cheek against the post, and watched the setting of the sun. The bright orange ball seemed to rest on the peaks of the distant mountains, turning the dark, pine-covered slopes a fiery red. Then the sun slipped slowly behind them. The fire-hot colors of sunset faded to a deep purple, announcing the coming of night. And, as the sky darkened from blue to pewter to black, she saw the first twinkling star above the tallest mountain.

Hawk's mountains. That's how she thought of them. Beneath their shadows, Hawk was probably getting ready to turn in for the night.

She sighed.

"What's troubling you, dear?"

"Oh . . ." She didn't turn to look as her mother gently closed the door and came to stand beside her. "Nothing, Mother."

"You've been sighing and moping all week long. It isn't like you, Bethany Rachel."

She shrugged. "I don't know, Mother. I just . . ." Again she sighed.

Virginia moved away from the rail and sat down in one of the chairs behind Bethany. "Are you unhappy here in Sweetwater? Is that it? Perhaps you'd like us to send you back to Philadelphia. I know Cousin Beatrice would—"

"No," Bethany answered quickly, turning around to sit on the wooden railing. "I don't want to leave Montana. I love it here. Really I do."

"But you've never said—"

"Truly, Mother. I don't want to leave Sweetwater."

"Then what is it, dear? Please tell me."

How did a girl go about asking her mother about love and men and . . . and kissing? She adored her mother, but somehow she just didn't feel as if Virginia would understand. After all, Bethany could count on the fingers of one hand the number of times she had seen Hawk Chandler. She couldn't very well tell her mother she lay awake nights thinking about kissing the man, wondering what it would be like to be held in those strong arms of his, to have his calloused fingers touch her cheek, and . . .

She was thankful for the darkness of the porch as the heat rose from her neck to her brow. Surely if her mother could see her face she would understand what troubled her daughter.

Bethany groped for something—anything—to say, as long as it wasn't about Hawk. She blurted out the first thing that came to mind. "I think Ingrid's in love with Rand Howard."

"I think there's a good chance she could be growing to love him."

"Do you suppose he'll ask her to marry him?"

"Yes, I think he will." Virginia rose from her chair and crossed to Bethany. She placed her hand beneath her daughter's chin and asked softly, "Is that what's troubling you? Is it the possibility of Ingrid getting married?"

The question slipped out without forethought. "How does it feel to be in love, Mother?"

"So that's what's been troubling you." It was Virginia's turn to sigh. "Quite wonderful, Bethany. And sometimes quite awful."

That certainly described the way Bethany was feeling. Wonderful. And awful.

"But . . . *how* do you know when you're in love?"

"Oh, you'll know, dear. When it happens, you'll know. That's how it was with me and your father. I'd practically grown up with him. He was always around our house when I was young. Remember, he and your uncle Frederick were close friends. One day, after he came back from seminary, he was at our house for supper, and I looked at him across the table and I knew I loved him. It had come on so slowly I hadn't even known it. I'd probably loved him for months without realizing it. But that's the kind of love that lasts."

"Ingrid hasn't known Rand very long. Don't you think their love will last?"

"Oh my, no. I don't mean that at all. Besides, even if Mr. Howard does ask Ingrid to marry him, they won't be getting married for some time, I'm sure. They'll have their period of engagement, perhaps even a year. Ingrid's a sensible girl. They'll have plenty of time to be certain this is what they both want." She patted Bethany's cheek and stepped back from her. "Don't worry, dear. Your turn will come. You're young. You'll meet the right man. And I pray you'll be as happy as I've been with your father." She paused, then added, "I think it's time we both said good night. It's growing late."

"Just a little longer, Mother."

"All right, dear. But not too long. Good night."

"Good night, Mother."

When the door closed behind Virginia, Bethany turned her gaze once again to the west. She could no longer make out the outline of the mountains against the inky darkness of the sky, yet she stared hungrily in their direction.

Wonderful and awful.

But Mother says love takes time to grow.

But Ingrid is in love with Rand, and they haven't known each other any longer than I've known Hawk.

But Ingrid's been with Rand more often in the past two-and-a-half weeks.

But I've kissed Hawk.

Wonderful and awful.

A cool morning breeze waved through the long range grasses, carrying with it the sweet scent of wildflowers in bloom. The long limbs of the willows swayed gracefully as the cottonwoods shed their cotton-white tufts along the river's edge. A flock of sparrows chirped noisily amid the verdant arms of the trees.

The beauty of the morning was lost on Bethany. She had slept little during the night, her thoughts continuing to be troubled by the remote Mr. Chandler, and now, as she followed her father and mother toward the tent, she felt anything but Christian. For no explicable reason, she felt angry at her parents, angry at Ingrid, angry at the world. But mostly, she was furious with Hawk Chandler—for no more reason than just because he was Hawk Chandler.

Ingrid's fingers tentatively touched her arm. "Please do not look so unhappy. Perhaps he will come with Rand today."

"I don't care if he comes or not," Bethany snapped in return, made even angrier by Ingrid knowing it was Hawk who was causing her black mood. "Why ever should I care at all what Mr. Chandler does? His soul is of no consequence to me. You were right. We'll never see the likes of him in church. He's nothing but a . . . a *heathen.*"

Ingrid's face fell. "Bethany!" she returned in

an aghast whisper. "You must not say such things."

Bethany stopped and whirled to face her friend. "Why mustn't I? It's the truth, isn't—" Her words caught in her throat, nearly choking her.

The object of her fury was riding through town beside Rand. Instead of his usual denim britches and open-necked shirt, he was wearing a dark suit and starched white collar. The brim of his black Stetson hid his handsome dark face from view, but there was no mistaking him. She would know him anywhere. She had long since memorized the wide cut of his shoulders, the way he sat his horse, the way his trousers fit against his sleek, well-muscled thighs.

Her heart quickened.

He had come. He had come after all.

Hawk saw her turn, saw her stop speaking as her eyes fell upon him. Unconsciously, he smiled. There were probably a hundred reasons why he shouldn't be so happy about seeing her again, but at the moment, he couldn't think of a one of them.

He and Rand stopped their horses not far from the two young women.

"Mornin', Miss Silverton. Miss Johnson." He touched his hat brim before stepping down from the saddle. He twirled the reins a couple of times around the hitching post, then turned toward Bethany.

She stood watching him, splashes of color in her cheeks, her eyes round and wondering. Her dark auburn hair was hidden beneath a fetching emerald-green bonnet, the satiny bow tied in a flourish near her right ear. A softer green shawl, nearly the color of her eyes, was draped low across her back and through each arm. In her hands she held a small black Bible. Her fingers were clenching it tightly.

What am I doing here? he asked himself as he shortened the distance between them with just a few quick strides.

Yet he knew exactly what he was doing here. He had come to see Bethany. He'd been counting the minutes until he would see her again. He didn't care if she was the daughter of a wealthy man, and he was just a working cowboy. He didn't care if she was more used to the glitter of Philadelphia society than the dust and sweat of a cattle ranch. He didn't care that folks would censure them both for what he was feeling and wanting. He didn't care about any of the possible differences that might separate them. He had come to see Bethany.

"Mr. Chandler . . . you came." Her voice was soft and pleasant.

"I couldn't very well turn down your last invitation, Miss Silverton."

He watched as her cheeks flamed even brighter. He could see she knew he meant the kiss and was embarrassed by his reference to it. Yet, even in her embarrassment, her gaze didn't drop away.

"Shall we go inside?" Hawk offered Bethany his arm.

She smiled, shyly at first, then brightening as

he took her hand and placed it against his arm as he escorted her toward the tent.

Vince stepped down from the buggy. There was only one other wagon and a couple of saddle horses in the field behind the Silverton home. He was still early. He'd wanted it that way. He wanted a chance before services to ask Bethany to accompany him out to his ranch for the afternoon. Of course, he'd be forced to invite the plain Miss Johnson to go along too as a sort of chaperone, but he was certain the reverend would give his permission. The reverend was a sensible man. He would know how difficult it would be to find a suitable husband for Bethany out here. The reverend must surely already know there was no one but Vince Richards to consider.

He leaned down and stepped into the tent. It was pleasantly cool inside, the morning breeze dancing in through the open flaps at the back of the tent and out through the front. He stopped just inside as his gray gaze whisked quickly over the mostly empty wooden benches.

His jaw tensed and his neck stiffened when he saw them. The two women were seated side by side on the first bench, just in front of the pulpit. On either side of them were two men. Rand Howard and Hawk Chandler.

Bethany turned her head and spoke to Hawk. Hawk looked down at her and replied.

Vince felt a twisting in his vitals as he whirled around and stepped outside, sucking in a quick breath through pinched nostrils. His teeth ground together. He'd be damned if he was going to let that breed interfere with his plans for Bethany Silverton!

But he would have to deal with it in another time, in another way.

Quickly, he made for his buggy.

After church, Ingrid and Rand stood away from the rest of the visiting, milling congregation. At five foot nine, Ingrid could almost look directly into Rand's brown eyes without tipping her head back. It constantly amazed her that this handsome, warm-hearted man should choose to be with her, should choose to love her. He made her feel almost pretty. No one else had ever done that for Ingrid before.

Rand took hold of her hand. "I started clearing a spot on my land this week. I know right where I'm going to build my house. Would you like to see it sometime, Ingrid?"

"I would like that very much."

He swallowed hard. She could see his Adams apple bob nervously. "I want you to tell me if you like what I'm plannin' to do." His gaze dropped to their hands, twined together between them. "You see, I want it to be your house, too."

She'd believed almost from the start that he meant to propose marriage to her. Yet, now that it had happened, she was struck dumb. Her pale blue eyes widened, and her mouth parted as a tiny "oh!" escaped on a gasp.

Rand cleared his throat as he looked at her

again. "I love you, Ingrid. Will you be my wife? I haven't much to offer, but I sure will love you."

She opened her mouth to speak but found her throat tight with emotion. Her eyes watered, and she knew any moment her face was going to be tracked with tears.

Suddenly, the hopeful, uncertain look on his face turned to one of despair. "I'm sorry, Miss Johnson. I knew I was bein' foolish, but—"

"Rand," she whispered, tightening her grip on his hand. "I would love to be your wife. I . . . I love you, too."

He moved as if he would kiss her, then glanced around at the worshipers still surrounding them and controlled the urge. But he couldn't stop a joyful grin. "Wait 'til I tell Hawk."

"Wait until I tell Bethany."

In unison, their heads turned, their eyes seeking out their friends. The couple in question was standing near the tent, visiting with the reverend and his wife.

"I never thought Bethany could do it. And in only a couple of weeks, too."

"Do what?" Rand asked.

"Get Mr. Chandler to come to church. Now I must pay her the five dollars." Suddenly, she stopped speaking as her fingers came up to cover her mouth.

"What are you talkin' about, Ingrid?"

She turned her face toward Rand once again, feeling a blush stealing up from her neck. "I cannot tell you, Rand," she said softly.

His gaze told her she must.

"You must not ever let her know I told."

"Told what?"

Quickly, Ingrid explained to him about the wager and how it came to be made. "She did not mean any harm by it," she finished, her eyes turning toward Bethany once more.

Rand's frown disappeared, and he began to chuckle. "No, I guess there's no harm done. But wouldn't it just scorch Hawk to know his comin' to church earned Miss Silverton such a nice sum."

Hawk hated to end the morning's pleasant interlude. It gave him a heady feeling, having Bethany sitting or standing beside him, her shimmery green gaze so often lifted toward him. But there was work to be done at the ranch, Sunday or no.

He held out his hand toward Nathaniel Silverton. "It's time I was heading back for the Circle Blue, Reverend. I enjoyed your sermon."

"We hope you'll come again, Mr. Chandler."

Hawk glanced at Bethany, saying softly, "I intend to, sir." Reluctantly, he pulled his eyes and thoughts away from her and turned both toward Rand. With a wave of his hand, he indicated it was time they were off.

A short time later, the two men were mounted and headed out of town. They rode in silence, each of them thinking about the woman he'd left behind in Sweetwater.

Quite unexpectedly, Rand began chuckling to himself.

"What's so funny?" Hawk asked, turning a questioning glance on his friend, a black eyebrow arching over one eye.

"Nothin'." And then the laughter grew.

Hawk grinned. "Come on, Rand. What's so funny?"

"I shouldn't tell you, Hawk. I'm not sure Ingrid will forgive me if I do. She just sorta let it slip or I wouldn't know either."

"Know what?" Hawk's curiosity was growing.

"Well, it seems that your comin' to church today was expensive for Ingrid. Cost her five dollars."

Hawk's grin faded and he looked at Rand as if he were losing his mind.

Rand lifted a hand. "I swear it's the truth, Hawk. Seems that first day we saw Ingrid and Bethany, I asked you if you was goin' to church, and you said no. Well, Bethany heard you and she made a wager with Ingrid that she could get you to come to church within a month."

"She what?" The grin was completely gone now, replaced by a dark scowl.

But Rand hadn't noticed his friend's lack of amusement. He was enjoying telling the story too much. "And she did it too. In just less than three weeks, if I recall right. That girl is really something, isn't she? Pretty as you please, she gets you to church whether you like it or not. You suppose she fills the reverend's church that way?"

So, it had all been a joke for Miss Bethany Silverton. Getting him to come to church was just a means to win five dollars from her friend.

It was all just a game to Bethany. Her coy looks, her shy smiles, even her innocent kiss had all been a sham. Just a lark. He should have known. He should have known Bethany wasn't any different from any other "lady" he'd ever known.

A smile reappeared on his mouth, this one tight and anything but humorous. "If you think this is so funny, Rand, care to make a little wager of our own?"

Rand stopped laughing and looked at his friend's profile. "What kind of wager?"

"Getting me to church wasn't all that hard. Miss Silverton might think a man like me wouldn't likely go to church, but I've been in plenty. It wasn't much of a wager to get me there again." His hard gaze swept over the rolling countryside, his blue eyes darkened with suppressed anger, an anger mostly hidden from his friend by the shade of his hat brim. "Now I'd like to wager over something a little more difficult. Something like getting a young lady of quality like Miss Silverton to agree to marry somebody like me. A breed."

"Wait. Hawk . . ."

"She's probably thought this was all great fun, flirting with the cowboy, but she doesn't have any notion of it being more than a game. Well, fifty dollars says I can get her to agree to marry me before the end of June. Fifty dollars says I can get her to be dying to marry me." His head swiveled around. His gaze locked upon Rand's wary face. "And not a word to Ingrid, either. This is between you and me."

"Sure, Hawk, but you don't want to marry her,

do you? I mean, you're not in love with her. Why put her and you—"

"Marriage isn't part of the bet. I only have to get her to *agree* to marry me. Nobody said anything about going through with it."

"Hawk, I think—"

"Think I can't do it, Rand?"

Rand shook his head, his face solemn. "You're wrong about this, Hawk. You're wrong."

"Is it a bet or not?"

"Sure, Hawk, but I don't like it. I just hope you know what you're doing."

Night had settled over Sweetwater and the Silverton home. The pale light of a first quarter moon fell through the hall window on the second floor. As Bethany tiptoed on bare feet past her parents' bedroom, she could hear her father's gentle snoring. Reaching Ingrid's door, she tapped lightly, then slipped inside without waiting for a reply.

"Ingrid? Are you awake?"

"Yes," came a mumbled reply.

"I couldn't sleep. Can we talk awhile?"

"Mmmm."

Bethany closed the door silently and hurried across the room. She sat on Ingrid's bed, tucking her feet beneath the quilt and drawing her knees up beneath her white nightgown to hug them against her chest.

All afternoon she'd wanted to talk with Ingrid about how Hawk made her feel, but there had been guests for Sunday dinner and then Papa had wanted to discuss plans for the building of the new church, which was to begin this week, and then it was supper time already. But now that she was here and could talk freely, she didn't know how to begin.

Ingrid pushed herself up against the headboard. "What is it, Bethany?" she whispered.

"Ingrid, are you . . . are you in love with Mr. Howard?"

Silence. And then, "Yes. Yes, I love him." Another pause. "Bethany, he asked me to marry him today."

"He did!" Bethany exclaimed in a hushed voice. "Oh, Ingrid, what did you say?"

"I said yes, of course."

Bethany launched herself forward, giving Ingrid a mammoth hug. "Oh, I'm so happy for you." She settled against the headboard at Ingrid's side. "Tell me how it happened."

"We were talking and he told me he was starting to build his own place . . . and then he said he wanted it to be my place too." The moonlight caressed her face as she smiled with the warm memory. "And then he told me he loved me."

Bethany felt gooseflesh rising along one arm. She closed her eyes to envision the scene, but instead of Rand and Ingrid, she saw herself standing with Hawk. She imagined him bending low to whisper those three wonderful words in her ear. Her heartbeat quickened as her eyes flew open once again.

"I do not want your parents to know yet, Bethany," Ingrid continued, unaware of

Bethany's wandering thoughts. "Not until we decide when we want to be married."

"I won't tell a soul. I promise."

Suddenly, Ingrid chuckled. "I will pay you the five dollars tomorrow."

"Five dollars?"

"The wager, Bethany. You did get Mr. Chandler to come to church."

It was her turn to laugh softly. "You know, I'd forgotten all about it. Our bet, I mean. I was just so glad to see him." She sobered. "Do you suppose I could be falling in love, Ingrid?"

"Only you can know the answer to that."

"But I don't know," she whispered, more to herself than to her friend. "I just don't know."

Chapter Eight

The invitation for a tour of the Circle Blue was delivered to Bethany by Gabe Andrews when he came to town for supplies on Monday.

"Papa, you simply must let me go. Ingrid's invited too, so it's not as if I would be alone with him, and Mr. Chandler said he'd ride into town for us tomorrow, so we wouldn't be without an escort away from town."

Nathaniel's eyes scanned the note once again, then he lifted his gaze to Bethany. She was standing beside his desk, her hands clasped before her. Her face was alight with excitement. Her beautiful green eyes pleaded with him, and he felt himself weakening.

He'd always given her too much freedom. He'd been told so time and time again by well-meaning members of his family back in Philadelphia. Common sense said she shouldn't be allowed to spend the afternoon out on the range with a man they barely knew. Not that he hadn't taken a liking to Hawk Chandler. He was certain he would treat Bethany with utmost respect. Still, his daughter was high-spirited and given sometimes to impulsive actions which later caused them all regret.

She cares for him too much already, he thought to himself as he perused Bethany's high color.

She reached out to touch his cheek. "I'm not a little girl any longer, Papa. Surely you can trust me to behave like a lady."

Nathaniel sighed. "I suppose if Ingrid goes too . . ."

"Oh, thank you, Papa!" She threw her arms around his neck and hugged him with tight enthusiasm. As she pulled away, she placed a kiss on his temple. "I must go tell Mr. Andrews. He told me he'd be at Eberlie's Mercantile." She whirled away in a rustle of fabric and was gone from the reverend's study in an instant.

Nathaniel shook his head as he rose from his desk and walked to the window. It wasn't easy, letting a child grow up. How much simpler it had been when she was a little girl, her long hair in braids with ribbons. He'd been the only man in her life then. How she had loved to go for rides in their carriage with him, calling on his parishioners. She had never been afraid to meet people, always looking for new adventures.

But how quickly she had blossomed from that pretty little girl into a beguiling young lady. Suddenly he'd been only one of many men vying for her attention. With a cock of her head or a bat of an eyelash, she could have almost anything she wanted. She was spoiled, true. But at the same time, she was an innocent, so open and honest, fresh and eager. Bethany had a kind and giving heart, and a zest for life like no one else he knew. He wondered now if he'd been wise to take her away from Philadelphia. The men out here—men like Hawk Chandler—were different from those she had known back east. If they'd remained there, she might already have married a man who could care and provide for her as Nathaniel had always done. She could already be living a nice, quiet existence with a home and servants and plenty of friends nearby.

He smiled to himself. What was he thinking? He couldn't quite picture Bethany Rachel ever living a "nice, quiet existence." It just wasn't her nature. Wherever she lived, her home would be filled with excitement and surprises. That was just Bethany.

But Hawk Chandler? Was he the right man for his daughter?

Nathaniel didn't know. All he knew was he didn't want Bethany hurt, even while he acknowledged to himself that everyone's life was filled with some hurts. Bethany's would be no different.

He'd been right, of course. He was a fool ever to trust a lady. Or any woman, for that matter. But his humiliation at Bethany's hands had struck much deeper than anything Alice had done. Alice, at least, had been honest. She had cared for him—in her own shallow way—until she learned of his mixed blood, and although her rejection had hurt, it had at the very least been an honest reaction. There had been no deception. She had simply told him she could not marry a man of mixed blood.

Bethany, on the other hand, had played him for a fool. She had made him believe his Indian blood didn't matter to her. She had flirted with him just to win a bet. He doubted the seeming innocence of her kiss was even honest. She probably had kissed and been kissed hundreds of times.

As he jogged his horse down Main Street, his face revealed nothing of his thoughts, nothing of the icy rage that surged through his veins, seeking his moment of revenge. He meant to see her humiliated before her friends as he had been before Rand. He would woo her. He would win her heart. And then, when she'd agreed to marry him, he would tell her just what he thought of her.

He stopped Flame at the white picket fence and dismounted. He noted the two horses saddled and tied at the side of the house. As his gaze flicked toward the front door, it opened, and Bethany stepped outside. A smile brightened her face as their eyes met.

Hawk felt a tightening in his chest as he beheld her once again. She was clad in a tan riding habit. The bodice fit snugly to reveal the enticing fullness of her breasts. The skirt was short and simply draped, accentuating the narrowness of her waist. A yellow cravat was tied in a bow at her throat, and a matching yellow gauze veil was wound around the crown of her tan silk hat.

He told himself it was a ridiculous outfit for

riding the range of Montana. She belonged back east with her society friends. She should be mounting up on some mincing mare to parade through a park or something. She didn't belong here.

Yet, even as he told himself these things, he couldn't deny how incredibly beautiful she was. It made him ache for what might have been if it weren't for . . .

"Good morning, Mr. Chandler," she called from the porch, raising her riding crop in greeting.

Her voice was melodic, like a mountain songbird. Had he ever noticed that before?

Don't be fooled by her, Chandler.

He wrapped the reins around a fence post, then opened the gate. "Morning, Miss Silverton."

"Ingrid will be right down. Won't you come in and say hello to my father?"

He stepped up onto the porch and removed his hat. "Be glad to."

Bethany's head tilted to one side as she glanced up at him. "It was terribly kind of you to invite us out to see your ranch." Her misty green eyes sparkled with excitement.

Hawk let his own gaze slide to her mouth, full and pink and inviting. He meant to kiss that mouth again before this month was out. Perhaps before this day was out. Winning this bet didn't have to be an unpleasant task, after all.

Bethany's cheeks suddenly flushed with color, as if she had read his thoughts. She turned her face quickly away and led him into the house.

Yes, that mouth should most definitely be thoroughly kissed.

Rand met them near the spring above the ranch house. They ate a light lunch in the shade of the willows, then they mounted their horses and rode leisurely across the range. Rand did most of the talking, his mood light and jovial. He told the two young women stories of his and Hawk's adventures on the trail and on the ranch, and he pointed out places and things of interest.

As he talked, Bethany glanced surreptitiously toward Hawk. He had spoken little since they bade her parents good-bye back in town. But it wasn't his silence that bothered her. It was the way he looked at her, the way he'd been looking at her all day. One moment she would swear there was a spark of—what was it? desire?—in his eyes, as if he wanted to kiss her. And then the next, his dark eyes seemed cold and blank and void of feeling of any kind. She didn't understand him. At times he almost frightened her. Yet, she didn't have to understand him to know she wanted to be with him.

"Would you mind, Miss Silverton?"

"What?" She turned her head abruptly toward Rand. "I'm sorry. I—I'm afraid my thoughts were wandering, Mr. Howard. What was it you said?"

"Before we take you ladies back to town, I'd like to show Ingrid my spot on the mountain. Would you mind?"

Bethany looked at Ingrid. The blonde's face was so alight with love and excitement, she was almost pretty. How could Bethany deny them a short while alone together? Her father need never know. "Of course I don't mind. I'll wait with Mr. Chandler at the house."

"We won't be long," Ingrid promised in a near whisper, her eyes locked with Rand's.

Bethany watched them ride away, then nudged Buttercup forward with the heel of her boot.

"Don't you think you know us well enough by now to call us Rand and Hawk?"

Her heart did a quick gallop at the sound of his voice. She was as alone with him as Ingrid was with Rand.

"And I'd like to call you Bethany, if you'd allow me that pleasure."

She didn't dare look at him. "I'd like that . . . Hawk."

They rode the rest of the way back to the ranch in silence. A sixth sense told Bethany that Hawk was watching her, that his fathomless blue eyes were studying her profile. She remembered the way he'd looked at her mouth this morning, and her heart quickened again.

They stopped their mounts beside the corral. Hawk swung down from the saddle and came around to stand between the two horses. His hands spanned her waist, and he lowered her slowly to the ground. He allowed his hands to linger in a delightful, almost intimate touch. Uncertain what to do or where to look, she stared at the open collar of his red shirt, but the sight of his dark skin beneath it only made her feel more uncertain.

"Bethany."

She could hardly breathe. He was going to kiss her. Surely, he was going to kiss her.

"Come with me. I've got something to show you." With that, his hands fell from her waist and he stepped away from the corral. When she didn't follow immediately, he glanced back at her. "Come on."

She felt a sting of disappointment. She had been so sure he would want to kiss her. Maybe he really didn't care for her. Maybe he just invited her here so Ingrid could be with Rand. Maybe she was just along as a chaperone. After all, Hawk hadn't been overly friendly today. Maybe he was just tolerating her company.

Well, *she* wasn't going to tolerate his toleration. She was bound and determined to *make* him enjoy her company if it killed them both. She didn't know exactly how she was going to go about it, but Bethany Rachel Silverton was no quitter.

"I'm coming," she said, putting some cheer into her voice.

You don't catch a man by mooning over him. That's what Eliza Carpenter always said back at Miss Hendersen's. Eliza was probably right.

Bethany followed Hawk into the barn. She stopped for a moment, giving her eyes time to adjust from the brightness of the outdoors to the dimness of the barn. A horse stomped its hoof and snorted somewhere nearby. The air smelled of hay and horse and dung, pungent yet somehow quite pleasant.

"Over here." He was standing beside a stall. His hand beckoned her onward.

Curious, she walked closer and peered over the stall door.

"This is Storm. Remember him?"

The black animal bobbed his head, causing his heavy mane to sway against his thick neck. The horse stepped closer, then pawed the barn floor before stretching his head forward to lightly nibble Hawk's hand where it rested on the stall door.

Bethany turned her gaze from the horse to the man at her side. "I'm sorry. I don't . . ." She ended with a puzzled shrug.

"He's the bronc I was breaking the day you first came out here."

"That's the same horse? But he looks as gentle as a lamb. He was so wild that day."

"A steady hand . . . a calm voice . . . a little time." Hawk's eyes held hers captive as his hand moved from the stall to her shoulder. "You can tame the wildest of creatures that way." His other hand came up from his side, settling beneath her chin. Tenderly, he tipped her head back.

She held her breath, waiting, hoping, even as her eyelids drifted closed.

The first brush of his lips against hers was so light, she wasn't even sure they were touching. In the next instant, an explosion of sensations spiraled through her as the kiss deepened. Involuntarily, her arms rose to circle his neck.

It was everything she had hoped a kiss would

be, and when he released her and straightened, she felt bereft, abandoned. He had let it end all too soon. She opened her eyes to look up at him, her breathing quick and shallow.

He saw the look of wonder in her eyes and was tempted to take her back into his arms and kiss her even more fully. He wondered if he was wrong. He wondered if she was, indeed, as innocent as she looked at the moment, her eyes shimmering, her cheeks flushed. It would be so pleasant to crush her against him. To feel those taut breasts pressing against his chest. To free her thick auburn tresses and wind his fingers through them. To let his tongue slip between her lips and taste the honey sweetness of her mouth. To . . .

Careful, Chandler.

Hawk stepped away from her, emotionally distancing himself as well. He couldn't allow himself to forget the rules of this new game he played, lest she become the winner before she even knew she was a player.

"We'd better go back outside," he said. His voice was low and husky. "Rand and Ingrid should be back soon."

"Yes," she whispered, tugging nervously at the lower edge of her basque, then fidgeting with the button at her throat. She spun away from him and walked with hurried steps back into the sunshine.

Bethany rolled onto her back and threw her arms onto the pillow above her head. The morning sunshine warmed her face as it fell through her bedroom windows. Eyes still closed, she grinned lazily and allowed a satisfied moan to slip out.

Once again she replayed yesterday's kiss with Hawk. Each time she imagined it, the kiss got longer and more passionate. She'd never felt so wonderful. She *must* be in love. And surely he must love her. He wouldn't have kissed her if he didn't love her. Surely he wouldn't.

Throughout the night she had thought of him. As the hours passed, Hawk Chandler had become taller and even more handsome. She forgot the cool look that could glaze his eyes. She forgot the firm set of his mouth which sometimes made him seem so harsh. She saw only his wonderful, rare smile. She heard only the gentle sound of his voice when he spoke her name. He filled her dreams and her wakeful moments as well. He was the hero every girl waited for. And he loved her. He must love her.

She opened her eyes, her heart beginning its rapid pace again. She wanted to be with Hawk today. She wanted to throw caution to the wind and hurl herself into his arms and let him kiss her. All she wanted to do at this moment was put a saddle on Buttercup and ride out to the Circle Blue.

But, of course, she couldn't do that. She would just have to wait, as a proper young lady would, until he called on her again. Sometimes she hated trying to be a proper young lady; it certainly wasn't easy. When he brought her home last night, he'd said he would see her again soon. *How soon*? she had wanted to ask, but she'd managed to refrain.

"Bethany, dear." Her mother's soft call was followed by a rap on her door. "Are you awake?"

"Yes, Mother." She sat up and waited as the door opened.

"Have you forgotten? The men are starting work on the church today. We need your help."

She felt a rush of guilt. Until that moment, she'd been oblivious to the sounds of hammering and sawing going on outside her window. She had forgotten everything except Hawk and his embrace. "I did forget, Mother. I'm sorry. I'll hurry."

Following a quick washing, she dressed in a white blouse and dark blue skirt, then tied her hair back at the nape with a matching blue ribbon. By the time she was downstairs, her mother and Ingrid were already busy making sandwiches and rolling dough for pie crusts. The men volunteering their time for the building of the church would be hungry come lunch time.

"What can I do to help, Mother?"

"Take out this pot of coffee and some cups for now."

Bethany picked up the tray as she was bidden and hurried out the back door.

The building site, between the Silverton home and the boarding house, was alive with activity. She saw her father standing with John Wilton and Fred Eberlie, all three of them pouring over the plans for the new church.

"Papa, I've brought coffee." She set the tray on a stack of lumber.

"Thank you, Bethany."

Noting the happy glow on her father's face, she knew he was picturing the church as it would be when it was finished. She smiled at him, sharing his joy. It was what he'd been working toward since the day he'd decided to leave Philadelphia. It was all the more satisfying knowing the reverend was respected and liked by all of Sweetwater.

How lucky they all were. They could never have known when they boarded that train in Philadelphia how happy they would be in this little town. A town they hadn't even heard of until a couple of months ago. Mother, of course, was happy any place Papa was. Papa was happy because he was fulfilling his dream. Ingrid, who hadn't even been a part of their family in Philadelphia, was happy because she was going to be marrying Rand. And Bethany . . . Bethany had found Hawk Chandler.

"Good morning, Bethany," his soft, low voice said.

She whirled, fearing she had conjured him up with her secret musings. He stood not more than four feet away. His shirt was open at the neck, and she caught a glimpse of his bronzed chest. His long shirt sleeves were rolled up above his elbows, revealing strong, dark forearms. A light beading of sweat glistened on his forehead and in the hollow of his throat.

"I'll have some of that coffee if it's for the taking."

"You never said you'd be here today."

"No, I guess I didn't." His expression was

inscrutable as his eyes held her captive. Then he offered a strange smile. "Coffee?"

Flustered now, Bethany spun away from him. "Of course. I—I'm sorry." She lifted the coffee pot off the tray and poured the hot brew into a cup. Then, holding the cup in two hands, she turned to face him once again.

His fingers touched hers as he slipped the cup from her grasp. She felt a sharp jolt. Her eyes darted up to look at him, wondering if he'd felt it too. But Hawk was quietly raising the cup to his lips, seemingly undisturbed by their brief contact. She watched as he slowly drained the cup. Occasionally, between sips, he would look her way, but he didn't speak. And Bethany seemed unable to think of anything to say to break the silence between them.

At last he held out the empty cup toward her. "Thanks." He glanced toward the piles of lumber and milling men. "I'd better get back to work." With that, he turned and walked away from her.

She felt a hot flush rising to stain her cheeks. Why—why that insufferable man! He'd acted as if they were scarcely more than acquaintances. He'd acted as if they'd never shared a kiss or spent an interlude alone in the barn at his ranch. He'd acted as if she were—as if she were nothing to him at all.

Well, you're not going to get away with this nonsense, Mr. Chandler. You may not be in love with me yet, but you will be. I'm going to see to that.

* * *

It was nearly sunset before Hawk rode his big stallion toward the corral at the Circle Blue. The stretch of muscles across his upper back and shoulders ached with fatigue, but it was a welcome feeling. He was ready to drop into bed and fall asleep, ready to get that green-eyed witch out of his mind.

Several times during the day, she'd brought a tray of food or drink to the laboring men. Each time she'd sought him out with her eyes and turned her beguiling smile upon him. And each time he'd felt a surge of wanting such as he'd never felt before.

The feeling angered him. How could she make him cold with rage and hot with desire at the same time? Her duplicity was flawless. If Rand had never told him about her little wager, he wouldn't have guessed she was playing him for a fool. Yet, even knowing the truth, he wanted her as he'd never wanted another woman. The kiss they'd shared yesterday had only whet his passion to know more of her.

In the dying light, Hawk unsaddled his horse and tossed the leather tack over the top corral rail. He scratched the animal beneath his mane, then ran his hand slowly across its withers and back.

"Women," he muttered.

Flame snorted and bobbed his head as if in understanding.

Hawk pushed open the corral gate, led the stallion inside, and pulled the bridle from behind its ears, gently easing the bit from its mouth. Rather than moving quickly away, Flame turned his head and nudged Hawk's belly with his muzzle.

"A man'd be better off with just his horse, wouldn't he, fella?" Hawk whispered as he scratched the horse once again. "A man would just plain be better off."

CHAPTER NINE

·——·

Bethany fingered the rose pink satin fabric and pondered again the gown she had in mind. If she could get her mother and Ingrid to help, she knew the dress could be finished by Sunday. Of course, it would mean two very long days, but it could be done. She knew it could.

"Good morning, Bethany."

"Oh. Hello, Martha."

"Is that for you?"

Bethany nodded. "Mmmm."

"It'll look real pretty with your hair."

"Thanks."

Martha walked around the counter to stand opposite Bethany. She leaned her elbows on the countertop and twisted a strand of curly brown hair between her fingers. "Hawk Chandler'd probably like you in that color, too."

"Do you think so?" The question slipped out before she had time to think. She was embarrassed to hear the eagerness in her voice.

Martha shook her head and frowned.

"Bethany Silverton, for a city girl, you're not very smart."

"What?"

"Don't you know it's not fittin' for you to be seein' a man like that?" Martha whispered as her gaze flicked over the mercantile to see if anyone was listening.

Bethany's voice dropped to a whisper in response. "A man like what?"

"Why, a breed, of course. Don't you know folks have been talkin' about you ever since the barn dance? And when my pa heard you'd been out to the Circle Blue, why he nearly burst a vein in his neck. Marched right over to see your pa to set him straight on a few things."

"But I thought everyone liked Mr. Chandler."

"'Course they do. But he's part Indian, all the same. There's some who'd just as soon string him from a tree as have him look at a pretty white girl like you. Sullied. That's what Pa says you'll be if you keep it up."

Bethany's surprise turned to anger. She stepped back from the fabric counter, her cheeks ablaze and her eyes sparking. "Believe me, Miss Eberlie, I am *not* sullied from my encounters with Mr. Chandler, nor do I intend to pick my friends by their family trees. God looks upon the heart, not the color of his skin. That's what *my* father says."

"You can say what you like," the younger girl responded with a shrug, "but that's how it is. Just don't think any decent man's going to give you a second look if you keep chasin' after Hawk."

Bethany's retort carried across the mercantile for all the customers to hear. "I am *not* chasing after Hawk Chandler."

With that, she whirled around and hurried toward the door. Only at the last moment did she see Hawk standing just inside. Had he heard her? Surely he had. Everyone in the room had to have heard her. The color in her cheeks deepened as she ducked her head and rushed on.

Hawk could imagine well enough what had been said to Bethany. He had witnessed her embarrassment and thought he'd seen a glimmer of tears in her pretty green eyes. He felt a moment of regret for his part in it. He shouldn't be subjecting her to the gossip and cruel words.

But then he thought again of her wager. She'd pretended his mixed blood didn't make any difference. She'd flirted and connived, all for the sake of five dollars. To her it was all a game. She had started it, but he meant to finish it. And when it was over, he wouldn't care what people said about him. They could all be hanged.

He pulled on the brim of his hat as he stepped back out into the sunlight. He didn't give himself any time to consider his actions. He had some courtin' to do, and it might as well begin now.

"You must understand it's your daughter's welfare I'm concerned with, Nathaniel." Vince leaned forward, bracing his forearms on his knees. "A small town like this . . . well, it can be cruel when one thwarts accepted behavior."

The reverend smiled tolerantly. "I'm sure you

mean to be kind, but I'm afraid I share Bethany's ignorance of prejudice. I happen to like Mr. Chandler, and I see no harm in us all being friends."

"Friends, no. But an afternoon at his ranch . . ."

The smile disappeared from Nathaniel's face. "She was not alone, Vince. She was with Ingrid and Mr. Howard."

Vince sensed he had nearly gone too far. "You're right, of course. I didn't mean to imply anything inappropriate. It's just that Bethany's such a sweet girl, and I don't want her being harmed by gossip." He stood and picked up his hat. "Well, I must be going. I still have business to conclude before I return to the Bar V. You won't forget the party out at my ranch tomorrow?"

"We'll be there," the reverend answered as he rose from his chair. He walked with Vince toward the door.

Before they reached it, however, the front door flew open and Bethany burst into the house. Her color was high. Strands of her burnished auburn hair had pulled free of their pins to curl around her temples and nape. Her eyes had a watery gleam. Had she been crying?

"Bethany, my dear, what's wrong?" Vince asked.

Her answering glance was anything but encouraging. "Hello, Mr. Richards." She folded her hands in front of her and composed herself. "Nothing is wrong. Why do you ask?"

Vince hid a grin. If his suspicions were correct, Bethany had just tasted a dose of the gossip he'd warned her father about. "You looked hurried, is all," he responded. He placed his hat on his head and turned toward the reverend. "Good day, Nathaniel. I'll see you and your family tomorrow at the Bar V." His gaze returned to Bethany. "I'm looking forward to having you in my home again, my dear."

She didn't reply.

Smiling now, he tapped his hat brim and walked outside to his waiting buggy. Tomorrow night would be a special night, indeed. He meant to dazzle Bethany Silverton with all he could offer her as her husband. He meant to propose marriage to her, and he had no intention of being rejected.

"What *is* wrong, Bethany?" her father asked as he closed the door.

She shook her head, not ready to talk about it yet.

"Does it have anything to do with Mr. Chandler?"

Her eyes widened. "How did you know?"

"Mr. Eberlie and Mr. Richards have both been kind enough to share their viewpoints on the matter."

Bethany turned into the parlor and sank onto a settee. "What do you think, Papa? Is it wrong for me to like him, just because his grandmother was an Indian?"

"Oh, my child, I wish I had an easy answer." He sat next to her and took her hand. "Bethany, there will be gossip if you show interest in a man of mixed blood. Some of it will be vicious and hurtful. Society has rigid standards, and we either obey those rules or we follow our hearts. Even ministers of the gospel can't agree on such a topic as this. What do you think is right in God's eyes, Bethany?"

"I don't know, Papa," she whispered, confusion evident in each word.

"You know, my dear, I would do anything to protect you from the hardships of this world, but I can't. And a parent who tries to shelter his children too much only does them harm. Some decisions, as difficult as they may be, you must make yourself." He stopped once again, obviously searching for the right words. Finally, he sighed and said, "I cannot find it in my heart to object to your interest in Mr. Chandler. My instincts tell me he's an honest, decent man, and that's what matters most to me."

"Thank you, Papa. I think so too."

It hadn't taken him long to find and pick the bouquet of wildflowers. There had been a moment, as he stood amidst the colorful sea of lavenders, cornflower blues, and sunshine yellows when he'd felt almost as gay as the flowers looked. It would have been easy to pretend he was on his way to spend an evening with a young lady who truly cared for him and he for her. He'd had to mentally shake himself. He'd had to remind himself that this was all for one purpose. To win fifty dollars. And that was the one and only reason.

As he stepped down from the saddle in front of the Silverton home, flowers in hand, he glanced quickly toward the site of the new church. There were several men hard at work. One of them, John Wilton, recognized Hawk and raised his hand in a friendly wave. Hawk returned it, then started toward the front porch.

Bethany opened the door in response to his knock. With his free hand, he swept his hat off. "Hello, Bethany."

"Mr. Chandler. Hawk. What a surprise." A soft blush warmed her cheeks.

"I . . . these are for you." He held the flowers out, feeling suddenly as awkward as a school boy.

"Hawk," she whispered, "they're beautiful." Her smile was gentle, reaching into her eyes as she looked from the blossoms to him. "Won't you come in?"

He nodded.

"Please sit down while I put these in some water."

But he didn't sit. He felt like a tight spring, filled with an abundance of nervous energy. He paced the floor, walking several times to the window and looking out, then turning away once again.

"Hawk?"

She had reentered the parlor while his back was turned. He swung around, thinking even as he did so about the way his name sounded from her lips, her voice so soft, almost like a caress. She was watching him with questioning, yet expectant eyes.

You should call a halt to this now, Chandler, he told himself.

"May I get you some refreshments?"

"No. . . ." He hesitated, then the words came in a rush. "Actually, I came to—to invite you to lunch, Bethany." Suddenly, he remembered the way she'd looked in the mercantile, the stricken expression on her face and the teary glitter in her eyes. If she was seen with him, the hurts would only increase. "Next week," he added quickly. "I'm in town for just a few hours today. I thought maybe we could do it next week. Maybe at Mrs. Jenkin's. The food's not fancy but it's good. Will you join me?"

Her smile brightened even more. "I'd like to have lunch with you. Very much."

"Good. Well . . ." Hawk slapped his hat against his thigh. "Guess I'd better be on my way."

He was out the door almost before she could bid him good-bye.

Damn! he thought as he swung into the saddle. This wasn't going to be as easy as it should have been. When she wasn't around, it was easy to stay angry with her and to know her for the flirt she was. But when he was with her, when he looked in those pretty green eyes or saw the blush on her fair cheeks or saw her heart-shaped mouth turn up in a smile, it no longer seemed to matter. He was just glad for the excuse to be with her.

Get a hold of yourself, Chandler.

He does care. He does care.

The phrase played in her head over and over as she watched him ride away. Her heart fairly sang with joy, and she couldn't keep from beaming openly. If anyone were to see her at that moment, they would have to know how she felt about Hawk Chandler. She didn't care that his grandmother had been a full-blooded Indian and his mother a half-breed. She loved him. It didn't matter one whit what anyone else thought. She didn't care if the whole world knew. She loved Hawk Chandler.

That same afternoon, Rand Howard sat on the edge of the sofa in the Silverton parlor, nervously sliding his hat brim through his fingers. His eyes shifted from the ornate carpet on the floor to the rosewood claw feet of the nearby love seat, then returned to his battered hat. He could hear the methodical ticking of the great mantel clock. The room seemed unbearably stuffy. His fingers came up to loosen the stiff collar that promised to choke the life from him before this ordeal was over.

"Well, Rand. Sorry to keep you waiting. I was working on Sunday's sermon. Ingrid tells me you wish to have a word with me. Nothing wrong at the Circle Blue, I trust?"

Rand hopped up. "No, sir, reverend."

Nathaniel's easy smile calmed him only slightly.

"Please, sit down, my friend. I can see you're distraught about something."

Rand obeyed, only too glad to sit down before his quaking knees gave way.

"Now, Rand, tell me what's troubling you."

Rand cleared his throat, his gaze returning to the well-worn, dusty hat brim. "Well, you see, sir, I've got this piece of land up in the mountains a ways. I've been clearin' it, gettin' it ready to build a place of my own." He drew a deep breath. He glanced quickly up at the reverend, then plunged ahead before he lost the last of his courage and his dignity. "Well, sir, I mean to build me a house fit for a wife. And I mean for Ingrid to be that wife. I've asked her and she says she's willin' but that I'd need to ask you for her hand, you bein' her guardian and all."

"Well, well," Nathaniel said thoughtfully.

"I'm goin' back up there this week and don't mean to come back 'til it's finished. And when I'm back, I want you to marry us. I figure it'll take me a few weeks or so to get it fit for Ingrid. It won't be nothin' fancy. She knows that. I don't own much, and I'll have to go on workin' for Hawk to support her. But she won't ever go without, Reverend Silverton. Not as long as I got a breath in me. I swear it."

Nathaniel grinned. "Swearing isn't necessary, Rand. I believe you. You seem to have given the matter a great deal of thought." There was a twinkle now in the reverend's eye. "And your proposal doesn't come as a surprise to me. If Ingrid's willing, I see no reason to withhold my blessing."

"You do?" Rand hopped up from the sofa again. "I can? I mean, you will?" He let out an unrestrained "Yippee!" all the while grinning with lunatic joy. As the echo died in the room, he tried to be properly contrite. "Sorry, sir."

The reverend rose, laughing aloud now as the women of the house came rushing into the parlor. "It's quite all right, my boy. Showing happiness is not something for which you should apologize." He turned toward Ingrid who was watching, wide-eyed, from the doorway. "Come in, my dear girl. Come in Virginia, Bethany. We have good news."

Ingrid came forward, her pale complexion glowing with a rosy hue, her eyes fastened upon the still smiling Rand.

"Mr. Howard has just asked for Ingrid's hand in marriage," the reverend told his wife as she stepped to his side. His arm went around her shoulder. "They're to be married as soon as he finishes building their home. In about a month or so, I should say."

Rand looked into Ingrid's glimmering blue-gray eyes. "I'll build it just as quick as I can," he said softly as he took her hand.

He wanted to kiss her on the mouth, but there were too many watchful eyes in the reverend's parlor. Instead, he leaned forward and lightly pecked her cheek.

"I love you, Ingrid," he whispered in her ear as he drew back.

His heart swelled in his chest when he saw the trust and love returned in her eyes of blue. By blazes, he meant to have that cabin built in a flash!

CHAPTER TEN

·——·

Sorry to do this to you, Hawk."

Hawk shook his head. "I understand. I guess I'd want to do the same if I were in your shoes." He held out his hand to Rand. "See you in a few weeks. You take care up there. Come and get me if you need any help."

"Thanks. But I'd kinda like to do this myself." With that, Rand pulled on the reins and turned his horse toward the mountains.

Hawk braced the sole of his boot against the lower fence rail and watched his friend ride away. They'd been together a long time. The place wasn't going to be the same without him.

An overwhelming aloneness swept through him, and on its heels came Bethany's image, promising to remove that aloneness.

He cursed violently as he pushed off from the fence and headed for the barn. What he needed was a drink. A good long drink. Anything to rid her from his thoughts.

Ever since he took her those blasted wildflowers, he'd been plagued by the memory of her face, her laugh, her voice, her smile, the way her hips swayed gently when she walked. He hadn't gone back into town to work on the church building again as he'd originally planned. He hadn't wanted to see her. He hadn't wanted to deal with the feelings she awakened in him. He'd vacilated between determination to get even with her for her wager and hoping he'd never have to lay eyes on her again.

He saddled his horse quickly, then led it behind him as he walked to the bunkhouse. Matt Cameron was sitting outside on a bench, quietly smoking a rolled cigarette. He could hear Rusty and Gabe's easy banter coming from inside through the open doorway. Caleb and Westy were out riding line for the next few weeks.

"I'm headin' for town. Care to come along?" he invited Matt.

Matt considered it, then shook his head. "Don't think so, boss. I still got me one helluva hangover from my last round at the Plains. Not to mention my pockets bein' a lot lighter. Think I'll just keep away from there for a time. You say hello to Bessie for me, though."

"I'll do it." Hawk swung up into the saddle. "Night."

"Night, Hawk."

Bethany paced from the parlor window to the dining room, then from the dining room to the kitchen, then from the kitchen to the parlor. She'd been at it for what seemed like hours. She stopped at the window and looked out at the town. It was still daylight but the sun was hanging low in the sky. Soon it would dip behind the mountains. Hawk's mountains. The mountains where Rand was building a home for Ingrid. She sighed in frustration.

All day long she'd had to show her pleasure over Ingrid's engagement, and all day long she'd had to fight the feeling of jealousy that had raised its ugly head to torture Bethany. By the time the rest of the family was ready to leave for the supper party at Vince Richard's ranch, she'd had a splitting headache and had begged off. Besides, the last thing she needed tonight was Vince watching her in that proprietary manner of his and telling her the Bar V was built for a woman like her.

She turned from the window again and flopped onto the settee, picking up the novel she'd left there a few rounds of pacing ago. She opened the book and trained her eyes upon the pages, but they might as well have been blank. Her thoughts were already traveling in another direction.

What was she to do? Whatever was she to do about Hawk? She loved him. Surely she loved him, for she was never able to stop thinking about him. But if he didn't come to town more than once a week, however was she to make him love her? The joyful confidence she'd felt when he left the house yesterday had faded, leaving uncertainty in its wake. Why had he left so suddenly? Maybe he'd had a change of mind. Maybe he wouldn't come next week.

Suddenly she remembered the way he had

kissed her in the barn at the Circle Blue. White hot heat seared through her veins at the memory. She'd thought then he must care for her. But he had acted so strangely ever since. Had she been too brazen to let him kiss her? Oh, that kiss!

She tossed the book aside with a whispered "oooh!" of frustration and rose once more to walk to the window. A few lights were beginning to appear, and she realized the room had become dim while she sat with her unread book. The sky had darkened, not just with the ending of day but with rain clouds. She heard a roll of thunder in the distance. It was a sad, lonely sound.

She almost wished she'd gone with the others to the Bar V. Half the town was probably out there tonight. It was a big social occasion. People had been talking about the Bar V supper for two weeks. At least, there she wouldn't have had time to think of Hawk. At least there she wouldn't have felt so lonely.

Bethany leaned her forehead against the cool pane of glass. "Why do you make me feel this way, Hawk Chandler?"

Her shoulders drooped as she turned away from the window and lit the lamp. Then, holding it before her, she climbed the stairs toward her room.

Her bedroom window was open, letting in a fresh breeze that promised to bring rain soon. Bethany set the lamp on the table next to her bed, then crossed to the window and closed it tightly before pulling the draperies over the glass. She unbuttoned her pretty mint-colored gown, donned this morning with hopes of seeing Hawk, and tossed it across the arms of a chair.

She shed her clothes before pulling a linen lawn nightgown from her bureau. Holding her arms above her head, she let the cool fabric slide over her skin. Then she picked up her hairbrush and sat on the edge of her bed as she loosened her auburn hair and began brushing the long tresses.

And all the while she performed these nightly routines, the thought kept repeating itself. *Why don't you come to see me, Hawk Chandler? Why don't you come?*

Bessie Stiles sidled up beside Hawk at the bar. "You look mighty lonely tonight, cowboy. How's about buyin' me a drink and I'll keep you company," she said above the noisy music and laughter.

Hawk looked at the painted face and wondered what she looked like beneath the heavy makeup. She couldn't have been more than twenty-one or -two, yet she seemed decades older in the harsh light of the saloon. Could she ever have been pretty? Could she ever have been as pretty as Bethany?

"I'll buy you a drink, Bessie, but I'd just as soon do without the company."

She shrugged her bare shoulders. "Whatever you say, Hawk."

After she was gone, Hawk tossed back another whiskey, letting the hot tentacles of the alcohol spread through his veins like a fever, warming his body. But the drink didn't make him feel any better. Nor had the three others before it.

"Hey, Chandler."

He glanced to his right. Leaning at the end of the bar was Jake Casper, one of the Bar V's less likeable hands. Short and stocky, with stringy blond hair and a thin mustache, Casper's brown eyes were bleary from too much drink. Hawk had had more than one unfortunate run-in with Jake Casper since Casper hooked up with the Bar V. He wasn't eager for another one tonight. He turned back toward the bar and finished the whiskey in his glass.

"Hear you're spoonin' the reverend's gal, Chandler. A little outta line, aren't ya?"

Hawk chose to ignore him. There was never any point in arguing with a drunk, especially not this particular drunk. Besides, he'd had several shots tonight himself. Discretion seemed the wise choice. He set his empty whiskey glass on the bar and turned toward the saloon doors.

"Chandler!" Casper's heavy hand landed on Hawk's shoulder.

He spun around to face his assailant, his anger hidden beneath a calm facade.

"You better keep away from that Silverton girl. There's some who don't take kindly to it."

"Mind your own business, Casper." Hawk's voice was deceptively cool and controlled. "And take your hand off me."

"Why don't you take it off for me?"

The pearl-handled knife was out of its sheath and pressed against Casper's throat in the blink of an eye. "I said, take it off."

Casper gulped. "Okay, Chandler. Okay." He backed away, holding his right hand in the air. He lifted his left hand to his throat, rubbing it nervously, but the skin hadn't even been nicked.

Hawk spoke in a deep, low voice. "Next time, I'll do more than warn you, Casper."

Hawk turned and headed out the swinging doors. He stopped on the boardwalk and drew a steadying breath, letting his temper cool. Finally, he turned his glance to the east. A dust devil spun across Main Street, sending a tumbleweed and dirt whirling up to smack against the board siding of Eberlie's Mercantile. The air smelled of rain. Thunder rolled in the west. A storm was brewing.

His intention as he stepped off the boardwalk and placed his boot in the stirrup was to head for the ranch. But somehow Flame ended up walking in the opposite direction, heading for the reverend's house at the edge of town.

It was useless to even think of sleeping. Her thoughts were as restless as the wind buffeting her window. Bethany slipped into a white cambric wrapper, picked up the lamp, and went down the stairs in search of that same unread book. Just as her foot touched the bottom step, she heard a knock at the door.

Somehow, she knew it was him.

"Who is it?" she asked as her fingers closed around the doorknob.

"Hawk Chandler."

She opened the door a crack. "It's late, Hawk."

"I'm sorry." He turned. "I'll go."

"No! Wait!" She opened the door wider. "You must have a reason for coming. What is it, Hawk?"

Before he could answer, a bolt of lightning streaked across the sky, followed almost immediately by a deafening crack of thunder. On the shirt tails of the rolling boom came the wind, carrying the stinging dust whirling before it. The flame of her lamp flickered and nearly died just as another bolt of lightning darted a jagged path from cloud to earth.

Startled, Bethany let out a squeal and reached for Hawk's shirt sleeve, pulling him inside before closing the door. She leaned against it, her heart beating rapidly in her chest as she drew several sharp gasps of air.

Slowly, she became aware of his gaze upon her. She looked up at him. The low-burning light cast strange shadows across his square jaw and aquiline nose.

"I . . . I hate lightning," she said softly, filling the heavy silence that cloaked the room. "I've been afraid of it since I was a child."

She couldn't see his eyes. They were hidden in shadows.

"Why have you come, Hawk?"

Why had he come?

He couldn't remember. He must have had something he'd wanted to do, something he'd wanted to say. But now his mind was blank of anything except Bethany. Bethany in the lamplight, her fiery auburn tresses spilling over her shoulders and down her back, the lush curves of her feminine figure adding an alluring shape to the white wrapper, her unique green eyes gazing up at him in a beguiling manner.

Heat spread once again through his veins. Like the whiskey, only better. He reached out and took her hand in his. Walking backward, he led her slowly into the parlor. He could feel her quivering, see the flickering of the light. He reached with his free hand and took the lamp, setting it on a table.

Lightning streaked across the roiling heavens once more. The sky cracked with thunder. Bethany jumped in fright again, and as she did, he pulled her into his arms.

As her body curved against his, her head fell back. She watched as his head slowly lowered, but with the searing touch of his lips against hers, she closed her eyes, giving in to the tumultuous whirlwind of feelings.

His arms tightened as he drew her up against him. She could feel the hardness of his chest pressing against her. The buttons of his vest dug into her breasts, but the pain was almost pleasant. Her hands slid up his chest to circle his neck, the fingers of her right hand twining themselves in his shaggy hair at the nape of his neck.

There was a strange, wonderful burning deep in the pit of her stomach. Instinctively, she moved closer to him, as if to assuage it.

Hawk groaned.

The room was lit once more with a flash of

lightning. The window pane shook as the heavens rolled. It was as if the elements were mirroring the storm inside her. Never, never had she dreamed kissing a man could be like this.

His mouth released hers and traveled from her cheek to her ear where he nibbled the tiny lobe.

"Hawk," she whispered, then copied his action.

She heard his sharp intake of breath, felt his hand move to the small of her back as he drew her ever closer against the taut muscles of his long body.

It was getting out of hand. He knew it was getting out of hand. He should pull away from her now and get out of here. He hadn't come here for this purpose. No matter what else Bethany Silverton was, she was not a girl to be used lightly. For all the eagerness of her kiss, for all the easy melding of her body against his, he could sense in his desire-and-drink-muddled brain that she was an innocent when it came to the passions of men.

Yet he couldn't obey the urgings of his common sense. The feel of her against him was too pleasant. Her breasts, released from the stays of her corset, filled him with a longing to bury his face in their ripeness. He claimed her mouth again, suckling upon her sweet breath, drinking the honeyed softness of her lips as his hands stroked the length of her back.

"Bethany . . ." he whispered into her open mouth.

CHAPTER ELEVEN

I love you, Hawk Chandler. I love you. I love you. I love you.

Now it was his turn. He must have come to tell her he loved her. No one could share such a kiss without love. It just couldn't be.

She opened her eyes to gaze into the face so close to her own. Her pulse raced; blood pounded in her head. Outside, the clouds had unleashed the rain, and it pelted the window, shaking the glass.

His blue-black eyes were glazed with a strange light, almost frightening in their intensity. His boldly handsome face was dark with passion. She held her breath, waiting for him to speak the words she knew he must say.

"Bethany," he repeated hoarsely.

His mouth dropped to the hollow of her throat. Her head fell back as a new wave of feelings washed through her. Her knees buckled, but his arm was there to keep her from falling, slipping beneath her knees and lifting her feet off the floor without ever moving his mouth from the throbbing pulse in her throat. There was a thundering in her ears. Even with her eyes closed, there seemed to be a constant flashing of lightning. A dizziness overwhelmed her, and she wondered if she could bear another moment.

Only when Hawk carried her across the room to the settee did he cease the sweet torture of his kisses. Only then did she feel able to draw a deep breath, momentarily righting the world. But then he sat, still cradling her against his chest, his left arm beneath her neck, his mouth returning to plunder hers once again.

His kisses were at once demanding and gentle, feather light one moment, fierce the next. His tongue danced lightly across her lips, then sought entry. It was a heady, intimate sensation. Like a moth to a flame, she was drawn to it, yet frightened by the heat.

Hawk. Hawk. Hawk.

His name echoed in her mind. She couldn't have spoken it aloud, even if he hadn't been kissing her. She seemed to have lost all control over her thoughts, her speech, her body. She was his to command, and command he did.

The fingers of his right hand slipped between the opening of her wrapper to caress her breast, only the light fabric of her nightgown separating flesh from flesh. She gasped into his open mouth as her hands clasped behind his neck. She felt the dizziness returning. Her body responded of its own will, seeking to be closer to the source of the scorching heat. Her nipples hardened; her breasts tingled. Heat spread from deep within her to the tips of her fingers and toes.

She was only vaguely aware of his fingers as they released the buttons of her wrapper. She felt the cool air against her hot flesh as the robe was pushed from her shoulder. There was a flash of shyness, a desire to cover herself once again, but it was quickly forgotten as his lips began a slow journey down her neck, across her shoulder, down her arm to the inside of her elbow, then back again.

The words were whispered near her ear. Unexpected and so soft she might only have imagined them. "Marry me, Bethany."

Marry him? Had he really asked that? Had he actually spoken or was it only part of the spell he was weaving around her?

Yes, Hawk, her mind and heart replied. *Yes!*

But she was still unable to speak. His mouth was moving again, leaving a path of tingling flesh wherever his lips touched. Her head fell back, her hair falling toward the floor. She didn't know what he was doing to her. She only knew she never wanted him to stop.

It was thus the reverend found them.

"What in the name of . . ."

Bethany's eyes flew open and she viewed her father from upside down. And right behind him were her mother, Ingrid, and Martha Eberlie.

With a suddenness that made the room spin, Hawk jumped up from the sofa and set her on her feet beside him. Bethany groped to pull her wrapper tight around her, feeling suddenly very naked, very exposed.

"Mr. Chandler, what is the meaning of this?" Nathanial thundered. His face was dark with rage.

"I . . . sir . . ."

"Papa . . ."

"Silence!"

She had never seen her father look this way before. The heat of desire of moments before was replaced with cold dread.

"Ingrid, please see Martha to her home. Virginia, take Bethany to her room."

"Papa . . ."

"Go to your room."

"Papa, I . . ."

The veins stood out on the reverend's forehead. "*Now*, Bethany Rachel! You and I will have a talk in the morning."

Tears welled up, blinding her. She wanted to look at Hawk but she didn't dare. Shame flooded her. Where everything had seemed right just minutes ago, now everything seemed awry. With a muffled cry, she darted past her father and up the stairs.

Bleary-eyed from a night of weeping and feeling more alone than she'd ever felt in her life, Bethany raised a hand and rapped softly on the reverend's study door.

"Come in, Bethany."

His voice was not the warm, loving voice she'd always known. It sounded remote and infinitely sad. It made her want to cry, but there were no tears left.

She opened the door.

Her father's face was etched with deep lines this morning. He looked ever so much older. But then, even she felt she must look older. She certainly felt older. Ancient, in fact.

"Good morning, Papa," she said in a small voice.

"Sit down, Bethany."

She sat.

The reverend sighed.

Bethany folded her hands in her lap and squeezed them tightly as she stared at them. She felt a fresh flush of shame. To have hurt her father this way. To have betrayed his trust in her. How could she make him understand she loved Hawk? Nothing had happened. Nothing really. Surely, since Papa loved her mother so much, he would understand. He must have felt this way about Mother sometimes. Was it wicked to want Hawk's kisses, to want his caresses?

She looked up, hopeful, but there was no understanding in the tired eyes perusing her from across the desk.

"I had a long talk with Mr. Chandler last night, Bethany. He has agreed to do the right thing by you. Of course, he had little choice but to agree. I'm sure you're aware of that. You're to be married in two weeks. It will be a simple affair."

Married. They were to be married.

"There's little we can do to stop the gossip now. I'm sure Martha has been unable to keep this to herself." The reverend paused and rubbed his eyes, looking as if the world were about to come to an end. "You have disappointed me, Bethany Rachel, and you've broken your mother's heart with your behavior."

"But Papa . . ."

He rose from his chair and turned his back toward her, then stepped to the window. "I know I'll forgive you, daughter. I know I *must* forgive you. But not today. Today I must grieve."

She'd thought she had no more tears, but they came suddenly to her eyes, spilling over to streak her pale cheeks. To have disappointed her beloved father, to have made him so sad. . . . She wished she could somehow make it up to him.

And then Nathaniel's words repeated themselves in her head. *Agreed to do the right thing . . . had little choice . . .*

Pain wrapped itself about her heart. She'd thought he wanted to marry her. Hadn't he asked her to marry him in the midst . . . ? Or had he merely been trapped by his own indiscretions?

"Why is he marrying me, Papa?" she asked.

Nathaniel's shoulders rose, then sagged. He sounded beaten as he answered, "Because he must after what we witnessed last night. He had no other choice and he knew it. It's not the way I'd pictured it for you, Bethany. Not the way at all."

She scarcely heard what he was saying as the terrible truth seeped into her heart. Hawk had never said he loved her. Not to her. Not to her father. He had mentioned marriage only in the heat of their embrace. Perhaps it had been the liquor talking. Perhaps passion. Whatever it had been had vanished beneath her father's stern glare. He was marrying her—but not from choice.

"Will I . . . will I see him again before the wedding?"

"No, Bethany. I think it best you don't. You are not to leave this house. You'll have much to do, getting ready for the wedding and your move to Mr. Chandler's ranch."

Bethany got up from her chair and moved to the side of the desk. She stretched out her arm toward her father's back as if to touch him, but too much space separated them. And not just space. They were separated by emotions now too.

She turned and walked listlessly to the door. She paused, her hand on the knob. Her chin dropped toward her chest, her eyes cast down.

"I'm so sorry, Papa," she whispered. "I'm so sorry to have disappointed you."

Virginia Silverton found her daughter by the river. Bethany's knees were pulled up beneath her skirts, hugged tightly against her torso. Her dark burnished hair fell loose over her back and hid her face from view.

"Bethany?"

The girl lifted her head, turning a tear-marked face toward her mother.

Virginia's shame and disapproval were no match for the heartbroken expression of her only child.

"Oh, Mother . . ." Bethany croaked as tears welled once again in eyes already red from weeping.

Virginia sat down on the grass and opened her arms. Bethany fell into them, sobbing in earnest now. Virginia's hand stroked the auburn tresses as she tried to calm Bethany's weeping, even as her own tears ran unchecked.

"Shhh, Bethany. It will be all right."

She wished she believed it.

Bethany hiccupped over another sob, then slowly brought her tears under control. Finally, she pulled away from her mother's embrace. Her head bent, her gaze on her lap, she wiped her eyes with the hem of her skirt, still sniffing.

"Here, my dear," Virginia said, holding out her handkerchief. "Blow your nose."

Bethany obeyed.

"Your father loves you, Bethany. I love you." She felt it was important for Bethany to hear those words. She seemed so alone and bereft.

"I . . . I didn't mean to do anything wrong, Mother," Bethany whispered, her voice strained. "It's just . . . we . . . it just seemed to happen." At last she lifted watery eyes to meet her mother's gaze. "I love him so terribly much." Her voice rose, strengthened by her passionate confession.

Virginia thought back to the scene that had met them last night. She'd never witnessed such unleashed passion. It had shocked her, almost frightened her. She had loved her husband for many years, but it was a gentle love. She never could have imagined herself caught in such an embrace.

Yet now, as she met Bethany's gaze, she knew beyond a doubt her daughter did love Hawk and it was right for them to be together. Still, she would have chosen an easier path for Bethany if she could.

"There'll be talk, Bethany Rachel. There will be townsfolk who will shun you. Not only because of what Martha tells them, but because he's a man of mixed blood."

"I don't care."

Virginia's hand lifted and she caressed Bethany's cheek, her fingers lingering a moment on her jaw. She had come out here to offer some sort of wisdom, yet the words didn't seem to exist. "It won't be easy," was all she was able to say.

"It isn't the talk that matters, Mother. I *want* to marry him. But . . . but he's only doing it because he's been forced to. I thought . . . I thought . . ." She was fighting tears again.

"It's all right, daughter," Virginia crooned as she opened her arms once again. "It will be all right."

Doc Wilton examined the ragged gash across the palm of Vince Richards' right hand. Then, looking over the rim of his glasses, he asked, "How'd you say you did this again?"

Vince's gray eyes were stone cold, his face as hard as granite. "It was an accident. Just sew it up."

Affronted, Doc grunted and turned his back on his patient. He didn't much care for Vince. Never had. Rich and powerful, he was a man who went after what he wanted and didn't much care who got hurt in the process. The doctor had seen men like him before. Vince Richards was a dangerous man.

"Well," Doc said as he returned with antiseptic, tweezers, needle and thread. "You won't be doing much with this hand for quite a while."

"Won't matter much. I'm left-handed."

"I'd say you were lucky then."

"Yeah. Lucky."

Doc worked in silence, plucking the tiny shards of glass from the bleeding wound. It almost looked as if the man had crushed a glass or bottle with his bare hand. His gaze darted quickly to Vince's face, then dropped again. Vince was watching the procedure with unflinching eyes, his expression hard and detached.

As the doctor reached for the needle and thread, Vince spoke. "I heard a rumor that the reverend was going to marry his daughter to that redskin at the Circle Blue."

"Yes, I believe Mr. Chandler and Miss Silverton are going to be married."

"*Mr.* Chandler." Vince snorted derisively. "And I thought the reverend was an intelligent sort."

Doc's eyes narrowed as he took the first stitch. "He is."

"Then somebody should have been able to convince him he's making a big mistake."

"I'd say it's nobody else's business."

"And I say it is. We can't have stinkin' breeds marrying our women. If we want folks back in Washington to take us seriously, they've got to be convinced we're civilized out here. This wedding's got to be stopped."

Doc tied off the thread, snipped it with the scissors, then raised his gaze to meet Vince's. "You might not take my advice, Richards, but I suggest you keep out of this one. Besides, I doubt the reverend's in a listening mood at the moment. Hawk Chandler's a good man, and I don't doubt but what he'll make Bethany a good husband. That's all that counts with me. I suspect it's all that counts with Reverend Silverton."

"Then you're as big a fool as the reverend."

"Perhaps," Doc Wilton answered grimly as he bandaged his patient's hand.

Hawk rose at the break of dawn, fixed himself a quick breakfast, stuffed his saddlebags with supplies, grabbed his bedroll, and headed out the door. He took Storm from his stall and saddled him, then led him outside and tethered him to the corral fence before walking toward the bunkhouse.

Rusty Andrews was just stepping through the doorway. "Mornin', Hawk," he said as he stretched and yawned.

"I'm headed out for a couple weeks, Rusty. Going to look over the range, see how Caleb and Westy are doing."

Rusty nodded and waited.

"While I'm gone, see if you can't get a woman in from town to do something with the house there. Clean it up real good. Maybe put some curtains in the windows or something."

Again, the old cowboy nodded, this time with a quirked eyebrow.

Every angle, every plane of Hawk's face had taken on a hard, unrelenting edge. His dark eyes coldly dared Rusty to challenge him. "I'm getting married when I get back. Get the place fit for a bride."

Rusty didn't even blink an eye. "I'll do it, Hawk."

Before the older man could consider asking who the bride was to be, Hawk turned on his heel and strode back to his waiting horse, mounted up, and rode off.

For nearly two weeks, he slept under the stars, ate hardtack and beans, checked the brands on the cattle, and kept his eye out for signs of rustling or sickness. And all the while, his thoughts churned.

Bethany. He was going to marry Bethany. He was trapped by her scheming. Trapped by her conniving. Trapped into marrying a woman who thought him a mere toy. Well, she was trapped too. It served her right. She was being forced to marry a quarter-breed cowpoke she didn't love. A cowboy with only a small cabin to offer her as home rather than a fancy house with fine carpets and white-capped servants. And it was her own fault. If she hadn't started things with that wager of hers . . .

And then there was the matter of his own

wager. He hadn't even beaten her there. She'd never agreed to marry him. She'd never given him an answer. It was her father who had decided they should wed. Hawk had no doubt Bethany wished she'd never laid eyes on Hawk Chandler, let alone wanted to marry him.

But despite it all, his thoughts were not entirely grim. He couldn't stop remembering the way she'd kissed him, the innocent passion that had flared upon her face. She might have been shamed into marrying him, but she wanted him, she did respond to his lips upon hers. They would have at least that between them. And she might give him a son. An heir for the Circle Blue.

Perhaps it would work out for the best after all.

CHAPTER TWELVE

She loved him. She was going to marry him. This should have been the most wonderful time of her life. Yet her own home was like a tomb and all the people in it mourners. Her mother's eyes were red with weeping. Ingrid spoke only in whispers. And her father still avoided her.

Bethany sat before her dressing table mirror and stared at her reflection while her thoughts traveled across the wide Montana range to the west. She'd heard not a word from Hawk in the entire two weeks. What if he didn't show up for the wedding? What if he hated her? What if he was as ashamed of her as her own father? Her stomach churned.

The bedroom door opened and Ingrid slipped inside. Their eyes met in the mirror.

"Everything is nearly ready downstairs," the blonde said in a whisper. "I have come to help you dress."

Bethany nodded, her heart breaking again. She didn't even have Ingrid anymore. An invisible wall had been thrown up between them, keeping Bethany from confiding her sorrow, her fears, even her love for Hawk to Ingrid. She was alone. Alone and miserable on her wedding day.

Tears teetered on the brink but she stubbornly called them back. She wouldn't appear before the few guests her parents had invited with tear stains on her cheeks. She had too much pride to let them see her distress and uncertainty.

Ingrid carried Virginia's wedding dress in her arms. In the past two weeks, the dress had been cut down to fit Bethany's petite size, and the belled satin skirt had been altered to drape more fashionably over a bustled petticoat. Bethany had often dreamed of the day she would be wed in her mother's bridal gown, but she had never dreamed it quite this way.

Bethany rose wordlessly from her stool and allowed Ingrid to drop the gown over her head. She closed her eyes and blanked out her mind while Ingrid's fingers nimbly fastened the tiny pearl buttons up the length of her back. She didn't even look when Ingrid lifted the white lace veil and pinned it into Bethany's carefully dressed hair, along with a spray of wild violets.

"You are so very beautiful, Bethany," Ingrid whispered as she stepped away from the bride. "Look."

She did look then. She stared at her reflection as if it were someone else's, someone she'd never seen before. The satin basque was high-necked and trimmed with Valenciennes lace. The skirt was trimmed with folds and bows of white silk. The satin train was beaded with tiny pearls. The veil fell in a mist of white over dark auburn hair and stiff shoulders, then down to the floor. The girl in the mirror was, indeed, beautiful. As beautiful as brides were meant to be on their wedding day.

But this bride's heart was cold with dread.

Her door opened again, this time for her mother. Virginia crossed the room in a rustle of petticoats and satine skirts. "The groom has arrived, Bethany. Your father is ready to begin the ceremony."

Bethany heard the tiny crack in her mother's voice and fought back her own tears. She longed to throw herself into her mother's arms and weep upon her breast as she had that day by the river. But the time for seeking comfort in her mother's arms was past. This day was one she must face alone, with her own strength. She was a woman now. She would soon be Hawk's wife. She could no longer act as a child.

Virginia's gentle hand cupped her daughter's chin. "Bethany, my dear." She forced Bethany's gaze to meet hers. "A marriage is for life. Yours isn't beginning in the happiest manner. Do all you can to see it goes better from this moment on."

"I will," she croaked over a sob.

Her mother left quickly.

Ingrid stepped in front of Bethany and lifted a hand to her cheek. "Be happy, Bethany." And then she too fled.

Bethany stared a moment at the closed door, then slowly began to turn, allowing her gaze to drift around the room. It had been her room such a very short time, yet it was home. This was where she was safe and loved and cared for. But in a short while she would be taken from here for good. She would be joining her life with Hawk Chandler's. She loved him. She wanted to be his wife. But she wanted desperately to know that he loved her too. Until he did, she would never be able to reveal her heart to him.

But her wedding wouldn't wait until he discovered his feelings for her. She would have to be satisfied to make him love her after their marriage.

With a quick squaring of her shoulders, she turned her back on her girlhood and left her room.

Two weeks on the range had convinced Hawk that he could marry Bethany, bed her, get her with child, and then relegate her to some forgotten corner of his mind. He had convinced himself that she was an utterly spoiled, malicious viper who deserved no consideration from him or any other man. She had played him for a fool and was merely getting her comeuppance.

But the moment she floated down the stairs in a cloud of white satin and silk, he knew his plans were flawed. He would not be able to use and forget her so easily. Her delicate, innocent beauty cast a spell over him. She was an angel. A lovely, frightened angel. The strain showed in the hollows beneath her cheekbones and in the misty green swirl of her eyes. He wanted to shelter and protect her. He wanted to hold her safely within the circle of his arms. Forgotten for the moment was the searing passion of the embrace they had shared, the passion that had brought them to this day. All that remained was a growing tenderness for his bride.

"Dearly beloved . . ." the reverend began as Bethany reached Hawk's side.

For Hawk, the rest of the ceremony was a blur.

She hadn't looked at him as she'd come down the stairs and crossed the room to stand at his side, but as her father spoke, Bethany dared to glance at her groom. He was so wonderfully handsome in his suit, his hair swept back from his dark face. She wished she knew what he was thinking about their marriage, how he felt about her now.

"Do you, Hawk Chandler, take this woman . . ."

As the reverend asked his question, Hawk turned his midnight-blue eyes upon his bride. Bethany's breath caught in her throat. For just an instant, she caught sight of something in their usually inscrutable depths. It wasn't hate or anger. Nor was it even the reckless passion that had burned in them on that night two weeks before. It looked almost like a tender wanting. Could it be he wanted to be here?

And then it was gone, vanished so quickly she doubted it had been there. Once more his expression was enigmatic. She saw only the firm set of his jaw and the sardonic tone of his voice as he replied, "I do."

Uncertainty knotted her stomach as her father turned his attention toward her.

"Do you, Bethany Rachel Silverton, take this man . . ."

Fred Eberlie watched the ceremony with disapproving eyes. He'd come only out of respect for the reverend, but it galled him to see a breed marrying a white woman. He didn't care if what Martha had said she'd seen was true. The Silvertons should have packed that girl back East rather than see this through.

Not that he hadn't done all he could to stop it. He'd talked himself blue in the face, trying to make Nathaniel see what a mistake he was making. He'd even gone out to the Bar V to see if Vince could lend him a hand in stopping this travesty. Unexpectedly, Vince's reaction had been one of violent rage. He'd actually thrown a bottle of whiskey at him, cutting his hand in the process. Then he'd ordered Fred out, telling him the reverend and his family could go to the devil for all he cared.

And surely that was exactly what would happen. To Fred Eberlie, there couldn't be a greater sin than the one he was witnessing now.

Standing beside her father, Martha Eberlie's thoughts traveled a different direction. She was thinking how lucky Bethany was to be marrying such a handsome man. Oh, she'd warned Bethany to avoid Hawk, but she didn't feel as strongly about it as her pa or Mr. Richards did. In fact, she couldn't help feeling a sting of jealousy. Why couldn't she get Davis Riley to kiss her the way she'd seen Hawk kiss Bethany?

Color flooded Martha's cheeks as she remembered what she'd seen. How she would have loved to have detailed it to the other girls in town! But her father had told her in no uncertain terms just what would happen to her if she revealed it to another living soul. It hadn't been easy to keep silent, but she didn't relish the thought of a thrashing at her age.

Doc Wilton grinned as he listened to the exchange of vows. Goll darn it, he liked that fellow. He didn't care what fools like Vince Richards said. Hawk was a fine, honest sort, and that's all that should have mattered. What the devil difference did it make who his father had married? It was the man he'd become that counted.

And Doc couldn't help thinking that this little snippet of a girl would be good for Hawk too. He'd watched her since the Silvertons arrived in Sweetwater. She had spunk, that one, and plenty of fire—just what Hawk needed. He'd be willing to bet these two would do fine. Just fine.

Oh, he'd heard the rumors about why this wedding was taking place. Martha Eberlie hadn't been silenced quite soon enough. But Doc Wilton suspected these two young people cared more for each other than even they knew.

Yes, given half a chance, they'd do just fine.

Sarah Wilton cradled her newborn son against her breast, her eyes locked on Bethany and Hawk, standing side by side. Never had she seen a bride so beautiful or a groom so handsome. She couldn't help thinking these two were destined to be together, just as she had been destined for John. There was just something about them.

Of course, Sarah had heard the whispers of the women in town. There had been plenty of talk about why the reverend's daughter was marrying so quietly and so quickly. There had also been plenty of caustic words spoken about her chosen groom.

She recalled Madge Delaney's visit, just a few days before. Seated in the Wiltons' parlor over the pharmacy, Madge had asked, "Have you heard about the Silverton girl? I hear she's going to marry that Hawk Chandler. Can you imagine a Christian allowing his daughter to wed a heathen? Why, it's enough to make a person wonder about his spiritual calling."

Sarah had quickly silenced the woman and invited her to leave. She had no patience with stupidity.

Her son wriggled in her arms, bringing Sarah's thoughts back to the present. She dropped her gaze to Chad's tiny face. A sense of wonder spread through her as John's arm slipped around her shoulders. Silently, she prayed Bethany and Hawk would find the same happiness she had found.

". . . and before God and these witnesses, I proclaim you man and wife."

There was a moment of absolute silence when no one moved or spoke. Then Hawk turned slowly toward his bride, bent down, and kissed her cheek. She felt frighteningly close to tears.

With a hand at her elbow, her new husband turned her around to face the guests who stood behind them. One by one, they came forward. As Bethany accepted their kind wishes, she felt her nerves stretching like a bow string.

Hawk stood at her side, so handsome in his black suit and white collar, his shaggy hair slicked back to reveal his bold features, his thoughts and feelings so impossible to ascertain. He never smiled or looked down at her, no matter how often she cast a furtive glance his way. Their few guests filed by, shaking his hand and congratulating him on his choice of bride. He nodded politely and thanked them, but Bethany wished she knew what he really felt. She could tell nothing by his expression or his tone of voice. This man, her husband, was a mystery to her. Almost a stranger.

If only he'll love me, it'll be all right.

Suddenly, his hand was on her elbow once again. "You'd better say good-bye to your family. It's time we were leaving."

The bow string stretched again.

She nodded mutely and moved from his side, gliding across the parlor toward her mother and Ingrid and Griselda. Silently, the three women accompanied Bethany upstairs to her room to help her change out of her wedding dress. It seemed no time at all before she was back downstairs.

It had been difficult, saying good-bye to her mother and Ingrid, but now she faced the most difficult farewell of all. Resolutely, she turned toward her father.

Nathaniel Silverton stood alone in the far corner of the parlor, exactly where he had stood as he performed the marriage ceremony. His face was tired and sad. She longed to take back the actions that had brought him such grief. She longed to give him back his smile and peaceful countenance.

She moved to stand before him. "Papa?" she whispered.

His hazel gaze dropped to meet hers. "It's time for you to leave, isn't it, daughter?"

She nodded.

"I pray you will be happy."

"Thank you, Papa."

"Bethany Rachel?"

Her answering "Yes?" could scarcely be heard.

"I love you."

"Oh, Papa." She threw her arms around his neck and pressed her face against his scratchy suit-coat. As his arms tightened to hug her, she stubbornly swallowed the sob that rose to choke her. "I love you too."

His hands gripped her shoulders, and he held her back from him. "Now it's time for you to go. Be wise, Bethany. I think your husband's a good man. Learn to love him for what he is and to overlook what he is not and you'll be happy."

Bethany nodded.

Nathaniel's right hand cradled her elbow as he turned her around and escorted her across the room. The reverend's eyes looked hard into Hawk's, and then he passed Bethany's hand into his.

"Take care of her, Hawk," he said softly.

"I will, sir."

"Go with God."

There was nothing left to do but leave. She had changed out of the wedding dress and into her traveling costume. Her trunk, filled with her clothes, had already been sent out ahead of them to the ranch. Her father's buggy, its black surface strung with colorful paper streamers, awaited the bride and groom by the gate of the white picket fence.

Hawk's hand settled against the small of her back, and with it, he guided her from the parlor and out into the glorious sunshine of the late June afternoon. He assisted her and her abundance of skirt and bustle into the buggy, then went around to the other side and slid in beside her.

Panic assailed her as he lifted the reins and slapped them across the horse's broad backside. With a jerk, the buggy jumped forward. She clasped her hands in her lap and fought the urge to hurl herself from the buggy right into the middle of Main Street. She stared straight ahead, her mouth clamped shut, her jaw so tight it ached.

The bow string stretched a little more.

Hawk sensed her unease and cursed himself for not staying in town until after supper. Anything to have delayed their return to the ranch in the middle of the afternoon. If they couldn't find three words to say to each other during the trip from Sweetwater to the Circle Blue, what in heaven's name were they going to do to fill the rest of the time until sunset? By sheer will, he kept his thoughts from straying to all the delightful possibilities that a wedding night promised.

"I had a woman in to sort of clean the place up."

Watching from the corner of his eye, he saw Bethany jump at the sound of his voice. Her unconscious reaction hit a nerve, leaving him feeling frustrated and a little angry. She had no call to fear him. He meant her no harm. It was her own actions, after all, that had gotten them into this mess.

He bit off the rest of his comment in a terse voice. "If you want to change anything, just let me know. I'll do what I can to oblige."

"I . . . I'm sure everything will be fine, Hawk," she replied meekly.

He was immediately repentant. He was being unfair. If he hadn't called on her late at night, if he hadn't gone into her home, if he hadn't had as many shots of whiskey, if he hadn't kissed her . . . Of course she was nervous. Of course she was afraid. Wasn't he on edge as well? And he hadn't been forced from his family and home. At least he had his friends and his work at the ranch. Everything familiar to Bethany had been taken from her.

He turned his head now and looked at her. She was his wife. She would be sharing his home, his bed, his life. The tender ache returned to his chest.

There was a time, just a few short weeks ago, when he had hoped he could share something special with Bethany Silverton. Perhaps she *hadn't* meant any harm with that wager of hers. Perhaps he *had* overreacted to it. And perhaps, just perhaps, she really did like him. If there was any chance she cared for him, even a little, what he did, what he said in the next few hours could make a big difference to them both.

Three times she had been to the Circle Blue, but as the buggy approached the ranch buildings, she looked at everything with different eyes, for now this was her home.

There was the barn, large and sturdy, and the bunkhouse where the cowhands slept and ate. There were several corrals and a couple of smaller outbuildings. There was an air of growth and permanency about the place. It had a good feel about it.

And then there was the house. Although she'd been to the ranch before, she'd still never been inside the house. It wasn't anything fancy. Just a square log cabin with glass-pane windows and a roof that looked weather tight. Not much to look at, to be sure, yet for some reason she felt strongly attracted to it. Once again, she thought how at home she felt.

This is where I'll spend my days with Hawk. And my nights.

The thought made her pulse quicken.

Hawk eased back on the reins, stopping the horse near the front door. He hopped down and came around to assist her to the ground. Then he guided her to the front door. He reached forward and opened it before her.

Bethany hesitated on the threshold, overcome with uncertainty. She had never been a wife before.

Hawk sounded almost as uncertain as she felt when he said, "I've got to tend to the horse. The men are all out on the range for a few days. Go on in. I'll be in in a minute or two."

She stepped inside, alone. The main room had a stone fireplace at one end. The center of the board floor was covered with a rag rug. There were two straight-backed wooden chairs on either side of the hearth, and beneath the window —with its obviously new calico curtains—was the velvet and satin brocade love seat her mother had brought from their home in Philadelphia. It had always been in her parents' bedroom. Bethany's eyes misted at the sight of it, knowing her mother had meant it as a very special gift.

Beyond the main parlor was an open doorway leading to the kitchen. She could see the massive black iron cookstove from where she stood. Cautiously, she moved forward for a closer look.

The middle of the kitchen was filled with a heavy wooden table and four chairs. Pots and pans hung on nails in the wall. There was a neat stack of firewood next to the stove, and beside it was a small, new-looking icebox. Beneath the window stood another table, taller and longer than the dining table, this one holding a large dishpan and two buckets. Against the far wall was a long, narrow washtub, which also looked new. Finally, next to the doorway where she stood, there was a tall cupboard, presumably filled with dishes.

She turned her back on the kitchen and let her eyes stray to the other two doors. One of them led to Hawk's bedroom. Their bedroom.

She felt a nervous twist in her stomach and hurried across the parlor to sit on the love seat. She sat ramrod straight, her eyes locked on a loose thread in the center of the rug as her thoughts ran riot. Tonight she would share a room with Hawk. The thought left her quaking. She remembered the furtive whispers of the girls at Miss Hendersen's. She had giggled along with the rest, but she hadn't understood the innuendos. What she'd heard had made very little sense to her, but now she wished she'd listened more closely.

Bethany heard his footsteps approaching, and her heart seemed to falter as he entered the house.

"There. That's done."

She glanced his way. He had removed his suit coat and starched collar. He'd opened the top button of his shirt and rolled up his sleeves. His skin was strikingly dark against the white of his shirt. She was acutely aware of his unusual height, the breadth of his chest and shoulders, the lean cut of his waist and hips. She felt herself blushing as she realized the path her gaze had taken.

He saw the way her eyes traveled down him and read her embarrassment as her gaze fell once again to the floor. He felt a sudden sting of wanting but quelled it. He would have to move with patience and care or she would bolt like a wild colt. What he must do was to make her think of something else, anything else.

Hawk tossed his coat across a chair and walked over to stand before her. "Are you hungry?"

She shook her head.

"Well, I could use a bite. I didn't eat this morning."

He watched as a look of horror replaced the blush of moments before. "Hawk, I . . . I can't cook."

He stared at her a moment, and then he began to laugh. He hadn't given much thought to the everyday aspects of marriage. He'd concentrated only on getting through the wedding ceremony itself and the night that would follow. But the look on her face as she confessed her inability to cook struck him as extremely humorous.

"Lucky for us, I can." He held out his hand. "Take off your bonnet and find an apron and I'll show you what I can do in the kitchen."

Her response to his laughter lightened his heart even more.

She smiled. Not the hesitant, skittish smile she'd offered him a time or two today, but a real smile, one that reached her eyes. She accepted his hand, allowing him to pull her up from the love seat, then together they walked into the kitchen.

CHAPTER THIRTEEN

·——·

Bethany was surprised to discover she was hungry, and when Hawk finished rustling up his specialty of fried potatoes and onions, she joined him at the table and ate her fill. The day ended with surprising swiftness, but they were unaware of it until the kitchen began filling with dark shadows.

"I could use a walk after that meal," Hawk said as his chair scraped against the floor. "Will you join me?"

The pleasant interlude seemed at an end. Her nerves were taut once again. She was uncertain. "I . . . I should do the dishes." She forced a nervous smile as she looked up at him. "I *do* know how to wash dishes."

"The dishes can wait until morning." His voice was deep and somehow very intimate.

She tried to joke with him. "Griselda would be horrified to hear you say that."

"Griselda isn't here, Bethany."

She knew that. No one was here. No one was here but she and Hawk.

He stepped around the table and pulled out

her chair. "Join me, Bethany. It's a pleasant time of day for a walk."

Hawk was right. It was pleasant. A nearly full moon, only a sliver missing from one side, threw a silver-white light over the undulating range land, giving it a surreal quality. The heat of the day had died with the setting of the sun, and a refreshing breeze stirred the long grass and tugged at the hem of Bethany's skirt as she walked at Hawk's side.

They walked a long time in silence, Hawk's hand so lightly on her elbow that she wondered if she only imagined it was there. They left behind the house and barn and outbuildings and moved up the skirt of the mountains until they reached an outcropping of rocks. Hawk motioned for her to sit down on a smooth boulder, then sat beside her. Below, the moonlit grasslands of Montana spread before them like an ocean of white-capped waves.

Leaning forward, Hawk braced his elbows on his wide-spread knees and dropped his hands, his fingertips touching, between them. His head was erect, his eyes locked on some distant point on the horizon. The chiseled features of his face were bathed in the silvery glow of the moon. And Bethany, who had found the courage to turn and look at him, thought she'd never seen anything or anyone more beautiful than Hawk Chandler at this moment.

"I'm sorry you were forced to marry me, Bethany. It doesn't make things easy for either of us."

I want to be here, Hawk. Please don't be sorry we're married.

"I don't have much practice with ladies like you."

She saw the tightening of his jaw, felt the sinking of her heart.

"I like to think my mother taught me to be a gentleman, but the truth is, I'm a cowboy. I've spent more time with other men and cows than with women since I left Chicago. And the women I've spent time with weren't ladies." He glanced pointedly her way. His eyes looked black as ink, and there was scorn in his voice. "*Ladies* don't seem to want much to do with a breed."

It doesn't matter to me, Hawk. I love you just as you are, and if only you'd tell me you love me, I could tell you too.

"It took me a long time to find this place. It's my home now. Someday, there'll be a fine ranch house and an even bigger barn. We've got enough land. I don't mean to be the biggest rancher in the territory. But the Circle Blue's going to be a name people know and respect. The best cattle are going to come off this range. I'm proud of it, and I mean for my children to be proud of it too."

His children. They'll be my children too.

"My children will have Indian blood, Bethany." There was a challenge in his voice as his gaze continued to study her mercilessly. "There'll be men and women who won't want anything to do with them because they're . . . breeds." Hate for that term was clear in his tone. "Just like their father."

She understood what he was saying and rose to the challenge. "What has that to do with who you are? Such people are ignorant fools."

"Yes," he replied, his voice more gentle now. "Yes, they are fools."

His hand rose to cup her chin, tilting her head back. A thrill moved up her spine. She swallowed hard, half wishing she could really see into the dark blue eyes she knew watched her so intently, half glad she could not.

He was like a hawk, scouting his prey. His mouth hovered over hers, awaiting the moment to strike. She watched, mesmerized, her blood pounding in her ears. Slowly, his hand moved from her chin to the back of her head. One at a time, he pulled the pins from her hair, loosening the heavy locks from their bondage, setting them free to spill in disarray over her shoulders and down her back.

"You're so very beautiful," he whispered as his mouth drew near. "I'll try not to hurt you."

I trust you, Hawk.

His lips met lightly with hers. His gentle touch was agony itself. Too much, yet not enough. A strange wanting seemed to be squeezing the pit of her stomach. She shivered.

"You're cold," he said, his lips still touching hers.

"No."

"We'd better go back to the house."

She didn't want to go in. She wanted to keep sitting here beside Hawk on this rock, feeling his fingers in her hair, feeling his breath upon her lips, indulging herself in the sweet closeness of this moment.

She had no idea what effect she was having on him, her face turned to the moonlight, a look of wonder and trust written in her eyes. All his encounters with women since Alice were with those who knew exactly what they wanted from Hawk and made it clear. Bethany was different. And that made him want her all the more.

He stood quickly, pulling her up with him. "We'd better get back," he repeated.

We'd better get back before I'm tempted to make love to you right here on the mountainside.

He was already tempted. The thought of her naked in the moonlight was nearly more than he could resist.

He began walking, his long strides carrying him quickly down the mountain, his arm beneath Bethany's elbow nearly dragging her along with him. He didn't realize how difficult it was for her. He was running from temptation before he did something he would later regret. By the time they reached the house, Bethany was panting for breath.

Hawk left her standing just inside the door and went to light a lamp. When he turned and looked at her again, he knew the temptation had followed him here. The desire came back a hundredfold. She was an angel. She was a temptress. She was everything he could have wanted.

Bethany's hair was wonderfully unmade, the tousled and wind-blown tresses making her look as if she'd just gotten out of bed. Her cheeks were pink from exertion, and her misty green eyes had darkened to the shade of a stormy sea. She stood across the room, her breasts rising and falling in rapid succession. Her hands were knotted in the folds of her skirt.

"Bethany . . . come here."

Her eyes widened.

"Now, Bethany. Come here."

He was almost afraid she wouldn't come. What would he do if she scorned him, if she refused his lovemaking? Would he force his rights upon her? No. He could live with her without love, but he would never take her against her will.

Hawk raised a hand toward her in invitation. "Bethany . . ."

She came. She floated across the floor and into his arms, as naturally as if they'd been doing it a lifetime. Hawk's arms closed around her, pulling her rounded curves up against the hardness of his male body. His mouth sought hers in a hungry, possessive kiss. She was his wife. Whatever strange twist of fate had brought them to this moment, she was now his wife and he was thankful.

He lifted her from the floor, cradling her against his chest as he would a child. In comparison to him, she seemed hardly more than a child. His Bethany. His wife. Tenderness mingled with desire, an almost heart-stopping combination.

Hawk opened the door to the bedroom and carried his bride across the threshold.

The moon bathed the room with a silvery glow, but Bethany was unaware of it. Her eyes were closed, her face pressed against Hawk's chest. She breathed deeply, memorizing the scent of his clean skin, a scent that was all his own. She knew she would never forget it any more than she would anything else that had happened tonight. Or whatever was still to happen.

Her feet were slowly lowered to the floor.

"Open your eyes, Bethany."

She loved the way he said her name. It was like warm honey spreading over her heart.

"Bethany . . ."

She lifted heavy lids and let her head drop back so she could look up at him.

"I'm going to undress you, Bethany. Do you know why?"

She tried to remember what she'd heard at Miss Hendersen's, but it was fruitless. She started to nod yes, then shook her head no.

"Are you afraid?"

She started to shake her head no, then nodded yes.

"Don't be, Bethany. Don't ever be afraid of me. I'm not a savage. I'm just a man."

First, he sat her on a stool against the wall. He knelt before her and placed her foot on his knee, then slowly slipped the black kid carriage shoe from her foot. Next, his fingers slid up her calf and shin. She had never imagined the mere touch of a man's fingers on her leg could cause such havoc in her heart. He rolled the garter and stocking down with agonizing slowness.

Her shoes and stockings gone, he stood and pulled her up with him. His hands on her shoulders turned her around until her back was to him. While he loosened the tiny buttons of her dress, she turned her gaze upon the large four-poster beneath the window, now spotlighted by the moon. It was such a very large bed. Her stomach tightened.

She felt the cool air against her back as her bodice gapped open. Then his lips touched her skin just above her chemise. She gasped. His fingers brushed her hair aside as his mouth moved up to her neck. She closed her eyes and let her head fall back, scarcely aware of his hands brushing her bodice from her shoulders and pushing it down her arms.

Then his hands weren't touching her any-more. Yet she knew he was close behind her. She was afraid to move, afraid to breathe. She longed for his lips to return to her nape—and was afraid at the same time that they would. Every sensation was new to her. Strange and exciting . . . and frightening too.

Once again his hands turned her around. In the moments she had stood without his touch upon her, he had removed his shirt. Now he was before her, bare-chested, tall, rawboned and strong. The muscles in his chest were enticingly defined. She was intrigued by the smattering of dark chest hairs and, without forethought, reached out to touch them. They were strangely soft, yet wiry.

At the touch of her fingertips, she heard him make a muffled sound in his throat. Like the avenging hawk she had imagined earlier, he swooped down upon his prey and captured her mouth. His tongue danced along her lower lip, inviting her to open and let him in. It seemed scandalous and daring, and she opened to him.

Somehow, in the following minutes, her che-mise was removed, followed by her corset. Her dress fell in a puddle about her feet, quickly covered by her petticoat. She didn't seem to be aware of her disrobing until the string of her drawers was loosened and they too fell away. Suddenly, she was terrified. She wanted to grab her dress from the floor and cover herself from the hooded gaze she knew was watching her.

"Don't be afraid, Bethany," he whispered once again as he lifted her above the fallen clothing and laid her in the center of the enormous four-poster.

For an instant, she looked up at him, looming above her, and wanted to shout aloud her love for him, promise him she would never be afraid as long as he loved her too. But then he straightened. His hands moved to the waistband of his britches. In sheer panic, she clamped her eyes tightly closed and waited.

The bed gave beneath his weight. She could feel the warmth of his body as he lay close beside her, yet not touching. His lips brushed her cheek next to her ear. His breath, hot and shallow, sent a wave of chills down her side. His hand began a slow, sensuous exploration, leaving a trail of newly sensitive skin behind. His mouth sought out her throat, pressing tightly against her throbbing pulse, then moving to cover her lips in a demanding, possessive kiss that sent her spiraling upward, beyond consciousness and into a new realm of feelings.

She had no time to be afraid as she became familiar with the intimate touch of his hand upon her flesh. He caressed her full breasts, making them taut. His feather-light fingertips brushed across her belly. It was almost like a tickle, yet far better. Even when his touch moved lower, cupping, stroking, she was not afraid. She gave herself over willingly to every new, wonderful sensation.

Bethany felt the bed shift, knew he waited, poised above her. She was still ignorant, yet somehow understood what was about to take place. Her arms rose to circle his neck. She opened her eyes. The moon had moved beyond the window, and only a sliver of light remained. Yet, in what light there was, she read a white-hot passion in his face and instinctively rose to join her passion with his.

It was a splendid thing, this joining of two hearts, this melding of two souls, this union of man and wife. Time stood still for two lovers, lost in a world of their own making. And when it was over, her rasping cry dying in the shadows of the room, they lay beside each other, totally replete, their bodies languid and their breathing tired.

His lips in her hair, she heard him whisper, "Bethany . . ."

She was certain there was an "I love you" hidden within her name on his lips. She wanted to tell him then that she loved him too, but she couldn't reply. There was hardly strength enough remaining to breathe, never enough to speak. In the morning would be soon enough.

As she drifted into a deep, satisfied slumber, a tiny smile curved her heart-shaped mouth.

The girls at Miss Hendersen's hadn't known anything about it at all.

CHAPTER FOURTEEN

Bethany was alone in the rumpled bed when she awoke. Sunlight had replaced the glow of the moon. It was warm against her bare flesh. With a self-satisfied groan, she pulled the sheet up to cover her breasts. She wondered if Hawk would soon return to the bedroom. She wanted to tell him she loved him before another minute passed.

Then she smelled the delightful odor wafting in from the kitchen—bacon sizzling on the stove. Hawk was cooking their breakfast. She grinned, tempted to remain in bed and wait for him to bring it to her, but she discarded the thought. She could make coffee. She wouldn't have him thinking he married a lazy good-for-nothing. And she would learn to cook. She would learn to do anything that would please him.

She tossed aside the sheet as her eyes swept the sparsely furnished bedroom. Besides the bed, there was only one chair, a washstand and basin, a narrow wardrobe, and Bethany's own trunk, sent out before the wedding. She hurried over to it and opened the lid, searching through the folded articles until she found a wrapper.

Glancing quickly at the closed bedroom door, she went to the wash basin and filled it with water from the pitcher. After washing, she donned the attractive pink-and-white wrapper, then ran a brush hastily through her unruly auburn curls. She didn't try to tame them, somehow knowing Hawk would prefer her to look slightly unkempt this morning.

She went straight to the kitchen from the bedroom, but he was nowhere in sight, although the bacon still sizzled on the stove. As she turned to look behind her, she realized the front door was standing open. Then she heard Hawk talking.

To himself? She grinned at the thought.

She tiptoed across the room, intent upon catching him by surprise.

"You're joking, right?"

That wasn't Hawk.

"We were married yesterday."

"Why didn't you let me know?"

"It was all kind of sudden. Figured you'd better just keep working on that house of yours so you could get married yourself."

"Well, I'll be . . . You know, Hawk, you didn't have to marry her to win my fifty bucks. The deal was to get her to *agree* to marry you. I wasn't too sure you could do that much, but I never thought you'd go through with it if you did."

Rand's words, said with an accompanying laugh, struck Bethany like a slap in the face. She reeled backward. Her eyes widened. Her hand covered her mouth as the taste of bile rose in her throat.

A bet? Fifty dollars? A joke that had backfired? Was that all she was to him? She had been ready to proclaim her undying love, when all she was to him was a bad payoff on a gamble.

Suddenly, the sick, hurt feeling passed, and she saw red. Fury boiled up in her veins like a too-full kettle on the stove. She flew forward and out the door, her fists already swinging before she reached her unwary prey.

"How dare you, Hawk Chandler?" she screeched as she pummeled his back. "How dare you do this to me?"

"What the hell . . . ?" He swung around, his arms up to protect himself.

"I'll never forgive you. Never!" The fingernails of her right hand raked his cheek.

Hawk grabbed her wrists. "What're you doing, Bethany?"

"Take your hands off me! Let me go!"

She was only partially aware of Rand's quick retreat toward the barn as she faced her husband of less than twenty-four hours. His face was dark and rock-hard, his eyes relentless as he faced her rage. His hands were still fastened tightly about her narrow wrists, heedless of her demands to release her.

Bethany's voice dropped to a near whisper, icy and controlled. "Let go of me, you filthy savage."

She saw him flinch, then her wrists were set free.

"I regret the day I first laid eyes on you, Hawk Chandler."

"What is it I've done?" His question was asked in an emotionless tone.

"Ha!" The sound hardly resembled the laugh it was supposed to be. "You make me a subject of your crude wagers, and then have the nerve to ask what you've done? You lied to me. You *used* me."

"*I* used *you*?" He took a menacing step toward her.

She drew back, but her chin thrust up. "Yes, you used me. It was all just a joke, wasn't it? But you didn't win your stupid wager. Did you think I would ever really care for a man like you? You're not just a savage. You're a fool."

His hard, blue-black gaze pierced her. "Yeah," he said in a quiet voice, "I'm a fool. I should have told your father he'd have to shoot me before I'd marry a spoiled brat like you. Don't think I ever wanted to marry you, Bethany. I'd have as soon married a she-wolf." He touched the four red scratches on his left cheek. "Perhaps I did at that."

"Well, you won't have to put up with me for long, Mr. Chandler. I'm leaving. I'll not spend another minute under the same roof with you. If my father won't have me, I'll go back to Philadelphia. I'll go to the ends of the earth before I'll stay with you." She turned her back to him but had only taken one step before his hands spun her around.

The man who stood before her, cold eyes glaring, was no relation to the gentle man who had tenderly disrobed her in the moonlight, the loving man who had brought her such delight the night before. This man was dark and threatening. "You're not going anywhere, Bethany Chandler." His fingers squeezed into her arms.

She felt a chill wash through her.

"You're my wife. As much as you may dislike being married to a *savage* . . ." He drew the word out, making it sound much uglier than even she had meant when she said it. ". . . you're still my wife. We had only one night together, but we did have that. There's a chance you may already carry my child in your womb. You won't step foot off this place until I know you aren't."

Her fury was gone. She felt weak. Heartbroken. "And if I am?" she asked softly.

"If you are, you'll stay until the child is born. Remember, it'll be sired by a *savage*. You wouldn't want to take a *breed* back to Philadelphia with you to raise. You'll leave it with me. Then you can go where you want." His hands released her arms as he stepped backward. "And I don't much care where that is." Then he spun on his heel and headed for the barn.

Her vision blurred with sudden tears. A muffled cry tore from her throat as she too spun around, her flight carrying her into the house, her intended path leading to the bedroom. But the moment she was in the door, she was engulfed with heavy smoke coming from the kitchen. Choking and coughing, her eyes stinging, she ran forward to pull the frying pan, charred bacon and smoking fat within, from the stove. In doing so, she burned her hand on the skillet.

Overwhelmed by defeat and sorrow, the pain in her hand slight in comparison to the pain in her heart, she sank to the floor, let her face fall forward into her grease-spattered wrapper, and wept copiously.

"Hawk, I'm sorry. I . . ."

"Forget it, Rand."

"But I . . ."

"I said, forget it," Hawk bit off, still wrapped in a cold rage. Wordlessly, he saddled Flame, mounted, and galloped out of the barn.

He should have known better. He should have known better than to think he could marry a girl like Bethany Silverton.

You filthy savage . . . you filthy savage . . .

The pounding hoofbeats seemed to echo her angry words over and over again.

You filthy savage . . .

If only she hadn't overheard Rand the way she did. If only he'd had a moment to explain. If he could have told her that he did care, that she was beautiful, that he was glad they were married. If he could have expressed what their lovemaking had meant to him. If he could have found the words to express what was in his heart . . .

But the angry words they had hurled at each other could not be forgotten. She thought him a savage. She'd said what he was, what his mother had been, didn't matter. She'd lied. There was no taking back the hateful things they had said to each other. It was too late now for anything good between them. Too late . . . unless there was a child.

If only there could be a child before she left him.

* * *

Rand stepped out of the barn into the morning sunlight and watched his friend riding away. This was his fault. If he hadn't been so careless about talking about the wager . . . Hawk had actually looked happy when Rand met him out by the pump. In a matter of seconds, Rand had spoiled all that.

He stepped up onto the corral fence and sat on the top rail, elbows on his knees, head in his hands, and tried to decide what to do. He hadn't heard all that was said between them, but he'd heard enough. Perhaps if he spoke to Bethany, explained to her about how Hawk's wager had come about, maybe she would understand and forgive Hawk. Then again, maybe he would only make things worse by sticking his nose in where it didn't belong.

Rand debated with himself for a long time before he finally hopped off the fence and strode toward the ranch house. He rapped loudly on the still open door.

"Bethany . . . Miz Chandler . . . Can I come in?"

She came out of Hawk's bedroom. She had changed from the flowing wrapper into a cream-colored dress with lace and ruffles, a gown totally incongruous with the rustic cabin which was now her home. Her hair had been captured in a severe chignon at the nape. Her chin was high, her shoulders straight. There was still evidence of tears on her cheeks, but her demeanor would brook no sympathy.

"Please enter, Mr. Howard. You needn't knock. I believe this is your home too." Her words were spoken in a tone suggesting he was a guest come to call. She was all lady now, totally in control. No trace remained of the girl who had flown through the doorway to attack Hawk's back.

Rand cleared his throat. "Not anymore, ma'am."

"Please don't let my presence drive you out. I'm sure I won't be here long."

Rand looked down at his hat, held tightly in the fingers of one hand. "I hope that ain't true."

"I assure you, it is." Bethany turned abruptly and walked to the love seat beneath the window. She sat down, her back rigid, not touching the back of the seat. "I know Mr. Chandler is your friend, and so I won't tell you what I think of him—or of you either, for that matter. But I promise you, I won't be threatened by him. He's a brute. He only married me because my father forced him into it. And if it hadn't been for that wager between you two, even that wouldn't have happened. I will stay only—only as long as necessary."

Rand shook his head slowly. "You're wrong about Hawk. I suspect you're wrong about a lot of things you're thinkin'. And I'd tell you how that wager come about, but I don't think you're in a mood to listen. Besides, it goes back farther'n that. It goes back to Chicago. Sometime, if you're willin' to listen, you ask Hawk about Chicago."

Bethany's face was ghost-pale. Glittering suspiciously, her green eyes seemed almost too large, almost too round. Her chin jutted forward stubbornly. "I'm sure I do not care to hear anything Mr. Chandler would have to say to me."

"Have it your way, ma'am," Rand responded with another shake of his head. Then he spun around and left the house.

The hours crept away at a snail's pace. Bethany wandered around the small house with nothing to do but replay her memories time and time again. How could happiness become misery so quickly? She had been ready to tell him she loved him. Did she love him still?

She walked to the open door and stared out at the silent yard. A few horses stood in the corral, their heads drooping, their tails swishing. A warm breeze rustled the leaves of a nearby poplar. The silence, the aloneness, the heat—it all added to her sorrow.

She should leave him. She should defy him. She should saddle her horse and return home to her parents.

"Papa," she whispered, her father's face appearing in her mind.

But what could she tell him? That Hawk hadn't wanted to marry her? That was no surprise. They had both been forced into it by their reckless actions. Would she tell him about the wager? No. It was too humiliating. Besides, even that wouldn't change what had brought them to the altar. She couldn't tell her father Hawk had mistreated her. He had been gentle and kind, right up until the moment she flew at his back in a rage. No, if she went to her father and told him she was leaving her husband after only one day, he would just send her back. Marriage was a holy sacrament, one not to be taken lightly. As much as Nathaniel loved her, he would send her back to Hawk.

Her father's kindly image was replaced by Hawk's dark and brooding one. An ache tightened around her heart. How could she share this house with him? Even now a sweet longing stirred within her, a longing for the man who had prepared their supper, who had walked beside her on the mountain, who had pulled the pins from her hair, who had loved her in the moonlight.

Bethany bit her lower lip and turned her back on the bright summer day outside. She could never allow Hawk to know what he made her feel inside. Her pride couldn't bear it if he knew. She would never let him know how deeply she cared. And if this feeling were, indeed, love, he would never know that either. Not if she stayed in this house with him for a hundred years.

The moon was already up when Hawk turned Flame loose in the corral. He glanced toward the house, feeling an overwhelming sadness as he stared at the dark windows. He wondered if Bethany was asleep.

Unwelcome thoughts of their wedding night returned, bringing with them a burning desire for another night just like it. He had never wanted a woman the way he wanted Bethany. He didn't want just her body for a brief time of passion. He wanted all of her—heart, mind, soul, body.

His mouth hardened suddenly as the memory

changed from last night to this morning. There was no point in giving in to the wanting. Chances were good they would never share anything pleasant again.

He walked toward the well and began working the pump handle. In a moment, the water was filling a pail. He unbuttoned his shirt and removed it, tossing it aside. Cupping his hands, he dipped into the bucket and splashed water on his dusty face, washing away the day's heat and sweat as best he could, delaying just a little longer the moment he must face his wife.

His wife. Twenty-four hours ago, he'd been hopeful about those words. Now they were almost an accusation.

He straightened and drew his arm across his forehead. Once again, his gaze settled on the cabin. He should let her go back to her father, just as she'd wanted. If he were wise, he would send her packing in the morning. He knew the chances of her conceiving a child on their wedding night were next to nothing. It was only an excuse to keep her there, to perhaps punish her in a small way for her angry, hurtful words.

Or perhaps it was to punish himself, for he also knew, even as the thought crossed his mind, that he wasn't going to let her go. Not yet. He had no idea how long it would be before she knew she wasn't pregnant with his child— perhaps a few days, perhaps a few weeks. However long it was, he meant to keep her there with him.

Bethany heard him enter the cabin. She stared up at the ceiling, waiting anxiously for the bedroom door to open. Though the room wasn't cool by any means, she pulled the blanket up tight beneath her chin and waited.

She could hear his footsteps. A sliver of light suddenly slipped beneath the door. Muffled sounds continued as he moved about the kitchen. She wondered what he was doing, but eventually, the smell of meat cooking in a frying pan answered her silent question. Her stomach growled, reminding her she hadn't eaten all day.

It seemed an eternity until she heard him approaching the bedroom at last. He paused a moment—was he as uncertain as she?—then opened the door.

She lay very still, feigning sleep, forcing herself to breathe when all the while she could feel his gaze upon her, knew he was studying her face in the moonlight. Her heart quickened as she wondered what he was thinking, what he was feeling. Would he demand his rights as her husband?

The door closed. She wasn't sure he'd even moved until she felt the bed give beneath his weight as he sat down and pulled off his boots. Then he stood again and, piece by piece, shed the rest of his clothing before slipping beneath the sheets to lie beside her. Bethany could feel the warmth of his nearness. Her body was alert, waiting for him to reach toward her. She recognized the desire, the need for him, even while her mind commanded her traitorous flesh to behave.

It would never do for Hawk to know of the fire of wanting that burned within her. It would never do at all.

CHAPTER FIFTEEN

· —— ·

They lived together as polite strangers, an unspoken agreement existing between them. In fact, they rarely spoke at all. Bethany rose before dawn to prepare breakfast, the results not always appetizing but at least edible. Hawk ate whatever was put before him without comment. Then, more often than not, he saddled his horse and rode out. He returned when the day was already gone. Bethany, always in bed and always feigning sleep, would listen to him disrobe and wait for him to slip beneath the covers to lie beside her. The long nights were agony.

She filled her days with what housework there was, washing clothes, sweeping the floor, dusting the shelves. She worked harder than she'd ever worked in her life, trying to keep her thoughts from straying to her husband. Her efforts were unsuccessful. Again and again, she heard his angry dismissal of her, felt the heat of his rage, knew the despair of being unwanted. And again and again, she remembered the way he'd taken her to his bed and loved her. Only pride kept her heart from breaking.

At least she wasn't completely alone during the long hours he was away. Hawk's hired hands had returned to the bunkhouse after giving the newlyweds two days of privacy. Although most of them generally left the ranch each day, just as Hawk did, there was usually someone still in the yard or the barn. Bethany felt a little less lonely, knowing someone was there, but it was awkward as well. When they chanced to look at her, even from a distance, she could feel their curiosity over Hawk's frequent and lengthy absences and felt again the sting of humiliation.

July arrived with clear skies and an unrelenting sun, baking the Montana range and the small house at the Circle Blue. Two weeks had passed since her wedding, the most difficult two weeks of her young life.

Bethany was lugging a full bucket of wash water toward the shade at the side of the house. Beads of perspiration dotted her forehead. The underarms of her dress were damp, and there was a dull ache in the small of her back. She glanced up as she approached the washtub and saw two riders cantering toward her. She smiled as she recognized Ingrid, the first smile to crack her face in what seemed a lifetime. She set the bucket at her feet and raised her hand to wave.

Ingrid's horse trotted into the yard. She hopped to the ground, not waiting for Rand to help her down. Grinning widely, she threw herself into Bethany's arms. "Oh, Bethany, it is so good to see you! I have missed you so very much."

"I've missed you too," Bethany replied, returning the hug with vigor.

Ingrid stepped back and took a longer look at her friend. "You have lost weight."

"Perhaps a little." Bethany turned toward Rand, stopping momentarily the questions she knew were sure to come. "Good day, Mr. Howard."

Rand touched the brim of his Stetson and nodded, then asked, "Hawk around?"

"No. He left early this morning to check the cattle."

"D'you know where?"

She shook her head. "Rusty's working on something behind the barn. Maybe he knows."

"I'll see." He glanced at Ingrid and a private smile curled his mouth upwards. "You have a nice visit and I'll be back for you later."

Bethany studied Ingrid's face as the blonde watched Rand saunter toward the barn. Love had transformed Ingrid somehow. There was a radiance in her cheeks, a tenderness about her mouth.

Ingrid turned and caught her watching. She colored in embarrassment. "I am shamefully in love with him," she whispered.

"No, Ingrid," Bethany responded honestly. "There is nothing shameful in loving someone." Then she hooked her arm through Ingrid's. "Come inside. Hawk brought up ice from the icehouse this morning. We can have some lemonade. I just made it myself. And you must tell me all the news from town."

Ingrid laughed as they entered the house. "Nothing has changed, except the church grows. You will see for yourself tomorrow. Hawk told me you will be in church tomorrow."

"You've seen Hawk?"

"Of course, Bethany. I take the men sandwiches and coffee while they work on the church, just as before. Hawk has been a great help. He is a hard worker."

Bethany turned her back toward Ingrid, busying herself with tumblers and ice and lemonade while her thoughts churned. Hawk had been going into town and working on the church. He'd never told her. Could he, perhaps, be doing it for her? No. It was silly to even wonder such a thing. And it would be embarrassing to admit to Ingrid that her husband of two weeks didn't tell her where he spent his days.

"Bethany?" Ingrid's hand landed lightly on her shoulder. "Are you happy?"

For just a moment, she thought she might burst into tears. She swallowed hard and blinked several times, then forced a smile as she turned toward her friend. "I'm happy enough, Ingrid. I know we didn't start out right, but I think we're both content. Look!" She laughed as she waved an arm around the kitchen. "I'm even learning to cook and clean."

Ingrid continued to peruse her with an uncertain look.

Bethany turned away once again. "There . . . there is one thing, Ingrid."

"What is it, Bethany?"

"How would I . . . How does a woman know if she's . . . if there's going to be a . . . a baby?"

Ingrid squealed with joy. "Oh, Bethany! A baby. Are you going to have a baby?"

"I . . . I don't know. I don't know how to tell."

"But that is simple. You will have no monthly flow while you carry a child."

"Oh." Bethany wondered at her own calm response. Inside, she felt as if she were crumbling into a million pieces, like a shattered china cup. Her flow had ended two days before. There was no baby. She would not be having Hawk's baby. There was no more reason to stay at the Circle Blue. She could leave whenever she wanted. Why didn't the thought please her?

Ingrid picked up the two large glasses, filled with lemonade, and carried them to the table, oblivious to her friend's turmoil. "I hope Rand and I will have a family right away," she said dreamily. She sat down and waited for Bethany to join her. "That is why we came here today. The house is finished. Rand and I are to be married in two weeks. We have come to ask you and Hawk to stand up with us. You cannot say no, Bethany."

"I wouldn't think of saying no," she replied absently.

But she didn't listen to Ingrid's continuing chatter. Her thoughts were in an uproar. She couldn't leave Hawk until after Ingrid's wedding. How would it look to have them standing up for the bride and groom when their own marriage had failed? It would make everyone uncomfortable. No, she would have to remain at the Circle Blue until after the wedding. But what if Hawk didn't want her here?

Well, she just wouldn't tell him. He needn't know there wasn't a baby. Not yet. He needn't know yet.

From the moment Rand caught up with him, Hawk had been wondering if Bethany would tell Ingrid how things really were between them. He knew she hadn't done so the moment he walked in the door.

Bethany rose quickly from the love seat and hurried to his side, slipping her arm through his as her silver-green eyes pleaded with him to go along with her charade. "Isn't it wonderful, Hawk? Rand and Ingrid have set a date for their wedding."

"So Rand told me." He continued to stare down into her face, caught afresh by her arresting beauty. He'd forced himself not to look at her for so long now, he reacted like a man dying of thirst, drinking her in while the opportunity remained. He was a fool to do so, and he knew it. He would pay for it later when he lay beside her in bed, unable to touch her, unable to draw her to him and possess her as he longed to do. He would pay for it while he lay there, hot with a desire that couldn't be quenched.

While Hawk ogled his bride, Rand moved into the room to stand beside Ingrid. "We'd better get goin'. I promised the reverend I'd have Ingrid back 'fore it was too late."

"But we will see you in church tomorrow," Ingrid said quickly, a contented lilt in her rolling voice.

Hawk had forgotten tomorrow was Sunday. He'd forgotten he'd told the reverend he would bring Bethany in for church this week. There just hadn't been a logical reason not to agree to his father-in-law's urging to bring his bride into town for the Sabbath. And now he was trapped by his own words.

"Yeah, we'll be there," he answered, even as he wondered if Bethany would use this chance to escape from the Circle Blue—and from him.

Together they walked outside to bid their friends good-bye. Bethany's arm remained locked with his. In unison, they raised their outside arms to wave farewell and stood silently as Ingrid and Rand rode away. Then they were alone.

Hawk waited for Bethany to pull away, to free herself from his touch. But she didn't. She didn't move at all.

This is how it should be, he thought. *This should be us at the end of every day.*

Except it wasn't the end of the day. There was still plenty of daylight, and he was already at home with Bethany. The longing to crush her to him and drink the sweetness from her lips was almost more than he could resist. If he didn't do something now to stop himself, he would soon do something they would both regret. He would kiss her, caress her, possess her, no matter how hard she resisted.

He turned suddenly, pulling his arm from hers, and strode into the house. In a moment, he was back outside, clean britches, a towel, and a bar of soap in his hands.

"I'm going to take my bath in the creek," he snapped at her.

Their eyes met, hers round and luminous. Her mouth was slightly parted and inviting, even with the beading moisture above her upper lip. Cinnamon wisps of auburn hair clung damply to her forehead and nape. He felt a sudden tightening in his loins and knew he'd better get into that cold water fast.

"Hawk?" Her voice was tremulous.

"What?"

"May I . . . may I go with you? It's much too hot to bathe in the kitchen. I'll go downstream. I won't intrude. I promise."

He could feel the scowl on his face. "Get your things while I saddle your horse."

He didn't want her to go with him. He needed distance between them. But how could he deny her when she looked at him that way? Besides, it couldn't have been an easy time for her, living with a man she detested, held captive until the moment she knew there was no child. And she hadn't just lived there in idleness either. She cooked his meals and kept the house spotless, things he knew she'd rarely done in her life. She'd done it and without complaint. He owed her at least this small request.

They rode in their usual silence, Hawk leading the way to a secluded place he knew. If it had been only himself, he would have walked to the closest spot of creek, not caring who might have chanced to see him as he bathed away the sweat of the day. But Bethany deserved something better.

Nestled at the base of the mountains, the small pond to which he led her was surrounded by trees and brush, a private swimming hole about a mile from the mouth of the springs. The water here was clear and icy cold. They reached the pond as the sun dipped behind the mountain peaks, hinting at the end of day even while it was yet a long time in coming.

Hawk glanced back over his shoulder. "You stay here," he told her. "I'll ride on a ways. You holler out when you're ready to go back."

Bethany nodded, and he moved on downstream.

Leaving his horse to graze on the bank, Hawk shed his clothes and stepped into the water. Ignoring the sharp difference between the temperature of the creek and the heat of the day, he sat in the deepest part—perhaps a foot of water—and began to scrub himself with the harsh soap. But his thoughts weren't on the coolness of the water or the hot July day. Nor were they on the cattle or horses or anything else to do with his ranch. Nor even on church tomorrow and going into town. They were all on Bethany.

Right now, not far from where he sat, she was bathing too. Her creamy flesh would be glistening with water. Her nipples would be taut from the cold. Her hair, loosened from those blasted pins, would be floating on the surface of the clear water, swirling around her bare shoulders. He closed his eyes, willing the vision away, but it wouldn't leave him. He groaned. The cold water wasn't helping.

He tried to recall the anger he'd felt when he learned of her wager, but it seemed a small and insignificant thing. He tried to feel again the hot rage he'd known when she'd called him a savage, but even that had cooled. The only thing remaining was the wanting, the terrible, unrelenting wanting.

It wasn't only her body he wanted. He wanted to see her mischievous smile. He wanted to hear her melodic laughter. He wanted to see her misty-green eyes sparkle with something other than tears. And he wanted her passionate body as well. He wanted all this and more. He wanted all of her.

Hawk groaned again and laid back in the stream, holding his breath as the water rushed over his face. He burst to the surface even as her shriek split the air.

Bethany was unable to move. The dark yellow eyes kept her frozen in place, barely two steps from shore. The black wolf's grizzled head was dipped low. Its throaty growl lifted the corners of its mouth to reveal sharp, jagged teeth. She imagined those teeth sinking into her throat and felt her knees weaken. She didn't dare breathe. She didn't dare move.

Suddenly, the animal's head turned, its ears

cocking forward, the growl suddenly silenced. Then with surprising swiftness, it disappeared into the brush just as Hawk burst into view at the far end of the pond, his rifle in his hand.

"Bethany!"

She pointed at the spot where the wolf had been, her mouth open, but her words were caught in her still paralyzed throat. A sudden dizziness shot through her, and she groped blindly for shore. She didn't understand how he could have reached her so quickly, but he was there to catch her as she swayed forward into his arms. Her body went limp as a wave of blackness swelled, then receded, leaving her shaking violently.

"What was it, Bethany?" he whispered into her wet hair, his mouth nearly touching her ear.

"A wolf. Hawk, it was a wolf."

She felt the cords of his arms tighten around her, pressing her against the safety of his chest. "It's all right now. It's gone."

She nodded, burying her face against his damp skin. "I was so—so frightened."

"I know."

How long was it before she became aware of the feel of her bare breasts pressed against him and remembered her nakedness? How long before she realized he was naked too? How long before the reason for her shivering changed? How long before she recognized the overwhelming desire flowing like hot lava through her veins?

She pushed away from him, turning so she

couldn't see his face, horrified by the sudden shift in her thoughts. "Please go away, Hawk. I want to get dressed. Please don't look at me."

She felt him hesitate, then heard him step away. "I'll get my horse." The gentle comfort of his voice had disappeared, replaced by the all-too-familiar gruffness.

The moment he was gone, she sank to the ground and cradled her face in her hands. How could she? How could she be so shameless? How could she act so wantonly with a man who wanted nothing more from her than a child—and even that not bad enough to try again to plant one in her womb? Was she ready to throw even her pride to the wind? Pride was all she had left. She couldn't give it up too. She couldn't let him see how much she wanted him, how much she loved him.

Oh, yes. She loved him. She couldn't try to deny it any longer. It didn't matter to her about the wager. She didn't care why he had married her. It didn't matter how short a time she'd known him. She loved him with everything that was in her. But she couldn't tell him. She would clutch the tattered shreds of her pride to her until her last breath was spent, but she would never confess to an unrequited love.

Steeling herself, she rose and stepped back into the pond, rinsing away the leaves and blades of grass that stuck to her flesh. Then she dried off and dressed in a cool linen gown. She was already seated on her mare when Hawk finally returned, his face dark and stony.

"Hawk?"

His remote blue-black gaze met hers.

"I have a favor to ask."

He continued to stare in silence.

"When we . . . when we go into town tomorrow, may we pretend we're happy? For my parents' sake. Please."

"And how long are we going to pretend?"

Forever, she wanted to shout. Her eyes dropped to the pommel of the saddle. "If there's no baby, they'll know soon enough."

"And if there is?" His harsh question cut into her like a knife.

"Then when I return to them."

He grunted what seemed to be his agreement before jerking his mount's head around and starting back toward the ranch house.

Sunk in abject misery, Bethany followed her husband—the man she loved—knowing her days to follow him were numbered.

CHAPTER SIXTEEN

·——·

I'll be gone at least three months, Montoya. Do whatever you have to do to get that breed out of there before I get back. I don't want to know what it is. Just do it. And don't ever come 'round my place again. You've got your money, and there'll be more when I get back if the job's done right." Vince placed his hands on his desk top and leaned forward. "And, Montoya, make certain nothing happens to the woman. Do we have an understanding?"

The Mexican's stance was irritating and impudent, displaying a total disregard for the wealth and power of the man behind the desk. His black eyes glared back at Vince, cold and unemotional. "We have an understanding, *señor*. Have a good trip." As he spoke, he settled his black sombrero onto his head, the wide brim shrouding his face in shadows.

Vince had the unpleasant feeling that the man was sneering at him as he turned and left.

He leaned back in his leather chair with a sigh, glad that that business was settled. Tomorrow he would attend the wedding of the scrawny-faced Swede to that sidekick of Chandler's. He wished he could avoid it, but the reverend himself had extended the invitation. The two men had had their differences, but Vince wasn't about to insult him. In the short time he'd been in Sweetwater, Reverend Silverton had become very influential in the community, and Vince was too astute to make a man of the cloth his enemy. He just might need the reverend's backing some day. He would need proponents in every corner when it was time to make his political moves. Besides, he had every intention of making the reverend his father-in-law.

He turned his thoughts from tomorrow's wedding to his own travels. Tomorrow afternoon he would head for Cheyenne and then on to Washington. He meant to grease a few pigs, so to speak, while he was back there, strengthening his ties to the powers in control. The time was ripe. The Northern Pacific would soon be completed. The land was being snatched up quickly, the population growing. Ranchers were becoming rich off the cattle and sheep that roamed the vast ranges. Now it was time for him to make his move. When the day came for Montana's statehood, he meant to be sitting in Helena at the head of its government.

Vince swiveled his chair to the side and stood, walking across the room to the open window. A cool, light breeze stirred the air, a pleasant change from the heat of recent weeks. As he did so often, he turned his gaze upon the western mountains. His mustache twitched as he began to grin. When he got back, the breed would be gone. Dead, most likely. That was how a man like Montoya usually worked. That would suit Vince best, of course, for when Hawk Chandler was dead, Bethany would be a widow.

Bethany a widow. What a delightful thought.

And then his thoughts drifted back in time, to the day he'd first heard she was to marry Hawk. It was Jake Casper who'd brought him the news . . .

"You're lying!" Vince roared as he jumped to his feet, the abrupt action sending his chair over onto its back.

"No, sir, Mr. Richards. It's the truth. I heard the preacher's gal was—well, I guess the reverend didn't have much choice than to tell them they had to marry. After all, Eberlie's girl was right there and saw it all."

A sharp pain stabbed Vince behind the eyes, nearly blinding him. In a rage, he slammed his wine goblet against the table. The glass shattered, tiny shards imbedding themselves into the palm of his right hand. Blood spurted from the wound, staining the white tablecloth. But Vince scarcely noticed. He was oblivious to everything but the fury Casper's news had caused.

Bethany marrying Hawk. That blasted redskin was stealing something else Vince wanted.

Vince had tried to reason with the reverend, tried to make him see what a mistake he was making, but the fool wouldn't listen. He'd thanked Vince for his concern but told him his daughter would be marrying Hawk Chandler as planned. He hadn't even seemed to consider

Vince's offer to marry the girl himself. And then, as an added insult, the reverend hadn't even invited Vince to the wedding.

Well, perhaps things had worked out for the best after all. His chance to wed the comely Bethany would come again, and when the Widow Chandler married him, he would also be acquiring the Circle Blue. It was a much easier, less expensive means of obtaining the land he wanted so desperately.

Yes, things had definitely worked out for the best.

Bethany sat on the edge of the bed, the bedroom growing dim in the gathering dusk. Her dress was pressed and ready for tomorrow, as was Hawk's black suit. She had even polished his best pair of boots. Now she waited for him to return home.

The past two weeks had been spent much as the previous two, except they went to church on Sundays. Those Sundays were equally wonderful and terrible for Bethany. On those days she was allowed to touch Hawk, free to slip her arm through his, free to look adoringly up at him. He never knew she wasn't pretending, for as soon as they left Sweetwater, she withdrew and cloaked herself once again in her pride. The six days that passed between Sundays were spent in loneliness and silence, with Hawk out on the range, returning after she was already in bed, as had become his pattern.

But tonight her charade would end. There would be no more Sundays with Hawk. There would be no more nights in his bed, as frustrating and painful as those had become. She would not be fixing him any more breakfasts nor washing his britches nor ironing his dress shirt. She would never again bathe in the pond and chance to be crushed, naked, against the protection of his chest. For tonight she meant to tell him there would not be a baby, and tomorrow, after the wedding, she would remain in Sweetwater while Hawk returned home.

Dear God, she prayed silently, her hands clenched, her eyes closed. *Don't let him let me go*.

There was a full moon again, just as there had been on their wedding night. And just as on their wedding night, it was bathing the bed in a silvery-white glow when Hawk's boots touched the floor outside the bedroom door. As she'd heard him do so often, he paused before lifting the latch and entering. He stopped, surprised to see her still up.

"Bethany, is something wrong?"

She stood, her hands twisting within the folds of her peignoir. "I needed to speak with you, Hawk. About . . . about tomorrow."

Hawk nodded and walked toward the bed, loosening his shirt as he came.

Bethany's heart rose to her throat as she looked at him. She didn't think she could speak. If only she could go back in time . . . If only she could change things. . . .

With a sigh, Hawk sank to the bedside, his back toward her, as he asked, "What about tomorrow?"

But there was no way to go back in time.

There was no changing the things she had said to him. "I won't be coming back with you after the wedding."

She saw his shoulders stiffen.

"There's no baby, Hawk."

There was a long, tense silence before he spoke. "I suppose it's just as well." His voice was low and emotionless.

Bethany swallowed back the thickening in her throat and forced herself to continue. "I don't want anyone to know until Rand and Ingrid are away. It would spoil things for them."

"Sure."

"You . . . you'll send my trunk to town later?"

He removed his shirt and tossed it onto a chair. "Sure," he said again.

Bethany lifted the covers on her side of the bed and slipped between them. Lying on her back, her gaze locked on the ceiling, her eyes swimming with unshed tears, she silently mouthed the words, "I'm sorry, Hawk. I'm sorry for everything."

"I want you to talk to Bethany tomorrow, Nathaniel. I can't shake the feeling that something's not right."

Nathaniel put aside his reading glasses and closed his Bible. He glanced over his shoulder at Virginia, already in bed. "I don't know why you think that, my dear. She's looked perfectly happy when we've seen her on Sundays."

"But she's not happy, Nathaniel. A mother feels these things. Now you promise me you'll try to talk with her."

Nathaniel grinned to himself as he reached for the lamp to turn down the wick. "Why is it that *you* have the feeling but *I* must do the talking?" He slid his legs beneath the blankets and held out an arm to draw his wife into the pillow of his shoulder.

Virginia nestled against him, an arm thrown over his chest, the position a familiar one after twenty years. "Just because, dear." She paused, then added, "She loves him a great deal, you know."

"Yes, I know."

"Then you'll speak to her and find out what's wrong?"

"I'll speak to her, Virginia. I promise."

She tightened her arm and lifted her lips to kiss his jaw. "Thank you, dear."

As Nathaniel drifted off to sleep, it was with a silent prayer of thanks to God for his wife and another prayer for happiness for his daughter.

Hawk led the horse and buggy from the barn just as Bethany stepped out the door. She was wearing an embroidered and flounced teal-green gown of fine lawn. A matching embroidered satin bonnet, trimmed with plumes and strings of satin ribbon, covered her auburn tresses and shaded her eyes.

His stomach felt like lead as he moved toward her. After today, he wouldn't see her stepping out into the morning light again. He wouldn't see her across the breakfast table. He wouldn't hear her even breathing in the bed beside him at night. As filled with tension and heartache as these past weeks had been, he was going to miss her.

For just a moment this morning, he'd considered asking her to stay, asking her if they could try again. He'd thought of the way she clung to his arm when they were in town, the way she turned that sweet smile up at him, and then had tried to tell himself what he imagined in her eyes was real. But the thought had been only a brief one, replaced quickly by the memory of the way she had shrunk from his touch and pleaded with him not to look at her when they were by the pond. No, it wouldn't work. She was a great actress, his Bethany, but she wouldn't be able to pretend to care for him when it was just the two of them.

Then he reminded himself of her duplicity, trying as he had so often to renew the flames of anger, forcing himself to hear her calling him a savage. Although the anger didn't come, the truth remained. She despised him for what he was and for what he'd done. No, it was better to let it end now. He had forced her to remain with him long enough. There was no baby, no more reason to keep her here against her will. If she remained, eventually their silent treaty would be broken, and they would again find themselves speaking cruel words to each other. Better to let it end while the bitterness was least acute.

Reaching the house, Hawk held out his hand to Bethany and helped her into the buggy, then walked to the opposite side and climbed up beside her. "Ready?" he asked briskly, not daring to glance at her profile for fear he would weaken and ask her to come back with him after the wedding.

"I'm ready."

Bethany felt her father's eyes upon her again. She turned her head and smiled, hoping beyond hope it didn't look as forced as it felt. Then, quickly, she dropped her gaze to the cup in her hands before he could see the heartbreak in her eyes. She didn't want to tell him anything until Rand and Ingrid departed and the guests began to disperse. That would be soon enough to face his disappointment.

"Your beauty eclipsed the bride's, Bethany."

She stiffened as she looked up. "I doubt there was anyone near as beautiful as Ingrid today, Mr. Richards."

"Ah, yes. All brides are beautiful." He smiled. "I'm sorry I missed your wedding. You must have been ravishing."

Bethany wished he would go away and leave her be. She didn't have the strength to deal with Vince Richards today.

As if in answer to her silent wishing, he said, "I'm leaving for Washington this afternoon. Paying a visit to a few senators I know. This territory's going to be a state someday, and we'd better be preparing for it."

"How long will you be gone?" The polite conversation was almost automatic, even though her new wish was for him to stay in Washington forever.

"Several months, I should imagine. Will you miss me while I'm away?"

Bethany was taken aback by his audacity. She drew herself up and lifted her chin in indignation. "Mr. Richards, please remember that I'm a married woman."

Vince seemed to shrug off her words as unimportant even as he said, "I beg your pardon." His smile widened as his voice dropped to a whisper. "*I* shall miss *you*, Bethany. No doubt you think I should give up on my plans for us to wed just because you married that breed. But don't worry. I don't think a woman is bound by any vows with a redskin. Someday you'll realize I'm right. You'll join me at the Bar V as my wife." Then he nodded. "Good day, ma'am." Still smiling, he turned and left her.

A wary shiver passed through her as she watched Vince making his way through the crowded parlor, pausing to speak a few pleasantries, shaking hands and smiling. He almost oozed wealth and power, and people responded to him as if he were royalty. Was she the only one who saw through the mask to the man behind it? Vince Richards was dangerous, she was certain of it. And he had singled her out for his attentions, despite her marriage to Hawk. What would he do when he learned she'd left Hawk?

She shivered again.

Suddenly, the sense of fear passed, replaced by a feeling of safety. She turned her head once again, somehow knowing what made her feel that way. Hawk was standing in the far corner, talking to Doc Wilton, but his dark blue gaze looked across the sea of people to meet hers. It reminded her of the first time they had seen each other and how disturbed his enigmatic gaze had left her. Her heart started thumping in her chest. What was it his eyes were telling her? She sensed the message was tenuous. She must grasp it now or lose it. If she had only a moment more . . .

"Bethany?" Ingrid's fingers closed around her forearm. "Rand and I are going to leave now."

Startled from her reverie, she knew the fragile link was broken, the message lost. Hawk returned his attention to Doc just as Bethany turned to look at Ingrid.

"I will come visit you soon," the blonde whispered as she hugged Bethany. "We will be living not so far away."

Bethany stopped herself from speaking the denial. Ingrid would know soon enough. "I'm so glad for you, Ingrid. You and Rand are going to be terribly happy. I just know it."

"Before we go," Ingrid continued, still speaking softly, "you need to tell me. Is there going to be a baby?"

Bethany shook her head and felt the sharp pain of disappointment.

"I am sorry." Ingrid stepped back and offered an encouraging smile. "But there is still much time. Perhaps we will both have babies at the same time."

"Perhaps."

Rand came to his bride's side. "Let's go, Miz Howard. We got a long ride ahead of us 'fore we're home."

"I am ready." Ingrid beamed at him, obviously relishing her new name.

Rand's dark brown eyes darted toward Bethany, and she knew he was wondering about her and Hawk. She forced another smile onto her face and another lie onto her lips. "Hawk and I will see you two soon. Now get going." Impulsively, she stood on tiptoe and kissed Rand's cheek. "You make her happy, you hear?"

"I plan on it, Bethany. I plan on keepin' her real happy."

Sometime during the following minutes, after the bride and groom had left and as the guests said their good-byes to the bride's foster parents, Hawk slipped away unnoticed. Then, suddenly, Bethany was standing alone in the parlor. She heard the front door close for the last time and waited for her parents to join her, steeling herself for their questions. As much as she dreaded it, it had to be faced.

"Oh my," Virginia sighed as she stepped into the parlor and sagged into the closest chair. "I'm exhausted."

Nathaniel patted her shoulder. "It was a wonderful wedding, my dear." Then her father turned his gaze upon Bethany. "I'm glad you haven't gone yet. I've scarcely had a chance to say hello. Where's Hawk? Out getting the buggy ready?"

"He's gone, Father," she answered in a small voice. To still the quiver, she lifted her chin and clenched her hands, calling upon her pride to bring her through just one more time.

"Gone?"

"I'm not going back to the ranch with him. I've left him."

"Bethany . . ." Her mother's voice was soft and worried.

"Will you let me come back to stay with you?"

Virginia and Nathaniel exchanged glances before her father spoke. "Bethany, you can't be serious. Are you sure this is what you want to do?"

Virginia rose from her chair and crossed the room to stand before her daughter. "You love him, Bethany." It was not a question but a statement of fact.

A sob caught in Bethany's throat.

Her mother's arms wrapped around her. "Oh, my darling. What has happened? Tell us."

"He doesn't want me," she replied hoarsely. "He just doesn't want me."

"But . . ."

More sobs punctuated her words. "I—I said some horrible things to him. Un—unforgivable things. He—he has a right to—to hate me."

She cried then, cried as she hadn't cried since that first morning after the wedding. Cried as she'd never cried before. Great racking sobs and a storm of tears.

When they were spent, she discovered she was sitting with her mother on the sofa, her face still nestled above the older woman's bosom, the fabric of Virginia's bodice soaked with tears. As she pulled away, still hiccupping, the reverend held out a handkerchief.

"Dry your eyes, Bethany Rachel." His voice was surprisingly stern. It was the tone he used from the pulpit when he warned his congregation of the dangers of sin.

She looked at her father as she swept away the tears and blew her nose, wondering if he were too ashamed of her to allow her to come back. It had never occurred to her he might disown her altogether. What would she do then?

"Now you listen to me, young lady. This is your home *if*—and I emphasize if, my dear—you truly need it. But I want you to think very hard about what you're doing. Your mother is right. You love Hawk Chandler. We've both seen it. I'd find it difficult to believe he's mistreated you."

"He hasn't," she interjected quickly.

"Marriage isn't something you try and then throw away if it isn't easy, my girl. And real love is a rare and precious thing. I don't know what's gone on between you two, and I don't think it's my business to know. But I *do* know my Bethany Rachel was never a quitter. She's always been a fighter. And I know one other thing about her. She's as stubborn as the day is long and has more pride than any ten people should have. Pride can be a lonely partner in life, Bethany." He paused for emphasis before asking, "Have you done everything you can, Bethany, to make him want you to stay?"

Her green eyes widened. No, she hadn't done everything. She'd never told him she was sorry for the ugly things she'd said. She'd never told him their fight was all her fault. She'd never told him she loved him and wanted to be his wife. She'd never told him there was nothing she wanted more than to bear his child.

Nathaniel saw the answer in her face, and his

own expression softened. "You go upstairs to your old room, Bethany. Stay for a few days and think things through. Then I'll take you home myself."

Home. Home to the Circle Blue.

The old determination returned. She wasn't beaten. It would work. It would. She would make him love her. Somehow, she would make it happen.

CHAPTER SEVENTEEN

Bethany spent the next four days pondering every moment since she'd met Hawk Chandler, doing her best to truly understand the man she'd married so she would know how to win his love. She couldn't just go back to the ranch and blurt out her love to him. She knew she had to *show* him, not just tell him. Words were too easily spoken. To find proof of that she only had to look at her own reckless tongue when she'd called him a savage and a fool.

On the morning of the fifth day, she awoke early. As she lay in bed, she remembered something Rand had said to her, something about Hawk and Chicago. He'd said it would help her to understand Hawk better. As much as she hated to intrude on the newlyweds, she was going up to see Rand and ask a few questions. And then she was going home.

She tossed the light coverlet aside and slid her feet to the floor, her gaze moving to rest on her trunk, waiting in the corner, never unpacked.

She smiled, feeling truly happy as she hadn't in weeks. She was going to see Hawk today.

Bethany took special care with her toilet. She brushed her hair until the auburn locks gleamed. Then, instead of the usual chignon, she fastened it high and allowed it to fall in a cascade of curls down the back of her neck, knowing Hawk liked it that way best. Tiny tendrils curled at her temples. She dabbed a lilac-scented cologne behind each ear and more on each wrist before turning to her wardrobe to choose a gown.

"Miss Bethany!" Griselda's frantic cry outside the door shattered her feeling of well-being.

"What is it?" She threw open the door, not bothering to pull a wrapper over her chemise and drawers.

"It's your mother. The reverend says to come at once."

Almost before the words were out of Griselda's mouth, Bethany was fairly flying down the hall and into her parents' bedroom. The reverend was holding his wife as she violently emptied her stomach into the wash basin.

Nathaniel looked up. His face was pale and drawn, his hazel eyes slightly feverish. "Get Doc Wilton, Bethany. Hurry."

"What—?"

"Hurry!"

Bethany spun away, racing back to her room. She pulled on the first dress her hand touched and was still fastening the buttons as she tore down the stairs and out the front door, her bare feet tossing up a cloud of dirt in her wake. She held her skirts high and ran as she hadn't since she was a child.

She burst into the apothecary. "Mr. Wilton," she gasped as the pharmacist looked up from behind his counter. "Where's the doctor?"

"Eberlie's. Called down there in the night and hasn't been back."

Bethany was gone before he could ask her what was wrong.

Bethany's heart was pounding in her ears when she reached the mercantile. She took the stairs at the side of the building two at a time, dragging in a ragged breath when she reached the landing. She pounded on the door and waited impatiently.

It was Doc Wilton himself who opened the door. There was something about the way he looked at her that made her think he wasn't surprised by her coming.

"Who's ill, Mrs. Chandler?" he asked.

"It's Mother. Please, come quick."

"What's wrong with her?"

"I—I don't know. She was vomiting when I went to her room. Father sent me for you."

She saw his shoulders sag. "I'll be there directly. Go back home. Give her plenty to drink. Make her drink even if she doesn't want to. Wait!" he called after her as she turned to hurry down the steps. "Boil all your drinking water first."

Bethany's eyes widened in question, but the doctor simply turned his back and disappeared into the Eberlies' home.

She was frightened more by what Doc Wilton hadn't said than by what he had, more by that

weary look in his eyes, almost like defeat before
he'd even seen his patient. Surely vomiting
wasn't that dangerous. Hadn't Bethany been sick
like that more than once while she was growing
up? Surely nothing was really wrong with her
mother.

Hiking up her skirts, she began running again.

Nathaniel gently rolled his wife back onto the
bed and covered her with a sheet. Then he
stooped to pick up the soiled bedding and carried it from the bedroom. His head ached and he
felt feverish, but he couldn't allow himself to fall
ill too. Not while Virginia needed him.

"Dear Father in heaven, help me," he whispered as he descended the stairs and turned
toward the kitchen. "Griselda?" he called, but
there was no reply. Rather than leave the soiled
linens in the kitchen, he carried them outside
and dropped them in a heap beside the step.
They could be washed later.

As he hurried back toward the stairway, he felt
a sudden cramp in his stomach and nearly
doubled over. Beads of sweat broke out on his
forehead. He grabbed for the back of a nearby
chair and held on tightly until the pain in his
belly had passed. A sour taste of bile rose in his
throat.

"Papa!" Bethany's cry preceded her into the
house. She came to an abrupt halt when she saw
him standing not far from the stairs. "The doctor says he'll be here directly," she panted.
"How's Mother?"

The reverend shook his head, still not certain he could speak.

"Doc Wilton says she's to drink lots of water, but I'm to boil it first. I'll do it now. Is Griselda in the kitchen?"

"I don't know," he answered.

For the first time, she seemed to really look at him. "Papa, are you all right?"

He nodded and began to climb the stairs. "Boil the water, Bethany. I must get back to your mother."

"It's cholera."

"Cholera?" Bethany echoed the doctor.

"And your father's ill too."

"Papa" She felt numb. She knew little about the disease, except it was feared and usually fatal.

"The Eberlies have it too. Both Fred and his daughter."

"But—?"

"Burn the sheets, Bethany. Handle any of their soiled things carefully. Destroy them. Wash your hands before touching any food. Cook all fruits and vegetables. Keep boiling all your water. Until we find what's caused it, we can't stop the cholera from spreading. And keep forcing them to drink. We've got to stop the dehydration if we can."

"But, Doc, I don't know—"

His voice was harsh. "Then you're going to learn, and quick. We may have us an epidemic on our hands."

She pressed the knuckles of one hand against her mouth and stared at him with wide, frightened eyes. Those were her parents in there. They couldn't have cholera. Not Nathaniel and Virginia Silverton.

"Find that maid of yours. You're going to need plenty of help." His voice softened a little as he reached out and gently touched her shoulder. "Pull yourself together, Bethany Chandler. We haven't time for hysterics now."

Bethany drew a deep breath and forced a nod. "I'll find Griselda," she whispered.

The older woman wasn't in the kitchen, nor was she outside anywhere that Bethany could see. At last, when there was nowhere else to look, she checked the servant's room. Griselda was in bed. The room smelled of sickness.

The reverend's house became a hospital, not just for the Silverton family and their maid, but for others too. Fred and Martha Eberlie were the first to sicken but not the first to die. The miller and his wife went first, followed by John Wilton's youngest son and one of Miss Olivia's girls.

Water boiled in kitchens up and down the main street of Sweetwater. Disinfectant fires filled the air with smoke, a smoke that grew worse when the source of the cholera was discovered. The miller's grainery had rats. The men burned the storage shed to the ground, along with the infected flour. But it was too late for many.

Bethany sat beside the bed and pressed the cup against her mother's lips. "Please, Mother," she encouraged her gently. "Please swallow just a little more water."

Her eyes were bleary from lack of sleep. She'd been awake for more than forty hours now. But the weariness was more than physical. It came from the heart as well. Griselda had died that morning. And as much as she longed to deny it, her mother would be gone before midnight.

Bethany wouldn't have recognized the woman in the bed as her mother if she hadn't cared for her through the agonizing hours of illness. Her eyes were sunken, her cheeks hollow. When Bethany touched her, her skin felt cold and was covered with a clammy sweat. The watery diarrhea persisted but the cramps had lessened somewhat in the past hour or so.

"Your father? How is he?" Virginia asked, her voice hoarse as it passed through the raw throat.

"He's better," Bethany lied, knowing the reverend wasn't far behind his wife. "He'll be in to see you soon."

"You must take care of him for me. He's never been alone, you know."

Bethany felt like crying but her eyes were dry and sandpapery. "Papa likes it ever so much better when you take care of him."

"But I won't be here, Bethany Rachel."

"Oh, Mama."

Virginia's hand lifted slightly off the bed to cover Bethany's. "You haven't called me that since you were a little girl. You always call me Mother. It sounds nice . . . Bethany."

"Mama," she said again, the tears suddenly coming.

"Be happy . . . Bethany." Virginia's eyes closed as she drifted a step closer to death.

Bethany bit her lower lip to keep from crying out. The tears fell silently as she stared at her mother's comatose form. It wouldn't be much longer now.

The bedroom door opened, admitting the doctor. "You'd better come, Bethany. I'll stay with your mother."

Bethany raised her mother's limp hand to her lips. "Good-bye, Mama," she whispered over a choked sob. Then she lay the hand gently at her mother's side and rose from her chair.

The walk across the hall seemed a mile long. Bethany paused just inside the door and stared at her father's still form on the bed, forcing back the agonizing wail that strained to escape. Nathaniel's appearance was much as his wife's had been. The dehydration and accompanying cyanosis made his face blue and pinched. The skin of his hands was drawn and puckered, and she knew if she touched him he would feel cold.

"Bethany?"

She realized he was looking at her, and she forced a wan smile. "Yes, Papa."

"Your mother?"

"She's nearly gone."

He nodded and turned his face toward the wall.

Bethany approached the bed and knelt on the floor, taking her father's hand between both of hers. She lifted the withered fingers to her tear-dampened cheeks. "Papa . . . I'm so afraid."

Nathaniel Silverton turned his head once more on his pillow. "We mustn't fear death, Bethany. Not if we are ready to meet our Maker. Your mother and I have served the Lord for many years. We have tried to follow His commandment, to love Him first, and then to love our neighbors. I do not regret leaving this world to live in His kingdom forever." His hazel eyes caressed her. "I will miss you, but your mother and I will see you again someday."

"I'm not a very good Christian, Papa," she confessed, the fear washing over her again as she watched him slipping further away. "Oh, Papa, however shall I survive without you?"

"Put your trust in the Lord, my child. Others will fail you. I've failed you. But Christ never will."

There was something in the way he spoke, something in his eyes that told her he was ready to leave this life for the next.

"Papa, please don't go!"

But even as she cried out, she knew all that remained was the shell of the man who had been her father. Nathaniel Silverton had gone home to his Master.

CHAPTER EIGHTEEN

·——·

It was the two buzzards circling in the gray-clouded sky that drew Hawk to the north. Cresting a ridge, he spied the lone, white-faced calf. It wasn't until he'd nearly reached it that Hawk saw the cow. She was lying nearby, her head and neck at a peculiar angle. The orphaned calf bolted a short distance away as Hawk rode closer, then it began to bawl. Hawk drew up his mount beside the dead cow. He was quick to find the cause of her death; he knew right where to look. There was a bullet hole in her forehead, just as there had been in each of the three cows he'd discovered over as many days.

Hawk's gaze swept the range as he silently cursed whoever was doing this. He knew it was only harassment at this point. Someone wanted him to find the cows. Someone wanted him to know what they were doing. Hawk just didn't know why or who.

He turned his attention to the calf even as he slipped his fingers around the lariat. He'd have to carry it back to the ranch house across his saddle. He hoped Storm would put up with it. The black stallion was still a bit green.

"Hawk!"

Hawk twisted in the saddle. Gabe Andrews, leaning low over the saddle, was madly galloping his horse toward his boss. Even from a distance, Hawk could see Gabe's horse was exhausted and heavy with sweat. He tensed. Only more bad news would cause his youngest cowhand to ride his horse so hard. Hawk jerked Storm's head around and rode to meet Gabe.

The young cowboy slid his horse to a stop, the animal's nose pointed skyward as it sat on its haunches. "Caleb sent me to find you," Gabe puffed as the dust settled around him. "He just got back from Sweetwater."

Hawk immediately thought of Bethany. "What's wrong?"

"They've got cholera. Caleb said he heard the reverend and his wife are dead and—"

Hawk's spurs dug into Storm's ribs. Startled by the unusual roughness, the stallion reared, then shot forward.

Cholera. The Silvertons dead. Bethany!

He rode the horse mercilessly toward the ranch, mindless of the heavy lather coating the black neck and underbelly, mindless of the sound of thundering hooves, mindless of anything save getting to Bethany.

He never should have let her go. He should have made her stay at the Circle Blue no matter what. If she died—

Caleb already had Flame saddled and waiting for him. Storm hadn't even stopped before

Hawk was vaulting from his back. He hit the ground running. His fingers closed around the pommel and he swung up onto the copper stallion even as Flame jumped into motion, sensing his master's urgency.

Hawk drove all thoughts from his mind. He wouldn't allow himself to think of what he might find in Sweetwater.

"She's going to make it, Mrs. Johnson," Doc Wilton said as he straightened from the little girl's bedside.

Mary's mother gasped and then sobbed as she bent to kiss her daughter's cheek. "Thank you, doctor. Thank you."

The doctor's eyes moved toward the weary young woman on the opposite side of the bed. "Why don't you get some rest, Bethany? The worst is over now."

Bethany nodded mutely. She glanced once again at the child. She was glad little Mary Johnson was going to live. By now Bethany knew children and the elderly were the easiest victims for this ugly disease. By now she knew far too much about cholera to suit her.

With a sigh, she turned and left the room. As she walked down the hallway and descended the stairs, she realized how silent the house had become. The patients who had survived had gone home now to be tended by their families. The remains of those who had died had been quickly burned. Only little Mary remained in the house, and soon she would be gone too. Then Bethany would be alone.

Alone.

The word echoed painfully in her heart, but she quickly snuffed it out. She wouldn't allow herself to feel it. She wouldn't allow herself to think about her parents. She willed the numb feeling to remain, protecting her from the realities she was still unready and unable to face.

At the foot of the stairs, she paused, as if uncertain what to do next. No one called to her. No one demanded attention. No one needed a drink. No one needed to die. No one needed Bethany. There was no one left.

The door crashed open before Hawk, and there she stood at the bottom of the stairs. Her head turned quickly toward him. Her eyes widened. Her mouth formed a little "O" in surprise. He stood still, framed in the doorway, drinking in the sight of her. She was alive. Pale and wan but alive.

"Hawk." Her voice was a mere whisper.

Quick strides carried him across the entry hall. "I came as soon as I heard."

"Hawk." The sound had become a whimper.

His arms reached to circle her, and she crumpled into them.

"I'm taking you home with me," he told her softly as he lifted her feet from the floor and cradled her head against his chest. "No arguments."

She made no response.

As he turned on his heel, he heard a sound at the top of the stairs and lifted his gaze. Doc

Wilton was watching him with dark-rimmed eyes, his face haggard.

"I'm taking Bethany back to the Circle Blue." His voice was stern, daring the doctor to tell him he couldn't.

"You go ahead, Hawk. She's done more than she should've had to. She's a strong girl, that wife of yours. Fine lady, too." The doctor turned away, his voice trailing after him. "Fine lady."

Hawk glanced down at Bethany. She was sleeping, the victim of exhaustion. She seemed to weigh no more than a feather. There wasn't even a promise of color in her cheeks, and her eyes were sunken behind dark shadows. Instinctively, his mouth lowered to brush across her forehead as an invisible hand squeezed painfully around his heart.

Once on the trail, he rode slowly, resting his mount and giving himself more time to hold his wife against him. He didn't know how long she would be willing to remain with him. He wasn't fooling himself. She had lost both her parents. She was alone in the world. He had come when she was vulnerable, and she had turned to him in her despair. When she was stronger, she would leave once again. Reverend and Mrs. Silverton's deaths didn't change the facts. He was still a savage and Bethany was still a lady.

She slept around the clock, unaware that her husband held her in his arms throughout the night. It was the deep, dreamless, untroubled sleep of one whose body had reached its limit. On through the next day she slept, Hawk at her bedside, watching her sleep, his own eyes bleary.

It was night once again when she awoke. It was like climbing out of a long tunnel, her trek back to consciousness. First there was the sensation of floating, and she wondered, *Am I dead, too*? She was lying down. Was this, perhaps, her casket?

With effort, she forced open her eyes. It was dark. Terribly dark. A spark of fear shot through her. She gasped and tried to sit up, but she couldn't. Something held her captive. Terror rose in her throat, but before the scream reached her lips, she heard his soft whisper.

"It's me, Bethany. You're safe now."

There was a moment's hesitation, a sense of disbelief. "Hawk?" And then the tears began, tears accompanied by great, racking sobs.

His arms tightened around her as he pulled her head against the expanse of his chest. His hand stroked her hair. But she was scarcely aware of the comfort he offered. She was embroiled in a multitude of ugly memories, memories she longed to forget. Her parents were gone. Dead. Never again would she hear her father's words of wisdom or her mother's words of love. She was alone. So utterly, terribly alone.

Bethany raised a hand to Hawk's neck, lacing her fingers through the shaggy black hair at his nape. Instinctively, her arm tightened, pulling him closer to her, hanging on lest he be snatched from her too. She felt him mouthing words against her hair, and slowly, her sobbing began to still.

Finally, she spoke aloud the truth she had fought to avoid. "They . . . they're dead. Both of them."

"I'm sorry, Bethany. I wish—"

"Hawk, I'm so afraid." She tilted her head back, turning her face toward his in the darkness. "I'm all alone and so afraid."

He kissed her forehead. "Shhh. Don't be afraid, Bethany." He kissed her cheek. "You're not alone."

For a long time—perhaps hours—they lay within the other's arms, Hawk's hands stroking her hair and back, Bethany clinging to him for all she was worth, the tears coming and going, like the rising and ebbing tide.

Sometime in the darkness, Bethany's response to his caresses changed. She could no longer lie passively beside him. She knew too great a need, a tremendous longing to escape the blackness, the emptiness that surrounded her, invaded her, held her prisoner. She wanted to touch life. She wanted to escape death. She wanted to feel love.

She pressed herself against the hard length of Hawk's body, her hands tangled in his hair. Her mouth sought and found his. At the touch of his lips, a raging fire flashed through her veins, sending her whirling in a flood of light. She closed her eyes as his tongue danced with hers, giving herself up to the cascading sensations he sparked within. Her skin tingled. Her loins burned.

When he tried once to pull away, she protested. "No, Hawk. Don't leave me. Please don't leave me." She heard his soft groan as his arms embraced her once again.

There was no need for patience or gentleness. She wanted to hold his naked body against her. She wanted to be joined with him and feel his life filling her. In unison, they shed the night-clothes they wore and came together again, heated bodies touching, arms and legs entangled, mouths searching and exploring. There was no time for thought or reason. This was a time to feel, to soar. It mattered not what had happened yesterday or what would happen tomorrow. This was now, a moment in time meant only for the two of them. And with abandon, Bethany gave herself over to a raging torrent of emotions, giving him back measure for measure.

Throughout the long hours of that night, they shared a desperate passion—Bethany seeking to feel life, and Hawk seeking to give it to her.

With the harsh light of dawn, Hawk considered what he'd done and cursed himself for the fool he was. When he'd carried her home, he'd acknowledged the differences that still separated them, yet at the moment she was most vulnerable, he had taken advantage of her, trying to assuage her loneliness and fear with his body instead of with the comfort of understanding words. He should have pulled away. He should have waited until her reason returned. Hadn't he also lost both his parents? Didn't he understand the way she felt? It wasn't Hawk she'd wanted. It was to forget all she'd been through. He should have known better than to give in to his desire, but it was too late now.

He was waiting for her in the kitchen when she came hesitantly out of the bedroom. She had fastened her long auburn tresses up on her head as best she could with the few pins he had left beside the bed. His chest constricted at the sight of the dark circles still lingering beneath her eyes.

Hawk rose and pulled out a chair for her. She glanced quickly up at him, then dropped her gaze as she sat down. She clasped her hands tightly in the folds of her gown. Hawk cleared his throat and sat down again.

They began in unison.

"Bethany—"

"Hawk—"

"Go ahead."

She shook her head without looking at him. "No. Please. You first."

Silently, he agreed. It was just as well he said what was on his mind and got it over with. "Bethany . . . I'm sorry about last night. I never should have . . . Well, it wasn't right, and I'm sorry. I want you to know I don't expect you to stay here."

"Not stay? But where—?" If possible, her face grew even paler.

"I know you won't want to go back to your— to the house in town. You said once before you might return to your family in Philadelphia. I'll see you get safely back to them. I'll take care of all the arrangements. You needn't worry about that."

"I see."

"Once you're settled, you can let me know what you want done with . . . with everything here." He paused and swallowed, then pushed onward with grim determination. He wanted it all said and done with. "Eventually I suppose you'll want a divorce. I'll do whatever I can to help. I mean, I won't fight you. You've a right to make a new life for yourself, once you're ready."

Bethany's chin lifted a fraction. Her sea-mist green eyes rose to meet his. "You've given this a lot of thought, haven't you?"

"Yes."

"Very well, Hawk. I'll leave on the first available stage." She stood abruptly and turned her back toward him.

"Bethany?"

"Yes?"

But what was there left to say? He couldn't ask her to stay. He could never make up for the mistakes he'd made. *All* the mistakes he'd made. It was better to end it all now, once and for all.

"Nothing, Bethany."

She didn't move for the longest time. Then her head turned slowly until at last their gazes met once more. The lost, wounded look in those misty green eyes would haunt him for weeks to come.

•

CHAPTER NINETEEN

Ordinarily, I wouldn't think of having a ball at such a time, but what was I to do? You know Harvey and I have been hosting our Harvest Moon Ball for years. Invitations went out weeks before I learned about Cousin Nathaniel. Well, I do hope you understand, my dear."

Bethany stared out the bedroom window at the expanse of green lawn behind the Worthington home. "It's all right, Cousin Beatrice. I truly do understand." It was difficult to care much about anything anymore.

Beatrice's chubby hand alighted on Bethany's shoulder. "I wish there was something I could say or do to make it easier, Bethany. It breaks my heart to see you so sad."

"I'll be fine," she whispered, swallowing the tears that always seemed to be threatening. She turned from the window, tilting up her chin. "Now, please stop fussing. You'll have guests arriving in no time at all, and you're not even dressed for the evening."

Beatrice glanced at her elegant dressing gown. Her round cheeks blanched. "Oh my! I'd forgotten. Dear me, where has the time gone?" With that, she rushed out of the bedroom.

Bethany let out a long sigh as her father's cousin disappeared. Then she walked across the room and firmly closed the door. Turning, she leaned her back against it. She'd almost forgotten just how wearing Beatrice Worthington could be. The portly matron never seemed to cease moving or talking. And her husband, Harvard Worthington, was cut from the same cloth. The pair of them were pillars of Philadelphia society, always in the midst of every social function of any note. But for all the bustle and bluster and ceaseless activity, Beatrice and Harvey had good hearts. They cared genuinely about Bethany and grieved with her over her loss.

She allowed her gaze to move idly around the large bedroom which was now hers. *Too large*, she thought as her mind brought up images of a much smaller bedroom in the two-story house in Sweetwater, followed by the memory of an even smaller bedroom in a log cabin to the west of town.

"No!" she whispered angrily. "I won't think about *him* anymore. Not today. Not anymore today."

Lifting her chin another notch, Bethany pushed away from the door and hurried toward the dressing table. She swept her black taffeta skirt to the side and sat down on the stool, then turned her eyes to the mirror. Her cheeks still looked pale and hollow. She'd lost even more weight since coming to Philadelphia. She had no appetite and she was so often tired.

"I feel so very old," she told her reflection. "I'm only eighteen and I feel one hundred."

What you need is some fun. Why don't you go to the ball?

Go to the ball? She couldn't. Her parents were scarcely dead a month. What would people think?

What does it matter what other people think? You know you loved them. You know you miss them. You don't need to hide away to prove your broken heart. Even Papa had said some conventions were for show and didn't necessarily mirror a person's heart.

But it wouldn't be seemly.

What do you care? You'll be a scandalous divorcee before long. She winced at that thought. *People expect divorcees to act unseemly.*

But was her cousin's ball the place to thwart convention, to begin her "unseemly" escapades? After Cousin Beatrice had been so kind to her, was this how she would show her thanks?

Why not tonight? You have to start living again sometime. Why not tonight?

"Yes. Why not?" she said aloud, the sound of her voice bolstering her courage and determination. "I want to feel alive again. Papa would understand."

And Beatrice would forgive her. Perhaps not tonight, but she would forgive her. And if she didn't, Bethany didn't have to remain in her home. She had her inheritance. She could live wherever she chose.

Anywhere but where you want to live.

A vision of the Circle Blue intruded on her reflections, a vision that fairly shouted, "This is where you belong."

"No!" Her hand slapped down against the dressing table, surprising even Bethany, the impact stinging her palm.

It was painful enough thinking about her parents. She couldn't bear to think about him too. She *wouldn't* think about him. She would do anything to wipe Hawk Chandler from her mind, tear him from her heart. He'd rejected her once too often, one final, terrible time. If she must anger every person in the city of Philadelphia by her flouting of social customs in order to rid herself of her heartbreaking memories, then so be it.

Bethany jumped up from the stool and hurried to her wardrobe. A quick look through the dozen or more mourning gowns found just what she wanted. The black satin was simply cut, modest and proper, yet somehow quite elegant and perfect for a ball. Hastily, she pulled it out and tossed it across the bed, then turned to the jewelry case atop the dresser. She found the lustrous choker of gray pearls and matching earrings and lifted them from the velvet-lined case. Yes, they would do just fine.

With a glance at the mantle clock that announced the growing lateness of the hour, Bethany shed her black taffeta and replaced it with the glossy satin gown. For a moment, she considered sending for Beatrice's maid to dress her hair, then discarded the idea. Rose would go right from this room to Beatrice if she knew what Bethany was planning.

Bethany seated herself once again before the dressing table mirror and began the tedious task of working the auburn mass of hair into an obedient twist. Finished at last, she eyed her work. Something more was needed. Something . . . She knew just what it was. Rising quickly, she went to a hat box on the floor of the closet and lifted off the lid. But she didn't pull out the hat which lay inside. Instead, she plucked the long black feather from the brim and carried it back to the mirror. It only took a moment to weave the quill into her hair and secure it with a few more pins.

"Done," she muttered, then drew a deep breath.

She wondered if she really had the nerve to show herself at the Harvest Moon Ball when propriety said she must hide away for months to come. Staring at her reflection, the first hint of a smile in weeks curved the corners of her mouth.

Yes, she had the nerve. As her father had said more than once, Bethany Rachel was nothing if not stubborn.

Vince Richards stepped into the brightly lit entry hall, his gray eyes quickly assessing the stately grandeur of the Worthington mansion. Every inch, every corner spoke of generations of wealth and influence. Someday, many years from now, he meant for someone to think the same thing when he stepped into the Richards family home in Montana.

"Senator! How wonderful to see you. We were afraid you wouldn't make it down from Washington."

"And miss your ball, Beatrice? Perish the thought." Senator Wright bowed toward his hostess, his long white mustache brushing her hand before his lips could do the same. When he straightened, he stepped aside and glanced back at Vince. "I hope you don't mind, my dear. I've brought a friend with me from Washington. Vince Richards, may I present our charming hostess, Beatrice Worthington, and her husband, Harvard."

Vince acknowledged the introductions as his mind carefully recalled bits of information the senator had told him about the Worthingtons. Despite his unassuming looks and stature, the jovial, rotund man before him—known to one and all as Harvey—had a lot of clout with men in places of power. Vince would do well to make a friend of him.

Following the senator, he moved on into the house. The strains of a waltz floated out to meet them as they made their way toward the ballroom. Along the way, Morris Wright repeatedly introduced Vince, and between introductions, the senator filled in helpful details about the other guests.

He smiled secretly, pleased that he had accepted the senator's invitation to accompany him to Philadelphia. This night was shaping up to be well worth the trip.

A half an hour later, the ballroom was a swirling mass of dancers. Vince was talking with a Philadelphia banker, the two of them standing near the patio windows which were thrown open to catch the slightest of late September breezes. As the music ended, Vince chanced to let his eyes wander from his new acquaintance to the doorway of the ballroom.

It was just then she appeared, her head held high in a regal, challenging pose. At first, he couldn't believe it was her. It had to be someone who just looked like her. But no. There couldn't be two Bethany Silvertons.

"Excuse me," he muttered to the banker and moved closer to the door.

She was clad in a gown of black, the only relief a string of gray pearls around her long white throat. But she was as beautiful in black as she'd been in pastels. He paused near a column and perused her. She was thinner than he remembered. And she looked older, more mature. There was something different about her.

Black. Good heavens! Could she be in mourning?

Vince couldn't stop the smile from tweaking his pencil-thin mustache. So the Mexican had killed Chandler after all. He would have to give Montoya a bonus. Bethany made a beautiful widow.

Bethany could hardly breathe. She felt as if a thousand pairs of eyes were staring at her, judging her, and finding her wanting of any social breeding or manners. She resisted the urge to bolt toward the stairs and the safety of her room. As usual, her impetuous nature had made her act hastily, bringing her—as it often did—to the brink of disaster. But she was intent on seeing this evening through. She would not run and hide, no matter what people thought of her.

She let her gaze move slowly over the room, keeping her eyes fixed just above people's heads. The massive ballroom was lined on two walls with gilded mirrors which reached from the glistening tile floor to the high ceiling above. A third wall was covered with life-size figures of waltzing couples, the artwork so wonderfully real a person had to look hard to know it was just an enormous painting. The fourth wall, at the rear of the ballroom, had two sets of French doors which opened onto a stone patio, a patio nearly as large as the ballroom itself. The patio was lined on all three sides with tall evergreens. Beyond it were the extravagant gardens of Worthington Manor.

"Why, Bethany, dear. I had no idea you intended to come to our ball." Beatrice, a sparkling tiara in her silver-gray hair, appeared out of the crowd to take her arm. "Look, Harvey. Bethany feels well enough to join us. Isn't it wonderful?"

Bethany would have kissed her cousin if they'd been alone, but for now, a smile would have to do.

Beatrice drew her toward a cluster of guests. "Look, everyone. Our dear cousin has come down to join us. Peter, you remember Bethany, don't you?"

She was surprised by the warmth with which

she was welcomed. Although some might have been appalled by her appearance at such a gala festivity, no one displayed their feelings openly toward her. (In truth, they probably wouldn't have dared in front of Beatrice Worthington.) Most had kinds words of sympathy to share with Bethany regarding her parents' deaths, and a few reminded her of happier times they had shared with the reverend and his wife.

For a brief time, she nearly forgot the loneliness that had driven her to the ball. For a time, she forgot Hawk and the way his memory crept into each and every thought. But finally she wearied of the sympathetic attention. The ballroom was too crowded, too noisy. A terrible longing for wide open spaces and the vast blue skies of Montana filled her. A longing for the simplicity of a log cabin and a swim in a mountain pool. A longing for . . .

She slipped away from the chattering people around her and worked her way toward the French doors and the dark solitude of the September night outside. But the light from the brightly lit ballroom spilled through the doors onto the stone patio and the noise spilled with it. Almost in flight now, she hurried across the patio and down the steps, then followed the pathway into the garden until she reached the fountain at its center.

Bethany sank onto a stone bench and closed her eyes, breathing deeply until the rapid pace of her heart began to slow. At last, feeling calm once again, she raised her eyes toward the starry heavens, looking like a black velvet cloth sprinkled with tiny diamonds. There were so many, all so bright. They dispelled the feeling of darkness, turning the gardens into a frosty wonderland.

Could Hawk be looking up at this same sky?

She squeezed her eyes shut again, angry at herself for allowing him to return to her thoughts so easily.

"You're a twit," she scolded beneath her breath. "A silly twit. And you'd better learn to forget him."

It was then she heard a man's voice at her shoulder.

"To think, I traveled all the way from Montana only to find you again. Good evening, Mrs. Chandler."

Her green eyes widened in surprise as she turned to look at Vince Richards, standing so close beside her.

He grinned. "Surprised to see me? No more, I trust, than I was to see you."

"I—I thought you were in Washington."

"I was. But fate has brought me here tonight." Another waltz began to play. "Would you dance with me, Bethany?" His hand lightly brushed her back.

She stepped away from him. "I'm sorry, Mr. Richards, but I'm not dancing tonight. As you can see, I'm in mourning."

"It's I who am sorry." His expression did, indeed, look apologetic. "You looked so beautiful, I didn't even notice you were wearing black. What happened to Hawk? Or is it too cruel of me to ask?"

Bethany felt a tiny sting in her heart and, in response, lifted her chin to give herself courage. "Hawk is fine, Mr. Richards. It's my parents who are gone. Along with many others in Sweetwater. There was an outbreak of cholera."

Vince was left obviously speechless by the news.

"I couldn't bear to stay in Sweetwater, so I came to stay with my cousin." All of Philadelphia would someday know she had left her husband, but she wasn't about to tell Vince so. She remembered too well the way he'd kept insisting she would be his wife one day.

"Your cousin?" He glanced toward the ballroom. "Do I know him? Or her?"

"I'm sure you must. She's your hostess."

It was another surprise for Vince. His dark brown eyebrows shot up, one slightly higher than the other. "Hostess! You don't mean Beatrice Worthington is your cousin?"

Bethany nodded.

"Well I'll be . . ."

Bethany took another step backward, then glanced around. "If you'll excuse me, Mr. Richards, I'm suddenly feeling very tired and must say good-night. I hope you have a pleasant trip back to Washington."

Quickly, she turned away and made her retreat from the ballroom and everyone in it.

Chapter Twenty

Hawk strapped the Peacemaker to his hip. His face was chiseled in harsh, angry lines.

"Let me go with you," Rand said for the third time in the past ten minutes.

"No. I need you to look after things here."

"Whoever's behind this ain't goin' to play fair, Hawk. He's lookin' for trouble."

Hawk turned a hard blue gaze on his friend. His voice was dangerously low as he replied, "So am I."

Rand tapped his dusty cowboy hat against his thigh twice, a frown drawing his brows close together. He stared at the tips of his boots. When he lifted his gaze toward Hawk once again, his brown eyes admitted defeat even while he mouthed the continued protest. "You oughta wait for the law to handle it."

"What law? Since Sheriff Cook's daughter died of cholera, he hasn't done a thing but sit in his office and nurse whiskey. And I'm not going to sit by and have my hands shot down one by one like my cattle."

"Okay, Hawk. But take Caleb or Rusty with you if you won't take me."

"I'm going alone." With that, Hawk grabbed the pommel and swung into the saddle.

Rand stepped back and watched as Hawk rode away. He had a bad feeling about this.

Ever since he'd put Bethany on the stage for Miles City, Hawk had been moody and out of sorts. He wasn't in the right frame of mind to be tracking down a gunman. And Rand didn't doubt for a moment the fellow Hawk was hunting was a hired gun. Everything that had been happening with the cattle and now Westy pointed to it. First rustle a few cattle, then kill a few more, and finally, pick off some of the cowhands. Just keep making everyone look over their shoulder all the time. Make 'em wonder if they're next.

"Rand?"

He turned at the sound of Ingrid's voice just as her light touch settled on his shoulder.

"You could not stop him from going?"

He shook his head. "Nope."

Her pale blue eyes turned in the direction of Hawk's departure. "He will return."

"I hope so, Ingrid."

"I know it. He must be here when Bethany comes back."

Rand gave a half chuckle as he settled his hat over his hair, pushing it back on his forehead. "What makes you so sure she's comin' back?"

"She will come. She loves him."

"I hope you're right about that, too, Ingrid. He sure could use that gal about now."

* * *

Hawk stopped his horse and eased out of the saddle. Hunkering down, he ran his fingers lightly over the ground. The man was leaving a clear trail. Either he wasn't very smart or he was leading Hawk into a trap. He was pretty sure it was the latter.

Sitting on his heels, he lifted his gaze and scanned the range to the east, then swept up the mountainside to the west. His black mood deepened. If he hadn't been so caught up in his own self-pity these past weeks, maybe things wouldn't have gone this far. He should have been out tracking this man down when all he'd been shooting were Circle Blue cattle. It was a miracle Westy hadn't been killed. Only chance had caused him to move at the right moment, causing the bullet to pass through his shoulder instead of his heart.

Another thought plagued Hawk. Who was this man and why was he taking vengeance on the Circle Blue? His first suspect was always Vince Richards, but he'd been in Washington for over a month now. Still, this was just the kind of dirty work Vince would have a hand in. But there was no proof, nothing to hang Vince with. If Hawk were to put a stop to this sort of thing, he needed to catch this man and wring a confession from him, find out who was paying him to kill Circle Blue cattle and men.

Hawk straightened and reached for his canteen. With a quick swallow, he slaked his thirst, then swung up into the saddle again. He wiped an arm across his forehead before pulling his hat brim lower to shade his eyes from the glaring September sun.

It seemed he had little choice. He could follow the trail and take his chances, or he could let the would-be assassin get away scot-free. There really wasn't any choice. He had to find him.

Bethany was alone in the sitting room. She had been staring out the window, unseeing, for over an hour. She held a black fan in one hand and slowly moved it, creating only a slight relief from the humid heat of the afternoon.

"Excuse me, Mrs. Chandler. There's a Mr. Richards here to see you."

"What?" Drawing back to reality, she turned to look at the housekeeper with a bemused stare.

"A Mr. Richards, ma'am. He says he's a friend of yours from Montana."

She was about to tell Chloris to send him away, to tell him she wasn't receiving visitors, when he stepped into the sitting room.

"I'm sorry to intrude, Bethany, but I wanted to see you before the senator and I return to Washington."

Bethany's irritation dissolved as she watched Chloris redden with indignation. Bethany had no doubt that, at a word from her, the huskily built woman would toss Mr. Richards out onto his ear. She was tempted to see it happen, but her mother's strict training in good manners kept her from doing so.

"It's all right, Chloris. Mr. Richards may stay. Please bring us some tea."

"Yes, ma'am," the housekeeper grumbled as she stepped around Vince and disappeared from view.

Bethany closed her fan and motioned with it toward a chair. "Do sit down, Mr. Richards."

"Thank you, Bethany." However, as he spoke, he settled himself into a closer chair than the one she'd indicated. "You look beautiful today, as always."

She made no reply, only returned his gaze with one of indifference. She hadn't liked Vince when she'd met him in Sweetwater, and she liked him even less in Philadelphia. She felt more vulnerable here without her father, without . . .

"Bethany, I'm afraid I was so stunned by the news the other night, I failed to properly express my condolences on the death of your parents. The reverend was a fine man, and I considered him my friend. And your mother was a lovely woman, always so very kindhearted and considerate."

"Thank you, Mr. Richards."

"I wish you'd allow yourself to call me Vince."

Again she remained silent.

"My dear, I'm afraid it's no secret you are here because you've left that husband of yours. But you needn't worry. A careful word or two to the right people, and we can have the marriage dissolved in no time. People will understand why you couldn't stay with him once you'd learned the truth about his—well, shall we say, his less than upstanding family background. Society will forgive you. You are young, and the young can be foolish sometimes. Divorce needn't be a stigma if it's handled properly. I will help in any way I can."

Bethany stiffened and her eyes flashed twin daggers. "Mr. Richards, I have no intention of discussing Hawk or our marriage with you. It is no one's business but ours what goes on between us, least of all yours."

"You're wrong," he replied, his voice sugary sweet as he leaned toward her, so close she could feel the warmth of his breath. "It's very much my business, since I intend to be your next husband. I won't hold it against you that you've lain with that redskin. I'll rid you of the memory of his touch. I'll make you clean again."

Her hand shot forward. The stinging crack echoed through the sitting room. Instantly, she was on her feet. "How dare you! You're not fit to lick an Indian's moccasins, let alone speak so of my husband. Get out!"

He rose slowly from his chair as he lifted a hand to gingerly touch the red mark on his cheek. His gray eyes were icy cold with restrained rage. "You'll regret you did that, Bethany, but it won't change the facts. You *will* be my wife."

"Never! Not even if I had to choose death instead."

Vince stared at her for an interminable time. Lust and hatred warred in his eyes, a look that frightened her beyond her anger. In a gesture of self protection, she raised her hands to her chest as she side-stepped around her chair.

With deliberate slowness, Vince placed his hat on his head, his gaze never leaving her. "Good day, Bethany. We shall see each other again.

Soon, I think." He touched the hand-shaped red mark on his cheek once again. "Yes, very soon."

He passed Chloris as he left the room. The housekeeper glanced at him, then looked toward Bethany. One look at the young mistress's face, and she set the tea tray on the nearest table and hurried across the sitting room.

"Are you all right, Mrs. Chandler?" Her arm went around Bethany's back as she urged the younger woman toward a chair.

Bethany drew a deep breath. "Yes," she whispered. Then stronger, "Yes. I'm fine, now that he's gone."

"Let me get you that tea, ma'am."

When Chloris returned, Bethany looked at her as she accepted the cup. "Chloris, don't ever let that man into this house again. Please."

"Not a chance of that, Mrs. Chandler. I didn't like the looks of him the moment I set eyes on him."

Suddenly, a sharp pain shot through Bethany's temple. The china cup and saucer clattered to the floor as her hand flew to the left side of her head. Tiny black specks clouded her vision. Her ears rang, and she felt the room spinning away from her.

"Hawk!" she whispered, and then fainted.

Hawk hit the ground and rolled into the brush, even as he drew his Colt from its holster. For a moment, he felt blackness threatening to overwhelm him. He raised his fingers to his left temple and felt the warm blood flowing where the bullet had grazed him. He clenched his jaw and shook his head in an effort to clear his vision.

He'd been lucky, just as Westy had been. He didn't dare allow himself to think this man was just a poor shot. If he hadn't felt the saddle slip, if he hadn't suddenly leaned forward to check the latigo and cinch, he would be lying dead beside his horse.

Hawk drew back farther into the thicket beside the mountain stream. He listened for any sound that didn't belong, for any hint the gunman approached. Except for the gurgling creek behind him, the forest was silent. No birds sang, no squirrels chattered. Even the mountain seemed to be holding its breath, waiting out the life-or-death drama.

Hawk's dark blue gaze scanned the mountainside above him. The shot must have come from that thick grove of trees. For the moment, the gunman had the advantage. Hawk couldn't move away from his cover without being an easy target. But night was coming fast, and then the advantage would be his. He knew this area as well by night as he did by day. He doubted his assailant could say the same.

He settled in to wait, his eyes shifting, watching, always wary. With his free hand, he once again touched the side of his head. Already the blood had slowed and thickened. Once again, he realized how lucky he'd been. But if he'd been paying closer attention, even this wouldn't have happened. He would have realized he'd reached the logical place for the man to attack. But he hadn't been paying attention. With the monotonous sway of the saddle, he'd allowed his thoughts to stray where they so often strayed. To Bethany.

He'd pictured her again as he'd last seen her, standing beside the stagecoach. She was wearing that pink dress of hers he liked so much and holding up the parasol to shade her creamy complexion from the sun. A few stray wisps of auburn hair curled at her nape. Only briefly had she allowed her eyes to meet his, eyes void of feelings or emotions, yet eyes that accused him of failing her when she'd needed him most.

Damn! He shook off the recurring memory. *She'll be the death of me yet.*

The faint snap of a twig was his only warning. He rolled and fired, instinct rather than sight guiding his aim.

The short, stout Mexican looked at him in surprise. His gun wavered a moment as he tried to fire in return, then it dropped to the ground. A ragged gasp rattled in the Mexican's throat before he toppled face down into the stream.

Hawk jumped quickly to his feet and scrambled through the water to pull the man out, still hoping the Mexican was only wounded. He needed to take him alive. Hawk needed to find out why he'd been killing Circle Blue cattle and why he'd tried to kill Hawk.

Grabbing the man by his boots, he dragged him onto the bank and rolled him over. Blank black eyes stared up at the sky. He was dead, and any hope for information had died with him. Grimly, Hawk picked up the body and carried him toward his horse.

He was walking toward her, shirtless, his blue denims riding his hips in a provocative manner. His blue-black hair waved in the breeze above a face hidden in shadows. She felt her pulse quicken. Her breath caught in her throat. He was coming for her. He was coming for her. . . .

Bethany jerked her head away from the vial of smelling salts, protesting the pull back to consciousness. But try as she might, her vision of Hawk wouldn't return.

"Mrs. Chandler?" Chloris's worried voice drifted to her ears. "Mrs. Chandler?"

With a hand, she waved away the smelling salts. "I'm all right, Chloris," she grumbled, forcing her eyes open.

"You fainted, ma'am. And nearly hit your head on the table, too. Are you sure you're all right?"

"Yes." She pushed herself up from the floor and leaned her back against the sofa. A slight ringing remained in her ears, but slowly, even that faded. She tentatively touched her left temple, recalling how sharp the pain had seemed and how certain she'd been that Hawk was feeling it too.

"Here, Mrs. Chandler. Let me help you up." Chloris's hand gripped Bethany's elbow as she drew her up from the floor and settled her onto the couch.

Bethany looked at the housekeeper. "I've never fainted in my life."

"Maybe I'd best get Mrs. Worthington and have her send for the doctor."

"Nonsense." Her voice was firm once again. The weakness had passed. "But I would like more tea. I promise not to spill it this time."

"As if that mattered," Chloris mumbled as she left the room.

Bethany rose from the sofa and walked across the sitting room to the large window facing the street. Tall trees shaded the front of the house, creating a leafy canopy. Her gaze moved idly up the street, pausing to study the elegant, stately mansions, each of them filled with proper, elegant people.

The thought came to her slowly, so subtle she nearly missed it. Once she had belonged here. Once she had been one of them. But no more. She belonged in Montana. She belonged with Hawk.

"I'm going to go home," she whispered to the world outdoors, her eyes widening as excitement welled in her breast.

Proud and stubborn, her father had called her. And she recalled something else he'd said to her. *Pride can be a lonely partner in life, Bethany.* She could hear the loving inflection in his voice. She could see the wisdom in his eyes.

Pride had driven her from the Circle Blue. She knew that now. Her own willful pride. Too proud to tell him she wanted to stay and try to work things out. Too proud to stay and teach him to love her the way she loved him. Well, she didn't mean to live alone with her pride. She was at least as stubborn as she was proud.

Stubborn as a mule, Nathaniel used to say with a teasing grin, *but nicer to look at.*

She was going home. She was going to make him love her, no matter what she had to do. Oh, it wasn't going to be easy. She knew she wasn't going to change overnight. She'd keep on stumbling over her own pride. But she would keep trying until she'd won his love. Pride was a terrible thing to have to swallow, she realized, but somehow she would manage it.

Her jaw set with determination, she whirled away from the window, ready to begin her packing. She had taken only a few steps when Beatrice scurried into the room.

"Dear heavens, Bethany. Chloris just told me what happened. Whatever are you doing on your feet, my dear? Sit down. Sit down."

"Cousin Beatrice, I'm fine. I just—"

"Sit down, I said."

"Really, I don't . . ." Her voice died in her throat. Then, with a resigned sigh, she obeyed.

Beatrice sat beside her. "Chloris said you didn't want the doctor. Are you sure I shouldn't send for him? He's a very competent man."

"It was just the heat, Cousin Beatrice. That's all. I'm perfectly fine now."

"Well," Beatrice said skeptically, her hazel eyes studying the younger woman. "You do have some color in your cheeks. I suppose . . ."

Bethany wondered how she was going to tell her cousin she was leaving. She had grown so very fond of Beatrice, had come to think of her as a friend, not just family. Beatrice and Harvey had welcomed her into their home with open arms, had comforted and sheltered her throughout the past difficult weeks.

"Fainting is such a bother for some women. Your mother, bless her soul, was a fainter. She was so strong in so many ways, but she was prone to swooning now and again."

"Mother? I never saw her faint."

"Oh my, yes. I remember one time . . . . How long ago was that now? She frightened me nearly half to death. I know what it was. It was when she was expecting you. She fainted right out in the middle of the street while we were out shopping, just the two of us. Created quite a spectacle, I'll tell you. Now I've never fainted a day in my life. Not even when I was pregnant."

"You were pregnant, Cousin Beatrice? But I thought—"

"Oh, I never carried a baby to term. There are five little Worthingtons waiting in heaven for me. Boys, every one of them."

"I didn't know."

"Of course you didn't. My goodness, that was years ago. The youngest would have been just about your age. Virginia and I found out we were expecting just about the same time. She used to come over and pray for me that I would be able to keep that baby. But it wasn't to be. I lost him in my seventh month."

"I'm so sorry."

Beatrice leaned forward and patted the younger woman's hand. "Don't be. Who's to say why things happen? We know so little, Bethany, in terms of eternity. And my life with Harvey has been very full, very blessed."

It was Bethany's turn to lean forward, kissing her cousin's cheek.

"Oh my! It won't do to get me in a state, my dear. I become quite hopeless once I've begun." Beatrice sniffed back the threatening tears.

Yes, it was going to be difficult to tell Beatrice she was leaving. For a moment, while her cousin was telling about her pregnancies, Bethany had been distracted from her earlier decision, but once she'd mentioned the full life she'd had with Harvey, Bethany's thoughts had returned instantly to Hawk.

"Cousin Beatrice, there's something I must tell you."

"My, you sound serious, child."

"I'm going back to Montana."

Instead of the argument and protests Bethany had expected, a satisfied expression covered Beatrice's plump face. "And it's about time, too. I wondered when you were going to come to your senses and go back to that man you so obviously love."

Speechless, Bethany stared with rounded eyes.

"When do we leave?"

"We?"

"Of course, we. I've been dying to see what drew your father to the west. Virginia always wrote such glowing letters. And if that's where you're going to make your home, now seems to be the right time. Besides, I can't allow a young woman to travel alone across the country, now can I?" She reached forward and took hold of Bethany's hand, her quick chatter ceasing as her expression grew serious. "You won't mind me coming, will you, dear? From what you've told me about this Hawk Chandler of yours, your task may not be an easy one. You may need my company, if only for a short while."

"Of course I don't mind, Cousin Beatrice. I think I would like your company very much."

"Then it's settled. We'll start making preparations at once."

CHAPTER TWENTY-ONE

.———.

My good man, you will drive this vehicle at a reasonable speed. I will not tolerate injury to me or my young companion because of your fool recklessness. Nor will I see harm done to my carriage or my horses. I am paying your salary, and I will dismiss you if I must. I'm sure there are other men willing to take on your job."

"Sure, lady." He glanced at the endless countryside. "And where you gonna find one of 'em out here?"

Beatrice Worthington's sharp hazel gaze impaled the driver. "I shall drive this carriage myself if I must. Do we understand one another?"

"So all right," the man grumbled. "I'll slow down if that's what you're wantin'."

"That is, indeed, what I'm *wantin'*, Mr. Gibbins. Now, if you'd be so kind, let's proceed at a gentler pace."

Bethany stifled a grin as she watched her cousin pull herself back into the carriage. "I'm really not so fragile, Cousin Beatrice. If you had ever ridden in a stagecoach out here, you would know what a tender ride we've been enjoying."

"Good heavens, child. I know that. It's the principle of the thing. I won't put up with impudence from my servants. Besides, you're in my care until your Mr. Chandler decides to come to his senses as you have, and I mean to see you're taken care of."

There was no more use arguing with Beatrice now than there would have been back in Philadelphia when she'd decided to personally accompany Bethany to Sweetwater. And, as it had turned out, Bethany had truly enjoyed her company. The long journey on the train had seemed less tedious with Beatrice along, and the days and nights had passed much more quickly than she'd dared hope they would.

But the issue of the Worthington carriage was almost too humorous for Bethany. Beatrice had insisted on shipping the carriage by rail all the way from Philadelphia, along with a matched pair of chestnut carriage horses. When it had been unloaded and assembled in Miles City, it had been the talk of the town. And it hadn't been easy to find a driver for the vehicle either. Still, Bethany was glad for it now. She remembered all too well the uncomfortable passage by stage. This well-sprung carriage, with its softly padded seats and backs, was by far a much more pleasant way to travel.

"I don't know what you find so appealing about this country," her cousin muttered, smoothing her dust-covered skirt and straightening her hat as the carriage jumped forward.

"Don't you, Cousin Beatrice?" Bethany asked,

noting the spark in the older woman's eyes. "I think you've enjoyed every moment of this trip."

Beatrice harrumphed indignantly, then sheepishly admitted, "Well, perhaps it has been the slightest bit entertaining." That said, she returned Bethany's knowing grin.

Bethany turned her gaze out at the passing range. She thought back to the day, just a couple of weeks before, when she'd decided to return to Montana. How different the scenery was now from the street outside the Worthington home! Instead of tall brick and stone mansions and the spreading tree limbs that obscured the sky from view, she could see for miles and miles in every direction she looked, the gently rolling range a mixture of golds and greens and browns.

"We might be able to see Hawk's mountains when we make camp tonight," she said, not recognizing the wistful note in her voice.

"We're so close?"

"I think we'll reach Sweetwater tomorrow, even at this speed."

"Good. One more night under the stars is as many as I can stand. It will be heaven to sleep in a comfortable bed. Harvey tried to warn me, you know. 'Bea,' he said, 'you are not on your way to Paris. This won't be an easy trip.' He does love to warn me about my escapades, even when he knows it won't do any good. I do wish he could have joined us. He would have loved it. I remember the time he . . ."

Bethany listened with only half an ear as Beatrice continued to chatter. It didn't matter if she replied. Her cousin was perfectly capable of carrying on an entire conversation by herself.

The steady rocking of the carriage, the sameness of the passing countryside, and Beatrice's endless monologue eventually lulled Bethany into sleep.

Hawk sat astride Flame and gazed down at the pool, remembering the day they had gone there to bathe, remembering her frightened cry and the way she'd stumbled from the water and into his arms, the feel of her against him, the smell of her hair beneath his nose.

He cursed himself and then cursed her. Nothing he did seemed able to wipe her from his memory. Everywhere he looked, she was there. She'd been with him such a short time, and yet she filled every nook, every cranny with her memory. He'd known a lady would mean trouble. He should have followed his instincts.

Not for the first time, he considered leaving the Circle Blue. Rand and the men could handle the place just fine without him. After Hawk killed the Mexican—a man whose identity and motive they had yet to discover—things had quieted down. There hadn't been any more trouble. Hawk could easily leave and not come back for years. Rand could handle anything that came up. In the past, of course, he would have expected Rand to ride with him, but things had changed. Rand was a happily married man now. He couldn't be following Hawk across the country. Fact was, Rand wouldn't even want to.

Yes, the more he thought about getting out of here, the more right it seemed. He could head for Texas. Or maybe he should go somewhere he'd never been before. California, maybe. And he would stay away until he could go through an entire day, maybe even a week at a time without thinking of her.

Again he saw her in his mind, like a water nymph, her fiery auburn hair hanging in damp tendrils over her shoulders and down her back; her white breasts, taut and round, glistening with droplets of water; her unique green eyes staring up at him. He wanted to protect her. He wanted to crush her to him and keep her there forever.

What would he do differently if he had it to do all over again? Would he still marry her or would he tell the reverend to find someone else? Would he have let her return to her parents' home when she told him there was no child? Would he have let her go to Philadelphia after her parents died?

Hawk jerked Flame's head around and started the copper stallion down the side of the mountain toward the ranch house. There was no point in pondering what he should have done or could have done differently. The past was the past. He'd be smart to put it behind him.

California looked more and more inviting all the time.

The October sky began to cloud over as the Worthington carriage approached Sweetwater. As it pulled to a halt in front of the Silverton home, the first raindrops started to fall.

Bethany threw open the carriage door without waiting for the hired driver to get down and open it for her. She stepped quickly to the ground, her eyes already glued to the white, two-story house. Not waiting for Beatrice, she opened the picket gate and hurried up the walk to the front porch. She paused there a moment, then reached forward and tentatively tried the latch. The door swung open before her.

As she stepped into the foyer, she felt an urge to call out, *Papa, I'm home!* The silent cry echoed in her mind as a shout would have in the empty house.

"How quaint, Bethany. The house is simply charming. I wasn't expecting anything so nice after the country we've passed through. So vast and empty. However does one find one's way about here? I would be lost in no time at all."

As Bethany turned toward Beatrice, she noticed the sound of raindrops and realized the sprinkle had turned into a cloudburst.

"I sent the driver to find the stables," Beatrice said. "I told him to deliver our things to us after the rain has passed. There is a stable in Sweetwater, isn't there?"

"A stable? Yes. Yes, there's a livery just down the street." Bethany reached around her cousin and closed the door, then loosened her bonnet and pulled it from her head. "Welcome to Sweetwater, Cousin Beatrice. Welcome to Reverend Silverton's home."

She turned from her older cousin's intuitive stare, trying to keep her from seeing the confused feelings in her eyes. She was so glad to be here, yet so sad to have come.

"Well," Beatrice said with authority, "let's get

these dust covers off the furniture so we can sit down in comfort. Just think. A seat that isn't moving. Heavenly."

Watching Beatrice Worthington bustling about the small parlor, pulling dust covers off the sofa and chairs and opening the window draperies without the help of a maid, did much to lighten Bethany's spirits. Her cousin was always surprising her. Here was a woman who had scarcely even poured herself her own cup of tea, and yet she had traveled all these miles without real complaint, slept under the stars through long, cold nights, and endured the jostling carriage ride across the plains.

"I'll check the kitchen and see if there's anything edible, but I suspect we'll want to dine at Mrs. Jenkin's Restaurant tonight. We can pick up supplies at Eberlie's Mercantile tomorrow." A pained expression passed across her face. "I forgot. Eberlie's is—it must be closed now. Mr. Eberlie died in the epidemic." Her gaze moved toward the stairs and the dark second story.

Beatrice's arm went around her shoulders. "It's all right not to be strong all the time, my dear."

"I haven't been back since . . ." Bethany felt her throat thicken. She blinked away unwanted tears. "I'd like to go over to the church, Cousin Beatrice. Will you go with me?"

"But it's raining, Bethany. Shouldn't we wait until it stops?"

Her voice sounded small, even to her own ears. "No. I'd like to go now. I need to do this. Will you come?"

Beatrice patted her shoulder. "Of course I'll come. Let's find some wraps."

Papa's church.

Bethany ran her fingers over the smooth wooden back of a pew. Someone had taken great care to craft it. Someone who had helped her father build this church. Or perhaps her father himself.

She lifted her eyes toward the front of the church. Muted light filtered through the stained-glass window. That glass had come with them from Philadelphia. Her father had taken great care over all those hundreds of miles so it could one day grace a church in the west.

She swallowed hard and started down the narrow aisle.

Behind the whitewashed pulpit stood an altar. A white altar cloth, lovingly stitched and embroidered by her mother, fell in gentle waves to the floor. At the back of the altar was a tall gold cross, and at its base lay an open Bible.

Bethany stepped up onto the riser. She paused and let her hand rest lightly on the pulpit. She wondered, if she closed her eyes, whether she would be able to hear him, his resonant preacher's voice booming forth with the message he'd believed all his life. A strong but loving voice.

Oh, Papa. I need to hear your voice. I need to hear your message. I miss you and Mother so much. Why did you die when I needed you so very much?

Where were they? Was Papa happy? Was heaven really what he'd thought it would be? *Was* there a heaven? Were he and Mother together? Why did they have to die? Why?

She turned away, awash with despair. A ray of sunlight, set free for a moment by the parting of rain clouds and turned radiant gold by the stained glass above the altar, pierced the darkness of the church and caressed the open pages of the Bible. Bethany stepped closer, her eyes drawn to the lighted passage.

Jesus said unto her, "I am the resurrection, and the life: he that believeth in me, though he were dead, yet shall he live: and whosoever liveth and believeth in me shall never die. Believeth thou this?"

And suddenly her heart was lifted. They weren't dead. Not really. They'd just gone home.

She believed.

As quickly as it had come, the sunlight vanished behind yet another cloud and the church fell dark again. But it didn't matter now. She'd found the peace she had sought.

I'm okay, Papa. I'm going to be all right. I still miss you, but I'll be all right. And Papa, I've come back. I'm going to follow your advice. I'm going to do everything I can to make him want me. I may not do it just like you would, but I'm going to do it.

She smiled wistfully, remembering.

You know how stubborn I can be.

With that, she turned from the altar and headed toward her waiting cousin.

"Let's go put the house in order, Cousin Beatrice. There's much to do."

The forge was white hot. Sweat ran down his forehead and into his eyes. Hawk set the iron shoe, red and glowing, onto the anvil and tapped it a few more times, then lifted it with the tongs and dropped it into the waiting bucket. A protesting hiss rose with the steam as the metal cooled.

Hawk placed a hand on his bare back and straightened, forcing out the kinks in his weary muscles. Of all the chores that made up a rancher's life, he liked this one the least. Even on a blustery October day like this one, working beside the forge was like working in hell. The heat never seemed to let up.

He pulled the cooled shoe from the bucket and moved to the waiting horse. Running an experienced hand down the leg, he lifted the animal's right foreleg and placed the shoe against the hoof. It was a good fit.

"Hawk?" Westy pushed open the barn door. "You got a visitor."

"Who is it?" he asked without looking up.

"Wouldn't say. Just said she's come to meet you. I showed her into the house."

Irritated, Hawk grunted and dropped the horse's hoof. "What—" he began, but Westy had already turned and left. Still frowning, he patted the animal's shoulder, then reached for his shirt. "Wait here, boy. I won't be long."

As he stepped through the doorway, he saw the fine black carriage with its intricate scrolling waiting near the house, a pair of matching chestnut geldings tethered to a nearby post. He didn't recognize the team as being from around Sweetwater, and the carriage was obviously a newcomer to the area. His frown deepened. He hadn't time nor was he in the mood for mysteries or silly women's games.

Long strides carried him across the yard from the barn to the house. He pushed the door open, stepped through, and closed it soundly. The plump, gray-haired woman jumped at his sudden entrance. Her hazel eyes rounded as they rose from his boots to his face.

"My goodness," she whispered.

Hawk felt a flash of regret for his ill temper. "Westy said you'd come to see me. Have we met, Mrs.—?"

"Of course not, Mr. Chandler." The startled appearance vanished from her face, replaced by a cheerful smile. "Yes, I could have guessed you would be Hawk Chandler."

"I'm afraid you still have me at a disadvantage, ma'am."

"Oh my," she fluttered, "of course, you don't know who I am. I'm so used to everyone knowing me. You know, back in Philadelphia, the Worthingtons have been around so long that just everyone knows us and I'm afraid I just assumed you would too. But then, there's no reason why you should. We only just arrived in Sweetwater a few days ago. But I couldn't wait any longer to come meet you, young man."

Philadelphia? He felt a strange clenching in the pit of his stomach.

"Bethany has been very busy, cleaning the house and all. It's been difficult for her, dealing with the memories as she went through her parents' things. But I just couldn't wait any longer. She's told me so much about you, I wanted to see for myself." She motioned for him to step closer. A sharp gaze assessed him once again. "My, my. You are every bit just as she described you."

Hawk backed up to the nearest chair and sat down.

"And I still haven't introduced myself, have I? That's what Harvey always complains of. He says I chatter much too much. I say it's nonsense. I'm merely making conversation." She laughed, a twinkle in her eyes. "But there I go again. I'm Beatrice Worthington."

"Bethany's in Sweetwater?" There was a mixture of joy and bitterness locked in his words.

"But of course. She couldn't very well stay in Philadelphia when she longed for Montana. And when I found out she meant to return, I insisted that I be allowed to come too. It wouldn't do to have a delicate young woman like Bethany traveling alone. I'm sure you, her husband, wouldn't have approved."

"How long have you been here, Mrs. Worthington?"

"Nearly a week. No, not that long, but several days. Yes, several days. Now you must promise me you won't tell her I've come to visit. She wouldn't want me to do it, you know. She just has to do things her own way, dear girl. Do you know she's planning to open a bakery? She's determined to make her own way out here. Won't take any help from me."

"A bakery!" Hawk exclaimed. "She can't even cook."

Beatrice shrugged. "I don't think she means

to let that stop her. After all, she's a woman living alone, with no father or husband to take care of her." The woman's gaze was so innocently naive.

"As you said earlier, *I'm* her husband," he replied in a clipped tone.

"Oh dear. Of course I know that. But since you're out here and she's in Sweetwater, it's rather a moot point, isn't it? A woman alone is a woman alone." She stood and turned with surprising fleetness for a woman of her ample size, picked up her reticle from the sofa, and headed across the room. "Now, I must be running. It's a long drive back to town." She paused at the open door. "It may be belated, Mr. Chandler, but welcome to the family. I think I shall like you once I get to know you."

Bethany opened the door and let out a little squeal before opening her arms to receive Ingrid's hug.

"I will not forgive you, Bethany," Ingrid said sternly as she stepped back, her hands still on her friend's shoulders. "To be in Sweetwater for four days and not send for me! I had to hear the news from the grocer."

Bethany took hold of Ingrid's hand and led her into the parlor. They sat, side by side, on the settee. "I'm sorry, Ingrid, but I just couldn't send for you yet. I needed some time alone here in the house." Her grin vanished. "It hasn't been easy, being back in this house again."

"Is that why you came back? Just to see the house?"

"No," she answered softly, shaking her head, a warm feeling spreading through her. "I wanted to come home."

There must have been something in her voice, something in her expression that another woman in love could easily hear and see. Ingrid seemed to recognize it instantly. "I knew you would. I told Rand you would. You could not stay away when you love Hawk."

Bethany sighed deeply. "Why is it you can see it and he can't?"

"Because he is a man," Ingrid said with a laugh, a smile lighting her cool blue eyes. "Be patient, Bethany."

Bethany's chin tilted upward in a characteristic show of determination. "I don't know if I can be patient, but I don't plan to give up. Not ever."

Hawk watched as the carriage pulled away from the house, his mind a whirl of confusion. What had brought Bethany back to Sweetwater? He wanted to think he might have had some part in it, but he discarded the idea. Apparently, her parents hadn't left her as much money as he'd thought. Knowing Bethany as he thought he did, she wouldn't want to take charity from her cousins. She had come back to live in the house left to her by her father and to make her living as a baker.

He couldn't help the amused look that stole onto his face. The thought of Bethany baking breads and cakes and pastries was preposterous. He remembered all too well her attempts at cooking. Oh, she'd improved in the short time they'd lived together as man and wife, but surely no one would *pay* to eat her food.

So, what was he going to do about it? After all, he *was* her husband—as Beatrice Worthington had so needlessly pointed out to him. Just what was he going to do about Bethany Chandler?

CHAPTER TWENTY-TWO

Bethany took her time riding out to the ranch. She wanted to savor every moment. It was a part of coming home, getting close to Hawk's land. Everything was the same, yet different. Fall had splashed colorful paints across the countryside, darkening the blue of the sky, deepening the browns of the earth. The willows and aspens had exchanged their verdant robes for ones of scarlet, mandarin, and gold. A brilliant sun blazed overhead, its rays cooled by a brisk but pleasant October breeze.

She'd known the moment she awoke that this was the day to pay a call on Hawk. He'd had several days now to stew and think over what Beatrice had said to him.

I hope Cousin Beatrice is right, she thought as her mount ambled slowly toward the Circle Blue. *I hope he'll want what he can't have.*

"You mark my words, Bethany," Beatrice had said to her. "I took his measure, and that's a man who's likely to rise to the bait. I saw that look in his eyes. He cares more than either you or he knows, or I'm not worthy of the Worthington name. You stay just close enough to make him think of you, but far enough away he can't have you. Before long, he won't be able to stay out of town."

"But that seems so dishonest," Bethany had replied. "Shouldn't I just tell him I love him?"

Her cousin had frowned. "Perhaps if he were a different sort, but I think Mr. Chandler had best discover it on his own. From what you've told me about the circumstances of your marriage, I'm not sure he'd believe you, dear."

Beatrice was probably right. At least, Bethany hoped she was. It seemed too late to change things now. She'd already rented the small bakery shop and put up her sign. *Bethany's Bakery.* Not very original, but hers.

She grinned now, imagining just how Hawk had sounded when he'd told Beatrice his wife couldn't even cook. Wouldn't he be surprised? Bethany could do anything when she set her mind to it. And baking bread wasn't the only thing she'd set her mind on this time.

At last, cresting a shallow gully, she reined in and feasted her eyes on the house and outbuildings of the Circle Blue.

"Home," she whispered, then sent a silent prayer heavenward that Hawk wouldn't be out on the range.

Somehow he'd known she would come today, and he'd been watching for her. As she rode slowly into the yard, he dried sweaty palms on his pant legs, ran his fingers through his shaggy black hair, then stepped out the front door to await her.

She was wearing a doe-colored cloak over a darker brown dress. Her fiery auburn hair was capped by an attractive umber bonnet. He felt a sudden thumping in his chest as he reacquainted himself with each delicate feature of her face—her slightly upturned nose, her heart-shaped mouth, the sea-mist green of her eyes, those same eyes framed by dark sable lashes. His memory hadn't done her justice. She was even more beautiful than he'd remembered.

"Hello, Hawk," she said softly.

"Bethany."

"May I come in and speak with you a moment?"

In answer, he stepped forward and placed his hands at her waist, lifting her from the sidesaddle and lowering her slowly to the ground, keenly aware of the tiny span of flesh and bone between his fingers and the full rounding of bust above her ribs. He caught a wisp of fragrance, fresh and sweet, and his pulse quickened further. A sting of longing filled him, possessed him. A feeling so strong, it caused him almost physical pain.

Hawk stepped back from her abruptly. "Come on inside," he said and turned away. As he opened the door, he added, "Sit down and I'll get us some coffee."

In the kitchen, he leaned against the stove and drew a deep breath into his lungs as he sought for control. What he wanted to do was turn back to the sitting room and take her into his arms and kiss her. What he longed to do was carry her into his bedroom and lose himself in her loving. And he hated himself for wanting those things, hated himself for wanting her.

But it didn't change his wanting.

Bethany sat on the love seat beneath the window and swallowed the lump in her throat. She had hoped and prayed he would welcome her back, that he would want her here. But it was clear from his stiff greeting that it was otherwise.

With trembling fingers, she loosened the tie of her bonnet and lifted it from her head, placing it on the love seat. Her fingers paused long enough to stroke the velvet and satin fabric her mother had so carefully chosen.

Hawk's cool words interrupted her thoughts. "I didn't know if you wanted me to ship that to you in Philadelphia or not. You didn't write to tell me."

"I didn't know myself," she answered, raising uncertain eyes to meet his dark gaze.

He handed her a cup of coffee, then sat opposite her in one of the wooden chairs near the hearth. He waited silently, his gaze never faltering.

I love you, Hawk. Why must this be so difficult? Her hands clasped and unclasped in her lap, and her eyes dropped to look at them, as if they belonged to someone else.

"What brought you back, Bethany?"

There was an instant when she came close to blurting it out, but she seemed to hear Beatrice's voice in her mind, warning her that Hawk wouldn't believe her yet. She still had to win him and his love. It might take a long, long time. She had to be patient.

The nervous clasping of her hands ceased, as did the trembling of her fingers. She lifted her chin, defiance and determination sparking in her green eyes. "It didn't take me long in Philadelphia to realize it wasn't home anymore. After all, I own the house in Sweetwater. Papa left it to me. And this is where my parents died. So I decided to come back."

"And why did you come out to see me?"

Was he wondering if she was going to divorce him? Did he want it or dread it?

"Things were so strained between us when I left, Hawk, I hoped we could somehow make things better. Do you suppose we could learn to be friends?"

There was a strange look on his face. She wished she understood men better. She wished she could guess what it meant.

Instead of answering her question, he said, "I hear you're opening a bakery."

"Yes. Papa left me a little money. I thought I'd better do something worthwhile with it."

The look changed. It was like a cloud passing overhead, darkening Hawk's countenance. "If you need money, you could ask me for help. I'm still your husband. I'll do what's right by you."

"I wouldn't think of asking you for money." She hadn't meant to sound quite so appalled.

"Well, if you try to support yourself with your cooking, you and your customers will all go hungry."

Bethany's anger was quick to flare. All the

words she had planned to say to Hawk evaporated in a mist of fury. She jumped to her feet. "A lot you know, Hawk Chandler. If I choose to be a baker, I can be the best one you'll ever see."

He was standing just as quickly, mirroring her anger. "That'll be the day—*Mrs.* Chandler."

"Well, I can see it was a waste of time to come out to see you." Bethany headed for the door. "Good day, *Mr.* Chandler." She slammed the door behind her before he could follow.

Hiking up her skirts, she swung a leg over the side saddle and jabbed the unsuspecting animal in the ribs with both heels. The horse squealed in protest but jumped forward into a canter.

"I'll show him," she muttered, her temper far from cooled. "He'll eat my bread *and* his words before I'm through."

Ingrid placed the plate of hot food on the table, then sat on the bench beside her husband. "We must do something," she said, more to herself than to Rand.

"Best thing we can do is stay out of it." Rand cut a slice of beef and speared it with his fork.

"But they are our friends, Rand. They need our help."

"I'm tellin' you, Ingrid, we'd best keep our noses out of their business."

Ingrid sighed and pushed her food around on her plate with her fork. It just didn't seem right that she should be so happy and her friend so miserable. Bethany and her family had done so much for her. If they hadn't taken her in, if they hadn't brought her to Sweetwater, she never would have met Rand, she never would have become Mrs. Howard, and she wouldn't be this happy now. Rand was wrong. It was up to them to help Hawk and Bethany. Now, just how could she do it?

"Swede," Rand said in a low voice, using the nickname only he could make sound soft and feminine, "you're up to somethin'."

She turned her eyes upon him and offered up an innocent smile. "I was just thinking. Bethany has never been up to our place. I think it is time we had her come to dinner."

"Alone?"

Ingrid shrugged. "Unless someone else just happens to drop by."

Bethany looked around the attractive shop front. Although it had not been meant as a restaurant, she had placed three small tables near the outside walls for customers who might prefer to eat their desserts right there. She had covered the tables with pretty floral-print table-cloths and set two wooden chairs at each table. A tall glass case at the rear of the room displayed her breads, pies, and pastries. The kitchen, with its enormous oven and long, flour-covered table, was behind a wide door that swung in either direction on its hinges. Everything looked in order for next week's opening. Her stomach fluttered nervously.

"Are you ready to go back to the house, Bethany dear? I'm afraid I'm completely exhausted."

Bethany turned toward Beatrice. Her cousin was wiping her hands on an apron as she stood in the kitchen doorway. There was a dusting of flour on the tip of her nose.

Bethany nodded. "Thanks for your help tonight, Cousin Beatrice. Without it, I'd have never been ready by Monday."

"My goodness, whatever is family for if not to help? And everyone I've talked to is very eager to taste your wares. Why, you're going to be an enormous success, Bethany."

"I hope so." She wanted so badly for her bakery to succeed. She had something to prove, not just to herself but to Hawk. He'd been so certain she would fail, and there were still times when she was afraid he'd be right. Never more so than at this moment. Sometimes she wondered if she wasn't more determined to prove him wrong than to win his love. Yet even as she wondered, she knew it wasn't true. It was more important that he love her. Still, until he did, it would bring some satisfaction to have him admit he was wrong when it came to her ability as a cook.

Shaking off that thought, Bethany snuffed out the lamps one by one, then slipped into her wrap and followed her cousin out onto the boardwalk. A chill wind whistled down Main Street, carrying with it the brassy tinkle of piano music mingled with noisy laughter from the Plains Saloon. Bethany turned her head toward the saloon. She wished she felt as gay as the voices sounded.

"Evening, Mrs. Worthington." There was a long pause before the deep voice continued. "Evening, *Mrs.* Chandler."

Bethany's head came around and her eyes

rose up the length of him. It was too dark to really see his face, yet she could sense his gaze upon her. Her heart beat a funny rhythm in her chest. He'd come to see her.

"I hear Monday's the opening of the bakery. You all ready?"

"We will be," she answered softly.

"Good." Hawk nodded. "I wish you lots of luck."

"Thank you, Hawk. You'll come to the opening, won't you?" She knew she sounded too eager, but she couldn't help it. She wanted him there. She wanted him there to see her succeed, but most of all, she wanted him there because she just wanted him near her.

"Sorry, Bethany. Got too much work at the ranch to come into town too often."

She stiffened, feeling once again his rejection. Then she reminded herself he had come to see her tonight anyway. She could at least take some comfort in that. It was a small step, but it was something.

"Well, it's a bit cold to be standin' outside like this. I was just on my way to the Plains for a drink 'fore I head back to the ranch. Would you ladies like me to walk you to your house first?"

It was like a slap in the face. He hadn't come to see her. He'd just been on his way to the saloon. "No, thank you. We're not afraid to walk to our own house. Good evening." Bethany stepped around him and grasped Beatrice's arm. "Come along, cousin."

To her surprise, Hawk took hold of her other arm as he fell into step beside her. His tone when he spoke was stern. "I think I'll go along anyway. You can't tell who might be out this time of night."

"Disreputable sorts?" she snapped. "Someone like you, perhaps?" She hated the petty anger in her voice as she tried unsuccessfully to pull her arm away.

He chuckled. "Perhaps."

It rankled even more to have him laughing at her when she was so angry with him. He wasn't supposed to find her amusing. Alluring, beautiful, irresistible—but never amusing. She felt a sharp retort rising in her throat, but Beatrice's fingers, squeezing her arm, silenced her before the words were spoken.

Bethany clenched her jaw as she stared ahead. The noise of the saloon faded behind them, swallowed up by the rising wind. No one spoke as they followed the boardwalk past the mercantile, Mrs. Jenkin's Restaurant, and the Delaneys' Boarding House. The dark silhouette of the church stood against the star-studded sky, drawing Bethany's gaze as they neared the white picket fence of the Silverton home.

I'm not doing very well, Papa, she thought. *He's even more difficult than I am.*

"Thank you very much, Mr. Chandler. Bethany and I will be fine from here." Beatrice's authoritative voice dismissed Hawk politely but firmly. "Good evening."

"Good evening, ma'am." Hawk's hand dropped from Bethany's elbow. "Good luck next week, Bethany."

Smug, that's what he was. Well, she would show him.

CHAPTER TWENTY-THREE

Y ou'll come for dinner tomorrow afternoon. Ingrid won't take no for an answer."

Hawk nodded as he tossed his cigarette into the dust and ground it out with his heel. "Told you I'd be there."

Rand swung up onto the saddle. With both hands, he lifted the collar of his coat as his gaze swept the lead-gray sky. "Looks like we're in for a bit of weather. Might snow."

"Might."

"Hope the storm doesn't hit 'fore I get a chance to taste one of Bethany's pies. Her bakery opens Monday. You goin'?"

Hawk's eyes narrowed as he looked up at his friend.

Rand shrugged. "Up to you." He turned his gelding's head. "See you tomorrow."

Hawk stayed outdoors until Rand had disappeared up the trail into the mountains, then he turned and went inside. Feeling the chill, he crossed the sitting room and tossed another log on the fire, sending sparks flurrying up the chimney. He sat in one of the straight-backed chairs near the fireplace. Staring into the flames, he rolled himself another cigarette. He reached down for a piece of kindling, stuck it into the fire, then brought the burning tip to the cigarette and puffed until it caught. As he tossed the wood into the fire and watched it burn, he rocked the chair back onto two legs.

The cabin was quiet except for the crackle of burning wood and the wind whistling around the corner of the house.

Too quiet, come to think of it.

Hawk had always thought himself a loner, yet he was discovering he'd been wrong. He missed Rand's company in the evenings.

No. Truth is, I miss Bethany, not Rand.

Shoot, he'd almost gotten over her before she came back. Well, maybe not over her exactly, but he'd been on the way there. He'd been planning his trip to California. He would've gotten her out of his system there. Ladies like Bethany Silverton were just trouble. He'd known it from the very beginning. He should have hightailed it the minute he laid eyes on her. And here she was, back in Sweetwater, causing him even more trouble. Why hadn't she stayed in Philadelphia where she belonged?

A bakery. Hurrumph! What did she know about running a business?

Folks would be saying he couldn't take care of his wife. Look at that breed, they'd say. He shoulda known better than to marry a white woman. Shoulda kept his place.

Well, he *could* take care of her. He could support her if she'd just let him. Stubborn female. What he should do is go into town and haul her back out here and put her in his bed where she belonged and keep her there. That's what he should do.

Five months. Five months was all he'd known her, and she'd managed to turn his life upside down. There he'd been, just minding his own business. He'd had his few friends—cowboys like himself—and his ranch and his cattle. He'd had everything he'd needed to be content. And now look at him. Lonely. Trouble sleeping. Thinking about her all the time. And, to make it worse, winter was coming. He'd have all those long months with little to do but think of her.

It wouldn't be so damned hard if I just didn't love her.

The chair fell forward with a jolt.

Love her? Good lord, I love her!

Why hadn't he realized it before? All this time, and he just hadn't faced the truth. He was in love with his wife.

It was like discovering something in a dark corner of a closet, something he'd never known was there. He took out this new feeling and carefully examined it. How long had it been there? And now that he'd found it, what was he going to do with it?

All his memories of Bethany flooded his mind. He must have been falling in love with her from the first day they met, from the moment he'd loosened her skirt from that nail outside the

Plains Saloon. He'd already loved her when he learned of her wager, only he'd been too stupid and mule-headed to recognize it. He loved her smile and her laughter and her eyes and her mouth and the way she walked and the stubborn set of her chin and her short temper and . . .

As he thought about all the ways he loved her, he realized something else. He realized she must love him too. The times she'd looked to him with trust in those beautiful eyes of hers. The patience she'd shown toward him. And look what he'd done to her. He'd told her she was useless to him if she wasn't with child. He'd sent her away after her parents died, sent her away when she needed him most. Time and again, he could have told her he loved her and won her love in return, but he'd been too big of a fool.

So now he had to begin again. He had to win her trust. He shook his head. It wouldn't be easy. She was headstrong and stubborn, his Bethany, and she had a lightning temper. And he wasn't much better.

But this much he knew. He wasn't going to let her get away again. He'd lay odds on it—and he didn't intend to lose this wager.

"You really didn't need to come into town for me, Rand," Bethany said as the buggy sped along the road.

"Glad to do it. Besides, Ingrid wouldn't've heard of you comin' out all alone for your first visit to the place."

Bethany returned Rand's grin, then turned

her gaze upon the road. A long sigh escaped her. "Actually, I'm glad to get away. We've been so busy. And with our opening almost here . . ."

"Don't like your shop?"

"Yes, actually I do. I think it's going to be great fun, but . . ." But what she wanted was to be baking for just one person, not many.

"Yeah. I understand."

Bethany thought he probably did.

The Howard cabin was nestled in a small clearing, surrounded by tall pines. It was a simple, two-room affair, but Bethany could feel the happiness that dwelt within it the moment she entered.

"Bethany!" Ingrid cried before enveloping her friend in a hug. "I am so glad you have come. Sit down by the fire. You are cold. I can feel it in your cheeks."

Bethany did as she was told, sitting in a rocker by the stone fireplace and rubbing her chilled hands together.

Ingrid placed another log on the fire. "Are you hungry?"

"Very. It smells delicious."

"It is venison. I have prepared a stew."

The door opened, sending another burst of cold air swirling into the cabin. Rand stepped through the doorway, followed quickly by Hawk.

"Look who's here," Rand announced with a grin.

Bethany's gaze was captured at once by his. She sensed Ingrid and Rand were talking, making excuses for why Hawk was there just when she was, but she knew they'd planned it. She should have felt irritated, but she didn't.

"Hello, Hawk."

"Hello, Bethany."

"I didn't expect to see you."

Hawk glanced sideways at his friend before removing his hat and placing it on a peg near the door. "I wasn't expecting it either."

Rand grinned and shrugged.

"Take off your coats and sit down by the fire," Ingrid instructed them. "I will have our supper ready soon."

Bethany felt a strange shortness of breath as she watched Hawk shrug out of his sheepskin jacket. An overwhelming need to be kissed by him swept through her, leaving a hot sensation in the pit of her stomach. She swallowed and dropped her eyes to the floor.

"How are you, Bethany? You look tired." Hawk sat in a nearby chair.

"It's not easy, opening a business."

"I hear it's going to be a great success."

Was there an apology hidden in his words? She glanced up at him. As usual, his expression was inscrutable. "I hope so."

He nodded and looked away.

Rand's voice broke the awkward silence that followed. "Come sit down at the table, you two. Supper's on."

Hawk stood and held out his hand to Bethany, but she feared he was merely being polite. Somewhat reluctantly, she placed her fingers against the palm of his hand and allowed him to lead her to the table. She wished he would look at her again. She wished he would smile. She wished she could tell him she'd missed him. Why did he have to be so blasted remote and withdrawn? Why couldn't he make this easy for her? Was there ever any hope of his loving her?

The silence continued at the table, despite Ingrid's and Rand's attempts at conversation. Finally, Rand lay down his spoon and stood up.

"Ingrid and me have got somethin' we wanted to tell you two tonight, and I guess now's as good a time as any." His gaze settled lovingly on his wife for a moment, then returned to his guests. "Don't know how to say it except to just come right out and say it. We're gonna have a baby."

"A baby?" Bethany turned toward Ingrid. "Really? A baby?"

Ingrid nodded, her face flushed and joyful tears brimming in eyes of blue.

"Oh, Ingrid! That's wonderful." Bethany's chair scraped across the floor as she jumped up and hurried around the table to embrace her friend. "Why didn't you tell me sooner? When is the baby due?"

"I could not tell you. I was not sure until I saw the doctor."

Rand answered her second question. "Doc says the baby'll be here around May."

"Congratulations, Rand." Hawk's hand slapped against Rand's shoulder. "I'm happy for you."

"Thanks, Hawk. We're pretty happy ourselves."

As Bethany turned back to her chair, her eyes

met Hawk's. He smiled, a warm, intimate smile. And suddenly, the whole room brightened.

"You sure you don't mind seein' Bethany back to town?" Rand asked at the door. "She could sure spend the night here."

Bethany shook her head and answered before Hawk could speak. "I can't stay, Rand. Cousin Beatrice is expecting me tonight. She'd be worried if I didn't come back."

"Well, you'd better get started." Rand glanced skyward. "Feels almost cold enough to start snowin'."

The couple was barely down the mountain when Rand's words proved to have been prophetic. The first sporadic flakes were large and lazy, floating through the air like giant white butterflies.

"How pretty," Bethany whispered as she held out a hand to try to capture one.

Hawk smiled to himself as he watched her, thinking it was she who was pretty.

But soon enough the snowflakes became smaller but more intense, and Hawk was no longer smiling. The air grew thick with them until he couldn't see the road before him. The wind rose and temperatures dropped perceptibly.

"I'm heading for the ranch!" Hawk shouted to Bethany.

Lead more by instinct than by sight, Hawk guided the horse in what he hoped was the right direction. His fingers felt frozen around the leather reins. Stinging snow pelted his forehead and cheeks.

A fleeting thought left him colder still. *What if I'm headed the wrong way?*

He glanced at Bethany again. Her face had nearly disappeared inside the collar of her coat as she leaned forward into the storm. The top of her head was covered with tiny crystals. She shivered uncontrollably, and he knew the snow was soaking through her wool cloak. As if sensing his look, she raised her chin from her chest and met his gaze.

I've got to get her to safety.

She seemed to read his mind. She managed a brave smile as she reached out to touch his arm in a reassuring gesture, her eyes telling him she trusted him.

He nodded and grimly turned his attention back to the storm. He slapped the reins against the horse's snow-encrusted rump and prayed he was headed toward the ranch. The temperature had taken another sharp drop as the wind grew in intensity. They wouldn't last long in this blizzard if they didn't find shelter soon.

Bethany was frightened, yet somehow she never doubted Hawk would get them to safety. She wasn't surprised when they suddenly found themselves behind the barn at the Circle Blue. Hawk quickly sheltered the horse, then guided Bethany toward the house. When she stumbled, he swept her into his arms without hesitation and carried her the rest of the way.

Hawk slammed the door behind him before setting her on her feet. His hands remained on her arms a moment, as if to steady her. She tilted her head and looked up at him, aware now of the silence around them.

His hand brushed her forehead, flicking away the snow that clung stubbornly to her hair. "You'd better get out of those wet clothes. I'll get a fire started."

"But I haven't anything else to wear."

"Put on one of my shirts. It'll almost make a dress on you."

She was shivering. She knew she was cold. But it was the way he looked at her that caused goosebumps to rise on her arms.

"Go on." He offered a gentle smile. "You're dripping all over the floor."

Her own smile blossomed in response. She nodded and scurried toward the bedroom. Her fingers shook as she struggled with the buttons on her dress, but soon she had shed the wet garments and clothed herself in one of Hawk's large work shirts. A glance in the dresser mirror told her it didn't quite make a dress on her as Hawk had promised. The shirttails barely reached the top of her knees. A shapely length of leg was left exposed.

A rap sounded at the door. "May I come in?" Hawk asked from the other side.

Her stomach jumped, and she felt a sudden heat in her cheeks. She nodded mutely.

"Bethany?"

"Yes."

The door opened slowly, and she turned toward it. Hawk's eyes told her all she needed to know about her appearance. She felt a gnawing want flare in her belly. Her mouth went dry. There was something special about this moment. She'd felt it coming all afternoon, ever since Hawk had followed Rand into the Howards' cabin. Even the blizzard hadn't been able to dispel it.

She saw Hawk swallow, then heard him say, "Go sit by the fire, Bethany, while I get changed."

She nodded again, this time where he could see her. He stepped aside, and she wondered if he felt the same pull she felt as she moved past him. A pull to turn into his arms rather than walk by.

When he came out of the bedroom moments later, Bethany was standing near the fire, her back to the flames. The room had grown dark except for the flickering firelight.

"Are you hungry? I can fix us something to eat."

She shook her head. "I'm still full of Ingrid's stew."

"Me too." He came closer.

Bethany felt her stomach knotting in anticipation. He was going to kiss her, and she wanted that kiss very, very much.

"If this storm keeps up, it may be several days before we can get to town and let your cousin know you're all right."

"I know."

He stood before her now, his face trapped in shadows. "Rand'll probably be worried too."

"He'll know you took care of me."

"Bethany . . ." His voice trailed off.

"Yes, Hawk?" Her head tilted back.

His mouth descended toward hers, each of them straining toward the other, yet allowing their touch to come slowly. A tiny shock shot through Bethany's veins as their lips met. His kiss was light, tender, and dizzying. Her hands rose to clasp around his neck. It was either that or collapse into the fireplace.

The kiss lengthened, deepened. His lips parted and his tongue traced the edges of her mouth. A sigh escaped her, and with the parting of her lips, his tongue moved inside to explore. His arms tightened around her back, drawing her up against the length of him.

The desire grew inside her. It burned in her loins like a raging fire. Never had she imagined she could want him so.

I love you, Hawk, she thought as his mouth released her at last, leaving her with ragged breath.

She opened her eyes to see him watching her, his gaze intense and questioning.

Yes. Yes. Yes.

She heard the little groan deep in his throat before he kissed her again. His hands moved up and down her back, then slid forward to cup her breasts, his fingers kneading the taut nipples.

Tell me you love me, Hawk. Please tell me.

Again his tongue invaded her mouth. This time the groan was hers. She wanted it to last forever, yet she wanted it to end before she went insane. She pressed closer to him, driven by a need beyond thought to become a part of him.

"There's a fire inside me," he whispered near her ear, "that only you can quench."

Tell me you love me, Hawk.

"I want you to come back, Bethany. I want you to forget the bakery and come home."

"Why, Hawk?" she asked through a parched throat.

"Can't you feel why?"

"Why, Hawk?"

His head moved away from hers, and he stared hard at her in the dim light. "Good lord, woman. Because I want you. Because you're my wife. Isn't that enough of a reason?"

It was like a bath of cold water. "No," she answered stiffly.

"Damn it all, Bethany," he cursed as his hands gripped her upper arms. "You're my wife, and I'm telling you to forget that ridiculous shop of yours and come home. You belong here. I promised your father I'd take care of you. Folks are talking."

"You think I care what folks say?"

He silenced her with another kiss, this one hard and demanding. But she didn't respond. She was too angry. How dare he *demand* she come back to him?

"You wanted me too," he whispered as his mouth moved a hairsbreadth from hers.

"Wanting isn't enough, Hawk. We've tried that, and it just isn't enough."

She turned from his arms to face the fire. She

cursed herself, wishing it was enough. But it wasn't, and she couldn't come back. Not if he didn't love her. Not even if the wanting drove her crazy.

There was a long drawn-out silence behind her, and then he said, "I'll sleep in the spare room."

Frustrated and angry, Hawk spent a restless night, knowing Bethany was in the next room. Why did she have to be so pig-headed? Couldn't she see that he wanted and needed her? Couldn't she see that he loved her?

Well, love her or not, he'd be hanged if he'd beg her to stay.

The sleigh came to a silent stop in front of the Silverton house. The horse's breath froze in tiny clouds near his nostrils.

Bethany lifted the fur lap robe and hopped to the ground before Hawk could come around to help her. "Thank you for bringing me home," she said stiffly, refusing to meet his gaze.

"Glad to do it." His reply was just as coldly spoken.

"Would you care to come in for a cup of coffee to warm you before you head back to the ranch?" The invitation was automatic and perfunctory.

"No thanks." He picked up the reins again.

As the sleigh slid past her, she allowed herself one quick peek at his profile. His jawline was hard and ungiving. His midnight-blue eyes stared mercilessly ahead.

"Ohhh!" she muttered and whirled toward the gate, tripping over a snow drift and nearly toppling into the wet, white stuff.

At that moment, the door flew open and Beatrice rushed out onto the porch. "Dear heavens! Bethany! You're home! I've been worried sick. I was about to send for the sheriff to form a search party."

"I'm fine," Bethany grumbled, feeling anything but fine.

"Was that Rand who brought you home?"

Bethany climbed the porch steps, holding up the wet hem of her gown. "No, it was Hawk. We had to take shelter at the ranch during the storm."

"My, my. Hawk, did you say?"

Bethany's anger was already fading, replaced by the more familiar sense of despair. "Nothing happened, Cousin Beatrice. Nothing's ever going to work right for the two of us. Why don't I just admit it and go back with you to Philadelphia?"

Two days she'd been shut up in the cabin with him with scarcely a word spoken between the two. It had been worse than those days before she'd returned home for Ingrid and Rand's wedding. At least then they'd pretended to be civil. All pretense was gone now.

"Nonsense, Bethany Rachel. You're not giving up that easy. Do you still love him?"

"Yes." Reluctantly.

"Then we'll just have to think harder is all. There must be some way to make that man come to his senses and take you back to the ranch."

"Oh, he already said he wants me to come back." Bethany began climbing the stairs toward her room.

Her cousin's surprised voice stopped her. "He what? Oh my, I am confused. But you just said nothing would ever—"

"He wants me back because folks are talking about his wife having to work. It's because of his pride, that's all."

"Mmmm."

Bethany resumed her climb. "I'm going to lie down, Cousin Beatrice. I'm chilled to the bone."

"Don't give up, dear," Beatrice called after her. "We'll think of something."

Vince Richards stared out the plate-glass window of his drawing room, surveying the white blanket of snow that covered the range. Winter had come early. He was lucky he'd arrived back in Montana before the storm hit.

While his eyes stayed on the snowy scene before him, his thoughts drifted. His months in the East had been fortuitous and full of possibilities, yet he'd felt little satisfaction there. Not since he'd learned Bethany Chandler had left Philadelphia to return to Sweetwater.

His fingers moved to touch his cheek as his jaw tightened. It was as if he could still feel the sting of her slap. It galled him every time he thought of the way she had spurned him for that redskin husband of hers. A husband she still didn't live with. A husband who obviously didn't even want her.

And then, of course, there had been the bad

news about Hawk himself. Still alive. Montoya had failed. It was a bitter pill to swallow, that one.

Vince turned from the window toward the mantel above the fireplace. Taking up his pipe, he sat in a comfortable leather chair and pondered what the winter would bring. Two things. Two things he meant to accomplish over the next few months. He would see Hawk Chandler gone from this range—either dead or run out, he didn't care which—and he would make Bethany Silverton Chandler his wife.

CHAPTER TWENTY-FOUR

·—·

Three weeks later, a surprise Chinook blew in, melting the snow and turning the streets to sludge. The sun was pretending it was spring, lulling everyone into a false expectation of more nice weather to come. Bethany was chief among those who wanted to believe winter was over before it had really begun. She took the warm winds and yellow sunshine against a clear blue sky as a sign of winter's reprieve and decided to ride out to Ingrid's, despite her cousin's very vocal protests.

"I refuse to stay cooped up any longer, Cousin Beatrice. I'm beginning to feel like a lump of dough myself. The day is pleasant. The sun is shining. And I promise to return long before dark. Now stop your fussing."

She hadn't meant to speak so sharply. She knew Beatrice was only concerned for her welfare. But if she was forced to remain inside today, she would be a screaming idiot before supper. Beatrice's nonstop chatter was beginning to get to her. Besides, she had been suffering with a headache for nearly two weeks now. And to make matters worse, she always felt just the littlest bit sick to her stomach. Mornings were worse when she was at the bakery. Even the smell of fresh-baked bread wasn't a pleasant one.

Dressed in a woolen riding habit, her fingers encased in leather gloves and her ears hidden beneath a fur-lined bonnet, Bethany gave herself over to the enjoyment of a beautiful day seen from horseback. There were still patches of white on the shady side of gulches and gullies, and where the snow had melted the ground was a deeper, richer shade of brown. The sky was the same shade of blue as the cornflower coverlet her grandmother had made for Bethany when she was a little girl. Fluffy puffs of clouds dotted the horizon. The mountains to the west rose like proud soldiers, guarding the range below, their purple peaks hidden beneath caps of white.

She drew a deep breath, then shook her head as she noted the snug fit of her habit, especially around the waist. Working in the bakery was adding inches where they didn't belong. She would have to be more careful about how much sampling of her own work she did. But this wasn't a day to think about the bakery or even the weight she might be gaining.

She turned her face toward the sun, reveling in the warmth against her skin. Strange how the air could be cool and warm at the same time. Then a sad smile slipped over her lips. How her mother would scold her for being careless with her complexion.

But this wasn't a day to think about her mother being unable to scold her, either. This was a day to enjoy just for the sake of enjoying it. She eased her hold on the reins and allowed the mare to break into a jog, mindless of the mud clods thrown up behind the trotting hooves.

Bethany's thoughts raced ahead to her destination. It would be good to see Ingrid again. There was so much she wanted to talk to her friend about. She needed a confidante closer to her own age. As much as Beatrice tried to help, sometimes Bethany just didn't think her cousin could understand what she was going through, loving and wanting Hawk so much, yet feeling furious with him at the same time. But Ingrid would understand.

There was no warning. Suddenly, her mare stumbled to her knees in the mud, and Bethany went flying forward, landing with a splat in the middle of the road. Although the air was knocked from her lungs, her fall was softened by the sodden earth. She gave herself a moment to collect herself as she wiped the mud from her face and sputtered angrily beneath her breath. Then she scrambled to her feet, her sodden skirts dragging heavily around her legs and ankles.

"Look at me," she muttered, shaking her hands to fling away the clinging mud.

She turned toward her buckskin and her complaints ceased. The mare's head hung low as she gingerly held her right front hoof off the ground.

"Oh, Buttercup. You're hurt."

The mud sucked at her boots as she tried to

hurry to the injured animal. She leaned over and carefully ran her hand over the knee, cannon and fetlock. At least the leg didn't appear to be broken. With luck, it was just a bad sprain.

"Well, now what do I do?"

Bethany straightened and glanced around her. She could start walking back to town or she could head for Ingrid's, which was closer but would be a climb. Of course, her other choice was to strike out toward the Circle Blue, which was closer yet.

No, she wasn't about to do that. The last thing she needed today was a lecture from Hawk Chandler about riding alone on the range.

She picked up the dragging reins and tried to coax the mare forward. The horse refused to budge.

"You win," Bethany whispered. "I guess you'll be all right until I can get back."

Again she glanced toward the mountains, then with a sigh she turned her back to them and started walking toward Sweetwater.

What a sight she was! Trudging and slipping her way toward town, her dress burdened with the clinging wet soil, her hat askew. Hawk had found her mare a couple miles back and had sent his own mount forward at a reckless pace until he'd spied her. Even from the back, he could tell she wasn't hurt, just angry. He could just imagine the muttering going on beneath her breath. He slowed his horse to a walk and followed behind her.

He smiled to himself. He'd awakened this

morning, and for the first time in a long time, his thinking was clear. He'd understood why Bethany had refused to stay with him when he'd asked. No, he'd *demanded*, which was even worse. He'd acted as if the only reason he'd wanted her with him was to warm his bed. Well, today he was throwing his damnable pride to the wind, and he was telling her he loved her. Whether or not she loved him in return, he was going to tell her.

Suddenly she stopped and her head slowly raised. She tensed, then turned around. He saw the flash in her silvery green eyes as she recognized him, and he couldn't help his own return smile.

"Nice day for a walk, isn't it?"

"I'm *not* out for a walk, you idiot. My horse took a spill."

"I know. I found her." He nudged his gelding forward, then stopped. "Need a lift?" There was still a trace of humor in his voice. He couldn't help it. She did make quite a sight.

Even beneath the dried mud on her cheeks, he could see the flare of color. "Not from you. Thank you, Mr. Chandler."

"Now, now, Mrs. Chandler. Don't be so hasty. It's still quite a ways back to town."

She turned her back toward him. "I'll manage."

Stubborn as the day is long, he thought as he started his horse after her at a slow walk.

"You know, Bethany, I've told you before it isn't safe for a woman to ride out alone."

"You've told me."

"So why don't you listen to me?"

Bethany whirled around, fists on her hips and head thrown back. "Because you don't ever say anything I'm interested in hearing."

A retort was already on his lips when she suddenly lifted a hand to her temple. Her eyes rounded, then closed as she fell unceremoniously backward. Hawk vaulted from the saddle and rushed to her side.

He was riding the black stallion, his right arm flung high as the horse bucked and twisted beneath him. She'd never seen anything so wildly wonderful as the two of them, fighting to see who would conquer and who would be conquered. She longed to be a part of it all. She longed for Hawk. . . .

"Bethany?"

She was reluctant to leave the dream. "Mmmm?"

Fingers tapped her cheek. "Bethany?"

"Hawk," she whispered, reluctant to leave the scene by the corral but being pulled uncontrollably away.

"Yeah, it's me."

"Hawk?" She opened her eyes. It really was him. Had she been at the ranch? Was he breaking horses in the middle of winter?

Concern furrowed his brow. "What's wrong, Bethany? You fainted."

"I fainted?"

He stood, lifting her with him. "Come on. I'm taking you back to town. We'll have the doctor take a look at you."

Her head had completely cleared now, and she remembered all that had transpired just before she blacked out. She felt silly for fainting. She was not that kind of withering female. And besides, he'd been laughing at her. She certainly didn't need him to tell her what to do now. "I don't need a doctor."

"Well, you're going to see one anyway."

"Hawk Chandler—"

"We're not arguing over this, Bethany." His midnight-blue eyes were uncompromising as they met her gaze. "You're going to do as I say."

Funny. She couldn't have argued if she'd wanted to. Suddenly, just looking at him, she went all weak inside. Meekly, she nodded.

Hawk carried her over to his horse and set her on the saddle, then mounted behind her. Once settled, he pulled her close against him and commanded her to put her arms around his neck.

"I don't want you fainting again and falling off."

Again she obeyed without comment.

As far as Bethany was concerned, the ride to town was all too short. Once they arrived at the house, she would have to move her head from Hawk's shoulder and unclasp her hands from around his neck. She tried to tell herself it was just as well.

If you weren't so stubborn, you'd just go live with him whether or not he loves you.

She could almost see her father shaking his head and telling her she was acting foolishly. But she couldn't help herself. It made her angry to have him telling her what to do. And it broke her heart to have him want her only out of pride and not because he loved her in return.

How does it feel to be in love, Mother?

She remembered the night she'd asked that question as if it were yesterday. And she could still hear her mother's reply.

Quite wonderful, Bethany. And sometimes quite awful.

It certainly was both of those.

Hawk was sorry when he had to pull his horse to a stop in front of the white picket fence. He was reluctant to lose the wonderful feeling of having her there in his arms. But they *were* there, and he *did* have to stop his horse.

Bethany's raised her head. "We're back?"

"Yeah. You think you can stand?"

"Yes."

He slid her gently to the ground, his hands under her arms until he was certain she was steady, then he dismounted. Before she could offer any protest, he'd swept her back off her feet and carried her up the walkway to the front porch.

Beatrice appeared from the back of the house as the door closed behind them. "Good heavens . . ." she breathed.

"It's nothing, Cousin Beatrice."

"That's not true," Hawk countered. "She needs the doctor. Will you see she gets into bed, Mrs. Worthington, while I go for him?"

"Of course. Of course. My, my. I knew she

shouldn't go for a ride by herself. I told her it wasn't safe."

Hawk carried Bethany up the stairs and into her bedroom, Beatrice close on his heels.

"I'm all muddy, Hawk," Bethany protested as he set her gently on the bed.

"It'll wash." He turned toward her cousin. "I'll go for the doc. See that she stays put."

At the door, he glanced back at her one more time. She was watching him with questioning eyes. There was a helpless, uncertain quality about her at that moment that tugged at his heart and made him want to return to her side. He longed to hold and comfort and reassure. He'd been all set to make things right between them, but now it would have to wait. And if there was anything really wrong with Bethany . . . if he lost her now . . .

"I'll go for the doc," he repeated as he stepped out of the bedroom.

Doc Wilton turned from the washbasin as he dried his hands on a towel. Then he rolled the sleeves of his white shirt down from his elbows. Bethany watched him as he methodically straightened his tie and then his eyeglasses. When he finally looked at her, there was a stern expression on his face.

"Well, my girl. There's to be no more horse-back rides for you for a while. Not until summer, I think. I don't want you taking anymore spills."

She hadn't really been worried until that moment. After all, she'd taken a pretty hard fall from her horse. She'd only fainted because she'd had the wind knocked out of her. Anyone might have fainted after that. But now the doctor's grim warning was causing her some alarm.

"What's wrong with me, Dr. Wilton?"

"Nothing that about six more months won't take care of."

"Six months?"

"My dear Mrs. Chandler. You are expecting a baby."

A baby. The words echoed in her head over and over again. *A baby!*

Doc Wilton reached for his black leather bag. "About early May, I'd say. Around the same time as Mrs. Howard."

A baby in May. Why hadn't she realized it before?

"Shall I send in the father so you can tell him the good news?"

Bethany was pulled from her musings by his question. "No!" she exclaimed, then added more softly, "I don't want him to know yet."

The doctor frowned.

"Doc, you know we've been estranged for some time now. I don't want us to confuse the issue more with our child."

"He must be told, Bethany."

"I know, but not yet. Please, Doc. Let me try to work this through in my own way."

"I don't know . . ."

"Please."

Still frowning, he nodded. "All right, Bethany. I won't tell him. Not if you promise you won't wait much longer before *you* do."

"I promise," Bethany replied.

"But I've got to tell him something. He's waiting outside."

"Tell him I fainted because of the fall I took. It could be the reason. Tell him I'm going to be fine. That's true, isn't it?"

"There's no reason you shouldn't have a normal, easy pregnancy. Just remember, no more horseback rides."

"No. I won't. I promise." She shook her head, her expression thoughtful. "I need just a moment to think, Doc. Give me a little time before you send Hawk in."

The doctor sighed heavily and turned without another word.

A baby. Hawk's baby.

Bethany's eyes drifted closed as her hands moved to cradle her abdomen. Inside her, a little bit of life was growing. Their lives joined together to create a new life. A baby. Their child. There was only one night it could have been conceived. The night Hawk came for her after her parents had died.

Somehow it was comforting to know that life had begun anew at a time when death had taken so much from her.

The bedroom door opened slowly. Bethany watched as Hawk's worried face appeared.

Hawk's baby, she thought and smiled.

"Care if I come in? Doc said you're going to be fine."

"I just had the wind knocked out of me," she answered. "Really, Hawk. I'm just fine."

The furrowed brow smoothed. "That's good news."

I've even more good news, if only I dared to tell you.

Hawk cleared his throat as he sat down in a chair near the bed. "Bethany . . ." He paused, and his gaze dropped to his boots.

"Yes?"

"Bethany," he repeated, lifting his eyes to meet hers once again, "I was on my way to see you this morning when I found your mare. There's something I need to tell you."

His expression was so somber. She could read nothing in his eyes. Suddenly, she was frightened of what had brought him to her.

"We've made a lot—*I've* made a lot of mistakes, Bethany."

Her hands clenched beneath the blanket.

"But I've discovered something recently, and I think you ought to know."

He was leaving Montana. He was seeking a divorce. She felt just the slightest bit faint again.

"When you were at the Circle Blue, I should have told you. I meant to tell you, only—only I got angry and acted like a fool."

"What is it you need to tell me, Hawk?" Her question came out in a quavering whisper. How she dreaded the answer.

"I need to tell you I love you."

The shock of his reply caused her blood to run hot and her fingers and toes to tingle. She felt light-headed. There was a strange roaring in her ears, and she knew she was staring at him dumbly.

"I know it's a lot to ask, after the way I've treated you, but I'd like you to come home, Bethany." He was watching her intently, his expression even more grim than before. "I've been a fool, and I know it. I'm sorry. I'd like us to start over, you and me. I think we can make it. I think you could learn to love me."

The smile began in her heart, then appeared on her lips. "You *are* a fool, Hawk Chandler," she answered as her heart swelled with joy. She reached out and took hold of his hand. "I've loved you for so long now. I couldn't learn to love you more than I do already."

They sat in silence, staring at each other, both holding their breath as the truth of their declarations sank in. And then she was in his arms, her face buried against his neck, as he whispered again his words of love. She clung to him, not out of desperation, but with a thrill for the love she had found with him.

She kissed the underside of his jaw, then worked her way up to his mouth. Gently, tenderly, she sought to acquaint herself once again with the sweetness of his kisses. There was joy in each second of rediscovery.

When at last they drew apart, Hawk looked into her eyes and asked, "Will you come back with me today?"

"Yes," came her breathless reply.

"What about the bakery?"

"I'll close it."

"Are you sure?"

A secret smile tweaked the corners of her mouth, and a twinkle appeared in her green eyes. "I couldn't have worked there much longer anyway. Not with a baby to see to."

"A . . ."

"Baby," she finished for him when he continued to stare at her blankly. Her smile broadened. "That's why I fainted, Hawk. I'm going to have a baby."

When he gathered her into his arms this time, it was as if she were made of fine porcelain. "I love you, Bethany Chandler."

"And I love you, Hawk Chandler. I'll always love you."

CHAPTER TWENTY-FIVE

·——·

Bethany knew before she was entirely awake that she was alone in the bed. She opened her eyes with reluctance. A bleak November sun was throwing a splash of light onto the comforter. She snuggled deeper beneath the quilts, wishing Hawk was still there to warm her. A contented grin slipped into place as she thought of the many ways he had of warming her. She sighed and buried her face in her pillow. Never would she have dreamed she could be as happy as she was now.

Oh, Papa, she thought, *you were so right. I didn't go about it as you would have, but he loves me all the same. I wish you and Mother were here. I wish you could see how happy we are.*

For a moment longer, she allowed herself to stay in bed and think about her parents and how glad they would have been for her, how excited they would have been about their first grandchild. Then, with another sigh, she tossed aside the thick blankets and hurried to dress. She had a busy day ahead of her. Beatrice was leaving this morning, and Bethany had to go into town to see her off and close up the house.

Even as she finished buttoning the bodice of her dark brown wool dress, she heard the front door close and knew Hawk had come in from his morning chores. She should have had his breakfast all ready for him. What a lag-a-bed he would think her. She ran a quick brush through her auburn hair, then tied it at the nape with a ribbon and hurried out of the bedroom.

Hawk was in the kitchen, a slab of bacon on the counter and a pan already heating on the stove. At the sound of her footsteps, he glanced over his shoulder. A grin split his face and his dark eyes caressed her. "Good morning, Mrs. Chandler."

She loved it when he called her that. And she loved even more the way she could read his feelings in his eyes now. They were no longer closed to her, no longer remote and cool. They held a world of emotions, an eternity of love, all for her.

She slipped beneath his arms and hugged him, dropping her head back so she could look up at him. "Good morning, Mr. Chandler," she echoed. "May I say, you have a sleepyhead for a wife, and she should be thoroughly chastised for letting her husband be about without a proper breakfast."

He kissed the tip of her nose. "You mustn't say those things about her. I love her too much to listen to any complaints."

"Oh, Hawk." Bethany pressed her cheek

against his chest. "Do you have any idea how happy I am? I'm almost afraid, I'm so happy."

"Don't be afraid, Bethany." His voice was low and full of tenderness. "I'll always be here for you."

Beatrice Worthington watched the driver with a stern glare. "You be careful with that, young man. That trunk holds some items which can never be replaced. Memories of my cousin and his wife."

"Yes, ma'am," the fellow grumbled in reply, never looking her way.

"My goodness," Beatrice muttered as she turned toward the house. "You'd think he was doing me a favor. It's only what he's being paid to do. Won't I be glad to get back to civilization again."

She glanced up as her foot touched the first step. Bethany was standing in the doorway, a carpetbag clutched in her hands.

"Here. Put that down, my dear. Haven't I told you you're not to be lifting things?"

"It's not that heavy, Cousin Beatrice."

"Don't argue with me, child, or I'll bundle you up and send you right back to that husband of yours."

Her threat, if that's what it was meant to be, hardly had the effect she might have wanted. At the mere mention of Hawk, Bethany began to smile. Her eyes glowed with a special inner happiness that could never be faked or forced.

In response, Beatrice grinned too. After all, she felt some measure of credit was due her.

Hadn't she guided and advised Bethany until the silly feud between those two lovers was over? Hadn't she helped her young cousin mend the hurts and find this happiness? Of course, she had. And now that it was done, it was time for her to return home. To get back to her own husband. My, how she missed Harvey, and from the tone of his letters, he missed her too.

"Well, dear, except for that bag in your hand" —She took the item from Bethany even as she spoke—"I think I have everything. I'm ready to leave."

"I'm going to miss you, Cousin Beatrice."

She leaned forward and kissed the girl's cheek. "Of course, you will." She chuckled. "But not very much. You'll be much too busy taking care of that wonderful husband of yours. And soon enough that baby will be here, and then your hands will truly be full."

"I can't thank you enough. You worked so hard, bringing me out from Philadelphia, helping me with the house, helping me with the bakery."

"Pooh!" Beatrice waved her hand, shaking off the thanks. "You're family, my child. I did nothing more than you'd have done."

There was a glitter of tears in Bethany's green eyes. "You'll come out again soon? And bring Cousin Harvey with you?"

Beatrice slipped her arm around Bethany's shoulders and started walking back toward the Worthington carriage. "You couldn't keep me away. I've got to see the baby, haven't I?" She glanced down the street. "Now, where's Hawk? I want to tell him good-bye."

Beatrice was having a difficult time controlling her own tears. She was going to miss Bethany. In these past few months, Bethany had become the daughter she'd never had. She had replaced all the business, all the bustle of society life with something even better. She was sorry to leave her behind. Not that she would ever want to drag Bethany back to Philadelphia. Heavens, no! Bethany belonged here in this vast country. They were suited to each other, just as Bethany was suited to Hawk.

"There he is," Bethany said, interrupting the older woman's thoughts.

Hawk was jogging his copper stallion down Main Street. His dark hair was covered with a black hat, and he was clad in a fleece-lined coat. Beatrice silently acknowledged his virile good looks, but it was his less obvious qualities that made him so special. Strong yet patient. Determined yet tender. He was a good man for Bethany Rachel. People could say what they wanted about his mixed blood. He was a good man, and she was proud to call him cousin.

He hailed her as he drew his mount to a stop. "I was afraid I'd miss you."

"Not a chance, Hawk. I wasn't about to leave without telling you farewell."

He hopped down from the saddle and strode over to where the two women stood beside the carriage. In the wink of an eye, Bethany had slipped to his side, her arm around his waist, his arm over her shoulder. Beatrice saw his fingers gently squeeze Bethany's shoulder and watched as the glow brightened his young wife's cheeks.

A satisfied grin tweaked the corners of her mouth. It was definitely time to go home. She was only in the way. An old cousin from Philadelphia was the last thing those two lovebirds needed around the house.

She stepped forward and placed a hand behind Hawk's neck, drawing him down so she could kiss his cheek. "You take care of our girl now, Hawk Chandler, or you'll have me to answer to. Do we understand each other?"

"We do."

Beatrice turned to Bethany, pecked her on the cheek as she'd done Hawk's, and said, "And you do the same with Hawk."

"I will."

"Good. Then I'll be on my way. Heaven only knows what sort of mischief my Harvey's managed to get himself into while I've been away. It could be anything. When I think—well, I'll find out soon enough. I suppose there's no point in borrowing trouble."

She turned quickly and scrambled into the carriage, not waiting for anyone to help her. Besides, she was too close to tears again, and she didn't want them to be seen.

"Let's go, young man," she called to the driver, then waved quickly at the young couple and closed the carriage door.

Hawk tied his stallion to the back of the buggy before climbing onto the seat beside Bethany. As he looped the reins through his fingers, he glanced briefly at his wife. Her lips were compressed in an effort to control her emotions. Her hands were clenched in the folds of her coat. He wished he knew what to say to help her. Saying farewell to Beatrice had been difficult enough, but closing up her parents' home again had nearly undone her.

"Let's go," he said, gently smacking the reins against the horse's rump.

Bethany sniffed. "Life's full of changes, isn't it?"

"All the time."

"I'm going to miss her a lot."

"Me too. I was kinda fond of the old gal." He grinned and looked at Bethany once again.

She returned his smile as she flicked away a tear. "Cousin Beatrice would certainly hate to hear you call her old."

"She'd probably wollap me one."

Bethany laughed. "Probably."

Still smiling, Hawk turned his eyes back on the road. He transferred the reins to his left hand and slipped his right arm behind Bethany. With a gentle pull, he drew her close against his side.

An overwhelming sense of contentment swelled his heart. He could hardly remember what his life had been like without Bethany by his side. And he couldn't imagine life without her ever again. When he thought how close he'd come to losing her forever. . . .

"I love you, Hawk." She spoke as if she'd been reading his mind.

He looked at her. She was watching him, her green eyes glittering with gladness.

"And I love you."

Sometimes it surprised him how easily those words came to his lips these days. Words he had stumbled over for so long. Words he had refused even to speak, let alone feel. Now, they were as natural as breathing. He couldn't help but say them to her.

"I love you," he whispered once again, then bent to kiss her mouth.

Vince saw their buggy approaching and slowed his horse to a walk. He felt the anger heating in his belly as he observed their tender kiss. They were oblivious to anything around them. If he'd wanted to, he could have—

He fingered the butt of his revolver, then moved his hand away. Now was not the time. When it happened, Vince Richards had no intention of being a suspect in Hawk's untimely demise.

He stopped his horse as they drew closer, still unaware of his presence.

"Good afternoon, Hawk," he called in greeting.

Startled, they turned in unison. Hawk's gaze was instantly wary.

"Mrs. Chandler, it's good to see you again." Vince touched his hat brim with a gloved finger.

"Mr. Richards," she responded stiffly.

"I'd heard you returned rather suddenly to Montana. I was concerned there might have been some sort of problem."

"I wanted to be home before the cold weather began."

"Very wise. Very wise." His gaze shifted from Bethany to Hawk. "I'm glad to see there wasn't any emergency with your loved ones. Hawk, did your wife tell you she and I spent some time together in Philadelphia? Very enjoyable company, I might add. The Worthington ball was especially nice."

"I thought you were in Washington," Hawk said.

"I was, but how could I stay away from Philadelphia once I learned Bethany Chandler was staying with her cousins?" His hazel eyes shifted once more to Bethany. He offered her an intimate smile. "I was disappointed to find you gone." Unconsciously, his fingers touched the spot where she'd slapped him.

From the corner of his eye, he saw Hawk's jaw tighten and knew he'd gone far enough for the moment. Hawk and Bethany would be exchanging words before he was hardly out of hearing distance.

"Well, it was a pleasure seeing you both." He touched his hat once more. "Good day to you."

A cold not due to the weather seeped into the marrow of her bones as Bethany watched Vince ride away. She'd always distrusted him. Now, suddenly, she truly feared him. She sensed an underlying threat in his comments. It was clear to her what he was trying to do, the trouble he was trying to cause between her and Hawk. But that wasn't really what bothered her. There was more. Something dangerous lurking behind his civil smile. And then there was the way he'd looked at her. . . . She shivered involuntarily.

"You didn't tell me Vince was in Philadelphia."

She glanced at Hawk and found him watching her with hooded eyes. She heard the unspoken question. Her fear of Vince was replaced by the sting of Hawk's distrust. It was bad enough hearing Vince's thinly veiled insinuations without having Hawk believing them.

She turned her gaze on the road ahead, stiffening her back and jutting out her chin as she replied in a clipped voice, "It didn't seem important enough to mention."

Without comment, Hawk lifted the reins and clicked at the horse. "Giddup there."

Silence accompanied the pair for the next mile or so. Bethany's spirits vacillated between indignant anger and heartfelt anguish. Surely Hawk couldn't believe Vince's innuendos! Surely he wouldn't let that man spoil their new and special happiness. How could he?

His voice broke the uncomfortable silence. "If it wasn't important enough to mention before, then it probably isn't worth thinking about now."

She glanced quickly his way. An apologetic grin was curving the corners of his mouth and warmth had returned to his dark eyes.

"Guess I'm still going to act like a fool now and then," he added as his arm wrapped around her shoulders.

Bethany allowed him to pull her close. "And I guess I'm still going to act stubborn too."

"A fine pair, aren't we?" he whispered close to her ear.

"Yes," she breathed with a sigh. "We're a fine pair."

CHAPTER TWENTY-SIX

·—·

With one quick motion, everything on the desk was swept away. The brandy snifter shattered into tiny shards, spilling the golden liquid across the polished wood floor.

"Are there no honest men left in Montana?" Vince shouted. But the room was empty, and there was no one to answer.

He turned toward the fireplace, slamming his fists against the mantel, his chin dropping to his chest. His face was mottled with rage and his eyes burned with frustration and fury.

"I'll find you, Casper," he muttered into the fire. "You won't get away with this. No one crosses me and gets away with it."

There was no doubt about it. Jake Casper had taken Vince's money, and then doubled-crossed him. He'd been paid to get rid of Hawk Chandler. Instead, he'd left the territory, taking Vince's generous advance with him.

It was plain that he was going to have to do it himself. Montoya had gotten himself killed, and Casper was a fool. And Vince didn't mean to wait much longer to take over the Circle Blue or the attractive young woman who warmed that dirty redskin's bed. It was up to Vince to handle this matter himself. And who better to do so than Bethany Chandler's future husband?

The wind whistled around the corner of the cabin, a sad, lonely sound. But inside, the room was cozy. A fire snapped and crackled on the hearth, its light dancing across the floor and casting shadows into the corners. Bethany sat on the sofa, deftly mending one of Hawk's shirts. Every so often, her gaze strayed to the door, her eyes anxious. She had expected Hawk before nightfall.

Resolutely, she forced herself to concentrate on her sewing. If she was going to be the wife of a rancher, she was going to have to get used to this sort of thing. Hawk would be all right. He'd been managing just fine before she came along, and she wasn't about to become a silly, worrisome female.

The door opened, banging against the wall as a gust of wind swept into the room. Bethany jumped at the sound and dropped her needlework onto the floor. Bundled against the cold, Hawk turned quickly and pushed the door closed.

"It's snowing pretty hard," he told her without preamble.

She rose from the sofa and went to him. She took his hat and hung it on a peg, then laid his gloves on a nearby table. "I was getting worried."

"It's hard to see out there. I was starting to

think I'd have to spend the night in one of the line shacks. I think you're about to be introduced to your first real Montana winter, honey. This snow isn't going to go away until spring." He bent down and kissed the tip of her nose.

The simple action caused her to smile. "Supper's on the stove. Are you hungry?"

"Starved," Hawk answered as he shrugged out of his knee-length, fur-lined overcoat.

"Hawk, you're soaked to the skin."

"Had to take a little swim."

"A swim? Hawk, you must be joking."

"Wish I was." He shivered suddenly. "I'll tell you about it later. I'm going to change."

"You're going to do more than change," Bethany replied in a firm tone. "I'm heating a bath for you. And then you're going to sit in front of the fire."

He grinned as he took her head between his cold hands. He tipped her head back as he softly replied, "Yes, ma'am. Whatever you say."

Hawk sank into the tub, ignoring the fiery prickles as hot water met icy flesh. Steam floated around his head like a cloud. He sank even lower into the water, closing his eyes as he let out a sigh.

He could hear Bethany filling another kettle and placing it on the stove. He grinned to himself, wondering if she meant to boil him too. She had stoked the stove and left the oven door open to warm the room even more. Lazily, he opened one eye and watched his wife moving about the kitchen.

Her hair had fallen free from the bun she'd fashioned that morning. It fell in fiery waves down her back, the auburn tresses capturing the hot glow from the stove's embers. He thought of how he loved to run his fingers through her hair as they made love. He thought of how it lay like a burnished cloud around her head. Remembering the way her misty green eyes gazed up at him, the way she whispered his name in the darkness, he felt a stirring of love deep in his heart.

She turned toward the cupboard, giving him a clear view of her silhouette. She was always shapely, but now there was a new ripeness in her breasts. Beneath the folds of her skirt, he knew her stomach was still flat, but soon that too would change. Soon they would feel their child quicken within her, a child resulting from the love they shared.

She turned, the steaming kettle in her hand, and caught him watching her. "Are you getting warm?"

He opened his other eye and nodded.

"Do you need more hot water?"

He shook his head.

She set the kettle back on the stove. "I'll get your dry things."

"Not yet," he said, stopping her. "Can I get you to scrub my back?"

He saw the little quirk of surprise in her eyebrow, but she came over to the tub without comment, picking up the soap before settling onto the floor behind him.

It was a good feeling, having her hand gliding

smoothly over his skin. And it was more than just the things she did for him. Just having her around was nice. He'd never known someone could fill every corner of the house with her presence. Nor had he guessed a woman would be able to fill every corner of his heart.

He remembered the rush of jealousy he'd felt when Vince told him he'd been with Bethany in Philadelphia. Hawk didn't want to share her with anyone, especially a man the likes of Vince Richards. Sometimes Hawk thought he'd like to throw everything into a wagon and take her away to some secluded place where they could live out the rest of their lives, just Hawk and Bethany and their children.

Bethany poured warm water over his back, rinsing away the lather along with his musings. He turned and looked at her and wondered what she would say if he told her his secret thoughts. But there was something in her eyes that told him she already knew and understood. Suddenly, he felt the hot stab of desire flaring in his loins.

"Hawk . . ." Her throaty whisper matched his heated emotions.

Sleek and muscular, he rose from the still steaming water and stepped out of the tub.

The blizzard lasted for five days. The world outside the cabin was a flurry of white, keeping Hawk and Bethany prisoners within the log walls. Willing prisoners. For nearly a week, they were able to forget everything except each other. It was a delightful interlude.

It was the silence that awakened Bethany. The wind wasn't howling. Snow didn't sting the window panes. The tall pine that stood just outside their bedroom wasn't whipping its branches against the log walls. The silence was total, as if the earth held its breath.

"It's stopped," Hawk said softly beside her.

Sensing their seclusion was nearing its end, Bethany snuggled closer against him, laying her head on his shoulder as his arm embraced her.

"I'll have to go out with the men and check on the cattle. I'll probably be gone several days."

"Do you suppose many died, Hawk?"

He lightly kissed the top of her head. "Cattle aren't very smart. They've got a tendency to just stand and let the snow bury 'em instead of finding a wind break. I've seen them freeze right in their tracks. But the Circle Blue's been through worse storms than this one, so don't go worrying yourself. We'll just have to hope for the best."

Bethany's hand slid across his chest. She sensed he was about to get up from the bed, and she was reluctant to let him go. She almost wished it could go on snowing until spring, just so she could keep him there, all to herself.

"The boys'll be ready soon," he reminded her.

With an inward sigh, she withdrew the arm she would have used to hold him in their bed. There was work to be done, her own as well as Hawk's. "I'll fix your breakfast."

They dressed quickly in the icy morning air, occasionally sharing a glance. Every time he looked at her, his eyes speaking his love, she felt a sudden jump in her stomach, and again she wished the storm had continued just one more day.

Hawk headed for the bedroom door. "I'll bring in some more wood so you won't run out while I'm gone."

Fastening the last button on her bodice, she hurried out to the kitchen. Hawk had already stoked the fire, taking the chill off the room. Bethany took a black iron skillet from its nail on the wall and placed it on the stove. Before long, she had bacon sizzling while she stirred up a mess of flapjacks.

"You know, my friend," Vince said as he leaned back in his chair, "the more I think of it, the more troubled I am. A nice white girl like Bethany Silverton, all alone on that ranch with that redskin. I don't care what the circumstances were. She never should have been forced to marry him."

Charles Delaney cleared his throat. "Well, from what Martha Eberlie said, the reverend couldn't very well have ignored things."

"But what if that girl was mistaken? Did we allow a misguided father to force Bethany into . . . Well, you know what I mean." He lifted the glass of whiskey to his lips but didn't drink. Charles and his wife Madge ran a pretty fair boarding house, but the man didn't know the difference between truly good whiskey and rot-gut.

"She seemed happy enough last time I saw her."

"Good heavens, man!" Vince exclaimed, his face darkening as he slammed the glass down onto the table. "She's got pride too. Do you think she wants the whole town to know what she's suffering out there?"

"No, I suppose not." Charles's expression showed his lingering uncertainty.

"And what sort of example is this for the young ladies of Sweetwater? What if another damned injun moves here? Would you want your girl taking up with him? Wouldn't you do something to stop her, even if she took a liking to him?"

Charles Delaney's voice raised in response. "Of course I would, but this isn't any of our business, Richards. Besides, Madge told me that Mrs. Chandler's going to be havin' a baby come spring. That makes it just a little late to change things, now doesn't it?"

Vince's mouth dropped open for a moment and his eyes widened in disbelief. Bethany was going to give birth to an Indian brat? He wouldn't believe it. He wouldn't allow it.

Hawk leaned forward as his horse lunged up the side of the ravine, the orphaned calf thrown across the saddle in front of him. He stopped at the crest and rested his weary mount, drawing a deep breath himself.. The hairs of his nostrils were frozen despite the wool scarf hiding most of his face from view, but his bulky buffalo coat kept most of the cold out. He closed his eyes a moment against the glaring white landscape.

The calf bawled and suddenly scrambled to be free. Hawk's arm tightened around its neck.

"Easy there, little guy."

"Hey, Hawk!"

He twisted at the sound of Rusty's voice and raised his free arm to wave in the cowpuncher's direction.

Rusty's horse plunged through the knee-deep snow. "Found about thirty head beyond that grove of trees," Rusty hollered as he approached. "They look fine. From the looks o' things, we're gonna pull through this first storm okay." As he jerked the scarf away from his face, his gaze darted to the brown and white bundle in Hawk's arms. "Lost one, huh?"

"Mother broke her leg and froze down there." He jerked his head toward the ravine. "I thought I'd take it back to the ranch house with me. I want to see how Bethany's getting along."

"I'm surprised you lasted this many days without headin' for the barn. Darned if I would've." Rusty grinned, showing a crooked row of tobacco-stained teeth. "The old line shack's none too pleasant anytime, let alone when you got a gal like Bethany awaitin'."

Sheepishly, Hawk nodded. He really wasn't worried about how his wife was getting along while he was out on the range. The truth was, he just plain missed her, and he was determined to see her by tonight.

Bethany opened the door.

"Good afternoon, Bethany."

She felt an instant dread as she met her visitor's eyes.

Vince removed his hat. "Hope you don't mind my dropping by. I knew Hawk would be out with his men after that storm we had, and I thought it wouldn't hurt if someone looked in on you to make sure you're all right." He patted his gloved hands against his upper arms, as if warding off the cold. "May I come in?"

She saw no way to refuse him without being outright rude. "Of course." She stepped to the side as she opened the door a little wider.

"Well now," he said as he moved into the parlor area. "What a change this is. You've made this into a home, Bethany."

"Thank you. Would you care for some coffee?" She didn't want to offer him anything. She just wanted him to leave. But her mother's admonitions about proper hospitality were too ingrained to be so easily ignored.

"I would at that."

While Vince removed his coat and made himself at home, Bethany went into the kitchen. Her hand shook as she poured the coffee into a cup. She set the coffeepot back on the stove, placed the cup on the table, and then closed her eyes, commanding herself to be calm. She was in her own home. He was no threat to her. Surely by now he'd accepted the fact that she was Hawk's wife and would never be married to anyone else.

Especially not him, she thought as another cold shiver moved up her spine.

An unwelcome memory followed in the footsteps of that thought. She heard him again as he told her she would be his one day. She remembered the fear that had shot through her then. It was with her still.

Stop this nonsense, Bethany Chandler, she silently scolded herself. *You will not cower before that man.*

She opened her eyes as she squared her shoulders. She raised her hands to smooth the chignon at her nape, then picked up the coffee cup and turned toward the parlor. Vince was standing right behind her.

Bethany gasped and dropped the cup, spilling the hot beverage down the front of her gown.

Vince's hands moved to hold her arms. "Are you all right, my dear?"

She stepped abruptly backward but found herself pressed against the table.

"Bethany, you're pale. Let me help you to the parlor."

She tried to shake off his hold on her arms, but he was not to be dissuaded from leading her to the sofa. She told herself there was no reason for panic. He'd merely startled her. Nothing more. Yet the fear wouldn't pass. She felt threatened and all too alone.

"Mr. Richards, I'm afraid I'm not feeling well enough for visitors," she said as she sat rigidly on the sofa. "I think I must ask you to leave."

"But, my dear, I don't think you should be alone now." He sat beside her.

"Don't call me that. And I will be perfectly fine as soon as you leave."

Hazel eyes narrowed. "As you wish, my dear Bethany." He rose slowly, his gaze still locked with hers. When he spoke, his voice was low and ominous in her ears. "You know I'm right, don't you? You *will* be my wife. And it *will* be soon. I'm not a terribly patient man."

"Get out." The order was a mere whisper.

"I'm going." He paused, then smiled. "I don't think I'd tell that breed of yours I was here. I'm afraid it would upset him, and there's no reason for him to be upset. I don't understand why he doesn't like me, but he doesn't." The smile faded. "Life is harsh out here, Bethany. All kinds of things can happen. A man can fall from a horse and break his neck. He can get mauled by a bear. He can be shot by renegade redskins. Winters like this, a man can get caught in a blizzard when he's out on the range. He can freeze to death, not even be found 'til spring. And when a man's angry, no matter how mistaken he might be, he's not always cautious. You want Hawk to be cautious, don't you, Bethany? You wouldn't want anything to happen to him, would you?"

She was shaking. "Get out!"

She heard his low chuckle as he turned away. Her gaze fell to her clenched fists as she waited for him to pull on his warm coat and take his hat from the peg near the door.

"Good day, my dear. I hope you're feeling better soon."

The door closed and still she didn't look up. She was staring at the coffee stain on her dress and trying hard to control the fear that gripped her. She tried telling herself she was being foolish. Hawk could take care of himself. And

Vince hadn't actually threatened to do either of them any harm. Perhaps she'd misinterpreted what he was saying. Oh, he still believed she would marry him someday, but it could be he was just waiting in case she should be widowed. Women were widowed all the time. Perhaps that's all he'd meant when he talked of accidents.

Yet Vince was right about one thing. Hawk would be furious if he knew Vince had been there. And his anger might make him careless.

No, it would be better if Hawk didn't know about Vince's visit.

Hawk saw Vince riding away from the ranch house. He spurred his tired mount through the deep snowdrifts. An uneasiness gnawed at his insides as he rode first to the barn, where he shut the orphan calf in a stall. Quickly, he unsaddled his horse and led it into a second stall, then threw it some hay before turning toward the house.

"Bethany," he called as he stepped through the door.

The bedroom door flew open.

"Hawk?"

She was dressed only in her chemise and petticoat. She held a gown in her hands, clutching it before her breasts. Her face was pale, her eyes round and luminous.

"Hawk, you're home."

He heard the tiny quiver in her voice. "What's wrong, Bethany?"

"Wrong? Nothing's wrong." She came toward

him then, melting into his arms, pressing her cheek against his chest, ignoring his cold, wet clothing. "I'm just so glad you're home," she whispered.

His hand stroked her hair. He hated himself for asking, but he couldn't stop the question. "Anyone been by while I was gone? Ingrid, maybe?"

There was a long pause before she answered. "No. No visitors. I suppose the snow's keeping everyone close to home."

Hawk's heart tightened. She was lying to him. But why? He knew she loved him. He knew there was nothing—had never been anything—between Bethany and Vince. So why was she lying about his visit?

He pulled away from her and tipped her chin up with an index finger, forcing her to meet his gaze. Despite her efforts to disguise it, he could read the fear in the misty depths. And for once, he knew better than to press her to tell him. Wisely, he kept silent. When she was ready, she would tell him.

I love you, he mouthed silently, then bent forward to kiss her lips.

"Oh, Hawk . . ." Her arms rose to circle his neck. "I'm so glad you're home."

As he hugged her tightly against him, he swore to himself he would learn what Vince Richards had done to frighten her so, and when he did, he would make certain Vince rued the day.

CHAPTER TWENTY-SEVEN

· — ·

The black wolf stepped from the shadow of the trees. His eyes glowed like amber lanterns in the frosty moonlight. He lifted his grizzled nose and sniffed the air, turning his head in a slow arc. Suddenly he stopped. His ears twitched forward, then back. And then he started loping on silent paws across the crusty snow. Almost immediately he was joined by seven other wolves.

The hunt was on.

Hawk slid from the saddle and knelt beside the bloody carcass. "Fresh kill." He glanced over his shoulder at Gabe Andrews. "Fifth one this week."

"I hear all the ranches is havin' problems. Wild game's scarce. Cows is easy pickin's."

"We'd better get the boys together and track this pack down."

Gabe grinned. Winters were long with little for the cowpokes to do until the spring round-up and summer trail drives. Except for the lonely task of line riding, checking to make sure the cattle weren't starving or freezing to death or both, the only real excitement winter offered up was wolf hunting.

Hawk straightened. His dark eyes surveyed the packed snow around the fallen animal. The wolf kills had begun earlier than usual this year. Heavy snows and frigid winds had taken their toll on the wild game. The wolves were becoming increasingly bold in stalking cattle. They had to be stopped soon. He couldn't afford to lose many more head to the predators.

He glanced up at the lead-colored sky. "We'll start first thing tomorrow."

Bethany woke up screaming, the nightmare's terror clinging like thick cobwebs in a dark room.

Instantly, Hawk's arms were around her. "Bethany, what's wrong?"

"Hawk, don't go today. Please don't go." Her words came out in tiny gasps. Her heart thumped loudly in her chest, blood roared in her ears, and an unnamed fear clamored in her heart.

"Why not?" he whispered, his hand stroking her back.

She laid her cheek against his chest. "I don't know. I had a dream, but I can't remember what it was about. I just remember you were in danger." She shuddered. "Please, Hawk. Please don't go."

"Bethany . . ." He spoke her name lovingly, tenderly. "You know I have to go."

"Hawk—"

"You *know* I have to go. It was only a bad dream. I can't stay home because of your nightmare."

She knew he was right. She was being silly. And wouldn't the cowpokes have a good laugh if they knew their boss cancelled a wolf hunt all because his wife had a bad dream. Worse, they'd lose respect for him. No, it wasn't even right for her to ask.

"I guess I am being foolish."

He kissed the crown of her head. "Nothing's going to happen. We're just going to go out and shoot a few wolves and then I'll be back. Same thing we do every year about this time."

Bethany nodded, but inside, the fear continued to gnaw at her. She could rationalize all she wanted. She still had a terrible sense of doom. Something was going to go wrong today. Something was going to happen to Hawk.

Her arms tightened around his neck, and she held onto him while she could.

Rand guided the sleigh along the snow-covered road. Ingrid was nestled up against his side, bundled under several blankets and a heavy buffalo hide. He grinned to himself, thinking how different his life was now from what he'd thought it would be. And not just his life. Hawk's too. Here they were, both of them married, both of them going to be fathers come May. It hardly seemed possible.

"What are you smiling about?" Ingrid asked.

He glanced at her. Her cheeks and nose were red from the cold, but he thought she'd never looked prettier. Each day he seemed to love her more. He'd never liked winter much. There just wasn't enough to do to keep a man from feeling lonely. But now he'd changed his mind. Now, except for a little hunting and a few other chores, he could stay inside his tight little cabin and spend his days and nights with Ingrid.

"I'm smilin' 'cause of you, Swede," he answered.

Her blue eyes twinkled. "I think you have been locked in our cabin too long these weeks."

Rand thought of their bed with its crazy quilts and feather pillows and the hours they had spent there. He grinned some more. Reading his mind, Ingrid poked him in the ribs through his heavy coat, and together they laughed.

"It will be good to see Bethany again," Ingrid said when the laughter had passed. "Has she grown large like me?"

Rand reached over and patted the rounded belly beneath the buffalo robe. "Not last I seen her. You'd never guess you and she were gonna have babies at the same time. I'd call Doc a liar, but I guess he knows what he's talkin' about. He did about you anyways, Miz Howard."

The horse pulled the sleigh into the Circle Blue yard and stopped in front of the cabin. Before Rand could help Ingrid from her seat, the door opened and Bethany stepped out.

"Ingrid!"

They hugged each other.

"I'm so glad you're here."

"Where's Hawk?" Rand asked as the two women parted.

"He's in the barn saddling Flame." Bethany stepped toward him, touching his arm as she looked up at him. "Rand, keep an eye on him for me. I'm frightened. I have a terrible feeling something's going to go wrong."

"Nothin's gonna go—"

Bethany's fingers tightened. Her sea-green eyes turned stormy. "Don't humor me, Rand Howard. Just stay close to Hawk."

"Okay, Bethany. I promise."

"And don't let him know." Her expression relaxed a little as she offered a wan smile. "He'd be angry with me if he knew I'd told you to take care of him."

Rand chuckled. "Yeah, I just bet he would."

For just a moment longer, Bethany pleaded with him with her eyes to take care of her husband, then she dropped her hand from his arm and turned toward Ingrid. "Let's go inside. It's freezing out here."

The five men—Hawk, Rand, Rusty, Gabe, and Westy—picked up the wolf pack's tracks near the mountain range around noon. As they followed them, low, gray clouds blew in from the west. The temperature warmed a little. It began to snow just as the hunters were closing in on their prey. Westy fired the first shot, felling a small female. The rest of the pack scattered quickly, and the men gave chase.

Hawk saw the large male separate from the pack. Likewise, Hawk turned Flame's head and broke away from the other cowboys. He wanted that black wolf.

The wolf darted quickly around trees and brush as it climbed steadily up the mountain. For a while, Flame kept an even pace with it, not gaining but not losing any ground. However, it was soon obvious the large black animal was going to win this time out. The snowfall was increasing, the tiny flakes stinging Hawk's cheeks and eyes; the temperature had dropped sharply; and Flame was tiring, his belabored breath apparent in the frosty air.

Hawk pulled in on the reins, drawing his stallion to a halt. He swore under his breath as the wily animal disappeared from sight. He was angry that the wolf had escaped, yet he had a reluctant admiration for the large predator.

"Another time," he muttered, turning Flame back down the mountainside.

Midway down, he passed through a narrow, rocky ravine. He was hunched forward in his saddle, his hat turned into the swirling snow. The thought had just passed through his mind that the storm had every sign of turning into another full-fledged blizzard and they all needed to get back to the ranch. Then, from the corner of his eye, a sudden movement caught his attention. He began to turn toward it when an explosion of pain erupted in his head. He groped for the saddle horn, but it wasn't there. Then everything went black.

Bethany rose from her chair near the fireplace and went once more to the window, moving aside the curtains and gazing out at the whirling white storm. Anxiety tied her stomach in knots. She felt almost sick.

"Bethany, please sit down. All this worry is not good for your baby."

"I can't help it, Ingrid." She let the curtains fall back into place and glanced at her friend over her shoulder. "Something's wrong. I can feel it."

"If something is wrong, there is nothing you can do about it now. Please come sit beside me. The men will be back soon, and you will see how needless your worry has been."

"I suppose so."

"I *know* it is so."

Bethany nodded, but her expression clearly said she didn't believe it. Hawk was in danger. Still, she returned to her chair and tried to make herself concentrate on what Ingrid was saying about Rand's plan to add a room to their cabin in the spring. But it wasn't long before her mind was wandering again.

Her thoughts roamed in a dozen different directions, lingering a moment to savor some memory of Hawk, recalling the way he looked, the way he talked, then moving on. She couldn't imagine her life without him.

Suddenly, there was a sharp pain in the back of her head, unlike anything she'd ever felt before. She groaned as a hand flew to touch the place.

"Bethany?"

The room swirled dizzily.

"Hawk," she whispered.

It had happened. Whatever she'd been fearing all day had happened.

As if from the end of a long tunnel, she heard Ingrid's worried "Bethany?" once again before sinking into a bottomless pit.

The first thing he noticed was the whistling wind, the next was the pain in his head. Hawk opened his eyes. While he'd been unconscious, sky and earth had become one. Everything was a blur of white. The blizzard raged around him, burying his still form beneath a blanket of snow.

He tried to push himself up and was rewarded with a blinding pain searing across his right shoulder and down his arm. He gulped for air and squeezed his eyes shut. He was certain his shoulder was broken. But as much as he longed to lie still to avoid the pain, he knew he couldn't. He had no idea how long he'd been unconscious, but he thought the day must be nearly gone. If he didn't find shelter soon, he would freeze to death.

Steeling himself, he pushed up with his good arm. Again, hot needles shot through his veins, but this time he ignored them and staggered to his feet. The utter whiteness of the storm was blinding. His eyes watered and blurred. His cheeks and nose felt numb, as did his fingers and toes. Holding his right arm against his body, he began walking, hoping he was headed down the mountain instead of up. It was impossible to tell.

To take his mind off the discomfort, he forced himself to replay the events just before he blacked out. What had happened to him? Something had struck him with great force from behind. Had a rock dislodged and fallen onto him? No. Not from that angle. Then what? The only logical answer was not what, but whom.

He remembered Bethany's fear that morning, her pleading with him not to go. She had sensed he was in danger.

And I promised her there wasn't anything to worry about.

Next time, no matter how far-fetched her dreams, he was going to listen to her.

Next time, I'll stay home with her.

And there *would* be a next time. He wasn't going to let anything separate him from Bethany and their child. Not anything.

White-faced, Bethany listened as Rand told her they would have to wait for the storm to break before they could go looking for Hawk.

"But it could snow for days," she protested quietly.

Rand couldn't look her in the eyes as he nodded. "It could."

Flame had shown up riderless about a half hour before the cowboys returned. It hadn't surprised Bethany, merely confirmed what she had known all along.

"I was certain he would be here, Bethany," Rand repeated. "Once it began to snow in earnest and we couldn't find him, I just . . ."

Bethany turned away and went to sit on the sofa. "It's not your fault. Hawk was determined to go."

Ingrid came out of the kitchen, carrying a cup

of steaming tea. She sat on the sofa beside Bethany and handed her the hot beverage. "Drink this. You will feel better."

No, she wouldn't feel better. Not until Hawk was home, safe and sound, with her. But she obediently accepted the cup.

Night came suddenly to the mountain, but just as the light faded, he found shelter in a shallow cave. The ground inside was covered with a thick layer of pine needles. With stiff fingers, Hawk scooped some into a heap, then dug out a match and set the dry needles on fire. The flames sputtered and nearly died, then caught and began to burn, whipped by the wind from outside.

Hawk held his hands over the meager fire. There was little warmth. He pulled his fingers back close to his face and blew on them, then rubbed them rapidly together. Suddenly, he was overwhelmed by the pain in his head. Wincing, he lifted his left hand to touch the throbbing place just above the nape of his neck. His fingers touched something warm, and when he drew them back, he could see they were covered with blood. Grimly, he acknowledged the seriousness of his situation. They'd better find him soon.

Bethany.

He sagged against the rock wall at his back and closed his eyes, praying for morning to come quickly.

CHAPTER TWENTY-EIGHT

· ━ ·

Bethany pulled on a pair of Hawk's trousers over her long johns.

"You cannot be serious, Bethany," Ingrid said, not for the first time.

"I *am* serious, Ingrid Howard, and nothing you or anyone else says is going to stop me."

"But you could lose your baby."

"I'm not going to lose this baby. I'm as healthy as a horse. But I'm not about to lose Hawk either. I'm going to help them find him." She picked up the heavy coat and turned toward the bedroom door.

The cowboys were all waiting for her. She could see their disapproval in their eyes, but she didn't care. She was Hawk's wife. That made her the boss when he was gone. And if she wanted to go looking for him, they darn well couldn't keep her from it.

Rand was standing nearby, holding the reins of a big dun gelding. "Bethany, are you sure you oughta—" Her stubborn glance stopped him in mid-sentence. "Yeah, I guess you're sure," he muttered.

Bethany needed his help to mount the tall gelding. The feel of the saddle was as strange as the man's attire she wore, and the winter air had a frigid bite. But none of these things were going to change her mind anymore than Ingrid or Rand or any of the others had been able to do. She'd been awake all night, wondering if Hawk was hurt or if he was even alive. She wasn't about to sit in that cabin and wait for news. She had to know now.

"Let's go." She jerked the gelding's head around and dug her heels into his wooly sides.

Vince sat down to a large breakfast, prepared to perfection by his Chinese servant. He eyed the food with pleasure. He had an enormous appetite this morning. In fact, he took an inordinate pleasure in everything this morning.

Outside the large dining room window, a rolling sea of white glimmered and glistened beneath a pale winter sun. Trees bent beneath heavy caps of snow. The clear sky was a brilliant shade of blue, mocking the memory of the clouds of yesterday.

"Mr. Richards, sir?" Ming Li appeared at the entrance, bobbing quickly at the waist. "Two men come."

Vince lifted a forkful of eggs from the plate. "Thank you, Ming Li. When they arrive, show them in."

Ming Li bowed once again and backed out of the doorway.

A few minutes later, the two cowboys were shown into the dining room. Vince fixed them with a quizzical stare and waited for them to state their business.

"Mr. Richards, I'm Caleb Moore. I'm a hand at the Circle Blue. This here's Westy."

Vince nodded. "How do you do?"

"We've had a bit of trouble at the ranch. Hawk Chandler got caught in the blizzard yesterday, and we've got search parties out lookin' for him now. I doubt he'd approve of my askin', but I was wonderin' if you could spare us a few men to help."

"Good heavens. How tragic. I'll call for some of the boys at once." He carefully folded his napkin and placed it next to his plate. "Ming Li!"

The servant appeared instantly.

"Have Chuck rustle up a few of the men. Tell them we've got a neighbor in trouble. And have him saddle my horse too. I'll be joining in the search."

Ming Li nodded.

"You boys make yourselves at home. Have a bite to eat if you want. I'll only be a minute."

As he left the dining room and started up the stairs, he grinned. How perfect that they should come to him for help. He couldn't have planned it better himself.

He quickly changed out of his black suit and into warmer clothing. There wouldn't be the blinding snow to fight today, but it would be bitterly cold. He wondered how long it would take them to find Hawk's frozen body. Perhaps they already had. Perhaps he'd be needed more to comfort the grieving widow than to find Hawk.

He hurried back down the stairs. "Well, gentlemen, shall we go?" As he led the way to the front door, he asked, "How is Mrs. Chandler taking her husband's disappearance?"

"Not good," Caleb answered. "She's out helpin' to look for him right now."

"She's what?"

Caleb nodded, his expression grim. "Yup. Wasn't any of us could talk her out of it. She was bound and determined to help find him."

Anger flared behind Vince's eyes. How dare she foolishly risk herself over that dirty redskin? Didn't she realize there were things a proper young woman didn't do? Especially not the future first lady of Montana.

He would have to guide the search party to Hawk's body quickly. It wouldn't do to have Bethany fall ill so close to their wedding.

Hawk fought his way back to consciousness. Groggy, his vision blurred and the throbbing worsening at the back of his head, he tried to concentrate on staying awake. He was cold, but it took almost too much effort even to shiver. He wondered what time it was.

He reached behind his head and gingerly touched his wound. At least the bleeding seemed to have stopped. The cold was his worst enemy now. The cold and time. Time was something he thought he had little of.

The big dun lunged up the mountain, sometimes sinking to his belly in the white drifts. As they climbed, Bethany's eyes scanned the area, looking for any kind of sign.

"Hawk!" she called. "Hawk!"

Somewhere in the distance, she could hear other voices doing the same.

"Bethany, pull up," Rand shouted at her.

Reluctantly, she obeyed. She turned in the saddle and watched as he drove his own horse through the snow toward her.

"Give yourself a little rest, Bethany," he said as he stopped beside her.

"I can't."

"You'd better. I don't have time to deal with a sick woman too. If you want to help Hawk, you'd better do as I say."

Her stomach twisted in knots. She had to find him. She had to. Desperately, she glanced around her. "Hawk!"

Rand shook his head, then nudged his horse forward, silently admitting defeat. Bethany immediately followed.

They were passing through a narrow ravine, the rocky sides jutting abruptly skyward, leaving Bethany with a terrible closed-in feeling. Suddenly, Rand jerked back on the reins. His horse snorted in protest at the sudden pressure on his mouth as he sat back on his haunches.

"What is it, Rand?"

Without answering, Rand hopped down from the saddle and walked over to one side of the ravine. Brushing away the snow, he came up with a hat.

Bethany rode up close to him. Her heart was in her throat. "It's Hawk's."

As Rand turned toward her, she saw something that caused an even worse feeling. The hat was blood-stained.

"We'll find him, Bethany." Rand was watching her anxiously, as if he expected her to swoon and fall from her horse any moment.

She drew a steadying breath. "Of course we will. He must have walked away from here. That means he's okay." She refused to think about what had caused his injury or just how bad it might be. She had to concentrate on finding him. She could succumb to her terror later. Not now. Not when Hawk needed her.

Through a constant roar in his ears, Hawk heard faint voices. He pulled himself up, gripping the rock wall of the cave.

"I'm here."

His words echoed in the small chamber, and his head rang in protest. He staggered toward the light.

"I'm here."

She would never be sure just what drew her to that spot at that moment. A few seconds sooner or later, and she never would have seen him. There was a sudden movement, caught from the corner of her eye, and then all was still. She almost ignored it, but something insisted she find out what it was. She dismounted and hurried through the snow.

Bethany discovered his unconscious form at the mouth of a small cave. He was lying face down. The back of his head was covered with dried blood, his black hair clumped and matted around the wound.

"Rand! Rand, hurry! I've found him!" She fell to her knees, clutching his shoulders.

He cried out in pain but never awakened. He was hurt, badly hurt, but at least he was alive.

"Thank God," she whispered. Her eyes misted. "Thank you, God. Thank you for keeping him alive."

She heard a rifle fire three times and knew Rand was alerting the others Hawk had been found. Soon he was beside her.

"How is he?"

"I'm not sure. His shoulder is hurt. When I tried to hold him, he cried out. He's unconscious. Look at his head."

Rand gingerly touched the head wound. "I'll send one of the men for the doc. He can meet us at the ranch." He glanced toward the cave. "We'd better get him out of this snow 'til the others get here. You take his feet. We gotta get him on his back first."

As they rolled Hawk over, he moaned in protest.

"Sorry, buddy," Rand muttered, then began dragging him back into the cave. Once they had Hawk out of the snow, Rand headed back outside. "I'll get a blanket for him."

Bethany scarcely heard him. She took Hawk's head upon her lap and smoothed his black hair away from his brow. "You must be all right, Hawk. The baby and I wouldn't know what to do without you."

Hawk's eyelids flickered, then opened. His blue-black eyes were dulled with pain and unfocused.

Bethany leaned closer. "I'm here, Hawk. You're safe now."

He frowned.

"Hawk?"

His eyes drifted closed once more.

Rand returned with the blanket and spread it over Hawk.

"He was conscious for a moment," Bethany told him, "but I don't think he knew me."

Rand's hand fell upon her shoulder, and he squeezed gently. "We'll get him outta here. You just keep prayin' for him."

"I've never stopped," she whispered, tears pooling in the corners of her eyes.

Vince bent over and stepped into the cave, followed by Caleb and Westy. Bethany was kneeling on the needle-strewn floor, Hawk's head cradled in her lap. She was wearing a bulky man's coat and trousers large enough to drown in. There were blood stains on the pant legs, and traces of tears were evident upon her winter-pink cheeks.

She glanced up at the three men. He saw the flash of surprise as she recognized him, but in the next moment, he was forgotten as her gaze returned to Hawk.

"We need to get him to the doctor quickly." Her fingers lightly traced a crease in his fore-head.

Damn! Hawk was still alive. Vince had been so certain he was dead. He'd left him lying in the snow, blood turning white to crimson. How had he survived the night? What did it take to be rid of that breed once and for all?

Vince stepped closer. "I'm sorry, Mrs. Chandler. But don't worry. We'll get him back safely to the ranch."

"Caleb," Rand said, breaking into Vince's thoughts. "You and Westy see what you can find to rig a travois. I think his shoulder's busted and he's lost a lotta blood. I don't think he could go down on horseback, even if he was to come to."

"I'll help them," Vince volunteered, his gaze still on Bethany. "I'm here to help."

She didn't like his being there. She didn't trust him. But she hadn't time to think about Vince or why he had become a part of the search party. More of the Circle Blue cowboys were arriving, and she could hear the chopping of trees to make a cot to carry Hawk down the mountain and back to the ranch.

"Bethany?"

Her name was scarcely a whisper on the air. She looked down at Hawk and discovered his eyes were open. This time there was recognition in them.

"What are you . . . doing here?"

"Looking for you. You got yourself in a terrible mess without me, you know." She offered a smile.

"Doc told you to stay . . . off horses."

"Our baby insisted on knowing where you were. I had to come. We're fine." She kissed his forehead as she fought tears of relief.

His eyes began to glaze again. "Someone . . ." His lids closed. "Some . . . one . . ." He moaned.

"Hawk?"

But there was no response. He had drifted beyond consciousness in search of a haven from pain.

For several days after their return to the ranch, Hawk's life hung in the balance. Bethany could sense how close he was to slipping out of her life forever, but she wouldn't let him go. She was with him around the clock, praying for him, changing his dressings, checking his shoulder, giving him sips of broth when he was able to take anything.

Stubbornly, she insisted he couldn't die. She wouldn't let him. Perhaps he heard her, for slowly he began his return to the living.

CHAPTER TWENTY-NINE

It was in the wee hours of the night. The darkest hours. A lonely wind whined at the windows. A tree branch rubbed against the roof. In the distance, a coyote raised its muzzle toward the moon and howled mournfully.

Beside her, Hawk slept. His breathing was steady, peaceful, and deep. Bethany slipped from beneath the heavy blankets, careful not to disturb him, and wrapped herself quickly in a warm robe. Bare feet carried her across to the window. She pushed aside the curtains and stared out at the night.

The sky was completely free of clouds and as black as tar. Against this ebony background, stars twinkled like tiny diamonds and cast a frosty glitter upon the stark white landscape below. Bethany felt the utter solitude and glanced over her shoulder, as if to reassure herself someone else was still with her, that she was not all alone in the world.

Hawk shifted in the bed but continued to sleep.

Her heart skipped a beat as she watched him. A smile curved her lips. How she loved him. And how very thankful she was that he was alive this day. It could so easily have been otherwise.

Hawk's convalescence had seemed to crawl by. His recovery was slower than either of them liked, and Bethany had discovered her husband was a very poor patient—irritable, demanding, and restless.

Her thoughts drifted back to last night as they'd prepared for bed. Hawk had rubbed the back of his head, as he always did when he was trying to remember something about his accident.

"Sometimes I think it's going to come back to me," he'd said, a deep frown creasing his forehead. "There's just something I can't remember, but I keep thinking it's important."

"Why don't you just forget it, darling. It's over, and you're almost well. What more matters than that?"

"I don't know. It just keeps nagging at me." He'd sighed as he swung his feet up from the floor and slipped beneath the layer of blankets. "Who knows. Maybe it wasn't even an accident."

Bethany had caught her breath. "Not an accident?"

"Sorry, honey. That was a fool thing to say. I'm just frustrated 'cause I can't remember anything. Shoot, I probably fell out of the saddle and Flame ran right over me." He'd motioned for her to hurry and get into bed. "Worst of it was losing the knife my father gave me. Soon as it thaws, I'm going up there to look for it."

Who knows. Maybe it wasn't even an accident.

Bethany's gaze returned to the lonesome winter scene outside her window. What was she going to do? She was positive Hawk was right. It *hadn't* been an accident. Someone had been waiting for him. And that someone was Vince. In her heart, she knew it was Vince Richards who had done this.

All kinds of things can happen, Bethany. A man can fall from a horse and break his neck. Winters like this, a man can get caught in a blizzard when he's out on the range and freeze to death. You wouldn't want anything to happen to Hawk, would you?

Vince's threats came back to haunt her now. She should have told Hawk about Vince's visit. She never should have lied to him. If he'd known, maybe he would have been more cautious. If he'd known, maybe he could have stopped Vince long before now. She'd let Vince frighten her into thinking she was protecting Hawk with her deception.

But she hadn't protected him. Instead, her silence had nearly cost him his life.

Yet she couldn't voice her thoughts to Hawk now. She knew what his reaction would be. He would be furious. He would want to confront Vince. But he wasn't strong enough yet, and Vince just might succeed with his threats the next time. She would have to handle this alone. Once and for all, she had to make it clear to Vince Richards that she wanted no part of him. She had to let him know she knew what he'd done, and that next time—heaven forbid there should be a next time—he wouldn't get away with it.

"Tomorrow," she said to herself softly. "I'll see him tomorrow."

Not wanting to find herself arguing with Hawk or telling him another fib about where she was going, Bethany waited until he'd nodded off to sleep after lunch before she asked Gabe to hitch up the sleigh.

"Tell Hawk I had an errand to run. I won't be long." She let the young cowhand help her into the sleigh as she spoke, then tucked a lap robe beneath her legs and picked up the reins.

Gabe was frowning but kept silent. The men had all learned Hawk's bride had a mind of her own. A bit of a maverick, that's what she was. And if her own husband couldn't keep her in line, it sure wasn't their place to try.

She knew this was exactly what Gabe was thinking even as she slapped the reins against the horse's rump. Ordinarily she would have been amused, but her thoughts were already running ahead of her to the unpleasant task at hand. It never occurred to her that she might be riding into a dangerous situation. Vince had threatened Hawk, not her, and nothing else mattered except putting an end to it.

"Young lady come."

"Is it Mrs. Chandler?"

Ming Li nodded.

"Thanks." Vince closed the ledger on his desk,

then rose from his chair and slipped into his suit coat. He glanced into the mirror beside the fireplace, smoothing his hair into place before heading for the front door to greet his long-awaited visitor.

"Ah, my dear Mrs. Chandler," he said as Ming Li ushered in a rosy-cheeked Bethany. "How nice of you to call."

"I have no time for your pleasantries, Mr. Richards. This isn't a social call." Her eyes had darkened to a stormy shade of green.

"Whatever—"

A gloved finger was shoved into his chest. "You don't fool me. I know it was you who bush-whacked Hawk. You tried to kill him. Did you think I wouldn't figure it out?"

"Me? What are you talking about? Bethany, you're distraught."

"Of course I'm distraught," she answered in a shrill tone. "You tried to kill my husband. And it's high time Sheriff Cook knew about it, too."

Vince's eyes narrowed. "That's a slanderous accusation, Mrs. Chandler. Have you proof to back it up?"

"You threatened him. When you came to the Circle Blue, you threatened him. I'll tell that to the sheriff."

He was enjoying this. She was a little too independent for his liking—he would have to change that—but she was beautiful and, most of the time, well-mannered. In the proper attire, with her auburn hair done up on her head and a diamond necklace glittering around her white throat, she would be stunning! She would be a flawless asset as his wife. Nothing was going to keep him from having her. Nothing.

Vince turned his back toward Bethany and walked to his office. He knew she would follow him, and he wasn't disappointed. He heard her clipped footsteps on the hardwood floor in the hallway.

"My dear," he said softly as he turned around to face her again. "It's your word against mine. I never threatened anyone."

"But you did!"

He grinned. "Perhaps I did, but if I tell them I didn't, they'll believe I didn't." He could read the confusion and frustration on her face. "Let me explain some things to you, my dear. I am a powerful man hereabouts. I am wealthy, and I'm white. Your husband, on the other hand, is a no-account breed. Yes, he has considerable land and some cattle and a few friends. But if it came down to it, I could see him hanged with very little effort on my part." He rubbed his chin. "Let's see. What charge could I bring against him?"

"But it's you who . . ."

Vince laughed aloud. "You really don't understand, do you?" He stepped suddenly forward, capturing her in his arms. "You *will* be mine, Bethany. I always get what I want."

He kissed her.

Bethany struggled and gasped for air. The instant Vince released his hold on her, her hand flew to her mouth to rub the feel of him from her lips. Angry beyond words, she delivered a telling slap to his cheek. Instantly, his fingers were clasping her upper arms, pinching painfully into her skin.

"I can see I've got to teach you some manners." His gaze was cold and unrelenting.

"Let go of me. When I tell the sheriff—"

"Ha!" With a thrust of his hands, he pushed her away from him. "Do you know what people are saying about you, Bethany? A girl who is discovered in a shameless state of undress with a—man like that? What do you think they call you behind your back?"

She felt herself pale. "It's not true."

"It won't be easy, but I mean to redeem you, my dear child. When you're Mrs. Vince Richards, I'll see that people soon forget Chandler ever lived, let alone that you lay beneath him like a common—" He stopped abruptly, his face contorted and mottled.

"You're crazy." She turned and headed for the front door. This was a mistake, her coming. What had made her think she could talk to him?

He was in front of her, blocking her departure, before she realized he'd moved.

"Yes," he ground out. "I followed him. I was waiting for him when he passed through those rocks. I hit him with the butt of my rifle. I think I could even hear his skull crack. Or maybe it was only my rifle stock. I discovered it was broken when I got home."

Bethany's hand went to her throat as her eyes widened.

"There was blood everywhere, but just to be

sure, I roughed him up a bit. I suppose it was then I broke his shoulder with my boot. Too bad I only bruised his ribs." Vince's fist struck the doorjamb. "I thought he was dead for sure, but damn him, that breed just won't die. No matter how many times I try to rid myself of him, he just won't die."

She felt sick. He was insane, and he was going to keep her there. No one knew where she was. What if he . . . ?

His gaze focused on her again. "Now let me tell you about *our* future, Bethany. I mean to see that he does die. He won't escape me next time. And when he's dead and your body has rid itself of his brat, we'll be married. Folks in town will understand your desire to marry again so soon. After all, they've heard how he mistreats you."

"But Hawk doesn't—" Her throat was thick with fear, and the words seemed to stick there, refusing to be spoken.

"Oh, but he does. Everyone knows what a mistake it was. A girl of your fine breeding and background, married to that no good redskin. Doesn't matter how watered down the blood, an Indian's still an Indian. Can't be expected to know how to treat a white woman. But what could you do? Your father—terribly mistaken, I might add—made you marry him after that unfortunate encounter, and your pride has kept you there when you should have asked for shelter with some of the good folks in town."

She stared at him in silence. She was confused, uncertain what to do or say. Did people really believe his lies?

And then, suddenly, her fear vanished, her thoughts cleared. The anger returned. How dare he spread such lies? How dare he so boldly admit to trying to kill Hawk?

"Get out of my way, Vince. I'm leaving."

He looked at her. His expression relaxed, then an evil smile twisted the corners of his mouth. "I'll make you an offer, Bethany. Leave Hawk and I'll let him live. Return to your house in town. Tell folks your marriage is over." His eyes flicked to her stomach, and he grimaced. "After the baby's born, you can give it to Hawk. You can give it away to anyone who'll have it. Then I'll help you get free of him once and for all. I have some important friends. We could get the marriage proclaimed invalid or get you a divorce. Then we will be married."

"Never," she whispered vehemently. She stepped around him and opened the door.

"Going home to tell Hawk what I've said?"

She didn't bother to reply.

As she hurried toward her sleigh, he called after her, "If he comes onto the Bar V or tries to make trouble, I'll see that he hangs. I can do it, Bethany. One word from me, and he's a dead man. Think of that before you tell him about your visit." His voice became more strident. "In fact, you'd better think about my offer if you want to keep him alive. I'll give you until spring. Until spring, Bethany."

She was shaking. Shaking so hard she could barely pick up the reins and turn the horse toward home.

It couldn't be true. Folks couldn't really be

thinking the things Vince had suggested. They liked Hawk. Folks knew he was good and kind and fair. He was an honest man. And she loved him.

But he was an Indian, and too many people thought the same way as Vince Richards. A white woman couldn't really love an Indian. After all, he was a savage by blood, and she was civilized just because she was white.

But surely they would believe the truth when she told them what Vince had done.

Then again, what if they didn't? What then?

If she stayed with Hawk, Vince might succeed in killing him. If she told Hawk about the threats, Hawk would go after Vince, and then Vince would see him hanged. She could save his life only by leaving him and seeking a divorce. No matter what she did, she lost.

Bethany jerked back on the reins and the sleigh slid to a halt. Her hands dropped to her rounded belly beneath the lap robe.

"What am I to do?" she whispered. "He's my life."

CHAPTER THIRTY

·—·

For Pete's sake, Bethany. Be reasonable." Hawk pulled on his coat and reached for the door.

"Don't go, Hawk. Please don't go."

His irritation was clear in each word so carefully spoken. "I've got a ranch to run."

"But you're not well enough. . . ."

He turned to look at her. There were dark shadows beneath her lovely green eyes. Her cheeks were pale and hollow. He knew she wasn't sleeping well—hadn't been sleeping much for weeks now—but when he tried to talk to her, she shut him out, told him nothing was wrong.

"We've been through this before," he said, more gently this time. "I *am* well. The doc said I was fine. Winter's nearly over, Bethany, and there's a lot of work to get done."

She reached out, as if to touch him, although she didn't. Her arm simply hung in the air, beseeching him not to go. "Please."

Hawk sighed. He was sorely tempted to give in

to her again, as he'd been doing for far too long. It hadn't mattered before. Winters were usually long and fairly idle. His hired hands were able to handle what work there was. But he was strong now and tired of his inactivity. He was ready to be in the saddle, working his ranch. The snow was beginning to melt. The promise of spring was already in the air. He couldn't allow Bethany to get her way again, no matter how helpless and fragile she appeared.

"I'll be back by supper time. Why don't you lie down and rest?"

She pressed her lips together in a tight line, but he could still see them tremble. He turned and left before the tears came. He wasn't sure he could resist her tears.

Rand was waiting for him next to the corral. "Mornin', Hawk," he said as he tightened the cinch on his pinto.

"Morning." Hawk tossed the split reins over Flame's copper neck, then swung up into the saddle.

The two men turned their horses toward the east range. They rode in silence. Hawk was unaware of Rand's studious gaze.

Finally, Rand asked, "Somethin' troublin' you?"

He turned to look at his friend, startled from his reverie, almost surprised to find someone there. He'd been lost deep in thought, trying to figure out what was wrong with Bethany, what was causing her to change, and searching for a solution.

"Don't have to tell me if you don't want to," Rand added as the silence stretched out.

Hawk shook his head. "It's Bethany. I don't know what's the matter with her."

Rand waited for him to elaborate.

"She's changed, Rand. She fusses over me like I'm an invalid. She jumps at the slightest noise. She cries at the drop of a hat."

Rand shrugged. "She's havin' a baby," he said philosophically.

"Is Ingrid like that?"

"Well . . . no."

"I didn't think so." Hawk's gaze swept back over the rolling countryside, a frown furrowing his brow.

"Has Doc seen her?"

"Yes, and I think he's worried too. She's lost weight, and she's not sleeping. It's like she's scared to death to let me out of her sight. Scared of her own shadow, almost."

He didn't add how much he missed the fire and fight in her eyes. He didn't admit how worried he was when he compared the stubborn, headstrong Bethany he remembered with the frightened young woman who shared his home. Something was terribly wrong, and his own helplessness was driving him crazy.

"Maybe I should bring Ingrid down. She's been feelin' a touch of cabin fever anyhow. Not long 'til these babies is due. Maybe now'd be a good time for her to come visitin'."

"I'd appreciate it, Rand. I'm at my wit's end."

"Heck, she's been after me to bring her down for weeks. It'll be doin' us both a favor, I guess."

Doc Wilton put his stethoscope into his bag and turned toward his patient again. "Mrs.

Delaney, I want you to stay in bed today, but you can get up tomorrow."

Madge Delaney nodded obediently as she buttoned the high collar of her white nightgown. "How's that sweet niece of yours, Doc?"

"Fine. Just fine."

"I hear we're going to have a couple more babies around Sweetwater this spring. Is it true, Doc?"

Doc was reluctant to answer. There wasn't a bigger gossip in all of Sweetwater than Madge Delaney. And he was certain she wasn't just enjoying a bit of idle conversation. She was fishing for information, as usual.

"That sweet Mrs. Howard. My, my. She was the nicest girl, for a foreigner. It must be difficult living up in those mountains and expecting a baby."

"She's doing fine."

"And, tell me, Doc. Is it true? Is that Silverton girl going to have a baby too?"

Doc's jaw tightened in irritation. "Do you mean Mrs. Chandler?"

"Yes. Yes, of course." She reached up and touched his arm as she spoke in a secretive voice. "I hear she's terribly unhappy, married to that Indian fellow. Sybil Bruce told me she'd heard he mistreats her, but she's too afraid to try to leave him."

The doctor stepped backward and picked up his black bag. He clenched his teeth together, resisting the urge to tell the old biddy just what he thought of her rumormongering.

Madge scarcely drew a breath as she continued. "I said at the very start, it was a sin for a man of God like the good Reverend Silverton, may he rest in peace, to marry his daughter to a heathen, no matter what the reason. Why, that Chandler fellow ought to be run out of the territory. He should know his place. And after folks around here have treated him as if he was one of us. Like an equal. Almost as if he was white like the rest of us."

Doc Wilton glared at the woman, groping for the right words to say. He'd seen what blind prejudice could do. It was a sickness that twisted a person's thinking, a sickness that could invade an entire community. "I assure you, Mrs. Delaney, that Mrs. Chandler is quite all right and completely happy with her husband."

But even as he spoke the words, he wondered if they were true. He'd been out to see her this past week, and he was worried. Ever since the new year had begun, he'd been witnessing a change in her. She was listless. She had no appetite. She seemed frightened all the time. He'd heard these same rumors before. Try as he might not to, he'd begun to wonder if there just might be a shred of truth in them.

Angry with himself now, he turned to leave the bedroom. "You send Ellen for me if the pain starts up again."

"I'll do that, Doc. Thanks."

Bethany was pacing the bedroom floor when she heard the dreaded knock on the door. Panic assailed her. She rushed into the sitting room and jerked open the door to reveal a tall, scruffy-looking stranger.

"What is it? What happened?" she demanded.

He squinted at her from beneath the brim of his hat. His mustache twitched, then he turned his head to the side and spat out a stream of tobacco juice. "Nothin's happened, ma'am. I just got a message for you if you're Miz Chandler."

"I am."

"Then I'm to tell you that spring's almost here. He said you'd know what it meant."

Bethany's fingers tightened around the edge of the open door. "Who said?" she croaked.

"Don't know, ma'am. I was just passin' through Sweetwater, lookin' for work, and the fella paid me to deliver the message. I figured you'd know what it meant."

"Yes . . . Yes, I guess I do know." She closed the door and turned away.

She was out of time. She was unable to keep Hawk with her any longer, and Vince—or one of his hired hands—would be out there waiting for him. For nearly three months now, she'd been racking her brain, seeking an answer. But the only way to save Hawk, to protect him from Vince's power, was to leave him. That seemed to be the only way.

Shoulders sagging, she returned to the bedroom. She pulled a carpetbag from beneath the bed, then stuffed what clothes she could inside. She would have to send for the rest of her things later.

I've done this before, she thought sadly, remembering her return to Sweetwater for Ingrid's wedding.

She ran her finger over the headboard of the

bed, then traced the quilt to the footboard. This was her home. She didn't want to be driven from it. Yet what else could she do? She'd been over it in her mind a million times. There was no other way to keep Hawk safe.

He'll never understand why you've left him.

But it was better that way. Better that he not know. If he knew, he would never keep away from Vince, and then there'd be trouble. And if there was trouble, Hawk would be blamed. She no longer doubted Vince could do exactly as he'd promised.

She carried her satchel into the kitchen and left it on the floor, then she walked to the small writing table in the corner. She dipped the pen into the ink bottle as she stared at the blank sheet of paper before her. There didn't seem to be any words that were right. How did you tell the man you loved more than your own life that you were leaving him?

Finally she wrote,

I've gone to Sweetwater to stay at the house. Please send my things to me.
B.

She blew on the ink, then placed the note on the kitchen table where he would see it. With a heavy heart, she picked up her carpetbag and left behind her home and the warmth within.

For hours she had wandered from room to room, touching the furniture, the walls, the draperies. Remembering her parents. Waiting.

So Bethany wasn't surprised when the front door was flung open and Hawk stormed in. She'd been preparing for it since the moment she'd left the Circle Blue.

"What the hell is the meaning of this?" he demanded, waving her note in the air.

She felt the blast of his anger but stood firm against it. "I can't stay with you anymore, Hawk. That's all."

"That's it? Just 'I can't stay'?"

She lifted her chin in a familiar, stubborn motion. "That's the only reason I can give you."

He stepped toward her, forcing her to look up at him. "Well, it's not good enough." He took hold of her arms. His voice dropped. "Bethany, what's wrong? Why can't you tell me what's troubling you?"

"Because I just can't." She heard the quaver in her voice and stiffened her resolve not to cry.

His dark eyes searched her face. She felt his confusion. She knew how he'd puzzled over her behavior this winter, yet she was unable to protect him and keep from hurting him at the same time. She would rather know his hurt and his anger. She would rather have him alive. She would have to learn to live with the pain in her heart.

"I won't come back, Hawk."

"And I won't give up, Bethany."

She thought of telling him she didn't love him, but she knew she couldn't speak that lie. And he would know it was a lie. There was no reason she could give him, and so she kept silent.

"I won't give up," he repeated, his hands

slipping up to cradle her jaw. "We've played foolish games before, Bethany, and we almost lost each other. I won't let it happen again. I'm going to find out what's at the bottom of this. And when I do, you're coming home." His mouth came slowly down toward hers.

She knew if he kissed her, she was lost. Quickly, she turned her head to the side so his lips met her cheek. He pulled back a few inches, eyes boring into hers. Bethany held her breath.

"I'll be back for you."

CHAPTER THIRTY-ONE

Ｍy goodness! Bethany Chandler, as I live and breathe. We haven't seen you in town in a coon's age."

Bethany turned from the mercantile counter. "Hello, Mrs. Bruce. It's good to see you."

Bethany felt Sybil Bruce's shrewd gaze assessing the hollowed appearance of her face before casting a knowing glance at Bethany's distended abdomen.

"Madge Delaney told me you'd returned to town yesterday. Is it true you're going to be living in the reverend's house?"

Reluctantly, Bethany nodded. "For a while."

Speaking in a low, confidential tone, Sybil continued. "Well, you know it was no surprise to anyone. We've all heard how difficult it's been for you. Not that we expected that kind of behavior from Mr. Chandler. I always thought he was rather a nice sort, despite his . . . well, you know."

"No, Mrs. Bruce, I don't know."

"Well, I suppose we couldn't expect a man of his—background to know how to treat a woman."

Bethany felt the heat rise to her cheeks. "There is nothing wrong with my husband's background, Mrs. Bruce."

The woman looked taken back by the abruptness of Bethany's tone. "Well," she huffed. "I was only trying to be sympathetic. No woman should be expected to endure—"

Bethany turned back toward the clerk behind the counter. "Have those things sent to me, please. I won't wait." Then she turned a hostile glare upon the Bruce woman. "I have endured nothing but love and patience from my husband. I won't have the town gossiping and saying things that aren't true. What's the matter with everyone? This is your neighbor you're talking about. He helped build this town. He helped build your church. So what if he isn't a blue blood. How many of us are? He's just a man like any other. No, he's *better* than any other. He has never mistreated me, and I'm happy and proud to be having his child."

"Well, I only thought . . . Since you'd left him, that is . . . I certainly . . ."

"Why I'm staying in town is not anyone's concern but my own." She pulled her skirts aside and stepped around the woman. "Good day, Mrs. Bruce." Chin in the air, head held high, Bethany left the mercantile.

Of all the ridiculous nonsense. Why were people so stupid?

She marched down the boardwalk, filled with

indignation and scarcely looking where she was going. Blinded by her anger, she nearly collided with Vince Richards as he came out of Mrs. Jenkin's Restaurant.

"Bethany, my dear. What a nice surprise." He removed his hat and smiled at her. "I hear you've moved to town just as spring is arriving. It's a wonderful time of year, isn't it?"

How she wanted to remove that insufferable grin from his face! "This is your doing, Vince Richards."

His expression was one of amusement. "What is my doing?" Everything about him seemed to be declaring his victory.

It was as if blinders had suddenly been removed from her eyes. Or perhaps she was just waking up from a dream. For three miserable months, she had cowered at the thought of this man. She had been a fool, playing into his hands, reacting just as he'd hoped she would. Where was her faith in Hawk? Weren't they to face things together? What was wrong with her that she'd allowed Vince to manipulate her this way?

"Let me walk you home, my dear." He reached for her arm.

Bethany jerked away from his touch.

Vince's face darkened, his eyes narrowed. "Don't do anything foolish, Bethany."

"I've been foolish, Mr. Richards, but I don't intend to be foolish any longer."

He seemed to understand her implication. "You'll rue your decision, Mrs. Chandler." This time when he reached for her arm, he caught it and held on tightly.

Before she could demand her release, she heard the softly spoken words coming from the street behind her.

"Take your hands off my wife, Richards. Now."

She whirled around, breaking free of Vince's hold. Hawk was sitting astride Flame, his posture deceptively casual. He was leaning forward, an arm resting on the pommel of the saddle. He looked relaxed, but she knew better. He was coiled like a rattler, ready to strike if necessary.

"She's left you, Chandler. You have no claim on her now."

Bethany swung back around. She was only vaguely aware of the gathering of faces at the restaurant door. "I *haven't* left him. I simply wanted a few nights in my parents' home." Then she turned back toward Hawk. With her eyes, she begged him to forgive her. "I love my husband. Nothing in this world could cause me to leave him."

The warmth of his gaze caressed her. "Are you ready to go home, Bethany, or did you want to stay in town a while longer?"

"I'm ready to go home, Hawk. I'm ready now."

Vince watched as Hawk dismounted, took Bethany's arm, and the two of them walked away. He could hear whispers coming from behind him. A blinding pain stabbed his temples, and impotent fury caused his hands to curl in tight fists.

He would tolerate no more from that breed—

or Bethany either. He would see that they paid and paid dearly!

Hawk kept his silence during the trip back to the Circle Blue. Bethany's inner struggle was palpable. He knew she was trying to find the words to tell him what had brought them to this moment. He glanced sideways, noting again the dark shadows beneath her eyes. Perhaps he should tell her it didn't matter, that they should just forget it. He should just let her rest. He'd seen a spark in her eyes today when she'd faced down Vince, a spark reminiscent of the fire he loved.

He stopped the buggy in front of their home and stepped around to her side. Bethany stopped his hands from helping her down.

"Wait, Hawk. I want to tell you what's happened. I should have told you months ago."

"You don't have to tell me if you don't want to."

Her eyes met his. The haunted look returned for a second, then vanished, replaced by a quiet confidence. "I want to. But first you must make me a promise."

"A promise?"

She nodded.

"What sort of promise?"

"I want you to promise me you won't do anything about what I'm going to tell you. Promise me you won't . . . Well, just promise."

Her misty green eyes flicked back and forth, searching his face for the promise she hoped to extract. He could feel her anxiety returning. At that moment, he would have promised her anything.

"All right, Bethany. I promise."

And so she told him. She told him of Vince's threat to make her his bride. She told him of his threat to harm Hawk. She told him how she'd confronted Vince about Hawk's accident and of his admission of guilt. She told him of Vince's warning to see Hawk dead if she didn't cooperate. He sensed also the things she didn't tell him. He could easily imagine the racial slurs she'd endured simply because she loved him. And with each softly spoken word, his rage grew.

Hawk stepped back from the buggy, then turned toward the corral.

"Hawk, where are you going?"

"To the Bar V."

"You can't. You promised."

He stopped and looked over his shoulder. "He tried to kill me and he threatened you. You can't hold me to that promise. I'm going to put an end to this, once and for all." He began walking again, his right hand slipping down to touch the handle of his Colt.

"Hawk!"

He almost ignored her cry of protest, but something made him turn once again, just in time to see her tumble from the buggy, skirts flying in all directions. He sprinted back across the yard.

"Bethany?" He knelt beside her.

She opened her eyes as he gathered her into his arms. "I'm not hurt," she mumbled. "I just tripped over my own dress. Help me up, please."

An amused grin tweaking the corners of his mouth, he obeyed. Unable to stop himself, he bent to kiss her. Forgotten for the moment was Vince and the trouble he'd caused. Hawk could only think how good it was to have his Bethany back again.

Suddenly, she gasped into his mouth. He pulled his head away. Her eyes were wide, her mouth slightly open.

"Bethany, what is it?"

"I'm not sure. I think—" Again she gasped as her hands dropped to her abdomen. "Hawk—I think it's the baby."

"But it's too soon."

Pain flitted across her features. "I don't think that's going to make any difference."

He swept her into his arms and carried her quickly into the house. Laying her on the bed, he said, "I'll go for the doc."

Bethany grabbed his hand. "Don't leave me, Hawk. Please. I'm frightened."

"Okay." He pried her fingers free. "But I need to send someone else. I'll run out to the bunk-house. I'll only be a minute."

Doc Wilton had explained to her some things about labor, but she hadn't expected the pains to be this hard this quickly. They came in great waves, beginning in the small of her back and sweeping around until they seemed to squeeze her in two.

Hawk returned to their bedroom and helped her change out of her clothes and into a clean nightgown. As he tucked her into bed, he smiled his encouragement. "It's going to be all right, honey. I sent Gabe. The doc'll be here soon."

She nodded but couldn't speak as another labor pain assailed her. Beads of perspiration broke out on her forehead and upper lip, yet she felt as cold as ice.

For a half hour—or was it an eternity?—the pains continued as they'd begun, hard and steady. Hawk wiped her face with a damp cloth and held her hand, whispering words of comfort. He brushed her hair from her forehead. He rubbed her cold fingers between his hands. Always he was there, encouraging her, comforting her, loving her.

Then, suddenly, impossibly, the labor grew worse, the pains more intense and lasting longer each time.

"Hawk," she gasped as a pain lessened. "I don't think the doctor's going to get here in time. I think . . ." Her fingers curled around the bed posts, her grip so tight her knuckles turned white. She bit into her lower lip to keep from screaming.

"Good gawdamighty," Hawk mumbled, awareness dawning in his eyes.

His expression would have struck her as humorous any other time, but at the moment, she had more pressing things to think about.

Shirt sleeves rolled up to his elbows, Hawk Chandler caught his daughter as Bethany pushed her from the safety of the womb. For a moment, the room was dead silent, then the tiny red and wrinkled creature in his hands caught her breath. A thin wail broke the silence. He stared at her in wonder, a strange feeling washing through him. A feeling of permanence, of belonging, of continuance. Then, coming to his senses, he tied off the cord with a string and deftly cut the physical bond that still bound mother and child. He cleansed her, then wrapped the infant in a clean, warm towel and laid her in her mother's arms.

Bethany's auburn hair hung in damp curls around her face. The dark shadows beneath her eyes were even more pronounced against the stark white of her complexion. Still, there was a glow in her green eyes that seemed to light the whole room.

"Look at her, Hawk. She's beautiful."

She was, indeed. She was tiny but perfectly formed. Her head was covered with silky black hair. Her skin tone had already softened to a rosy pink. She had ten miniature fingers, complete with nails. Perfect little fists flailed the air, complaining at her abrupt entrance into the world. Her wail had grown into lusty protest. She was beautiful, indeed.

"She should have a name," Bethany whispered as she drew the baby closer to her.

Hawk was silent as he looked at the child. He'd thought often enough about a name for a son, but this fragile bit of humanity, this daughter now nestled against her mother's breast, this child of his loins who already threatened to rule his heart . . . What name could he give this child?

"You name her," he said softly.

Bethany lovingly guided the baby's mouth toward her nipple, coaxing the infant to suckle. "She's so tiny. So delicate. Like a little bird. I would like to call her Phoebe." Silvery-green eyes, aglow with love, lifted to meet Hawk's dark blue ones. "The hawk is a fierce hunter, swooping down on its prey, soaring in the wind, and he has sired a child of shining beauty."

"If she's only half as beautiful as her mother, we'll have one heck of a time keeping the men of Sweetwater at bay." He leaned down to kiss Bethany's forehead. "I love you."

"And I, you."

Hawk sat on the bed then and placed his arm around Bethany's shoulders. Together, the Chandler family awaited the arrival of the doctor.

CHAPTER THIRTY-TWO

Vince leveled his gray gaze upon the short, stocky cowboy standing between the two taller men. He took pleasure in seeing the nervous tick in Jake Casper's cheek. He waited, letting the tension grow.

"It wasn't very smart to leave without doing the job you were paid to do, Casper," Vince said at last. "Not very smart at all."

"Like I tried to tell you, I got word my ma was sick. I didn't have any choice. I had to try to get to her."

"So you've said." Vince picked up a pen with his left hand and began to write on a piece of paper. The words were meaningless, but the action was carefully calculated.

Casper shifted his weight from one foot to the other, then back again. He nervously eyed the writing from across the room. Vince knew he must be wondering what it meant. Casper was a stupid man.

"Your mother died five years ago," he said quietly, glancing up once more.

Casper swallowed hard. Sweat had broken out on his brow.

"But you're lucky, my friend. I'm a forgiving man. I'm not going to hold this little mistake of yours against you. Not as long as you lend me a hand. You won't even have to finish the job I paid you for. I have another little task for you."

"Sure, Mr. Richards. Whatever you need." Relief washed over the man's face. He grinned. "You just name it."

"I want you to go with Joe and Ray into town. I want you to have a few drinks. And then I want you to mention to whoever might be listening that the reason you left was because Hawk Chandler threatened to kill you for flirting with his wife. You let folks know he waved that knife of his in your face—you know the one I mean; the one with the pearl handle—and you decided you'd better take off for a while until he'd cooled down." He smiled, showing a row of white teeth. "Do you think you can remember that, Casper? It's very important that you do."

Again the cowboy glanced at the two men on either side of him. Then he nodded. "Sure. I can remember that. I tell 'em I was flirtin' with that pretty wife of Chandler's and he got right jealous and pulled his knife on me. He told me he was goin' to cut me up one side and down the other if I so much as looked at her again. So I decided I'd visit a friend of mine down in Denver until spring." With a nervous grin, he looked at Vince for confirmation.

"Very good, Casper. Oh, one more thing. It

might be a good idea if the sheriff happened to overhear you, too. You repeat the story if you have to."

"Whatever you say, Mr. Richards. You can count on me."

Vince's smile warmed. "I know I can, Casper. I know I can." Then, with a flick of his eyes, he dismissed them all.

When he was alone once again in his study, he pulled open the drawer of his desk and reached inside, toward the back. A moment later, he pulled out a knife. The long blade was sharp and well-kept. It had a pearl handle.

He stared at the knife, thinking how fortunate it was that his men had brought back Casper just when they had. With a little prodding, folks would remember Hawk's argument with Casper last year, and it wouldn't take much for them to believe the story about Hawk threatening his life for flirting with Bethany. The people of Sweetwater already were beginning to believe the worst about the breed when it came to his white wife.

With growing satisfaction, he laid Hawk's knife on top of his desk. "Too bad you lost your knife in that snow storm, Mr. Chandler. Too bad, indeed."

Sheriff Cook found Casper's body a week later. His throat had been slit. A search of the area turned up a pearl-handled knife. It wasn't hard to identify the weapon as Hawk Chandler's. He'd seen it many a time in the past. He was sorry to have to do it, but it seemed there wasn't any choice. He had to arrest Hawk for the murder of Jake Casper.

Bethany couldn't believe what was happening. There were five men in the posse besides Sheriff Cook. Likeable, responsible men. Men who should have known better. How could they be doing this to Hawk?

"Sheriff Cook," she said again, turning her gaze on the bearded man as he fastened the handcuffs behind Hawk's back. "Hawk couldn't have killed that man. He lost his knife months ago."

"Sorry, Miz Chandler, but your word just isn't enough. He's your husband, and I'd expect you to say whatever you had to to get him free."

"But he's been at the ranch with me since our baby was born. He hasn't been out of my sight for more than a few minutes."

Sheriff Cook shook his head.

"But it's the truth, Sheriff."

"Sorry, ma'am." He pulled on Hawk's arm and led him toward his horse.

"Hawk!" Bethany followed, desperately grabbing hold of Hawk before the sheriff could force him to mount. "Hawk—"

His stoic expression softened as he looked down into her eyes. "It'll be all right, Bethany," he said softly. "Go up to Rand's. Tell him what's happened. And tell him about Richards' threats. He'll know what to do." He leaned down and captured her mouth in a tender kiss.

"Come on, Hawk." Sheriff Cook pulled him away.

Bethany could scarcely see. Her green eyes were awash with tears. She waited as the two men mounted their horses, then watched as they and the others cantered away.

Suddenly, the aloneness was frightening. All the men were out on the range. There was no one here to help her. What if they hanged him? What if she were without him for the rest of her life?

She spun around, hastily wiping the tears from her eyes as she hurried into the house. In a few minutes, she was back outside, Phoebe in her arms. She ran toward the barn, laid the baby in a pile of hay, and saddled her mare. Then, Phoebe held fast in her arms, she rode as fast as she dared up the mountain to the Howard place.

Doc Wilton paced back and forth across his office. He rubbed his eyes, then bent his head backward, trying to relieve the tension in his neck.

He couldn't shake his feeling that Hawk Chandler was innocent of Casper's murder. It was more than just because he liked Hawk. It was more than the gut feeling that Hawk wouldn't jump a man from behind and kill him in cold blood, no matter what the provocation. There was something about the murder itself. There was something he should be able to point to and say, "This murder wasn't committed by Chandler."

He returned to his examination room and pulled the sheet back from the corpse. Once again he looked at the sliced flesh at the base of Casper's throat. There was something he was missing. Something . . .

"Rand is not here, Bethany. He said he was going to look for strays up near Willow Creek. He will not return until dark, I think."

Bethany blanched.

"What is wrong?" Ingrid demanded. "You must tell me."

"It's Hawk. They've arrested him for murder."

"Murder? But . . ."

Bethany thrust the baby into Ingrid's arms. "Take care of Phoebe for me, Ingrid. I've got to help Hawk."

"But . . ."

"When Rand returns, tell him what's happened. Tell him Vince Richards is behind this. Ask him to hurry." Quickly, she bent over to kiss Phoebe's downy head. In a whisper, she said, "I've got to help your daddy, my little one. We'll be back for you soon. Mama promises."

Ingrid's expression showed her concern. "I do not know what you are about to do, my friend, but be careful."

"I'll be careful."

Hitching up her skirt, Bethany mounted quickly. She jerked Buttercup's head around and dug her boot heels into the buckskin's ribs. Seeming to sense Bethany's anxiety, the game little mare took off like a shot, racing pell-mell down the mountain.

It seemed forever before the Bar V came into view. Bethany tethered her lathered mare to a tree a good distance away, slipped the rifle from its scabbard, and stealthily made her way toward the house. She wasn't sure exactly what she meant to do when she got there. She'd never held a rifle in her hands before, let alone pointed one at a man with every intention of firing if he wouldn't cooperate. But she would do whatever she must. She wasn't going to let Vince get away with framing Hawk for the dead man's murder.

She made her way toward the back of the house, stopping to listen, watching for any signs of life. Everything was still.

"What other proof do you need, Sheriff? The man's guilty. You only have to look at him to know that."

"Listen, Delaney. I'm going to hold him here until the Circuit Judge comes. He deserves a fair trial, just like anybody else."

Hawk listened as more voices entered the fracas, then he turned his back toward the doorway of the sheriff's office and leaned against the black iron bars of his cell. Fair trial? He'd be lucky if they didn't string him up before sundown.

He closed his eyes and remembered the frightened look on Bethany's face. He'd told her it would be all right, but he didn't believe it. He'd seen the way the men in the posse looked at him. They'd already tried and judged him and found him guilty.

I'm sorry, Bethany.

He was sorry he wouldn't have more years with her. He'd become fond of the idea of growing old with her by his side. He was sorry he wouldn't have the chance to see Phoebe grow up. Oh, what a charmer she was destined to be. She was going to have his black hair, but he'd swear she was going to have eyes the color of a stormy sea, not quite green, not quite blue. He was sorry he wouldn't have a son who could take care of the Circle Blue for him, carry on his name.

His hands closed into fists.

And, *damn*, if he wasn't sorry he hadn't settled things with Richards first.

"Looking for something, my dear?"

With a gasp, Bethany whirled around. Vince was standing so close she could have touched him. He'd taken the rifle from her before she realized it.

"Most of my guests come to the front door." He put the rifle down with his right hand as his left closed tightly about her wrist.

"Let go!" she cried, trying to pull away. "Let go of me, you—you murderer. Did you think I wouldn't know? Did you think I wouldn't try to stop you? You black-hearted bast—"

"Come now, Bethany. Where are your manners? We can't have you talking like one of the hands. I think you'd better come inside and have a nice, long drink. It will calm you."

"I don't want a drink. I don't want to calm down." She struggled to pull away from him, but his grip only tightened. "You killed that man.

You did it, and you're letting Hawk take the blame."

Vince laughed. "Of course, I did it. How else was I to be rid of your husband?"

Instead of trying to pull away, she went for his face with the nails of her free hand. She caught his cheek just below his right eye. He let out a startled cry before he backhanded her, knocking her head violently to the side. There was a deafening ringing in her ears, and the world spun crazily, but she fought back all the harder.

The next time he hit her, she blacked out.

Ingrid stopped the buckboard outside the sheriff's office. Awkwardly, she scrambled down from the seat, then reached back for Phoebe before hurrying into the jail.

Deputy Palmer was leaning back in his chair, his boots propped up on the desk top.

"I would like to see Sheriff Cook, please."

"Sorry, Mrs. Howard. Sheriff's not in." He pushed his hat back from his forehead to see her better but didn't bother to straighten in his chair. "Somethin' I can do for you?"

"I would like to see your prisoner then."

Palmer shook his head again. "Sorry, ma'am. He ain't allowed no visitors."

"Please. This is his baby. I must see him."

"Well . . ." He glanced at the baby in her arms, then at her enlarged abdomen. "I don't know . . ."

"Deputy Palmer," Ingrid pleaded. "This is important or I would not have come all this way."

His feet dropped to the floor. He sighed as he got up from the chair. "Sheriff ain't going to like me doin' this, but I suppose . . ."

"Thank you, Deputy. You have a good heart."

He snorted. "Sure." He opened the door leading to the cells. "Five minutes. That's all."

"Thank you," she said again as she slipped past him.

Hawk looked up as she neared the cell at the back of the jail. The moment he recognized her, he was on his feet. "Ingrid!"

She reached through the bars to take hold of his hand a moment, then pulled it back again.

His dark eyes searched her face. "What is it? What's happened?"

"It is Bethany. I think she has done something foolish."

Hawk closed his eyes. A resigned expression passed over his face. "What, Ingrid?"

"Rand was not home when she came. She left Phoebe with me. I think she has gone to see Mr. Richards. She has gone alone."

She heard his groan, felt his fear and frustration. His hands clasped the bars and shook them. "God help me," he prayed, his eyes closed. "I've got to get out of here."

Ingrid understood everything he was feeling. She feared for Bethany. She feared for Hawk. She wished Rand was there to help, but he wasn't. She had to help these two before one or both of them perished.

Hastily, she glanced around. Behind the door leading back to the office was a potbellied stove.

On the floor beside it was a black scuttle. A plan began to form in her head.

Without a word to Hawk, she laid the baby on the floor at her feet and walked toward the doorway. Stepping behind the open door, she picked up the scuttle and turned around. She caught sight of Hawk's questioning look and shook her head, motioning for quiet.

"Deputy, come quick!" She put all her desperation and fear into those three words.

He was through the doorway in a flash. "What—"

Ingrid brought the scuttle down with every ounce of strength she possessed. The deputy never knew what hit him. He fell face forward onto the floor.

Even as she held her breath, waiting for him to move, she hoped she hadn't killed him. Then she lifted her gaze once more toward Hawk.

"The key, Ingrid," he reminded her. "Get the key."

CHAPTER THIRTY-THREE

Bethany opened her eyes slowly, fighting the nausea that left a bitter taste in her throat. Her ears still thundered, and the pain in her jaw was piercing.

Vince dragged her to her feet. "That was a foolish thing to make me do, Bethany." He touched her chin, forcing her to turn her head to the side. "You're going to have a nasty bruise." Shoving her before him, he entered the house.

He took her into his study and told her to sit. She longed to disobey him. She longed to go for his eyes again, and this time gouge them out. At least she got some measure of satisfaction from the angry red welts beneath his eye.

"Ming Li!"

The servant appeared instantly in the doorway.

"Get me some rope. Then go outside and find Mrs. Chandler's horse. Take the animal away from her and set it loose. Just be sure it's off Bar V land."

Ming Li nodded and left on quiet feet. He was back soon with the requested rope.

"I'm sorry I'll have to tie your hands, my dear." Vince tenderly touched his cheek and winced. "But I can't have you causing any more trouble." He bound her wrists behind her back, the rough hemp cutting into her flesh.

"They'll find out you've taken me."

"How, Bethany? Your husband's been arrested for murder. He's mistreated you in the past. Everyone in town has heard rumors of it. Why on earth would you stay?" Vince walked over to his desk and picked up a letter. "I think we should honeymoon in Washington. My good friend, Senator Wright, has invited us to stay with him. I told him some time ago that we were to be married."

"I'd die before I'd marry you, Vince Richards."

His gray eyes narrowed at the venom in her voice. He leveled a fierce gaze upon her. "That would be a shame."

A cold dread washed over Bethany. The man was insane. No, he was something even worse. He was evil to the core and knew exactly what he was doing.

"You're right about one thing," Vince continued. "I can't keep you here. My men will return later this afternoon. No one must even suspect you were here. I expected you, you know. You're quite predictable, my lovely Bethany. I knew you would come to plead your husband's cause. So I sent all the hands out just so we could be alone."

As he spoke, Vince came around the desk again and crossed the room to stand beside her. He stroked her cheek with his index finger, then let it glide down her throat and along the edge of her breast. Bethany flinched at his touch but couldn't escape him.

"I'm going to possess you," he said in a throaty voice, filled with wanting. "I've waited far too long. From the moment I first saw you, right here in this room."

Bethany closed her eyes. She knew if he used her as he planned she would want to die. With Hawk dead and her body defiled by Vince, there would be no reason to go on living.

But I'll take him with me.

She would kill Vince. She cared not what would happen to her after that.

Doc opened his door on the echo of the knock. "Mrs. Howard, what is it?"

Ingrid's blue eyes were wide with fear. There was a smudge of black soot on her chin and another on the tip of her nose. She was clutching a baby to her breast, but it wasn't her child for she was still large with her own pregnancy. Spying the infant's black hair, the doctor knew it must be the Chandler baby.

"May I come in, Dr. Wilton?"

"Of course. Of course." He drew her inside. "What's happened, Mrs. Howard? What's brought you here?"

"I cannot tell you," she replied. "Please let me stay."

Hawk knew he might not have long before someone discovered the trussed up deputy and a posse was formed to hunt him down. He had to find Bethany before then.

And if Vince had so much as harmed one hair

on her head, so help him he would kill Vince a hundred times.

Ingrid had never done anything like this in her life. She had struck a man over the head with an iron scuttle. She might have killed him. How could she have done it? What would Reverend Silverton have thought of her behavior? Yet what else could she have done? She'd had to do something. She'd had to help Hawk and Bethany.

As she sat in the doctor's office, little Phoebe asleep in her arms, she thought back to the shy, proper girl who had come west with the Silverton family. Was she that same girl?

Suddenly, she felt a little like laughing. There *had* been a moment of satisfaction when she'd seen the deputy lying on the floor. A sense of power had flowed through her. A feeling of confidence. She'd liked that feeling.

But it was gone now. Ingrid could hear the ticking of the doctor's clock and wondered how much time she had before the deputy was free and came looking for her.

Hawk left the horse and approached the house on foot. The yard was silent. No activity stirred in the barn or the bunkhouse.

It didn't feel right to have everything so quiet.

He stopped at the edge of the barn and drew a steadying breath. He didn't dare rush into it. Not when Bethany's life could hang in the balance. If only he knew for sure that she was there.

A movement just north of the house caught his

eye. A man on horseback. Hawk pressed himself closer against the barn.

The rider was Vince's Chinese houseboy, Ming Li. He'd seen him once or twice before. Hawk wondered what he was doing, out riding by himself. For some reason, it too felt unnatural. It just didn't fit.

Hawk's sense of danger increased.

Ming Li rode his horse to the back of the house. He tied the animal there and went inside. Then nothing. The silence was uncomfortable.

Hawk could almost hear his nerves stretching.

Doc jumped as his door flew open with a crash. Deputy Palmer strode into the room, a gun in his hand. He pointed the Colt revolver at Ingrid. His expression was furious.

"All right, little lady. On your feet."

"What's the meaning of this?" Doc demanded.

"She broke Chandler out of jail and tied me up. I'm placin' her under arrest."

Doc tried not to let his surprise show on his face. "I can't let you do that."

Palmer's glower switched to the doctor. "You can't stop me. I'm gonna put her in jail and then me and a posse's goin' after Chandler. And when I find him, I'm gonna hang him myself."

The doctor stepped between Palmer and Ingrid. "Where's Sheriff Cook?"

"He's not back from the Monroe place yet. Don't even know Chandler's busted out."

"Don't you think you'd better wait for him before forming a lynching party?"

The deputy waved the muzzle of his gun at

Doc, ignoring the doctor's question. "Out of the way, Doc. I got a job to do."

"So do I, Palmer." Doc's voice was stern, authoritative. "I cannot allow you to take this woman into custody. She could have her child at any time. Are you willing to take the risk of its happening when she's alone in your jail?" He stared hard at the deputy.

Palmer looked a little uncertain.

"Leave her in my care. She obviously hasn't tried to escape. She's here, isn't she?"

"Well . . ."

"I give you my word she will be here when you return."

"I suppose . . ." Finally, Palmer holstered the revolver. "All right. But I'll be back for her." Casting a meaningful glance past the doctor at Ingrid, he left.

Now it was the doctor's turn. He turned on his patient, his expression clearly stating he would tolerate no evasion of his questions. "Ingrid Howard, I expect some answers. Now." He pulled up a chair and sat close to her.

Her eyes downcast, she nodded.

"Tell me what happened."

Quietly, Ingrid detailed the events of that day, beginning with Hawk's arrest and Bethany's appearance at Ingrid's door a short while later. "I know she has gone to the Bar V. I fear she is in danger."

Richards.

Doc rose abruptly, knocking over his chair.

That's it!

He could see Casper in his mind. The man had

been grabbed from behind and his throat cut, but it was the *way* it was cut. That's what had been troubling the doctor. From right to left. The cut was from right to left. But a right-handed man would cut from left to right. Casper's killer was left-handed.

So was Vince Richards.

"Stay here, Ingrid. I'm going out to the Monroe place to find the sheriff. Watch for him. If he comes here and I've missed him, send him to the Bar V. Tell him I said Vince murdered Casper and Mrs. Chandler may be next. Tell him Palmer's talking of lynching Hawk. Tell him anything, but *get him out there.*"

The gun barrel touched his scalp just behind his ear.

"You know," Vince said in a soft, almost jovial tone, "this is exactly how I welcomed your wife."

Hawk started to turn around.

"Don't move, Chandler. Just drop your gun." The voice was harsher this time. "Now, get inside. Hands up."

The gun poked him in the back, guiding him through the rear of the house and into the study.

Bethany was there. Her hands were tied behind her, and she was bound at the ankles as well. Her hair hung in a tangled mass. Her eyes were luminous, frightened. There was a bruise darkening on her jaw.

Hawk, she mouthed but no sound came out.

An almost blinding fury rose in his chest, urging him to turn and go for his captor's throat.

But he swallowed it even as he cursed himself for allowing Vince to get the drop on him. He had to stay cool and level-headed, now more than ever.

"Before I turn you over to the sheriff, Hawk, I want you to know I plan to marry Bethany. Once they've hanged you, of course."

"I'm going to kill you, Richards," Hawk whispered in response.

Vince chuckled. "Of course you are." He jabbed Hawk in the ribs with the gun. "Sit down there."

Hawk glanced at Bethany. With his eyes, he tried to reassure her. Vince might succeed in killing him, but he had to get her free first.

Think, Chandler.

"You know what I have on my desk? Plans for the new Bar V. A bigger Bar V once I've married the Widow Chandler and her property becomes mine. Of course, Bethany and I might not be here long after we're married. Statehood will come soon. Five, ten years at the most. In the meantime, I'm running a lot of cattle, building my herd."

"You were behind the rustling, right?" Hawk asked, already knowing the answer but stalling for time.

Vince laughed again. "Of course."

"And the man who tried to shoot me?"

"Montoya? Yes, I hired the idiot. But I'm glad you killed him instead. I'd paid him far too much and didn't relish giving him the five hundred more I'd promised." Vince was warming to his story. "Would you like all the details, Chandler? I'll tell you and then we really must go into Sweetwater. I'm sure folks are wondering where you are."

Vince had just come to stand in front of him when Ming Li stepped into the study.

"Boss, I—"

Vince glanced at his servant. In that instant, Hawk dove toward him, knocking him back against the large oak desk.

Bethany watched as the two men grappled on the top of the desk, then crashed to the floor. Hawk's right hand gripped Vince's wrist. Twice, then again, he struck it against the side of the desk, trying to dislodge the gun.

She heard Vince's grunt, then saw the revolver go spinning across the hardwood floor. Her eyes snapped back toward the two men at the sound of shattering glass. But she couldn't see them any longer. They had fallen through the large plate-glass window. Sounds of the struggle continued out of her sight.

Bethany fought against the ropes, feeling them cutting even deeper into her skin. She ignored the pain and the warm blood trickling into her palms. She needed desperately to see what was happening.

Hawk knew the moment the fight was his. He could sense Vince's fear as he realized it too.

Hawk's fist slammed into his opponent's stomach. He heard the grunt, saw Vince double over and stumble backward. Without hesitation, Hawk followed, pressing his advantage as his hands closed around Vince's throat. They fell to the ground again, rolling over and over as Vince tried to pry Hawk's fingers free.

He saw Vince's face turning red, watched as the gray eyes bulged in their sockets, felt the struggle weakening. But he didn't let up.

The slaughtered and rustled cattle. The Mexican, Montoya. The ambush during the blizzard. The memories boiled within him, stirring up an uncontrollable rage. But it was the thought of Bethany's frightened eyes and her bruised face that gave his hatred impetus.

He meant to squeeze the life from Vince Richards.

He'd nearly succeeded when a bullet struck the dirt not far from his hands.

"Let him go, Chandler."

His fingers tightened.

"I said, let him go."

Knowing it was too late, that he wouldn't succeed, Hawk released his hold and rose to his feet. Vince rolled onto his knees and elbows, choking and gagging. Dispassionately, Hawk watched him. He'd been so close. He'd been so darned close.

"Get a rope, Delaney."

Bethany's heart nearly stopped at the sound of gunfire. She tried to stand, tried to get to the window, but she only succeeded in falling to the floor.

"Hawk!" Tears burned her eyes.

"Missy?" Ming Li leaned over her.

"Please help me," she begged, but expected

nothing. When she felt his hands loosening her wrists, she glanced over her shoulder in surprise.

"Missy hurry," Ming Li urged. "No time." He freed her ankles, then held out a small pistol for her to take.

"You're helping me?"

Ming Li nodded, his expression grim. "No time talk. Hurry."

He didn't have to tell her again. She grabbed the weapon and rushed to the door, not knowing what she might find beyond it. She certainly didn't expect it to be a group of men, most still on horseback. Hawk was in the center, a noose around his neck. Vince was standing just a few yards from the porch steps, his back toward her, the fingers of his left hand on his throat.

"Throw the rope over that beam," Deputy Palmer commanded.

Bethany raced down the steps. "Stop!" she yelled as she came up behind Vince. With shaking hands, she pointed the gun at his back.

All heads turned.

"You're hanging the wrong man. Vince Richards killed Casper. He confessed it to me."

"Mrs. Chandler," the deputy said, stepping toward her, "put down the gun."

"Not until you listen. And take that rope off Hawk's neck." Her eyes darted from man to man. "I'll kill him. So help me, I will."

"Mrs. Chandler . . ." Palmer's voice was placating.

Bethany turned her head slightly to the side, hoping they would see the bruise. "He was holding me prisoner so I couldn't tell anyone. He hit me, and then he tied me up."

"Don't listen to her," Vince cried in a raspy voice. "She's crazy."

"If you don't believe me, look at the rope burns on my wrists."

There was silence, then a low grumbling as the men noticed the raw sores.

"Lady tell truth." Ming Li stepped onto the porch. "Boss kill."

Vince's head jerked to the side. "Shut up, you damn chink." Then he turned his gaze back on the posse. "Are you going to listen to this babbling woman and some stupid Chinaman?"

"Not stupid. Ming Li know plenty. You want proof, you look in boss's desk. Boss not so wise to leave things for Ming Li to read."

Bethany's glance moved toward the posse. She saw the beginnings of doubt passing across their faces. She knew she had won at least a reprieve when Palmer removed the noose from around Hawk's neck. Her arm dropped to her side, and a flood of relieved tears sprang to her eyes, blinding her.

In that same moment, Vince also realized he'd lost. He spun on his heel. His right fist rammed into her chest as his left stripped the gun from her hand. She fell backward, but her blurred gaze was locked on the weapon as Vince turned it toward the porch. He fired at Ming Li. She saw the little man grab his shoulder and fall.

Then, as Vince quickly turned back toward the posse, she heard him say, "You won't escape me again, Chandler. Not again! I won't lose everything because of a damned breed."

Her vision now terrifyingly clear, she saw his finger squeezing the trigger. Her scream melded with the gunfire.

Bethany scrambled to her feet, but even as she rose, Vince's body crumpled and fell. She stared at him, dazed, hardly daring to hope. When she looked up, Sheriff Cook was approaching Vince's deathly still form. He was holding his gun at his side. Behind him, she saw Doc Wilton dismount and hurry toward the porch to check on Ming Li.

She was still afraid to look. Afraid of what she might find. Her heart in her throat, she turned her gaze toward Hawk. But he wasn't lying in the dirt like Vince. He was coming toward her.

Hawk caught her up in his arms and pressed her tightly against him. "It's over, Bethany," he whispered. "It's finally over."

"Hawk," she whispered in return.

She heard the sheriff clear his throat. "I'm mighty sorry about all this, Hawk. When Doc told me about the knife—well, I'm glad we got here when we did."

"So am I, Sheriff." Hawk's fingers splayed over her back as he drew Bethany ever tighter.

Bethany dropped her head back and looked up at him. "Let's go home, Hawk."

With a loving gaze, he agreed. Effortlessly, he picked her up in his arms, cradling her head against his chest, and headed for his horse.

CHAPTER THIRTY-FOUR

Bethany looked in the direction of the springs even as the orange sun slipped behind the highest peak. She could see the skeleton of their new home rising against the darkening mountainside. The sounds of hammering faded even as the daylight had. Hawk would be coming home soon.

She glanced at the sleeping infant in her arms, then lowered her lips to brush them lightly against the downy head. The miracle of this child still captured her heart. That their love could create something so perfect, so precious. . . .

Phoebe stirred. Her heart-shaped mouth—so like her mother's—sucked at the air. She frowned, as if suddenly realizing what she sought had yet to be found.

"Are you hungry, my little bird?" Bethany said softly.

Phoebe opened her eyes. Hawk swore they would be green; Bethany insisted they would be blue. For now, they were a color somewhere in-between. A mixture of sea and sky. A color as unique as Phoebe herself.

Bethany turned with a contented sigh and went into the house, leaving the door open to catch the late spring breeze. She sat on the love seat beneath the sitting room window, unbuttoned her bodice, and brought Phoebe to her breast. The infant latched greedily onto the nipple, slurping and sucking with gusto, causing her mother to laugh.

"You'll not stay small and petite very long with such an appetite."

But Phoebe paid her no mind.

The room was bathed in gray shadows when Hawk stepped through the doorway. He paused, caught by the picture mother and child made. He felt the familiar melting of his heart. He marveled again at the joy this woman had brought into his life. He found it difficult to remember why he'd ever resisted her.

She lifted her head and met his gaze. Even in the dim light, he could read the love in her eyes.

He thought suddenly of that day in April when they'd come too close to losing what they'd fought so hard to find. He remembered seeing Vince grab the gun from Bethany's hand, seeing him shove her to the ground. He remembered the fear that had shot through him, certain that Vince was going to kill Bethany before anyone could stop him. But it hadn't happened that way. The sheriff's bullet had pierced Vince's cold, black heart. He'd been dead before he hit the ground.

Hawk shook off the grim memory. Why think of death and fear, why think of the pain of rejection and prejudice, the ugliness that waited in the world when he could bask in the peace and joy within these walls?

Bethany was smiling at him now. He walked over to the love seat and bent down to place a kiss on the crown of her head, then did the same with Phoebe.

"She looks more like you every day," he told Bethany. "Beautiful."

Bethany lifted the sleeping infant into Hawk's waiting arms. While Bethany closed and buttoned her bodice, Hawk carried the baby into her bedroom and laid her on her stomach in the cradle. Phoebe wriggled, turning her head from side to side before settling peacefully back to sleep.

Hawk pulled a light blanket over her padded bottom, then let his hand linger on her back, feeling the rapid heart beat, overwhelmed by the sense of joy this tiny scrap of humanity gave him.

"Are you going to spoil her?" Bethany asked as she slipped up beside him.

He placed an arm around her shoulder. "Only as much as your father spoiled you."

"Then she's going to be a handful."

"I'm sure of it," he agreed with a chuckle, and she joined him with her own melodic laughter.

Bethany wondered if it was possible to feel too much happiness. Could a heart burst from an overabundance of joy?

As their laughter faded, she lifted her head.

Her gaze met Hawk's. She remembered how cold and closed up they had been to her at one time. So unreadable. So enigmatic. But now she thought she could see right into his heart and soul. She had become a part of him, and he of her.

He gathered her tenderly to him. His mouth lowered to claim hers in an achingly sweet, gentle kiss. Her heart beat an erratic rhythm in her breast. She held her breath, caught by the magic he could so easily weave around her. She felt his hand slide up her side to cup her breast. A wonderful, tingling sensation shot up her arm and set butterflies free in her stomach.

"I love you, Mrs. Chandler," he said huskily beside her ear, then nibbled her ear lobe.

Her faint moan escaped on a sigh.

"Perhaps we could have another daughter. Would you like another child, Bethany?"

Her body seemed to vibrate, the wanting was so strong. "I'd like a dozen children," she answered, "if they were all like their father."

Hawk's arm slipped beneath her knees and he lifted her off the floor. He carried her into their bedroom, then laid her gently on the patchwork quilt. Standing above her, he cupped her face in his large hands and lifted her chin toward him.

His blue-black gaze caressed her face. "No matter how many children we have, I'd bet they'll all be perfect."

Bethany swallowed the sudden rise of joyful tears.

"And you know how my luck runs," he continued as he moved to claim her mouth with his. "I can't lose when it comes to a wager with you."

Dear Reader:

The story and characters for THE WAGER were conceived when I was in the midst of another book. They insisted I put the other book aside and write their story. I'm glad I listened to them.

My personal life took a wild and sometimes difficult rollercoaster ride during the writing of THE WAGER. Along the way, I learned many valuable lessons about the myriad qualities, joys and heartaches of loving, the resilience of human nature, and the strengths wrought from close family and friends. Perhaps Hawk and Bethany learned these things too.

All my romantic best,
Robin Lee Hatcher

AUTOGRAPHED BOOKMARK EDITIONS

Each book contains a signed message from the author and a removable gold foiled and embossed bookmark.

PASSIONATE ROMANCE ON THE HIGH SEAS
BY ROBIN LEE HATCHER

PIRATE'S LADY. Lady Jacinda Sutherland had dreamed of a handsome knight who would sweep her into his fiery embrace. But Tristan Dancing was no knight—he was a ruthless pirate—yet his masterful touch brought a whirlwind of passion to her staid existence.

_____2487-X $3.95 US/$4.95 CAN

Breathtaking Historical Romance
Robin Lee Hatcher

"Lively, tempestuous romance!"
— *Romance Readers Magazine*

HEART STORM. From the New York theatre to the London stage, Niki O'Hara followed her dream to become an actress — and tried unsuccessfully to deny her feelings for the handsome, arrogant Adam Bellman.

_____2318-0 $3.95 US/$4.95 CAN

PASSION'S GAMBLE. After her first passionate embrace with Colter Stephens, Alexis Ashmore knew she could never love another. But the gamble she was forced to take to win his love would jeopardize their future if she lost.

_____2412-8 $3.95 US/$4.95 CAN

STORMY SURRENDER. Young Taylor Bellman was forced to marry a wealthy older man to save her family plantation. But it would take a gallant Yankee visitor to awaken her sleeping heart.

_____2585-X $3.95 US/$4.95 CAN

_____2595-7 HEART'S LANDING $3.95 US/$4.95 CAN

_____2487-X PIRATE'S LADY.   An Autographed Book-
         mark Edition. $3.95 US/$4.95 CAN

_____2638-4 GEMFIRE. Special refraction engraving on
         cover. $4.50 US/$5.50 CAN

INDIAN ROMANCE AT ITS PASSIONATE BEST
by MADELINE BAKER

"Madeline Baker proved she knows how to please readers of historical romance when she created *Reckless Heart* and *Love in the Wind*."
— *Whispers*

LOVE FOREVERMORE. When Loralee arrived at Fort Apache as the new schoolmarm, she had no idea she would fall into the arms of a fiercely proud, aloof Indian warrior. *An autographed bookmark edition.*

_____2577-9 $4.50 US/$5.50 CAN

RECKLESS LOVE. Joshua Berdeen was the cavalry soldier who offered Hannah Kinkaid a life of ease in New York City, but she was bound to the handsome Cheyenne warrior who had branded her body with his searing desire. The fiery sequel to *Reckless Heart*.

_____2476-4 $3.95 US/$4.95 CAN

LOVE IN THE WIND. Katy Maria Alvarez had decided to enter a convent, but fate had other plans for her. Katy's coach was attacked by Indians, and she became the slave of arrogant warrior Iron Wing.

_____2390-3 $3.95 US/$4.95 CAN

RECKLESS HEART. They had played together as children— Hannah Kinkaid and the Indian lad. Then Shadow and his people went away, and when he returned, it was as a handsome Cheyenne brave who awakened Hannah to a passion she had never known.

_____2255-9 $3.95 US/$4.95 CAN